ÏLLЦSÏVE HΦЯÏZΦЙ

Seeing isn't always believing.

Eric Lowans

TERRAPIN Group Publishing LLC

TERRAPIN Group Publishing LLC

ISBN: 978-0-578-25033-5

Cover Image by Eric Lowans
Cover Model: Crystal Northup

PRINTED IN THE UNITED STATES OF AMERICA

CHAPTER 1

The instructions had been clear enough, "Top of the arch, 0915." Barely into a new year, Mathias Karlsson struggled to understand what could be so important that he needed to drag himself hastily from his semi-retirement in the desert southwest, nine hundred miles, to St. Louis, by the most expedient means *possible*. But the message had nevertheless been marked urgent, as was typical in Washington's inimitable fashion, and he was now poised to present himself at the proper place and time.

After spending twenty-four years with the Army Special Operations Command, he had gone in to his first retirement emotionally exhausted, but ready to begin working on his life. It was what one was supposed to do when one completed military service. But, once he realized that the fabric that had held his marriage together all those years had actually been his extended absences, after an amicable divorce, he returned to the business as a contractor. Thus, for the past fifteen years he had been, for lack of a better term, a U.S. government counteragent; a man whose primary job was to dissuade or nullify enemy agents. Legally, when possible. Quietly, if not.

He was not a spy or intelligence operative in the ordinary sense of the term, even though he bumped into them from time to time. Neither was he a mercenary. He was a US soldier, regardless of whatever status the Defense Department stamped in his 201 file. He had scruples, allegiances, and ethics. He loved his country. Politicians, not so much.

Divorced and with few friends of either sex, he was, by occupation and preference, a loner. A psychologist would say that the key differences between Karlsson and a sociopath were the presence of impulse control and empathy. However, empathy was usually a personal emotion for him. When he was working, he focused strictly on the mission. This was an attribute that endeared him to his handler, who exploited his talents from a nondescript office building in Arlington, a couple of miles from the Pentagon.

Washington had been unconventionally different in the past few years, and his department - rather, his former department, was no exception. As usual, brevity was the order of the day, often at the expense of clarity. The phrase, *most expedient* meant quickly, but within reason. If he had chartered a private jet for the trip, there would have been significant financial fallout in the accounting office.

But, like any good company man, Karlsson dropped what he was doing, grabbed a puddle-jumper for Phoenix, and connected with the next available flight into St. Louis. It was after midnight when he arrived, so he rented a car and found a suitable hotel near the freeway that afforded him excellent access to the airport or to alternate routes out of town if that particular need arose.

Now, after straining his neck looking up at the stainless steel man-made-wonder-of-the-world, he entered the visitor center at the base, worked his way past the various security devices intended to ensure everyone's safety, by disarming them of course, and then frowned at the sixty-inch diameter hybrid of a diving bell and an iron lung that he was going to have to compress and contort himself into to make the sideways journey to the top. The truly scary part of this process was that there were five seats in each car, meaning that the designer intended five human beings to ride in the contraption at the same time. Luckily, the other visitors took one look at his six-foot, four-inch frame and opted for a different car, leaving Karlsson to his peaceful reflection on the bumpy, four-minute ride to the top. And when he again tasted fresh air of sorts, he was some six hundred feet higher than when he had started.

She was a good deal younger than Karlsson, not much over forty. Attractive and professional, she did not necessarily have to have been the one, but she was the only person in that hollow space at the top of the arch by herself, and she wasn't really dressed for sightseeing. Their eyes met briefly, and she confirmed her identity by using her left hand to brush her hair behind her ear, an innocent enough gesture, but one they teach everyone at the *Farm* that means, "Not now, follow my lead." Well, it was what they used to teach. Karlsson hadn't been to Camp Peary in more than ten years.

She was listening intently to the docent explain how and why this piece of steel had been erected. Off to the sides, younger attendees were spread out on an angled, carpeted section of floor, leading up to windows that overlooked the river and the city of St. Louis, a long way down. Karlsson had never been comfortable with heights, and the concept of leaning out like that to look down made him just a little uneasy. He had done some rappelling, and jumped out of a few airplanes in his time, but that was different. Many of those jumps were at night, but even during the day jumps, one never really had the perception of height. The jumper simply prayed the static line was well-connected and that the riggers had competently done their job.

Karlsson feigned interest in the lecture and when he saw her start towards the tram for the return to terra firma, he made sure that he got into the same car. They were alone.

"That's quite a challenge for a guy your size." She said as soon as the doors closed.

He smiled, "I've never really thought of myself as claustrophobic until today."

She laughed "This would certainly bring it out in anyone! This was my co-worker's idea of a joke. When she heard that I was travelling to St. Louis this week, she insisted that I take this tour." She extended her hand, "Jackie Biehn." It wasn't a perfect recitation of the inane sign-counter-sign verbiage that Karlsson had been told to listen for, but it was close enough, and he was far too old to be anal about it.

"Matthias Karlsson", He replied taking her hand. "Matt, to my friends."

"Nice to meet you, Matt. I was told to give you this." She reached into her purse and pulled out a gold challenge coin and handed it to him. Embossed on one side was the seal of the Secretary of the Air Force. Karlsson flipped the coin over and saw, to his amusement, a picture of a bulbous-headed alien with large eyes, peering out from behind some sort of arrowhead-shaped craft, surrounded on the edge with a Latin inscription, *Ad Gradum Proximum*.

"You know, Jackie, I've studied several foreign languages, but I have to confess that Latin was not one of them. What's the inscription?"

She looked him in the eye, "To the next level." She paused for a moment to see if it meant anything to him or maybe just to see if she could win the staring contest, and then continued. "The people on the team originally wanted something like *to the next dimension*, but they weren't sure that would have translated well, since the Romans never could have envisioned something like this."

"Something like what?" Karlsson asked, eyebrows raised. "I'm just a bit in the dark as to what I'm supposed to be doing here."

She lowered her voice to a whisper as if someone in the next car could inadvertently overhear some snippet of conversation, with all the clanking and other noise associated with moving a bunch of steel containers up and down an enclosed tram. "I can't say much here, obviously, but it has to do with the Apollo thing."

"The what?" Karlsson asked, honestly confused.

"Apollo. I thought you were briefed."

Karlsson smiled at the attractive forty-year-old who was obviously very physically fit. And not wearing a wedding ring. "Apollo? Greek mythology? One of the twelve Olympians?"

Biehn looked at him for a moment as if he might have been joking with her. "The...space program. Remember, we went to the moon?"

Karlsson frowned as he tried to process what she had just said and pretend like he knew what he was supposed to be doing. "The Apollo space program? I'm no authority on that subject, but didn't they run out of money and close that down in the mid-seventies?"

Biehn cautiously replied, "Well...the NASA program did shut down in 1975. No one told you what we were looking into?"

Karlsson shook his head. "Huh uh, but I'm all ears. You obviously know the right phone number to call in Washington, or else I wouldn't be here. So," He raised his eyebrows. "What is it that I can do for you?"

She ignored the question, "I'm at the Renaissance up the street, and I understand they have a room reserved for you as well. We need to split for a while when the car reaches the ground floor. But I would like to meet you for dinner. I've just come in from Italy, and I'm afraid that if I don't get some sleep pretty soon, I won't make any sense at all."

"No explanations necessary, Jackie. I've done my fair share of travelling and understand completely. But, since I already have a room in another hotel, why don't I just meet you in the lobby, say, five o'clock?"

"That would be great" she replied as the doors to their iron lung opened.

She bounced out of the car with seemingly unbridled energy, leaving him to carefully work his way out with an obligatory stretch to ensure that all bones, joints, and muscles continued to function as intended. He cursed Paul for setting up this meeting in such a ridiculous location. There were a hundred places in St. Louis where they could have done this, without him having to be uncomfortable. But then, Paul was never really concerned with his agents' comfort – only the mission.

Karlsson walked around the downtown area for almost an hour, snapping pictures of nothing in particular, and casually looking around to make sure that no one took the slightest interest in him. He had no idea what he was involved in, but it never hurt to be cautious. When he wasn't employed as a nefarious character, on contract to Uncle Sam, he'd actually made a pretty good living at photography, and his avocation had provided a suitable cover on many assignments. That was in the day when one had to tote numerous rolls of film and be careful not to waste shots. Now that everything was digital though, he could snap as much as he wanted, check the results on the back of the Nikon and decide to keep it or erase it. So, between framing, snapping, and reviewing, it afforded him a perfect opportunity to look around and see if anyone was tailing him. They weren't.

To further the perfunctory ruse, Karlsson even wandered into a riverboat casino of sorts, and lost forty dollars in an effort to see if he was being stalked. No one followed him, and no one took any interest in the fact that he had left much the same pauper as when he had entered.

Eventually, he returned to his rental car and drove back to his hotel in the suburbs, and when he got to his room, he used his special cell phone to call a certain number in suburban Washington.

"Seven six one three" was the curt answer.

"It's Prometheus, for Paul." He said, using the name they had given him some years earlier.

"One moment please." Said the voice on the other end, followed by a series of beeps.

"You made contact?" Paul never wasted time on pleasantries. He just didn't have the social skills.

"Well, I guess you could say that." Karlsson took a breath, "I met an interesting young lady who offered me an intriguing coin, but little in the way of explanation. She said that she needed her beauty rest and that she would feel much more inclined towards open communication over dinner. What gives?"

There was only a momentary pause before he began. "It's complicated. Some of our pessimistic colleagues would say it is a mess."

"I've tried to respect your retirement, Matt. You know you were one of my best and I can think of no better way to illustrate my gratitude than to give you your peace and allow you to find your soul again. But, for reasons that you will eventually learn, I cannot use any of my regular personnel on this. And, as you'll recall from when you joined our team, we are an elite group with a lifelong bond. As a matter of fact, we are so elite, there are times when even our own people wish that we never existed."

It was sometimes difficult to differentiate between his conde-scension and placation performances, so Karlsson got an uneasy feeling whenever Paul felt the need to explain himself. It usually meant that a listener needed to read between the lines so to speak, and carefully look for a hidden meaning in his speech. "We have a rather complex situation with the upcoming election. On one hand, we have a patriot who seeks to retain the highest office in the land and may be eminently qualified for that office. And, on the other hand, we have a Senator who may be leaning towards unconstitutional or illegal means to subvert the political process. Both of these men may attempt to use a classified program to their advantage and may be playing with fire. If allowed to continue un-checked, there is a significant possibility of global repercussions, especially from our Russian and Chinese friends."

He paused before continuing, "The Beltway is less stable now than I've seen it in decades and there are people in every organiza-tion, including ours, who place their personal and political needs above those of the nation. And now, we find that the Bureau has assigned agents and informants to key political campaigns, as well as other competitive federal organizations with whom they should be aligned."

"Situation normal." Karlsson replied.

Paul continued, "I need to lone you out for a few weeks. As, well, a security consultant of sorts. And, as I said, I can't use any of my current staff for this."

"Excuse me?" Karlsson asked.

"There's an aerospace contractor in Cleveland. They supply various parts for aircraft that do not officially exist; the kind that Ms. Biehn can tell you about during your dinner. While her role in this matter is to identify financial security weaknesses in the con-tractor's classified programs, and locate some missing government property, your role will become clearer after you meet with the company's principals."

"And they'll explain what this has to do with Apollo?"

The line was silent for a moment. "Don't mention that word to anyone other than me. I assure you; things will make more sense after your Cleveland meeting."

Karlsson grimaced at the phone, "Yes, sir". His team was not exactly in the security business, but if Paul thought they needed someone with his skills on this job, then so be it. But then, just before hanging up, Paul said something that scared him.

"Thank you."

Stan Marchand saw the clubhead of his new Ping G410 LST drive through the ball with his near-perfected swing. In his mind the ball would travel three hundred yards with a slight draw to the left, positioning him 132 yards from the pin, leaving an easy nine iron shot to set up for the birdie putt. From the blue tees, the second hole of the King's Course at Gleneagles Country Club in Plano was about 432 yards today. He had played this hole a hundred times and knew every nuance, every subtlety of it.

Unfortunately, his centered mind and graceful arc were interrupted at the top of his backswing by the cell-phone buzzing in the cart behind him, causing him to miss the sweet spot on the face of the club and thump his shot about 225 yards down the right side of the fairway.

"Gawdammit! Turn that fucking thing off!" He screamed as he watched his ball roll through the fairway before coming to a stop a few inches in the rough. He turned to George with a prayerful look and started to speak.

But, George Griffiths, now a *retired* oil man in his seventies, too quickly replied. "No way. You hit it; you play it!" Griffiths was worth more than a hundred million and could easily afford to lose every hole on the course. However, whether it was their standard ten-dollar-per-hole bet or a million, George was not about to give anything up. It was sunny, nearing sixty-three degrees, so he knew Stan couldn't blame the shot on the weather. "Besides, it's your phone!"

Stan stormed back to the cart and slammed his four-hundred-dollar club into his golf bag, before plunking himself into the driver's seat of the cart and reaching for his phone. He quickly glanced at the offending number and recognized the Virginia area code before deleting it. It was a number that he could not put into his contacts list. It was a number, which if anyone asked, was an annoying telemarketer. But he knew who it was.

Now retired from the US Secret Service, Marchand had a very nice pension to live on, as well as an inheritance that left him fairly comfortable. His divorce had been final fifteen years earlier, but even though it was his money now, he still enjoyed taking care of his two grown sons. He also felt obligated to take care of his ex-wife when she needed something, like paying her airfare to his oldest son's wedding in England the year before. After all, the breakup of the marriage was his fault. His masculine good looks combined with a somewhat hyperactive libido had brought many opportunities throughout the years to mingle with attractive women of all ages, from eighteen to eighty. However, now that he had turned sixty, the demographic tended to run more towards the more senior end of the range.

Nevertheless, family was important, and his sons meant everything to him. One had gone on to medical school, and the other to law school. In his heart, he loved them both, but that would not keep him from joking with friends, that one of his sons saved souls, and the other sold his out when he passed the bar exam.

He turned off the transgressing phone and tossed it back into the compartment in the dashboard of the golf cart. "Sorry. No do-overs?"

"No fucking way." Griffiths replied. "I haven't forgotten. Ten years ago, you made me lock my guns up when *W* came to visit my family and I. You don't never take a Texan's gun away from him son!"

Griffiths had been a huge contributor to Republican causes and candidates and was a personal friend of George W. Bush. Nevertheless, the Secret Service had protocols to follow and when

W, or George Forty-Three, as he was sometimes known, visited the oil man's eight thousand square foot house outside of Dallas, the Secret Service insisted on creating a safe space for the President, and that included not letting anyone other than Secret Service personnel carry firearms for the duration of the visit.

"Paybacks are a bitch!" the oilman recited calmly as his drive screamed 290 yards down the center of the fairway.

Griffiths grinned as he returned to the cart, "So, who the fuck is calling you nowadays? I thought you were retired."

Marchand frowned as he depressed the accelerator pedal on the golf cart and moved them down the fairway. "Nobody. Well, nobody I want to hear from until I whip your ass!"

Stan tried his hardest to concentrate on the game, but the cell phone call had achieved its intended effect. It had broken his focus. He could hit the distance with his clubs today, but his accuracy was deplorable. By the end of the round, the oil man had beaten him by six strokes.

"That's sixty bucks you owe me, government man!"

"Yeah." Stan said as he drove the cart up behind his Cosmos Blue Audi Q3. The mini-SUV gave him what he needed in the way of performance, but also gave him the cargo capacity he considered essential when he was working on his house or stocking the car for a vacation. A vacation from retirement. "Yeah...would you take fifty and a drink in the club house?"

George grunted and grinned, "Sure. Single malt, right?" he asked knowing Stan's predilection for expensive scotches. The club had a wide selection of single malt scotches ranging from twelve to eighteen years old. None of which were cheap.

They off-loaded their clubs; Stan into his Audi, and George into his camel-colored Bentley Flying Spur. The sedan version of the two-door Continental GT, it was perhaps a bit technologically inferior to other cars in its class, but it afforded the owner with the interior quality and comfort that one would expect when paying two hundred and fifty grand for a piece of machinery to get them to the grocery store and back.

"Still driving that English piece of shit?" Stan remarked, in an attempt to subvert the garish display of wealth.

"Just today. It's my wife's. We traded 'cause she's got my Dually." He replied, referencing his custom Chevrolet 2500 HD, with the 20,000-pound towing capacity and an elaborate steel bumper system that could probably go through reinforced concrete. The truth be known, no real Texas oil man would want to be caught dead in a Bentley. "Her sister bought another mare, and they ran to Pilot Point to pick her up."

Both men chuckled as they headed back to return the cart and find a table in the new 5401 Grille. Drinks and dinner ran them well past seven in the evening, and by the time Stan made it back to his house, he was too exhausted to work. Nevertheless, he turned his cell phone back on and looked at the incoming calls from the Virginia number. There was also a text, brief and to the point:

Check your email. Coordinate for your review. Urgent.

He could check his emails but reckoned that he was far too tired and probably too inebriated to comply with their wishes tonight. He knew what they wanted. They had sent him a coordinate that they wanted remote-viewed. Urgently. But, as he knew, and as did they, remote viewing was severely diminished when the viewer was under the influence of single malt scotch. Well, under the influence of alcohol in general, but single malt scotch to be sure. He was retired. Sort of. It could wait until tomorrow.

CHAPTER 2

D inner with Jackie had been pleasant, but only moderately informative. It turned out she was some sort of supersleuth working for the Air Force's Office of Special Investigations and had been hot on the trail of a government contractor known to be pilfering from Uncle Sam. The reason for the meeting being in St. Louis was because that just happened to be the location for the National Military Personnel Records Center. The official repository of millions of personnel records for everyone serving in the US military since World War I.

However, why she needed to personally visit a resource that offered its goods online, did not come up, and in keeping with Karlsson's long established history of minding his own business and keeping his country's secrets secret, he didn't ask. Apparently, she was high enough in the official pecking order that she could dictate where a meeting was to take place, and who would have to travel nine hundred miles to get there.

As far as the rationale for pulling Karlsson out of his well-earned retirement, the information was scant. She tacitly explained that part of his role was to determine if certain parts for secret aircraft, which were supposed to be made in America, according to US government regulations, might be susceptible to counterfeiting in foreign manufacturing facilities. And, while the term *counterfeiting* generally conjured up some preconceived notion of dingy back rooms or dark garages in faraway lands, many items that were illegally produced, were often made in a manufacturer's very own facilities. Sometimes with the knowledge of larcenous, or politically compromised management, and sometimes without their culpability.

She gave him an address in a Cleveland suburb, along with a couple of names, and asked if he could be there the day after to-morrow. The questions she had asked about Karlsson's background were innocent; the same types of questions two people might ask each other on a first date. But the nature of the questions told Karlsson that she did not know any more about him than he did her. She had wanted the meeting to look casual, but because of the public location in which she chose to dine, she was reluctant to talk about anything that might be remotely construed as secret.

That was fine with him. Based upon his brief conversation with Paul, he didn't get the feeling that she was running this show. The two made small talk through dinner and by the end of the evening, Karlsson found himself attracted to her. Well, physically anyway, maybe emotionally too. In some ways, she reminded him of his ex-wife Peggy. Just enough that it was too painful to push dinner any further than what it was.

Peggy had been gone for over a year now. It had been something quick. One day, her doctor found it, and a couple of months later, it killed her. He'd had an opportunity to talk to the kids at the funeral, but they were fully grown, employed and married. There was little he could say to them to make up for the lost decades. They were cordial and friendly. Her current husband remembered him from years passed and thanked him again for coming to their aid when they had needed his special kind of help. But even though they'd been apart for many years, as Karlsson left the services, he still felt a loss. So, whether it was her smile, or scent, or manner, as attracted as he was to Special Agent Jackie Biehn, he remained professional and aloof. Just as well. Unlike the old days, younger women were no longer attracted to older men, and he detested being a caricature.

And now, according to plans and promises, Karlsson had arrived as scheduled at the Bratenahl manse just before dawn, to light snow and fog. As he approached the large house, he noted the two sedans parked on the circular drive. From the bar codes and *No Smoking* decals on the windows, he surmised they were both rentals, but not from the same place, or at least the same time. One was showroom spotless, as if stored in a garage. And the other had been covered in snow and road salt, its windows hastily scraped off, probably that morning.

The heavy wooden door in front was open, but a glass outer door kept out the weather, which to Karlsson, seemed unseasonably warm for Cleveland this time of year. He decided that the open door meant welcome, and he also felt that knocking would be futile since the place was so big, no one would hear him anyway.

Among the first things to hit him about the place were the smells. The odor of old wood, old books, old leather upholstery, old money. Karlsson had done some internet research on the place the night before in his hotel room. Stately, majestic, built in 1928 by some US Senator, it had recently been completely refurbished. It had been purchased by a publicly traded corporation named Echo Aerospace about ten years earlier and converted for use as a corporate meeting place with some lavish VIP guest rooms. With seven bedrooms and seven and a half bathrooms, the joint occupied a little over seven thousand square feet on three acres of lakefront property. As he looked around, he wondered where the secret room was that was common in those days of prohibition. All the older mansions had them. A place for the rich to hide their booze, while hypocritically protesting the evils of demon rum during the day.

The voices emanating from downstairs led him to a narrow stairwell which took him to the lower level and a conference room that had an ample amount of glass overlooking Lake Erie. Or rather what he could see of it through the light flurries and dense fog.

There were two men, one of whom he had met briefly somewhere, maybe a couple years back. Italy seemed to ring a bell. The other was tall, lean, gray, like a CEO type, and introduced himself first, "Mr. Karlsson, I'm Arthur Collins." He extended his hand, "Thank you so much for coming so quickly". His handshake was moderately firm and practiced, but his eyes showed fatigue.

"No problem Mr. Collins, I'm happy to see what I can do to help you." The smell of coffee caused Karlsson to glance at the credenza with fruit, pastries and juices laid out, at which point Mr. Collins gestured for him to help himself.

After pouring a cup of black coffee, Karlsson nonchalantly took in the room. The conference table was dark cherry with a glass pad atop; a stretched hexagon shape with the center slightly wider than the ends, about 20 feet long. He wondered how they got a single piece of glass in here without breaking it. Around the table, expensive swivel chairs, pushed in, and equidistantly spaced signaled that the place was professionally maintained.

The chap that Karlsson had recognized from a past assignment came around the table offering his hand. The spry man tried to force a sincere smile, but it was obvious he was not used to exuding pleasantness. "I'm John Carroll. My friends call me JJ. When we met in Massa, I was suddenly called away and we didn't really have time for introductions." Carroll was in his early sixties, about five-foot-ten, but very lean and fit. He still had the crew cut that hinted at a Marine Corps career, but even with a more fashionable civilian cut, the way he moved would have given it away, regardless. "Please extend our gratitude to Mr. Scheller for allowing us to borrow you for a couple of weeks".

The use of Paul's proper name led Karlsson to believe that one or both of them, were not as in-the-know as they'd each like to believe. It had been a big secret in the outfit for a long time, but Karlsson had come across his real name, Princeton Scheller, almost by accident. In the business though, he was only known as *Paul*. "Please, sit down, Mr. Karlsson."

Carroll started the lecture, "Mr. Karlsson, the Iowa caucuses are over, and the presidential candidates are headed for New Hampshire. We've never seen the parties so polarized and so committed to winning, regardless of the methods." He paused to take a sip of his coffee, "Recently, one of our Divisional Vice Presidents became concerned because they caught one of their mid-level executives not only having confidential communications with one of the candidates, but also with the Chinese; a practice that is doubtfully legal, but most assuredly would embarrass the company and cost us a fortune if the relationship were to become known."

Mr. Collins cut in, "Did you ever hear of Aurora, Mr. Karlsson?"

"Aurora?" he grimaced, "Well, other than the one of Borealis fame, the only other context in which I've heard it bandied about was relating to some new super-steroidal replacement for the SR-71 Blackbird".

"That's the one." He put his hands in his pockets and stared at the floor as he moved away from the glass sliding doors. "A term that was used years ago in a congressional budgeting document, that all too quickly drew the attention of the Area 51 conspiracy buffs." He moved to the end of the conference table and pulled the chair out.

After he was seated, Collins continued with a light sigh, "Actually, Aurora was the name of my housekeeper at the time. Given such ridiculously short notice to change the name of something we'd worked on for the previous ten years, it was the best I could do. I'm afraid I'm not much at the cloak and dagger game. We were walking up the steps to the Capitol when one of the staffers asked me what I wanted to call it. I guess I was surprised that we couldn't call it what it was; Ares...after the Greek god of war."

He took a sip of his coffee, "I mean, the damn thing looks like the head of a spear, and the spear happens to be the symbol for Ares. Frankly, it was one of the project engineers who came up with it. According to mythology, Ares' strengths were fearlessness, decisiveness, and determination, but he also had some weaknesses. Ares was impulsive and bloodthirsty...always looking for a fight. It seemed to fit." After another pensive sip of coffee, he went on, "We're concerned that we may have a leak of sorts."

He paused for a moment to bring himself back to the topic. "We had one of our own men on this, a guy named Hadley, out of our London office. Retired Royal Marine colour sergeant, quite capable, but he went missing last week in Shanghai. He was following up on something and then we lost contact. Have you worked in Asia Mr. Karlsson?"

"A little. I've spent most of my career working in Europe and South America." Karlsson was not sure how much they knew about him, but they must have known something if they knew how to contact Paul. Their organization did not have a website, so a person would waste their time trying to find them through Google.

Carroll nodded at Karlsson but addressed the senior gent at the end of the table. "Right, Arthur. Mr. Karlsson was promoted to a management role several years ago, overseeing their operations in Europe and Scandinavia."

And, while Karlsson was of Scandinavian extraction and was fluent in Swedish as well as Spanish, the truth was that after thirty-some years in the field, he was told that he needed to slow down. He had not really understood Paul's rationale for putting him out to organizational pasture, but then Paul usually had his reasons. Initially, it had been Karlsson's own idea. As a matter of fact, he'd earlier discussed retirement with his boss. But, in the end, it came all too easy for everyone. Their group was now inundated with the new breed of academic super-humans that could run five miles in thirty minutes and could knock out their doctoral thesis on their iPhone at the same time. It was not as if he had not done his fair share of physically demanding stuff throughout the years, but any enjoyment of donning his gym shoes and taking the morning air was long since gone.

He had tried his best to integrate into the management role, *mentoring and empowering* the newer members of their team, as babysitting had come to be known. However, as was the case with most people in that line of work, office work became a prison sentence. After all, Karlsson, like most of his older associates, was not MBA material and he did not know the first thing about political correctness. He had tried his best, but office work was not for him, and eventually he picked up the phone and requested a quiet separation. It was his second retirement, so he knew what to expect.

Collins continued, "This is a pivotal election year, Mr. Karlsson. We've been working on Ares...excuse me, Aurora, for almost twenty years. Now that it is complete and we're ready to take orders, the project could be jeopardized if some presidential candidate decides to exploit any questionable connections with foreign governments and *out* us on prime-time television, just to get at his opponent."

Karlsson had a somewhat quizzical look on his face as the executive continued, "Think about it," he stroked his upper lip as if he'd once had a moustache, "An aircraft capable of sub-orbital flight that can take off and land from many military bases around the world and be on the other side of the globe in a few hours. Totally invisible to radar and thermal detection, and able to take crystal clear photographs that can read tire tread impressions from over 150,000 feet."

Karlsson savored his coffee. It was strong like the European blends, "I've heard the rumors. I watch the Discovery Channel."

Carroll was pensive. "This is big, Matt. This technology is probably the largest leap we've made in the space program since Michael Minovitch figured out how to use planetary gravity to slingshot unpowered spacecraft with pinpoint accuracy to the edge of our solar system. All with mathematics. Now, we may be re-writing some of those formulas and changing what we know about physics."

Carroll pulled out a chair and sat down, "The key to Aurora's success, is its secrecy. It's bad enough that there have been rumors and speculation about its existence out there for several years, but as long as that existence was never confirmed, then the opposition would have no concept of the missions Aurora can actually perform. If the Area 51 buffs want to think we're testing recovered alien spacecraft, then more power to them. Hell, we've even gone so far as to have pie-plate mock-ups made so that occasionally, someone gets a glimpse of something other-worldly peeking through a hangar door left carelessly ajar. We'll do anything to keep the public from discovering what we're really testing."

Collins interrupted. "Matt, with just a few minor changes to the propulsion system, this thing is capable of achieving escape velocity and going into orbit. Maybe more. Depending on fuel weight, and a secondary propulsion system, there's talk that it could make it to the moon and back." Collins looked at Carroll furtively.

Growing anxious Karlsson asked, "And you think your executive is selling your secrets to the Chinese, or is trying to politically sabotage the project by feeding a candidate's political agenda?"

"Either are possible, Mr. Karlsson." Collins interrupted, "And, both of those matters would be the job of the FBI to unravel."

"Then what is it that you want from me?" Karlsson prompted.

After a stifled breath, Collins looked at Carroll, who arose, walked over to the bookshelf on the wall opposite the glass doors, and returned with a white cardboard box, about four inches on each side, the company's name and logo printed in blue ink on the outside. He positioned it on the table in front of their guest.

Collins directed, "Go ahead and open it. You probably won't recognize that part, Mr. Karlsson. It is made of a new space-aged blend of titanium and another metal that we've kept secret for a number of years. It is a fuel system component for a Pulsed Detonation Wave Engine, or PDWE for short. Our packaging engineers tell us that the box looks genuine, and our chemists say that the ink used in the logo matches our ink's chemical profile. In short, anyone in the business would think it's genuine."

From Karlsson's expression, Collins immediately determined that their visitor hadn't a clue as to what they were talking about and offered an explanation. "In order to power an aircraft like Aurora, we had to develop a new propulsion system. Conventional jet engines can't push an aircraft to the speeds and altitude we need in order to fulfill the aircraft's mission."

"The PDWE propulsion system works by creating a liquid hydrogen detonation inside a specially designed chamber when the aircraft is traveling beyond the speed of sound. When traveling at such speeds, a thrust wall is created in front of the aircraft - that is to say; the aircraft is traveling so fast that molecules in the air are rapidly pushed aside near the nose of the aircraft, which in essence becomes a wall. When the detonation takes place, the airplane's thrust wall is pushed forward. This process is continually repeated to propel the aircraft."

"From the ground the contrails look like, well, donuts-on-a-rope.

Liquid methane or liquid hydrogen sometimes, is ejected onto the fuselage, where the fuel mist is ignited by surface heating. The PDWE works by creating a liquid hydrogen detonation inside a specially designed chamber when the aircraft is traveling beyond the speed of sound. This little component in front of you basically keeps the methane from exploding the aircraft."

Carroll cut in, "Listen, Matt, you can't begin to imagine the complicated regulations that this will stir up. Category Fifteen of ITAR; the International Trafficking in Arms Regulations. They cover defense articles relating to spacecraft and are rigidly enforced by the Department of State's Directorate of Defense Trade Controls."

Carroll opened a folder on the table in front of him and continued, "Some of the items on the Missile Technology Control Regime Annex are controlled by both the Department of Commerce on the Commodity Control List and by the Department of State on the United States Munitions List. Our legal team believes that this component would also be covered in Section 121.16 of the Missile Technology Control Regime Annex and controlled by Commerce and maybe even other federal organizations." He shook his head.

Karlsson's brain was overwhelmed, and he hoped he wasn't supposed to be taking notes.

Arthur Collins jumped back in, "Then there's the Invention Secrecy Act of 1951, allowing the government to impose so-called *secrecy orders* on patent applications that contain sensitive project data, thereby restricting disclosure of the invention and withholding the grant of a patent. This lets them impose a gag, even when the application is generated and entirely owned by a private individual or company without government sponsorship or support."

"It's a mess if this gets out." He gestured to the piece of metal Karlsson held in his hand, which seemed much lighter than someone might have thought for its size. "That simple component, by itself, took many years and millions of dollars to develop, and was one of the most closely guarded secrets of our program".

Collins added, "Matt, this is just the first step towards the stars. If we can create a similar propulsion system to move space-time instead of just air, we could actually move distant stars closer to us. We wouldn't have to travel the speed of light. We would warp space and draw these distant targets closer."

"And this is what you think your errant executive wants to sell to the Chinese?" Karlsson asked in an attempt to bring the discussion back to parameters he could grasp.

Carroll interlaced his fingers and stretched his arms out in front of him until his knuckles cracked. "No, Mr. Karlsson. That's the one Hadley anonymously purchased from them on an online auction site."

———«(◎)»———

Stan Marchand rolled over and tried to screw his eyes shut to prevent the daylight from dissolving his dream. He was with the most magnificent woman he had never met. They were on a bed in his grandmother's house and the woman of his dreams was there, sitting crossed legged, barefoot, asking him if he minded if she stayed with them for a few days. She was beautiful. Long blond hair, blue eyes, and a pouty nose that complemented her brilliant smile. She was exotic, mysterious. He thought he'd seen her somewhere, perhaps on television, or in a couple of movies, and fanaticized her being close to him. Now, he was about to finally have his wish, when the sunlight streaked through the blinds, penetrating his eyelids, and bringing him back to reality. Grandma had been gone for many years and Stan did not think about her that often, so it bothered him a bit that this was taking place in her house. A house that had been vacant and derelict for many years now. He reflected that some psychologist would have had fun with that one!

He knew it was fruitless to try to get the woman and the dream back again. With the morning light, she was gone. He carefully sat up and pushed himself out of bed, rubbing his head and his eyes in the process. With his age and medical history of injuries, he knew better than to rush the process. After a trip to the bathroom, he made his way to the kitchen to the smell of coffee, which had auto-matically started dripping an hour earlier.

In the cupboard near the sink, he grabbed a coffee mug and somewhat shakily poured a cup. As he first sniffed, then sipped, he looked at his cell phone on the island, which had been charging silently overnight. "Not yet." He said aloud.

He took his coffee and wandered from room to room, looking at the lavish contemporary furnishings. His furnishings. He had picked the colors of the walls and the fabrics and style of the furniture. It was *his* place. Well, his and the designer who had helped him pick everything out. Nevertheless, it was supposed to be him. But with-out a family, or at least a steady woman to help him enjoy it, he felt incomplete. Alone. Now that he was basically retired, he thought about it often.

When he finally made it back to the kitchen, the coffee had be-gun to take effect and he picked up the cell phone and touched the icon for text messages.

Check your email. Coordinate for your review. Urgent.

He laid the phone back down on the granite island and moved into his office. It took a few minutes for the laptop to boot up and for him to filter through his email. After deleting the bulk of the in-coming stuff, which was of little to interest to him, he hovered over the one titled, *Grand Emperor Insurance*. When he clicked on it, he recognized the familiar format of a tasking.

"I have on the desk in front of me, an envelope with the number J56122. Please tell me what you can about it."

For twenty-five years, Stan had been a credentialed Secret Service agent. A good one. He had risen through the ranks from field office work to tours on the Counter-Assault Team, a Presidential Detail and then the Special Agent in Charge of a former President's detail in Texas. His interests in psychic functioning had been an un-sanctioned sideline, a hobby of sorts, until one day when he vividly saw the potential for violence to erupt during a Presidential visit to the Midwest. He went out on a limb and reported the information to his superiors, under the guise of the information having come from an anonymous source. But, when the information was investigated, and found to be accurate, he knew that remote viewing could be a successful intelligence tool. That is, with proper training, approved protocols and of course, physical confirmation.

As a Military History major at the University of Cincinnati, Marchand had been fascinated by stories of World War II. But while his fellow students were more studious of the tactics of war, he was engulfed by the use of somewhat unorthodox intelligence practices. In particular, he was intrigued by Hitler's interest in the occult and paranormal, and how he was secretly using information from a variety of psychic sources to add to the Reich's capabilities and strength. Notable among these often forgotten or downplayed stories were Himmler's use of remote viewers to find Mussolini in 1943 after he had been placed in custody and hidden somewhere in the mountains of Italy.

Upon learning of Hitler's strong desire to rescue the deposed leader, Himmler supposedly called upon certain elements of the Vril or Thule Society, led by a mysterious woman named Maria Orsic. Himmler was eager to please his boss, but the problem they had created in their quest for a master race, was that most of Germany's psychics had been rounded up and put into concentration camps under a program called *Special Action Hess*. This was in response to Hitler's former deputy using psychic intervention as an impetus to take flight to the UK to supposedly broker a peace deal through the Scots. Hess was captured but survived the war. Himmler had not been so lucky. No one knows what happened to Orsic after the war.

Remote Viewing, as it had come to be known, emerged as a strategic weapon following WWII, and began to take shape in the early 1970's when engineers and physicists at Stanford University began lab experiments to see if there was anything to it. The Soviets believed there was. The CIA had maintained that the Soviets had been experimenting with the unorthodox discipline since the war and there was a concern in Washington, or at least Langley, that they may be getting ahead of us in the psychic space.

In short, remote viewing was the controlled laboratory practice of seeking impressions about a distant, unknown target using extrasensory perception. Viewers, through relaxation or meditation were able to clear their minds and interpret sensory input about people, events, or other specific targets, with surprising accuracy. Original exploration by Stanford Research Institute in California turned into a twenty-year program that was sponsored by the US government. The outcomes were that anyone could be taught remote viewing, although some individuals would be better at it than others, depending on their pre-existing psychic potential. And while skeptics argued that the studies could not be replicated or validated, the government knew that it worked. It was just that no one knew *how* it worked. It just did.

Over the years, Stan read everything he could get his hands on about the subject. But, because of his occupation, and the traditional mindset of his peers and supervisors, he was reluctant to talk about it openly. Even at home in his castle, he kept his books on psychic functioning and other paranormal subjects hidden in the basement like a teenager hiding pornography. It was not until he was near retirement that a chance meeting with some similarly gifted people in the law enforcement community gave him the self-confidence to explore the process more openly.

Marchand finished his run and then showered. After one more cup of coffee, he decided his head was as clear as it was probably going to get and returned to his office on the first floor. He had been careful not to watch the news or look at incoming messages for fear of front-loading. Many times, his so-called *urgent* taskings were about rapidly unfolding global events, and he did not want to bias his session with thoughts of what he had been following in the news. Besides, the news media had grown increasingly and irresponsibly political over the past couple of years, and consumers could no longer depend on the accuracy of stories anyway.

He pulled up his email and highlighted the task reference number. Somewhere in the Beltway, his tasker had an envelope on his or her desk with that reference coordinate written on it. He had seen the envelopes before. But in remote viewing, there was no need to see the target, or the envelope for that matter. The viewer just needed the coordinate; an identification number or letter series that connected the viewer to the target in question. It truly was not that secret. It was all over the internet.

He pulled several sheets of blank paper off of the printer, and found some pens, pencils and markers in his center desk drawer. After taking a couple of deep breaths, he wrote the target refer- ence number: J56122, his initials and the date in the upper right corner of the page that he had oriented into landscape position on the desk in front of him. In the upper left corner, he drew a nonsen- sical doodle; an ideogram that helped translate information from his subconscious into his conscious mind so that he could write it down on the paper.

After a couple more regulated deep breaths, he could feel his mind start to clear. He shut out the sound of the refrigerator motor, purring in the kitchen. Next came the barking dog, several hous- es away. In his world, all was silent and well. He was at peace. He deepened his breathing and felt his heart slow. His mind became a blank screen. He felt a momentary sensation of weightlessness. Opening his eyes, he gently retraced the ideogram he had drawn, and then lightly tapped it in different places.

He focused on the target coordinates. Someone had loaded that envelope. Someone knew what was inside. Therefore, that knowl- edge already existed in the universe. Stan just had to relax and let it come to him. The first perception hit him, and he wrote "EVENT" in block letters on the left side of the page and circled it.

He relaxed and allowed the randomly received sensory input an opportunity to punch through to his conscious brain. He began to write, "Occurred suddenly...but might have been predicted by one or two of the people directly affected. Maybe days or weeks before. Feelings of chaos...commotion...cramped...trapped. Intense heat... can't breathe."

Marchand's heart was racing. He took a deep breath and then a swig from his water bottle. "Can't get out. Scrambling...rapid movement...happening too fast...door blocked or something. Fire... intense smoke..."

He touched the ideogram again, "Can't breathe...can't be saved in time...anger...safety wasn't important...inferior material."

He sketched some crisscrossing structures, parallel and perpendicular lines. It didn't make sense to him, but that was okay. He was getting something. He pushed the sheet of paper to the side and grabbed a clean piece off of the stack. After writing his name and the date again, he drew another ideogram, which seemed very much like the first.

He took a couple of deep breaths and tried to relax. This was a powerful event. People around the world would hear about it. It occurred in the past. Way in the past, but in this century. Mechanical... electrical...explosive?

He drew the vertical and horizontal lines again and tried to connect them with supporting diagonals, but it just didn't look right. Something was missing. Frustrated, he pushed that page aside and began again. "LIVES" he circled on the left side of the page. Immediately below the entry, he began making additional notes, "Four lives... men... adults...some kind of container...round...like a submarine?" Off to the right he wrote AOL, indicating an analytic overlay.

During remote viewing, the viewer needed to report on the raw sensory input without trying to use his or her conscious brain to figure the message out. Psychic data does not come through in any particular language or order. Thus, when a viewer tried to connect the dots or fill in the blanks with something from their own life experience, they recorded it as an AOL and moved on.

"Round...tubular..." He wrote. "Powerful."

He concentrated on the images and feelings he was receiving. "Powerful, but incomplete. It is missing something...something boxy...ugly...not streamlined and sleek like the rest of the target." He quickly sketched an antique TV set on a pedestal of sorts. The old kind, with tubes. "Two pieces...but won't be needed until later."

He took a couple more deep breaths and lightly dragged his

pencil back and forth across the page until an image seemed to materialize. He drew a triangle with rounded corners, and then traced over the edges for a couple of moments before drawing four circles inside. The circles represented human life. He squinted his eyes shut momentarily as a malodorous sensation surprised him. In his mind, it smelled like spoiled, almost rancid buttermilk. As he made the notation on the left side of the page, a chill came over him. The four lives in the triangle were lost.

CHAPTER 3

As Karlsson familiarized himself with his own business class cockpit of sorts, he had to discard pillows, blankets and a couple of bags of travel trinkets that the airlines provide their business and first-class travelers to make them think that they're getting something that the poor fools back in steerage would die for. In reality, he would just as soon have had a guaranteed departure and arrival time rather than all of the extravagance of a pair of disposable slippers and eyeshades.

Still, the extra space afforded the folks in business class would reduce the thirteen-hour flight from sheer torture to mere annoyance. How anyone of normal size could survive a flight of that duration, while firmly enslaved in a coach-class seat, was beyond the wisest of minds. He cursed the pilots every time they repeated the trite and thoughtless phrase, "...just sit back and relax and enjoy the flight." Every time he heard that ridiculous recitation, he wanted to choke someone.

He managed to locate a remote-control device flush-mounted into his console on the left side. Studying it, he realized that it must control something, so after a brief search he discovered a video monitor that was tilted, twisted, and inverted in the end of the console. As he ostensibly fiddled with all of his passenger accessories, he tried not to look like he was noticing the people boarding the aircraft behind him.

He figured that since there was no first-class seating on this flight, they were as close to the cockpit as they could get, and therefore, at least one or two air marshals had to be close by. It wasn't that he would jump up to help them subdue any unruly passengers or misinformed radicals hell-bent on steering them into a symbolic target of interest. They had their job to do, and he had his, and Karlsson's group was definitely not a law enforcement agency. But, if there was a firearm around, call it professional curiosity, Karlsson felt obliged to know who had it.

He was more interested in who else from Echo Aerospace might be joining him on this trip. Carroll's admission that they had already sent their own man to Shanghai, led him to the conclusion that they had a lot invested in this; maybe too much to be entrusted to a washed-up old has-been government-type like himself. He certainly could not put it past them to send someone along to baby-sit and to keep an open channel of communications. All with good intentions, naturally, but an unnecessary complication in any number of scenarios.

His communications protocol was really pretty simple. Karlsson reported to Paul, period. On a loaner job like this, he might call one of their executives if he had something significant to report. But, if they were waiting for some sort of nightly update from him, they would have a long wait. The management team of a Fortune 100 defense contractor might very well want their own real-time intelligence as a project began to unfold. And there were a ton of companies that specialized in that type of corporate security work. Besides, the Chinese government had a nasty reputation for monitoring phone calls and computer traffic going out of their country, especially from western hotel chains. There was no reason to give them more information than they already had.

To further complicate a trip of this sort, the problem with having too many uncoordinated teams in the field at one time is that once the shooting started, there was usually no obligation to stop and ask which side someone was on. Karlsson's rules of engagement had always been a little more concise than those of his comrades in the law enforcement domain: if it represents a threat to your mission, neutralize it. He was alert, but for all of the so-called security planning, he didn't spot anyone who paid him the least bit of attention.

For some reason, Collins felt it would be better for Karlsson to fly out of Columbus, rather than Cleveland. This was, presumably, so that no one could possibly connect him to any official business in Cleveland. "Very security conscious, these guys." He mused.

The downside was that it was a two-hour drive to the Columbus airport, followed by an obligatory two hour wait in the departure terminal and then he had to change planes in Minneapolis. Because Columbus did not generate as much air travel as some of the bigger airports, one had to find a connection to get to about anywhere. In Minneapolis, he had to go through security again before boarding a flight to Tokyo.

Once in Tokyo, the company's travel plan had him changing planes to a Japanese carrier for the final leg into Shanghai. And, as he looked through his itinerary, he desperately hoped that the Chinese had forgiven them for the rape of Nanking, or rather *Nanjing* in Chinese. It would not do to have Chinese air traffic controllers deciding to aggravate Japanese pilots by giving them incorrect landing coordinates as payback for something that had happened in 1937.

After buckling in and paying close attention to the cabin attendant who was trying to tell everyone how to fasten their seatbelts, he buried himself in one of the SkyMall magazines until the roar of the engines indicated that they were scooting down the runway. By the time the captain had turned off the seatbelt light he was already getting drowsy. But, while he had never been able to totally fall asleep on an airplane, he was at least able to relax and think through the details of the previous day's conversation on the Lake.

"You mean, like EBay?" Karlsson looked up.

"Well, not really, but roughly the aviation equivalent to it. It's a web auction site that caters to the movement of aircraft parts from a variety of undisclosed sources. It was started by the Russians after the breakup of the Soviet Union. They had tons of military hardware, and no one at home was taking inventory. They couldn't even account for all of their submarines!"

Carroll interrupted, "The FBI goes after them from time to time, but because it's web-based, with listings from hundreds of international users, they rarely catch anyone. When they try to sting someone, they find they're selling from a country with which we have no enforcement authority or extradition, or they end up having their own fictitious username suspended because that website logs unsuccessful or suspicious transactions...just like other auction sites."

"Well," Karlsson thought out loud, "If Ares is so secret, and its development has been specifically for the U.S. Government, then why would anyone want to counterfeit a part that has no commercial value? You think someone else has been building another Ares somewhere?"

Collins responded, "Maybe, but it doesn't necessarily have to be an aircraft with the same mission as Ares. It could be used on any sub-orbital craft that might need this type of propulsion system. It could easily be converted to a weapons delivery platform."

"But the, uh... PDWE...was a revolutionary new thing, supposedly kept very hush-hush?" Karlsson posited.

They looked at each other with a hint of embarrassment and then Carroll spoke carefully, "We didn't necessarily have the original idea. I mean, the idea's been out there for many years, discussed openly in science and technology magazines. And, of course, we've had engineers come and go from the project over the years. We don't know if someone has gone into business for themselves, or if a competitive power has decided to race us into the *new space*. Or if someone has developed a strategic weapon using the same propulsion system".

Karlsson shrugged, wondering if Echo had, in fact, stolen the idea from yet another source. "As you said, isn't this a job for the FBI?"

Both men looked at each other rather sheepishly again and then Carroll resumed, "Traditionally, yes. But in this particular case, we'd rather not have the adverse publicity that could come out of an official investigation. Right now, there are a lot of players competing for privatized space ventures. The current market value is estimated to be more than three trillion dollars. And, we already have a suspect. It's not like there is a lot of investigation to do."

"Martin Jeffers is his name." Carroll slid a manila envelope across the table. Inside was a photo taken from Jeffers' company identification badge, and several pages of the usual notes relating to his job and personal lifestyle. "He started out with us fifteen years ago as an aerospace engineer and rose through several management positions. Recently, he decided to leave the corporate team for a similar job with one of our manufacturing divisions across town."

Karlsson looked quickly at the report and read, "Born in Florida to naturalized parents...both from the UK. No arrests, no convictions, one divorce, but no credit problems. He sounds like a model citizen."

He was a model employee, too." Collins interjected. He's always been an asset to the organization; numerous awards, several patents. Very gifted and a very capable manager, never had any trouble getting his clearances renewed through the Defense Department. No perversions, no gambling and no drugs as far as we can tell."

"I'm not a psychologist," Karlsson flipped through the report, looking for certain key words, "but it doesn't sound like he's the type to be involved in espionage or seditious acts. If he's truly up to no good, what would you feel his reasons were?"

"We don't know." Carroll admitted. "He's the only one who's had access to every layer of the project, and the only one who's traveled extensively in China. And of course...the only one we know to have had contact with Senator Layden in unusual places, at unusual times."

"Maybe he's just a fan of the Senator's work, or the head of his local Layden-for-President club."

Both men looked at each other and for a moment Karlsson was afraid that they had failed to appreciate his dry sense of humor, and then Carroll said quietly, "We have an...uh...asset, in the Senator's camp." After a moment, he continued, "Matt, you have to understand that this is not only about national security, but it's also about big business. We depend on government contracts and it is only prudent to ensure that no matter who wins the election in November, that we have to have open channels of communication with the White House. With the privatization of space, there are dozens of companies that are being given contracts on various pieces of the endeavor. Some are joining forces and others are competing against each other with a fervor."

Karlsson gave them his best poker face, "And?"

Collins paused to take a sip of his coffee, "Her name is Jenny Lu. She's on the Senator's communications team, so she has access to several of his schedules and meeting contacts. She also happens to be engaged, so they say, to Marty Jeffers."

Collins continued as Karlsson raised his eyebrows. "She and Martin became quite close over the months preceding his departure."

"Close?" he responded, remembering the divorce listed in the file. "As in they had an affair?"

"Yes." Carroll replied. "It could have been just a physical thing at first...but when we looked into her background, we found that her life here began with naturalization about ten years ago. We know nothing about Ms. Lu before her twenty-second birthday, which she celebrated as a naturalized American citizen. Now, Ms. Lu is engaged to Mr. Jeffers."

Karlsson had not let the word go by unnoticed. "You said asset? As in, she reports certain activities or interests of the Senator to you? If you don't know anything about her, then how and why did you recruit her to work for you?"

Collins and Carroll exchanged another furtive look between them before Collins explained. "Uh...we've created our own poison, so to speak. Martin and Jenny met at a fundraiser a few months ago, that we...uh... actually put together. They basically hit it off. As I said, we need open channels of communication with both candidates, because we simply can't predict who'll be in the White House next January."

"Martin reported the contact, as was appropriate under the circumstances, and we ask him to, you know, see if she might be interested in full time employment after the election. I mean, many of these staffers are volunteers, and successful candidates can't possibly offer everyone who worked on their campaigns, a position of importance. So, in light of her occupational credentials, we...uh... offered her a compensation package that would be nearly twice what she could earn in government."

"You bought her to keep her on your side?" Karlsson said as he took another sip of his coffee.

"Precisely." Carroll, the former Marine, said succinctly. "But now, we need to know if she's really on our side, or has gone into business with Martin, for reasons yet to be made clear."

───────

When the aircraft touched down in Shanghai, it was dark and raining. At a kiosk, Karlsson converted some currency to RMB and walked right passed the limo driver holding the handwritten cardboard sign with his name on it. He had not requested a limo, and he doubted that Echo would have advertised his name in the airport lobby. He went out into the cool night and found a taxi that would take him to the Radisson New World.

Collins' travel agent had booked him into a very nice Marriott, but his knowledge of the Chinese counter-espionage program combined with his client's botched attempt at investigation and their potentially self-obsessed paranoia, caused him to re-think the accommodations at the last minute and book himself into another property. Certainly, the Chinese would have the new room bugged as well, but at least he knew they were not going to be sharing anything with Echo Aerospace. There was no sense making it easy for everyone, and he could assure all parties concerned, that he was not bringing in or taking out anything of technical or cultural interest, which could immediately place him in violation of his visa.

The Pudong, or east side of Shanghai is a modern, brilliantly lit financial center for Asia, the city lights reminiscent of Manhattan or the Las Vegas strip. The buildings are tall and western, while the real China can be found just blocks away. Karlsson was tired from the trip and decided to catch some sleep before his body's internal clock reminded him that it was off by a half day and would proceed to mess up every biological pattern he had.

When after a restless night of interrupted sleep, he finally awoke around 0700 local time, he opened the drapes to a somewhat overcast day and thought to himself that when the fog burned off, it would turn out to be a uniquely beautiful city. Unfortunately, he would soon find that the fog was a product of questionable air quality and would not burn off for the duration of his visit.

He breakfasted on an occidental buffet of eggs and meats and then took a stroll through the People's Park across the street. There, to indigenous music being piped in through invisible speakers, Masters and students alike performed Tai Chi with military precision. He made enough turns in his wanderings to ensure that he had not attracted anyone's attention and then returned to the hotel.

The last person to have spoken with former Colour Sergeant Bryan Hadley was the Echo Aerospace Managing Director for Asia-Pacific Operations, Angelo Coelho. Born in Madagascar to Portuguese parents, he spoke a half dozen languages fluently and with his bachelor's degree from MIT, and a Harvard Executive MBA, he was a perfect fit. It was as good a place to start as any, so he had asked Collins to set it up as a casual meet and greet. Hadley had been on a confidential investigation for the home office, so there would have been no need for anyone to know he was missing, except for his boss, and whomever might have had a hand in making sure he was missing.

After several perilous minutes of what would have passed for reckless driving in the States, the taxi dropped him in front of a modern building of glass and steel. Symbolic of the new Shanghai, it could have been in any major city in the world. Upon arrival, Karlsson tried to guess at how many RMB there were to a dollar, before giving up and handing the driver the biggest tip he had probably received in a while.

He found his way to the elevators and was pleased to see that the architects had copied the US guide for elevator comfort, rather than the European, and had made enough room for eight or nine full size adults. They all rode in silence, and when the doors opened on the seventh floor, he made a mental note that he was the only one to disembark on that floor.

To the left, there was a wall with a solid steel door, requiring an access badge for entrance. On the other side of the hall, there were double glass doors, through which Karlsson could see the receptionist on the other side. When he entered, she looked up from what she was doing and smiled.

"Good morning, I'm Matt Karlsson for Mr. Coelho."

"Certainly, one moment sir." Was the reply as she picked up her phone and dialed an extension.

It was only a couple of minutes before the double doors opened with a hiss, and he was met by a rather striking blond, who in her heels, had to be close to six feet tall. "Mr. Karlsson? I'm Rene, Mr. Coelho's executive assistant. Would you like to come with me?"

He followed her down a carpeted hallway, flanked with office doors and pictures of aircraft on one side, and cubicles with busy workers on the other. She looked back over her shoulder with a smile, knowing that he was watching her move. "Can I get you a cup of coffee?"

"No, thank you." Karlsson replied as she opened the door to the corner office.

Coelho was tall, almost as tall as Karlsson, but obviously a little heavier. He looked to be in his late fifties, well attired in a fashionable blue business suit, but when he reached to shake hands Karlsson could tell he had not always been an executive. Large, beefy, farmer hands. His grip was firm and presented palm down, indicating that he was used to being in charge, and thought he was in charge now.

"Angelo Coelho." He said with a welcoming smile.

"Matt Karlsson." He answered, returning the smile.

Coelho gestured for his guest to sit down in one of the two armchairs facing his desk. Once seated, Karlsson began." Mr. Coelho...

Angelo…I know you're busy, but I want you to know how much I appreciate you taking the time to meet with me."

"Certainly." he replied. "Arthur said that this was a seriously high priority and to do whatever I could to help you." He made a steeple out of his fingers on the desk in front of him.

"I'm basically just here to go over some of the information that Bryan Hadley passed on to us and see what we can do to add to that inquiry. When was the last time you saw him?" Karlsson asked as he moved the chair away from the desk to afford a few extra inches of leg room.

"Hadley?" he thought for a moment, "Oh, yes, of course, the British fellow?" He looked over at his computer monitor and then typed and *moused* around for a moment.

"Bryan was here the last week of January."

"Was it just the two of you?" Karlsson asked, somewhat surprised at the executive's unfamiliarity with the recent conversation with a corporate emissary.

He looked confused for a moment, "Yes…is there a problem?"

"No problem," Karlsson shook his head innocently. "I was just curious if Martin Jeffers had joined you."

His eyes narrowed, "Martin? No, he wouldn't have been in that meeting as…well, he was the subject of the meeting."

"The subject? Angelo, I don't mean to sound suspicious, but what did you and Mr. Hadley discuss?"

He pursed his lips and frowned, "Well, since you are asking on behalf of Arthur, I guess I can tell you that Bryan felt that there were some irregularities with Martin's documentation of some of our projects. Mind you, Jeffers was only here two or three times a year and didn't report to me. But," he looked out of the window over the city of Shanghai, "I have to admit that I was a bit curious about some of the information he wanted to access on one project."

Karlsson shrugged, "So, what was the project? And what did Hadley seem interested in?"

"He wanted to look through the records of the plant where they make the *sprayer* and wanted to see what we had on the project.

So, we ran some numbers...you know, fixed versus variable costs. In particular; labor, square footage...project loads and timetables... manufacturing costs."

"The sprayer?"

"Yes, that's the project name. Not sure what it means or what it's used for. It's actually just a component that will be shipped to the US and paired up with other components that will make...uh...a sprayer of some kind for aircraft. Because of D-FARS, we often produce parts according to spec without knowing what they are for or how they fit into a particular project downstream."

Karlsson removed a notebook from his sport coat inner pocket and began to make notes. "D-FARS?"

"Yes, Defense Federal Acquisition Regulation Supplement. It is a set of restrictions for the origination of raw materials intended to protect the US defense industry from the vulnerabilities of being overly dependent on foreign sources of supply. It came out in May 2014. It basically says that we cannot knowingly procure counterfeit material, and we must use a risk-based approach to reduce the frequency and consequence of counterfeit materiel by applying certain preventative processes. It forces us to strengthen oversight and surveillance of critical materials and components. We're therefore required to document all occurrences of suspected and confirmed counterfeit materiel with the Department of Defense."

Karlsson scribbled in his notebook. "Can you tell me...show me those numbers that you ran? In particular, what did Hadley seem most interested in?"

"Well, he wanted to know how many projects were being run out of Puxi; the facility over there. Like I said, he asked basic questions about project integrity and costs. He seemed most curious if there was anything unusual about their financials."

"What about their financials?"

"He questioned why their cost of goods-sold went up during a certain period last year...the...uh...last quarter, I believe."

"You say, *goods-sold*? And, what goes into that?"

"Well, when we take on a project, we have to look at materials, labor costs, and fixed costs like floor space and utilities, you know. From that we can arrive at an estimate of what it costs us to make a particular item. If we're making something for ten dollars a unit and all of a sudden, it goes up to twelve...or even fifteen, then we need to know what factors contributed to an increase in our production costs."

Karlsson nodded. "And what did you find?"

Coelho shrugged and clicked through some files on his desktop. "There was in fact, an increase in unit cost for the Sprayer Project. About eleven percent."

Karlsson wrote the figure in his notebook. "So, to what did you attribute the increase?"

Coelho squirmed a bit in his seat and glanced quickly down at the desk before answering. "I'm not sure. Hadley was looking into it and was supposed to get back with me."

"Really?" Karlsson looked across the desk. "Well, since I'm not a manufacturing guy, could you tell me what some logical reasons might be that would drive this budget line up?"

It was obvious by his tone that Coelho did not like having to explain things to individuals he felt were subordinate to him. "It's like I said. There could be an increase in labor costs, or there could have been an increase in raw materials. There could have been a design change or a quality problem that required a recall and re-design. For all I know, the electric bill might have gone up."

Karlsson could sense that he had struck a nerve, or certainly put Coelho on the defensive. There was no way a key executive like Coelho could be naïve to such a significant loss, without initiating a comprehensive review of the project. And the mere presence of someone from the home office looking at his division should have given him cause to make sure everything was in order. Karlsson smiled disarmingly, "That makes sense. Like I said, I'm not really a business guy and so I wouldn't try to assert that I understand how things work in a manufacturing facility."

They discussed some of the other manufacturing operations that went on in Puxi, which had nothing to do with the sprayer. Largely automotive, some aviation. The company had numerous global clients so there was no expectation that a single component would keep all the lines running. Karlsson replaced the notebook in his jacket pocket and arose. "I appreciate the time you afforded me. I'm sure it's very valuable. If you could make a quick copy of that file for me, I'll be on my way."

Coelho looked at him for a moment. His reluctance was obvious, but Karlsson could not decide if it was the angst of giving proprietary information to a stranger or because there was something in the data that Coelho wouldn't want out of his control. On the other hand, Coelho knew that his guest was on official business for the Chairman of the company. "Um, certainly."

As Coelho inserted a small flash drive into his laptop and began to mouse and click again, Karlsson added, "Oh, and would it be too much trouble to get a tour of the Puxi factory?"

"Uhmmm...yes...yes. Ed...uh...Eduard Bodnar is the ex-pat who runs that operation. I'll have someone drive you." He hit a button on his telephone "Rene, can you ask Ling to take Mr. Karlsson over to the Puxi facility and set him up with a tour?"

Coelho double-checked that the file had copied and then withdrew the flash drive from his laptop. "Here you are. These are the files that Bryan asked about. Because they are proprietary, I would ask you to do your best to keep them confidential."

Karlsson dropped the tiny plastic drive in his jacket pocket as Rene softly opened the office door behind him. He reached to shake Coelho's hand and noticed that the handshake was not as firm, and Coelho's eyes barely made contact with his. "I'll guard it with my life. Thank you again for your time, Angelo."

He followed the graceful Rene back towards the lobby and the awaiting receptionist. She smiled warmly at Karlsson as she offered him her business card. "Li Min will get you to the parking garage and introduce to you our driver, Ling. Please let me know if we can be of additional service to you."

"Thank you, Rene. It was nice to meet you." He replied with a smile that she was probably used to receiving from men of most ages and nationalities.

Li Min, the receptionist, came around from behind her desk and gestured towards the elevators across the hall. When the doors opened, she pressed the button for the second floor, and explained that the parking garage was on levels two and three, and all Echo executives parked on two.

When the doors opened after the brief ride, there was an Asian fellow in a sport coat standing beside the right rear door of a turquoise Volkswagen Jetta. Or the Chinese variant, anyway. Volkswagen had a strange joint-venture relationship in China wherein their car models were known by different names in different cities. Between the requirement for all car manufacturers to have a local business partner and the already-existing overlap between sedan size and price, the Jetta could be called a Skoda Rapid or a Santana, while its slightly larger brother, the Passat could be known as the Magotan or Lavida, depending on where you were. Thus, it was difficult to tell a particular model at a distance.

Karlsson did a cursory visual sweep of the area, trying his best not to look like a guy that was well-trained to sniff-out evil characters, no matter what their motives. It was a typical parking garage that was fully packed. Seeing beyond the first couple of rows was next to impossible, so he decided to tempt the fates and get in. Once seated in the rear, Ling closed the door smartly and walked briskly around the car to the driver's seat in front. After strapping himself in, he looked over his shoulder, bringing the sides of his fists together several times. "You buckle?"

"I'm buckled." Karlsson replied as the VW lurched forward.

The key to surviving driving in Shanghai is, quite simply, to not look out the windows. They have rules there, but these rules are unlike anything known in the west, including Manhattan during rush hour. The streets are overcrowded, and traffic control devices seem to be mere suggestions. If there are five lanes of traffic merging into two, they abide by what could be called the *photo-finish* rule. In other words, whichever car is a millimeter in front of the other, automatically has the right of way, whether or not either driver has the safety of their passengers on their minds at the time.

They crossed the bridge into the Puxi side of Shanghai, and the driver made a turn to take them down along the Huangpu River, a seventy mile long tributary of the Yangtze that eventually empties into the East China Sea. Whether it was Ling's driving or a poor exhaust system on the Jetta, Karlsson was starting to feel a little queasy, and was thankful when he pulled up in front of a building that had bilingual signage indicating that they were at an Echo Aerospace facility.

Marginally nauseous and not being used to the chauffer treatment, Karlsson was out of the car by the time Ling made it around to open his door. "I wait?" He asked.

Karlsson disappointed himself with his attempt at the traditional Chinese expression of gratitude; "Xie xie ni", and added, "Thank you", since Ling's English proficiency was far superior to Karlsson's Chinese.

Ling smiled and nodded as Karlsson moved up the driveway towards the security station. There were two guards in the small shack who evaluated him with the same regard one gives a lab rat about to go through the maze. Karlsson dropped Ed Bodnar's name; the facility manager who was giving the tour, and that served only to whet their appetite for information as to who this visitor was and what he was doing there. The officers requested to see his company identification and Karlsson had a difficult time explaining that as a consultant, they were not issued company ID cards. Instead, he gave them one of the generic business cards used for such situations. But since it did not have Echo Aerospace printed anywhere on it, they were confused even more.

Finally, after two phone calls and some rapid chatter in what Karlsson presumed to be Mandarin, they gave his business card back, and had him sign a visitor logbook before pointing him at the double doors leading into the building.

Eduard Bodnar turned out to be a fifty-something gentleman who at one time had probably been in great shape. But now, his receding hairline and sloppy waistline signaled that he had abandoned fitness as a lifestyle and was now concentrating on greeting middle age with a stoic acceptance. In his college days, the six-foot blonde might have been a great football player, but over the years, the muscle had turned to fat and he was just big. A Ukrainian-born US citizen, he was responsible for all operations at the facility, making them make money in a communist environment where profit really was not the goal. Compliance was.

Through the tour, Karlsson learned that they usually ran two, but sometimes three shifts with three hundred fifty people in a facility encompassing about 300,000 square feet. Like his boss, though, as cordial as he tried to be, he still exuded a level of annoyance that suggested that he did not like interlopers from Corporate, sticking their noses into his business.

He admitted that Hadley had been there, but as far as he knew, didn't take away anything that might suggest there was anything inappropriate taking place on his watch, and therefore, offered Karlsson the same tour that he'd given Hadley some weeks back.

It was a sterile tour which probably followed the same itinerary that they offered anyone who requested one. After a brief orientation in his office, they moved through the production area, warehouse, and finished goods sections of the plant. But, during the tour of the packaging lab, Karlsson pretended not to notice the four-inch boxes on the rack, quite like what he'd been given in Cleveland. At a distance, to the casual observer, they appeared the same.

It seemed that the sprayer, as the component was known, was only a small part of the work that was being done there. The facility was actually tooled for a variety of automotive and aviation parts that were constructed to written specifications and then shipped out to other plants around the world for completion, including clutch and transmission components. The Plant had several different production lines, but the hours of operation were reduced to two shifts mid-year the year before to bring the place into budgetary compliance.

Bodnar walked Karlsson into the area where the sprayer component was fabricated. Upon visual examination, the part seemed to be identical to the one he had held in the Bratenahl mansion. It was extremely lightweight but was obviously missing the rest of the intricate components needed to make it work. When he asked his guide, Bodnar had explained that due to US government regulations, that was as much of the component as they could make overseas.

When the tour was over, Ling was waiting for him next to the guard station, with the back door of the Jetta open. As Karlsson got in, he couldn't help but notice that Ling wasn't quite as amiable as he'd been on the drive in, and the two security officers who had done everything but strip search him on the way in to the building, did their best to ignore him on the way out.

Ling closed the back door and ran around the rear of the car, jumped in, and was shifting into gear even before his door was closed. When they had had left the property and headed back towards the Pudong side, Karlsson tapped him on the shoulder, "Is everything all right?"

Without turning his head, or looking up at the rear-view mirror, he replied, "Everything fine. We go hotel?"

Karlsson thought for a moment and then said, "Actually, Ling, I would like to walk some. Can you drop me on the other side of the People's Park?"

It was then that Ling looked at his passenger in the mirror, "Park not good for you. I take you hotel."

"No. Take me to the park." Karlsson repeated firmly.

Karlsson could see the driver's shoulders tense for a moment before he gradually acquiesced, "Okay...I take Park."

When he pulled up to the north entrance to the park, instead of coming around to let Karlsson out, he canted his head over his right shoulder and said, "This where you want?"

"Yes, thank you." Karlsson replied, getting out and closing the back door. As Ling drove off, Karlsson could see him punching numbers into his cell phone and watching him in his rear view mirror. Karlsson wondered why his behavior had changed so significantly in the hour that he was touring the Echo facility. Similarly, the two security guards seemed to intentionally avoid looking at him when he left, making him even more concerned. Most importantly though, Karlsson wondered why did Ling want him at the hotel so quickly?

By the time he had innocently meandered through the park, in the general direction of the Radisson, he had his answer. On first inspection, it appeared that there were three of them. One was in the van in the pick-up area in front of the hotel, and there were two more of them, flanking the revolving door leading into the lobby. Karlsson's paranoia notwithstanding, he was fairly confident that they were there for him. The questions though were; who were they, what did they want, and what should he do about it?

Obviously, once he had recognized their ambush, he could simply turn around and walk away. It made a sensible Plan A, but Paul had not trained them to run away. Quite the opposite. Sometimes the game plan called for agents to allow themselves to be captured, just so they could more quickly identify who the bad guys were, making it easier to eliminate them. If there were only two of them, and the quarry had the element of surprise, a skilled operative could certainly take them out sans abduction. But that would not necessarily get the team any closer to the truth. Unfortunately, there were three and they were dressed like worker bees. Karlsson was after the queen. The other consideration was that Hadley had also been a well-trained Royal Marine, and might have faced the same decision, but no one had heard from him in a while.

Karlsson reasoned that he was supposed to be a security consultant on this trip and not a master secret agent with lethal tendencies. If a gent travelling on a non-official passport, was to be picked up for playing a role in the disappearance or death of two or three indigenous folks who happened to be loitering in front of a hotel, there could be repercussions not only for one tall skinny guy, but also for his country and several US businesses. Thus, directly engaging a numerically superior force in the middle of Shanghai was probably not the best plan either.

He looked at his watch. It was just after two in the afternoon. As he waited and watched from the park, a Plan-C began to take shape in his mind. He could wait them out and see if they were relieved by a new shift, or if they just gave up and went home. Or, if Ling let them know that he had dropped his passenger in the People's Park, then maybe they would start to search for him there. Either way, it would tell him something about their organization.

He didn't have to wait long. It wasn't fifteen minutes before he saw one of the door flankers take a call. From his viewpoint, Karlsson could tell by the operative's body language, that someone superior to him was passing along information or orders. The chap's eyes darted up and down the street briefly before his interest shifted across the street to the People's Park. It was a quick call and when it was over, he conferred with his partner before speaking through the window to his confederate in the van.

Moments later, the two door-watchers started across the street in Karlsson's direction. He watched carefully from behind a tree, knowing that if they spilt up and went different directions when they entered the park, they would surely find him. His pulse quickened. Nevertheless, they both went straight in as he moved around the tree in a manner that did not look suspicious to the other persons present. They didn't split up until he had the chance to move back towards the way from which they'd come. Towards the hotel.

He moved quickly across the street and came up on the van from the rear on the passenger side. Quickly and decisively, he opened the front door and got into the passenger seat. The driver turned with a start but Karlsson was too quick for him. His left hand went forcefully to a point midway between the driver's shoulder and elbow, and using pressure, forced his hand back up to the steering wheel. "You speak English?"

The driver looked at him, totally surprised and nodded his head.

"You're here for me, right?" Karlsson increased his grip on the man's upper arm.

He nodded again. "Yes."

"Then let's go! Don't wait for your friends. Tell me where you want to take me and who we're going to meet."

"I don't know what you mean." He replied softly in near-perfect English, looking out his window to see if he could see his partners.

"Sure, you do! You're the driver. You were told to wait for me. Your friends were going to put me in this van, and you were going to drive me somewhere. Well, I'm in the van and ready to go. So, let's go!"

There was a moment of hesitation before the anxious driver put the transmission into gear and carefully entered traffic. He was about to tap the horn when Karlsson stopped him with a sharp jab to his rib cage. "No! I'm not here to play games. I want to meet your boss and if you don't want to take me, I'll throw your body in the back of this van and go back to see if one of your friends would like do it instead."

The driver looked at Karlsson to try to gauge whether the threat was genuine or a bluff. Either way, he didn't seem the type to take chances. "It's not like that. It's not what you think."

Karlsson leaned close to him with a sardonic smile. "And what do I think?"

"You probably think we meant you harm." The driver's eyes darted between the chaotic traffic around him, and his rear-view mirror. "We were sent to make sure that you would meet with Zhou. Just meet."

"Never heard of him. Why would I want to meet with Mr. Zhou?"

"Business." He replied watching his side mirror. "It could be very profitable for you."

Karlsson stared at the driver for a moment before speaking. "Uh huh. You speak English quite well. Where did you learn it?"

"Army."

"What did you do in the Chinese Army?" Karlsson's curiosity was piqued.

"No. US. I was born in Santa Monica, did four years in Armor, before..."

Karlsson cut him off. "Where's Armor headquarters located?"

The driver looked at him briefly as he responded, "Fort Benning... Georgia."

"Is that where the Patton Museum is?"

"No, man. The Patton Museum is in Fort Knox." The driver replied, knowing that he was being interrogated.

Karlsson fired back, "Is that where they have Patton's pearl-handled revolvers on display?"

The driver smirked, "Come on. Didn't you see the movie? Patton said that only a pimp in a Louisiana whorehouse would have pearl-handled guns. His were ivory."

Karlsson smiled a bit. "What's your name?"

"Liu Wei."

What about your two friends back there? Were they Army too?"

Liu Wei shook his head. "I doubt it. They are more like cheap labor that Zhou uses from time to time."

"Uh huh. And what's your part in all of this. You're not US Army anymore. You are driving a van for a couple of street thugs with orders to take me to Zhou one way or the other. Are you cheap labor too, or is that what you want them to believe?"

"Let's just say I'm cheap labor until someone tells me otherwise." The driver answered, his eyes darting between the lanes as the cars around him seemed to move like marbles in the back of a moving pickup truck.

Karlsson didn't trust the man in the slightest. Flawless English, and a limited knowledge of US military operations didn't make him genuine. He was more intelligent and articulate that Karlsson might have imagined for a common thug. He was someone's asset for sure. But whose?

"Just talk? Yeah. Is that how it worked for Hadley?"

"Hadley?" Liu laughed. "Hadley's okay. I heard he decided to take an early retirement package and got set up in a cottage in Corfu. When given the chance, he decided to play ball."

"Play ball?" Karlsson raised his eyebrows. "Just like that?"

Liu Wei nodded his head. "Just like that. He already had some kind of pension from the British government, and I guess he was tired of working a regular job. Zhou offered him a passport and a briefcase full of dollars and Euro, and the last we saw of him was when they dropped him at the airport. His wife still receives his pension in the UK, and then they share a place on the Ionian Sea on the weekends."

"Really? A passport? What name, and what nationality?"

Dangerously taking his eyes off the traffic on the bridge back over to the Puxi side, Liu Wei looked at him again. "Third version Hong Kong Regional, with the biometric code, bi-lingual. It's legit."

"I thought you had to be a citizen of the PRC to get a Hong Kong passport?"

"You do now. Supposedly. After the transfer of sovereignty of Hong Kong from the UK to the People's Republic of China, the rules changed. But *shanzhai* is big business. The government makes money from it, so they're willing to bend the rules to keep their revenue coming in."

"Shanzhai?"

"Yes. It means, literally...mountain fortress. But the term generally refers to counterfeit or imitation products."

"So, is Zhou a counterfeiter or a government person?"

Liu Wei smirked and shrugged. "Maybe both. I don't know for sure. I just know that he is powerful in the business and you don't cross him."

Karlsson knew that counterfeiting represented close to four hundred billion dollars a year for the Chinese. With that kind of money on the table, people in government had to have their hands in it some way. He also felt that the driver was giving up way more information than a paid street bully would normally know or give to a guy that was seen as the enemy. Still, he believed him.

"What else? How many men will be where we're going?"

"Probably six to eight warehouse workers. They're not a problem, but will fight if told to, just to keep their jobs. Probably only two that are dedicated security people who will kill. Them, and of course, the woman."

"The woman?"

You can't miss her. She's blond and six feet tall." He looked at Karlsson. "Let's face it, you ain't that good looking. If she comes on to you, then it's because she was ordered to. Watch your ass if you meet her. You're probably not her type any more than Hadley was." He chuckled. "Or vice versa!"

Karlsson thought for a moment. Then all of a sudden, the description hit him like a ton of bricks. "Rene." How many six-foot blonds were running around Shanghai with a connection to Echo Aerospace? But why was his captor giving up so much valuable information? Karlsson had to know more.

"You seem knowledgeable about the culture in the US. Who do you think will win the Virginia state basketball championships this year? Williamsburg or Quantico?"

Liu Wei tried not to smile too much. "I don't follow Virginia high school sports anymore. But I think there's a school in Maryland that has a much better team to watch. Beltsville."

They'd played the coy exchange that two operators might play to try to communicate with each other until they found out whose side they were each on. Karlsson offered him Williamsburg and Quantico, which were the locations of the training centers for the CIA and FBI. Liu Wei came back with Beltsville. That was the location for the training academy for the US Secret Service.

The US Secret Service. Established in 1865, its initial mission was to suppress the counterfeiting of U.S. currency. The Secret Service was mandated by Congress to carry out the integrated missions of protection and investigations of a variety of financial crimes as well as protecting the President of the United States and several other key dignitaries. Counterfeiting. Were the Chinese counterfeiting US currency? Credit cards?

Karlsson felt a comforting chill as Liu Wei turned down a familiar street. It should have been familiar. Karlsson had been on it a couple hours earlier. As a matter of fact, they passed the Echo Aerospace facility on the right and then went two more blocks to a nondescript warehouse that seemed clean and well-lit, but otherwise presented no strong security presence.

"This is your stop, Mr. Karlsson."

Karlsson should not have been shocked that they knew his name. After all, they had been sent to kidnap him and would have gotten a serious reprimand if they'd brought back the wrong guy.

Liu Wei put the transmission in *park*. "There's a cu-zee nine on the floor in the back seat." He said, referring to a Chinese-made QSZ-92. The 9MM with the dual stack magazine held fifteen rounds of ammunition. "As soon as I drop you, I'm going to call in and say that you forced your way into the van, and then tossed it in the back when we got here, because you knew you'd be searched inside. You okay with that?"

Karlsson nodded. "Yeah. That's the story. Are you going to be okay?"

"Absolutely." He looked at him. "I was paid to get you here, and I did. I'm going to tell them that I'm headed back to the park to pick up the rest of the guys, and then we're going to come back here and do whatever we're told to do. You've got about twenty minutes before we get back and have to kick your American ass. Are you okay with that?"

"Twenty minutes? Yeah. Better than some of the deals I've gotten."

Karlsson paused, "The name? Hadley's new name?"

"Hudgens. Bryan Hudgens."

The van slowed in front of the main doors, Karlsson turned to the young man. "I don't know who you are...but for some reason I feel like wishing you good luck."

"You as well. Get out of my fucking van, Laowai."

CHAPTER 4

S tan Marchand looked at his unread email from Emperor Insurance. "Tell me more about the device you perceived as a television set. Task reference number: J56122B."

The television set? It was an AOL, an analytic overlay that didn't seem to make sense for the target he was working. It was an afterthought. Nevertheless, he grabbed a bottle of water from the refrigerator and placed it within easy reach on the corner of his desk. He went through his routine of stacking blank paper on his left, and a variety of pens and pencils on his right. Organization made him feel comfortable.

He slid out of his flip-flops and reached for the headphones dangling from the arm of his desk lamp. Once they were properly seated over his ears, he went into his music file and selected a one-hour track of soothing meditation music with a sub-audible binaural signal that would help him relax and clear his mind.

The toughest part of remote viewing was the process of clearing the junk out of one's mind to allow subconscious information to flow through to the conscious brain. The viewer needed a blank screen on which to project psychic data. Buddha said that the human mind was filled with monkeys that were noisy, undisciplined, and antagonistic. They were the nuisances that kept one awake at night with worry and concern. Relationships, work, politics, religion. There were two principal ways to quiet the monkeys; one was to temporarily escape with the help of chemical diversions like alcohol and the other way was to manage the monkeys through meditation. Alcohol and drugs were not supportive of remote viewing, whereas meditation was.

As he listened to the soft music that contained barely audible pure tones generated in his head as a result of the binaural process of injecting two separate frequencies into opposing ears, that were ten hertz apart, he took all of his concerns and problems and swept them into the dustpan so that they could be dumped into a box for safe keeping. They would be there when he returned. Some clinicians saw binaural beats as a mere illusion, a placebo of sorts, whereas other experts realized the therapeutic quality of such input to relax or rejuvenate. The truth was that people were different enough that some could relax by listening to a particular piece of music, regardless of frequency, and still achieve the intended effect. Sometimes, certain passages in songs generated perceivable changes in a person's feelings or behavior. It could be as subtle as a key change or the transition from a chorus to a bridge.

His breathing was slow and steady, and his heart rate safely hovered just above bradycardia, his worries were gone and the picture screen inside his mind was now clear. It was time to begin to focus on the new task: J56122B. He made a notation of the date and the task reference in the upper right corner of a blank sheet of paper and then doodled an ideogram in the upper left. He focused on the task and waited to record any input he received about the target. He tried to ignore the fact that the image or impression now being targeted had already come to him in the earlier session. He did not want to pollute today's session with any overlay that might have emerged as a result of the feedback. It was somehow important. They wanted to know more about it. Somewhere in the universe, someone knew what this thing was. What it represented.

He tapped the ideogram several times and then his pen stopped, seemingly on its own. "Metal." He wrote along the left side of the paper, and then drew a circle around it. Gestalts, perceptions began to surface, and Marchand wrote "complicated...complex ... discarded."

He deepened his breathing and then wrote "different" next to his notation of metal. Different metals. "Incomplete...not finished."

He drew a box-like shape and then used short diagonal lines

to round off the corners of the square. "Eyes...triangular eyes." Underneath he wrote, "Nose...not square...rectangular." He sketched something that looked like a boxy jack-o-lantern that rested atop a stand of sorts. Not a swivel stand in the traditional sense, but one that served as a base to allow movement of the upper piece.

"Moved...misplaced." He concentrated for a moment. "Hidden... concealed?"

He pushed the paper to the side and reached for a blank page off the stack. He drew another ideogram in the upper left had corner and traced over the device a couple of times.

He was receiving feelings, perceptions of significance. It was important. It had been important. How could it have been misplaced or forgotten? It was designed by many people...educated people. Exacting tolerances. An engineering marvel. A scientific coup of sorts. It received transmissions like a television, but it also transmitted something. It travelled. It moved. It was designed to work in an intolerable environment.

Marchand tried to step back and draw the image three-dimensionally. The top part looked like a boxy pumpkin that some kid carved for Halloween. The bottom had a base and four legs. Legs that came out at slight angles...not straight up and down. He unscrewed the cap on his water bottle and took a swig.

A ladder? There was something like a ladder on the front. A ladder? But it didn't reach all the way to the ground. A user would have to really jump to get from the ground to the bottom of the ladder. Or, vice versa, if jumping to the ground from the TV set. Expensive. It was extremely costly. Why would engineers build something so complex and costly, to exacting standards, and then attach a ladder that didn't reach the ground?

Flame. Fire. Power. New gestalts were entering Marchand's consciousness. Power...push...thrust. He wrote the words along the left side of the page and then reached for another sheet of paper. He began refining his sketch. It was too big to be a TV set. It was larger than a car, smaller than a house. It carried people. Far. It was intended to carry people to distant places. But not by itself.

It was lost. Administratively. Many people collaborated to bring this concept, of whatever it was, to fruition. Broken down into pieces. It was sent somewhere. And then somewhere else. Then, it was reassembled. It was dormant, useless for a year. Studied. Other people finished it. Someone put it back together.

Marchand steadied and deepened his breathing. Purpose was important. Not a television but loaded with electronic equipment. Language not right. Built by several groups… assembled…part of a bigger project. Important project. Too many companies. Too many people. Became lost. Stolen? Sold? "Shit!" He said out loud. He suddenly got an analytic overlay of an old Lunar Excursion Module. A spacecraft designed to be transported to the moon and then used to ensure a soft landing and an eventual return of its astronaut cargo to an orbiting Command Module, for the ride back to good old planet Earth. Along the right side of the page, he wrote AOL; LEM, 1960's.

As was typical in these types of taskings, the remote viewer never knew the purpose of the task, only the target itself. It made no sense that anyone would be looking for something that had ceased being useful several generations before. Nevertheless, he made the appropriate notations and kept viewing.

He closed his eyes and allowed the darkness to morph into shapes. Shapes. Feelings. It travelled. It went to a distant place. Another place. "The moon". He circled the word and then wrote AOL beside the notation. His conscious brain was now trying to fill in the blanks about the target. Once he had focused on a lunar lander, it seemed that he was no longer producing valid information as a part of the viewing. And, since remote viewing was not an exact science, he took that as a signal to write up what he had and send it back to the nebulous entity at the digital location of Emperor Insurance. They wanted the referenced *TV* remote viewed, and that's what they got. He was retired. It didn't have to make sense.

Karlsson shook his head as he got out of the van and watched it return down the street in the direction from which they had come. He had not expected the case to be simple. But on the other hand, he hadn't expected it to take shape so suddenly. In a matter of hours, he had developed a lead on the missing Hadley, and also tied a potential illegal counterfeiting operation to a nefarious character that he was about to meet. Then again, his intuition could be way off, and he was seconds away from a bullet in the head.

He didn't see a *Welcome* mat on the ground in front of the door, but since they were expecting him, he walked on in. There inside was one of the largest Asian men he had ever seen. At six-five or six-six, the guy had to weigh close to three hundred pounds. The vertical scar that ran from his forehead down through his right eye and deep into his cheek would have made him quite memorable. And, identifiable in a police lineup, if it ever came to that. Karlsson smiled. "I believe I'm expected?"

The man with the scar grunted and extended his arms out to his sides, "Raise arms."

Karlsson complied. "If you're looking for a gun, I left it in the car."

The giant ignored him, spun him around to face the wall and then forcefully ran his hands along Karlsson's body and through his clothing. He found the hotel room key in his left front pants pocket and pulled it out. After glancing at it, he returned it and grunted. "This way."

Karlsson quickly glanced around at the lobby office. It was small, a reception desk and a couch. A skinny Asian fellow on the couch stood and followed them down the narrow hallway that seemed to lead towards a large warehouse area. He surmised that if there were two people on the site that could kill, then these were probably them. They certainly were not warehouse workers. The large man had the look of an obedient minion. The skinny guy had the look of a psychopath who was in the game to hurt people. A salary was just an added benefit. He was in his early thirties, but his hands looked old and broken. There was no life behind his eyes.

Karlsson had seen that look in the Army. They were the kind of troops that the Army did its best to keep out of its ranks. If they had avoided prison up until their enlistment at age eighteen or nineteen, they might have been eligible for military service, but their sociopathy was an indication of serious trouble yet to come. The kind of trouble that would be bad for public relations and put other troops at risk. More risk than they already faced in a combat zone.

Scarface's physique blocked most of the view in the narrow hallway, but as the group neared the light at the end of the tunnel, Karlsson could hear a male voice speaking excitedly into a telephone from an office somewhere off to the right.

The emphasis on the ascending and descending vocal tones made Karlsson think that he was speaking Cantonese rather than Mandarin. Mandarin was the official language of China and spoken throughout most of the country. However, in Southeastern China, including Hong Kong, the locals spoke Cantonese. A more colorful and vibrant-sounding language to western ears. Vocal tones were important in Cantonese communication.

While both languages were technically Chinese, the two languages were not mutually intelligible. The written characters used for both languages descended from the same language group in ancient China, but Mandarin used simplified characters, established by the Chinese government in 1932, while Cantonese continued to use the traditional characters. Therefore, those who read traditional characters would be able to figure out the simplified characters, but those who were raised in simplified Mandarin would have a difficult time reading the traditional characters.

Scarface stopped suddenly at the end of the hallway almost causing a rear-end pile up as Psycho-boy had to stop short to avoid hitting Karlsson. A moment later, the phone call ended, and Scarface stepped into a more warmly lit office near the entrance to the warehouse area. The lighting appeared more conducive to a working environment than the standard fluorescent lights that seemed to dominate the Chinese commercial office-scapes and residences. He looked over his shoulder at Karlsson as he stepped aside. "You inside."

Karlsson nodded at the big man as he squeezed passed him. The Asian gentleman behind the desk could have been forty or sixty. Flawless skin with a few wrinkles around his eyes. Barely over five feet tall, the man still seemed to command a certain presence with his immaculate blue wool pinstripe suit and crisp white shirt. The red, white and blue diagonally striped tie had been knotted perfectly with a half Windsor and his desk appeared clean and organized. "Mr. Zhou, I guess? Nǐ hǎo."

"Mr. Karlsson. Good of you to join us." He replied in accented English, gesturing to the armless chairs in front of his desk. His face was relatively deadpan. No anger. No emotion. "I hope my staff did not alarm you with my invitation?"

"Let's just say that I was a bit surprised by it all." Karlsson replied honestly.

The corner of Zhou's mouth raised a bit as if to say he appreciated the attempt at sarcasm. "What brings you to Shanghai, Mr. Karlsson?"

"You already know that, or I wouldn't be here."

Karlsson was aware of Scarface's move towards the back of his chair. Zhou waved him aside. "That will not be necessary, Sam. Mr. Karlsson and I have much to discuss. Please leave us for a moment."

When the two men had left the room and closed the door behind them, Zhou continued. "Please forgive Sam and his associate. They are very loyal to me, but do not understand the intricacies of business negotiations."

Karlsson needed information, but he also wanted to establish a level playing field. "Is that what this is? A negotiation?"

Zhou nodded briefly, "Of sorts. You did not answer my question."

Karlsson saw no reason to try to deny anything or fall back on the name, rank and serial number routine. If they had bought off Hadley and had Rene from Echo's executive office on the payroll, they undoubtedly knew more about what he was doing there than he did. "Same as Hadley."

At last, a small smile formed on Zhou's lip. "And what do you think Mr. Hadley was doing here?"

Karlsson shrugged. "He was looking into some aircraft parts that found their way to the black market. He was told that the Echo facility up the street was a good place to start looking."

Zhou looked up at his computer screen and began typing as he spoke. "Ah. The so-called black market. Not to be confused with the gray market, or of course, shanzhai."

Karlsson looked at him without emotion. Zhou had opened up the discussion by mentioning three different types of illegal trade channels. He felt his silence would give Zhou the opportunity to talk more. So, with that brief silence, Zhou continued. "As you may or may not know, the *black-marketing* of goods generally refers to the movement of stolen products through a global supply chain. Goods are stolen. Sometimes they are re-packaged or re-branded, and then they are distributed at much lower costs than a customer would pay for legitimate, authentic products."

Zhou opened his center desk drawer and removed a pack of cigarettes. A popular US brand. "Cigarette, Mr. Karlsson?"

Karlsson shook his head. "No, thank you."

"For the black market to occur, crimes must be committed. There is the crime of the original theft, and other related offenses that might take place during that theft such as assault, burglary, and the like. And then, there is a secondary crime of receiving or disposing of stolen property, which will eventually occur somewhere else in the supply chain."

Zhou tapped the filter end of the cigarette on his desk and then lit it with what appeared to be an awfully expensive gold lighter. Perhaps a Dunhill or DuPont. He snapped the top shut as he exhaled a plume of smoke towards the ceiling. "On the other hand, there is the gray market. Sometimes the gray market is known as the diverted goods market. The way that works is that some companies, particularly US companies, like to be competitive in foreign markets. As such they will sell an item that might list for ten dollars in the United States, for two or three dollars in a country like

Aruba or Venezuela. Even though the labels for these goods might be printed in a foreign language...or often bi-lingual, entrepreneurs can buy truckloads of goods at these prices, and then re-route them back into the US to sell the goods cheaper than the manufacturer is selling them for in their regular distribution channels."

He pulled on his cigarette and paused to savor the toxic smoke in his lungs before exhaling. "In the gray market, no crime is being committed. A company pays for a trailer-load of goods, receives those goods after paying the appropriate shipping and customs fees, and can then re-sell them anywhere they want. The importer is the new owner. Usually, there is contract language between the manufacturer and the importer somewhere that prohibits these types of transactions, but that is a civil matter between two parties. No crime has been committed."

Karlsson nodded. "I understand."

The grin began to appear in the corner of Zhou's mouth again. "But my sources tell me that you are here to discuss a different business scheme. Correct?"

"Correct." Karlsson nodded again.

"The manufacture and movement of counterfeit goods. Specifically, aviation parts. Is that correct?"

Karlsson returned the grin with a bit of deference. "Correct, sir." Using the term *sir*, in a sincere fashion gave the impression of politeness, and did not make the recipient a bit more difficult to kill at the end of the conversation. On the other hand, using it sarcastically in a fashion that has come to pass for customer service in some companies, would make the recipient want to reach across the counter and choke the salesclerk so hard their eyes popped out. It was all in the delivery. It worked.

"So then, of course, there is counterfeiting. How much do you know about product counterfeiting, Mr. Karlsson?"

"Not much. Just what I see on television."

"There are many ways to counterfeit products. Sometimes, you simply buy a legitimate copy of the product you intend to duplicate and take it apart to see how it is made. Some companies call that reverse engineering. Every company does the same with their competition's goods, just to see how they are made. Then, depending on the complexity of the assembly, or the availability of similar parts or ingredients, you just make it yourself. A counterfeiter does not have to spend years in research and development, and certainly does not have to pass any type of US quality standards or regulations. And the US economy has embraced foreign *knockoffs*, as they are known in your country. People enjoy purchasing a fake purse with an expensive logo, to feed their ego and to impress others."

"However, our government has started to crack down on some forms... pharmaceutical or nutritional products, for example. If word leaks out to the world that inferior Chinese knockoffs have caused illness or injury, certain company presidents... and some government officials, have found themselves standing in front of a firing squad. After a trial, of course. We are not savages here."

"With more technical items, however, we've often found it more profitable to simply run a fourth shift at the manufacturer's own location."

"A fourth shift?" Karlsson asked.

"Yes. Many foreign-owned companies operate three shifts a day. A counterfeiter would simply work with a facility's manager to help him or her meet the necessary business plan for production, and then run an additional shift that their company does not know about. Often, you see, counterfeit items are made in the same factories, and with the same materials, where the authentic merchandise comes from."

Karlsson was quiet for a moment. He decided he had to give Zhou something in return in order to show that he had something to bargain with. "So, the only evidence of an operation like that might be when the unit cost of goods sold climbs without explanation?"

Zhou gave his first genuine smile of the meeting. "Precisely."

"The fourth shift uses materials and labor that are already on the company's books. But instead of producing five hundred units according to the forecast, they actually produce six hundred. And the only evidence of this scheme is that the company unknowingly goes through more raw materials than they had budgeted and doesn't see the fixed costs for operations have climbed, until compared with the actual output of finished goods."

"You learn fast Mr. Karlsson."

Karlsson was partly thinking out loud, "Thus, by including key management personnel, a so-called counterfeiter might actually be producing finished products for almost nothing?"

Zhou nodded. "Correct."

"And the facility manager makes a nice little bonus that his or her company doesn't know about."

"Again, correct." Zhou acknowledged. "Or your Internal Revenue Service. Part of our agreement would likely include the mechanism with which to appropriately conceal the additional wealth."

"You mean, like bank accounts in places that don't share information with the United States. Or the United Kingdom? Would that include some sort of identification allowing a person to access those funds without using his or her real name?"

"Naturally."

"So, what about Hadley? Lead or silver?"

"Excuse me?" Zhou was not familiar with the expression.

"Plata o plomo. It's a Latin American expression that means a person can either cooperate and take the silver...or refuse and take a lead bullet."

Zhou thought about the statement for a moment. "Interesting phrase, but we are not quite that dramatic here. You see, hypothetically, if a person decides not to cooperate, we can simply let them go on their way. Our cyber intrusion teams are unparalleled. Mr. Karlsson, we can see online activity that most of the anti-virus companies cannot fathom. If one solitary person decides to go up against us, they are literally going up against their own government. You see, Mr. Karlsson, we control elections now." Zhou seemed proud.

"Excuse me?"

"The troubles in your country, the riots, the destruction...those events may be orchestrated and financed by wealthy American ideologues, but they are part of the Russian move against you. The Chinese are much more sophisticated. The US government only owns about a third of your country's debt. China owns, overtly over a trillion dollars, more than ten percent. Covertly, through intermediaries, we own an additional twenty percent. To be more specific, we own the businesses that make your ballot boxes and computer systems. We own the companies that make your information networks. Depending on which Presidential candidate we feel will benefit us, it is a relatively easy maneuver to have hundreds of thousands of ballots suddenly show up...electronically or physically, at the last minute, to ensure a victory. The Russians have always been tactical brutes, whereas the Chinese are much more strategically astute."

Zhou felt like he was in control and kept rolling. "With our vast financial strength, what makes you think that we don't own so-called American businesses? The very businesses that your Defense Department claims to have thoroughly vetted. What makes you think that we don't own a portion of the largest arms manufacturers in the world?"

"Space is privatized now, Mr. Karlsson. Like it or not, you cannot even get to your own space station without begging a ride with the Russians. How do you think those privatized space operations are funded? This is nothing new. We've been doing this for many, many years."

Karlsson considered the gravity of Zhou's comments. An election was underway. One of the candidates was about to be a Chinese dupe, whether he knew it or not. But, somewhere in Echo Aerospace, someone in a key position was providing information and material that could also be used to sabotage the defense of the United States, or to advance a political campaign. Karlsson had to pass this information along, but he could not do it from China. He had to string Zhou along for a while.

"Mr. Zhou, are you saying that you really think that you can control US elections?" Karlsson asked incredulously.

Zhou regarded him for a moment as a father would his

impetuous son. "Please do not feign naiveté in these matters. Your Central Intelligence Agency has been inserting themselves into foreign elections for half a century. And, when those attempts have failed, you have bought off heads of state and other key diplomats just like we do. You do not seem like a hypocrite to me."

Karlsson thought for a moment. He had a point. "And Hadley?"

Zhou smiled as if he had accomplished his task and won the negotiation. "Hadley was a recent hire at Echo and his needs were more easily anticipated. Purely economic. He had no company allegiance and was only working to improve his conditions in retirement. You, on the other hand, are not an employee and have no social media profile that we can find. You are a contractor of sorts. But we do not know your goals. So, that concerns us. We need to know more about you."

Karlsson looked down at the floor as if he were ashamed of himself. "I'm in the same age group as Hadley, and probably in the same financial situation. I'm retired from the military and do consulting work as a means to supplement my income. My goals? Buy some land in New Mexico and raise a couple of horses."

Zhou drew on his cigarette and then stubbed it out in the glass ashtray on the desk. As he exhaled the stream of smoke from his nostrils, he smiled. "Then I think we can come to a mutually agreeable arrangement."

"It's not just the money." Karlsson interjected. "I have to give them something. Someone. If I go back with nothing to report and then suddenly begin spending money that I don't have, I'll be washed up in this business. People will know. And they will just send someone else, with whom you'll eventually have to deal."

Zhou shrugged as if it was only a minor obstacle. "How high up do you need to go?"

"Excuse me?" Karlsson looked up from the floor.

"Forgive my Eastern viewpoint, but we have almost a billion and a half people here in China. If we sacrifice one American puppet, we will find another in a matter of hours." He looked again at his computer screen and tapped on his keyboard. "I believe you met Mr. Coelho earlier, did you not?"

"Coelho? Yes...the..."

"The Managing Director for Echo's Asian Operations. He is a very astute businessman, but unfortunately, a loss like the one you and Mr. Hadley have discovered would seem to indicate that he was either grossly incompetent or was covering up some shortages on a project called The Sprayer. That information combined with some rather shocking video of him with his Executive Assistant, would probably be enough to allow you to close this case, would it not?"

Karlsson tried to act surprised. "The tall blond, Rene?"

"Yes. That is the one. It seems that Mr. Coelho enjoys some rather lurid proclivities with tall women and might have been using illegally obtained funds to help pay for her apartment. He will not want his wife and family to find out. He will go quietly. Would that be sufficient?"

Karlsson owed a debt of gratitude to a certain Asian-American van driver for the advance information about Rene. "Coelho and his assistant?"

Zhou smiled again. "I could send you the video, but I do not know how you would explain obtaining it to your client."

"That would be sufficient. But...what type of a...severance package did you have in mind for me?"

"A hundred thousand US dollars. Would you like cash, or an electronic transfer?"

And there it was. Karlsson had learned what he needed to learn. "Electronic transfer. I don't want to go through customs with that much cash."

CHAPTER 5

Thirty-some hours later, Karlsson landed at Cleveland Hopkins International Airport, unshaven, unwashed, and exhausted. The actual flying time through Tokyo and Chicago was about twenty-two hours. However, flight scheduling, plane changes and a need to send some quick text messages from Tokyo added several hours to the itinerary.

His first text had been to an anonymous number in Arlington, Virginia that was monitored by a twenty-four-hour operations center. It said simply "PROMETHEUS RETURNING WITH GROCERIES". It literally meant that he was bringing Paul something he could consume. Information. What Paul would do with the information would be up to him, and possibly outside of the scope of Karlsson's current assignment.

His next text was to AFOSI Agent Jackie Biehn. Since she was the one who had initially requested this presence on this case, he owed her the second communication. The text to her simply said "IN TOKYO. WILL BE AIRBORNE FOR 20 HOURS. WOULD LOVE TO MEET YOU IN CLEVELAND FOR DINNER TOMORROW".

Finally, he dispatched a text to J.J. Carroll, his official client, as far as anyone knew. He had to be careful how it was worded. "NO ACTION NECESSARY YET. ETA CLE IS TOMORROW AFTERNOON. HADLEY OK, REGRETS NOT GIVING WRITTEN NOTICE."

Zhou's parting comments were still clear in his head. "How high up do you need to go?" That meant that someone above Coelho's pay grade was also involved in the counterfeiting scam. Since he was not sure of the reporting relationships in Coelho's business unit, he didn't want to reveal everything he had learned until he was certain of his audience. And, if the senior leadership decided to act on partial or unverified information, it could be disastrous for the case as well as the company. Besides, he had not heard back from Paul or Jackie as to what his official report to a private company should include.

Most of the people involved in the case believed him to be a contractor of Echo Aerospace. The reality was that he worked for Paul. Paul had offered him to Jackie, and Jackie had steered him towards Collins and Carroll. But like the man who kept meeting people on his way to St. Ives, one could add as many personalities to the mix as they liked, but it did not change the fact that his boss was, at least for now, the US Government. His highest priority was to summarize the meeting with Zhou and see what direction Paul wanted him to take. Further complicating the matter was the fact that the parties involved didn't necessarily share the same goals.

He had carried his bag onboard the aircraft so there was no need to wait around the baggage carousel. Nevertheless, he moved towards the arrivals area and found a quiet seat to check his incoming text messages before booking a hotel for the evening, and then arranging transportation. His phone took a moment to boot up and then try to re-locate itself after a trip halfway around the planet. When it looked like he was connected to a local network, he tapped the icon for text messages. It seemed like they were stacked in the order that he had made them.

The first one from Paul was brief, "CALL ON ARRIVAL".

The one from Jackie was a bit longer, "DINNER SOUNDS WONDERFUL...WHERE AND WHEN?"

And the response from Carroll seemed a bit more complicated. "ANXIOUS TO HEAR MORE ABOUT HADLEY, AND WHAT YOU FOUND. ON PINS AND NEEDLES HERE!"

Karlsson dialed Paul's number and was excited when he answered on the first ring. "That was a fast trip. What do you have for us?"

Karlsson was tired and hungry but tried to keep his sense of humor. "Good news and bad news. Which do you want first?"

The monotone answer was to be expected. "Whichever makes more sense."

"The short answer is that Bryan Hadley is living in Corfu under the name of Bryan Hudgens. He took a payoff from a guy named Zhou, probably around a hundred grand in US currency and Euros. It may be easy to track the source; watch for a similar deposit in my Bahamas account. The money probably came through yesterday. The counterfeit aircraft part that has drawn such interest was produced in Echo's own facility. Zhou's operation is just a couple of blocks from the Echo manufacturing facility on the Puxi side of Shanghai. Zhou thinks I have accepted a payoff as well, and I am supposed to give the folks at Echo their guy, Angelo Coelho as the culprit, in order to close the investigation. He is the managing director there and apparently shares some romantic interests with his admin; a woman named Rene, last name unknown. But you can't miss her. Six feet tall, blond, and hot. Apparently, there's video if you want to see it."

Paul ignored the humor. "I'll take your word for it. Do you have anything firm on this or just Zhou's word?"

"I have a flash drive that has the financial data pertaining to the Sprayer, as it's known. The sheet shows that during a six-month period last year, the plant continued to produce similar units according to their plan. But a closer inspection shows that their unit cost for those pieces climbed without a logical explanation. The explanation is that Echo produced one hundred more of them than they thought. No idea where the other ninety-nine went."

"Let me see if I can work on that from this end." He seemed to be making notes on his side of the call. Was that the good news or the bad news?"

"That was the good news. Mission accomplished...sort of. The bad news is that Zhou has someone placed higher up in their organization than Coelho. He also has similar relationships with several other defense contractors, so the sprayer could be the tip of the iceberg. There's more."

Karlsson spent the next few minutes summarizing the

conversation with Zhou that focused on being able to manipulate voting software and machines to favor a specific candidate. When he was finished, Paul briefly commented, "We've known about the threat for a while, but this might give us additional information as to the source. Brief Special Agent Biehn at your earliest convenience. She may have some additional follow-up for you on this thing."

He paused. "Let Arthur Collins know what you've got relative to his inquiry. But leave out the part about potential manipulation of our election process."

"Understood. I'll check back with you tomorrow, I think. I'm so jet-lagged I'm not even sure what today is. I almost left my shoes on the TSA belt at O'Hare."

"Get some sleep." He said before ringing off.

While he was still relatively conscious, he sent a text to Jackie. "IM AT CLE...R U IN TOWN?"

While he was waiting for a response, he started to dial Carroll's number, but then stopped as he remembered Paul's specific instructions; to call Arthur Collins. It could have been an oversight, or he simply used the name because that was who requested his department's assistance. Regardless, Paul specified Arthur Collins, so he dialed his cell number.

"Arthur Collins."

"Mr. Collins, it's Matt Karlsson. I'm back in town and have some news for you. Are you available this afternoon?"

"Hi Matt. Yes, JJ let me know you were on your way home. We can both be available by three o'clock today if that fits your schedule?"

"Absolutely. Meet at the mansion in Bratenahl?

"Sounds great. I'll let Frank know we're coming." It took him a moment in his haze to recall that Frank was the house manager who lived onsite most of the week.

By the time the call ended, Special Agent Biehn had responded. "HOW ABOUT MARBLE ROOM 623 EUCLID AT 1830?"

Karlsson replied with a thumbs-up icon and then scrolled through downtown hotels to see which might have availability for one or two nights. He found a suitable property near the lake, not far from Burke Lakefront Airport, the general aviation executive airport serving downtown. Several large companies based in Cleveland kept their corporate aircraft there, including Echo Aerospace. It was only about seven miles west of the Bratenahl Mansion off Interstate 90.

Once checked in, he grabbed a shower and changed clothes before stopping in the first-floor restaurant for something to eat. Anything to eat. Modern air travel meant cramped surroundings and marginal service, at best. Since the attacks of September 11, 2001, cabin attendants ceased being actual attendants and thought of themselves more as junior Air Marshals. Their demeanor and tone were often condescending, and it was evident they cared little for a passenger's comfort. On the other hand, if one failed to turn off their electronic devices, they rejoiced in descending upon a paying customer like wolves chasing a limping deer. And, to that point, Karlsson had travelled on many private aircraft, flown by pilots who argued that cell phones did nothing to disrupt electronic equipment in the cockpit. Further, many passengers either forgot or refused to turn their phones off during a flight, and no one in the flight crew ever seemed to be aware of it. So far, no aircraft had crashed because of a cell phone. Additionally, the fact that airlines had shrunk the size of the seats and shortened the distance between rows so that they could cram more human cargo on board, was an overt way of saying their service was about revenue, not about comfort or convenience.

After a club sandwich, Karlsson felt almost human again. He returned to his rental car and after finding his way to the I-90 on-ramp, headed east towards Bratenahl. The ten-minute trip gave him an opportunity to think about what to say to Collins and Carroll, and how best to say it. They had some internal problems that would be difficult to ferret out. The question was whether the problem of product counterfeiting was entirely new to them. Certainly, they were aware that most successful products were copied at one time or another, and China was most assuredly at the epicenter of it.

They must have had scores of legal brains on the problem, as did most of the Fortune 100 organizations.

The FBI had been all over the problem for some time. Operation Chain Reaction, overseen by their National Intellectual Property Rights Coordination Center, was a comprehensive effort targeting counterfeit goods entering the supply chains of the Department of Defense and other U.S. government agencies. Chain Reaction began in June 2011, and other programs like Operation Engine-Newity specifically focused on illegal importation and distribution of counterfeit automotive and aviation parts.

It was not like it was a secret. Thousands of companies had representatives in the FBI's InfraGard program, a partnership between the Federal Bureau of Investigation and members of the private sector protecting critical infrastructure. The InfraGard program connected private companies to the FBI, providing education, information sharing and networking. US Federal agencies had a vested interest in protecting US commerce, particularly in the defense industry.

It was just before three in the afternoon when Karlsson arrived at the manse. He entered the circular driveway at the end of the lane and parked behind the black Mercedes S-450 bearing an Ohio license plate with a Cuyahoga County sticker. It had been cold and clear for the last few days, and the car was free of the road salt residue that seemed to adorn most vehicles in the area this time of year. He made a mental note of the license number for no reason other than habit and took the clean sidewalk to the front door. It was open, just as it had been on his last visit a week earlier, so he entered and found his way to the conference room on the lower level.

Arthur Collins and John Carroll stood side by side, looking out the glass doors towards Lake Erie. When they heard him enter, they turned in unison and offered anxious smiles as a patient does when the blood work comes back from the lab, but want to know what the doctor has to say.

"Hi Matt. Welcome back!" Collins said, rounding the end of the table to shake hands. "How was your trip?"

Carroll joined them at the end of the long table and shook hands as Matt replied to both of them, "Long trip without much sleep, but I think I'm awake enough to let you know what I've got."

"Great!" Collins gestured at the coffee pot on the credenza. "Grab yourself a cup and have a seat."

Carroll added, "Or if you'd prefer to stand for a while and stretch your limbs, that might feel more comfortable. I hate those international flights."

Karlsson nodded, and after he had a sip of coffee, pulled out one of the chairs and sat carefully. His *hindquarters* and lower back were still sore from the experience. "I suppose the logical way to start would be for me to tell you what I found, and then for you to ask questions about the information that might be relevant for you."

Both men nodded and Karlsson began. "First, your man Hadley was able to find the source of the counterfeit part that you were interested in. And, where it was made. When he confronted the suspected leader of this…group, he was offered a large sum of money to drop his inquiry. Since he was already retired, living on a pension from the Royal Marines, the cash was enough of an enticement that he literally took it and ran. I have no idea why he didn't send you a written notice, but my understanding is that he is now living in Corfu. Possibly under an assumed name. It's a popular vacation spot for Brits and I assume that he and his wife had visited there before and liked the place."

The two executives looked at each other, visibly angered. Carroll spoke softly and deferentially to Collins. "Dammit Arthur, I'm sorry. But I told you I questioned his commitment to the company."

Collins held up his hand. "I know. He seemed knowledgeable and quite experienced. This was probably foreseeable, but I wanted to give him the benefit of the doubt. I thought he was well compensated for what we asked of him."

Collins turned his attention back to Karlsson. "How did you learn about this, Matt?"

Karlsson shrugged, "It was actually pretty easy. A rather distinguished Chinese gentleman named Zhou, probably from Hong

Kong judging by his language skills, offered me a hundred grand to drop it as well."

Collins and Carroll looked at each other again before Carroll asked, "And, you turned him down?"

Karlsson shrugged, "Of course not! I absolutely took the money and had him wire it to an account in the Bahamas." When he saw the looks on their faces, he quickly continued. "First, it's the best way to track the source of the funds. Second, to make my defection look legitimate, I told Zhou that I also needed to have a sacrificial lamb to slaughter to get you to drop your case."

"A lamb?" Carroll asked.

"Yes. I told him that you'd never drop this case until you had someone to blame it on. I said that if I didn't hand them someone, then you'd simply send another investigator next week. Maybe someone from the FBI."

Karlsson reached into his jacket pocket and retrieved the flash drive that he had been given in Shanghai, by his lamb. "This is the information that your managing director there...uh, Coelho, gave to Hadley. He made a similar copy for me. That copy. That will show you several financial spreadsheets that illustrate that while production goals were being met in the Puxi facility, costs per individual item, I think you call it goods-sold, apparently jumped in the third and fourth quarters last year. That's because your plant budgeted for and produced five hundred units according to plan. What Coelho was covering up was that there were an additional one hundred units produced in your facility, with your materials and your labor, that went out the back door to Zhou."

Collins picked up the flash drive. "Coelho? The ex-pat from Madagascar?"

Karlsson nodded. "Yes. But I'm afraid there's more."

He had their attention, so he laid it out for them in a way that addressed their interests. "Coelho was undoubtedly successful because he was a shrewd businessman, perhaps, but you have to consider that the depth of this problem indicates that his operations; his materials and labor had to be supported by the Chinese government. Someone within their system made sure his workers showed up and they made their production goals every month in order for them to produce extra units of your Sprayer, and whatever else they are making there for an alternate market. And they had someone planted on him to verify what was going on, and to ensure his cooperation. Rene.

"Who?" Carroll asked.

"A rather striking blond who serves as his executive assistant, who coordinates his schedule, and has electronic access to everything that he does. In a matter of minutes, you should be able to pull her personnel file and find out when she was hired, and who she listed as references. She got in the position somehow. My information is that Zhou has some video of her and Coelho engaging in some naughty behaviors that your Human Resources department would object to. Probably on company time and probably using company funds. You could fire her when you fire Coelho, but that might not get you closer to the source."

Karlsson took a sip of his coffee. "Zhou doesn't know that we know about her. He only gave us Coelho. So, whomever you put in to replace him should understand the relationship and know that he or she will be subject to attempts at corruption, and if they fail to cooperate could find various problems suddenly developing in their facility."

"This is, unacceptable!" Collins bellowed. "To think that we've been...infiltrated like this with apparent ease."

"And, for a long while." Karlsson added. "Zhou alluded to the fact that he has had people in most western organizations for a long time, and the Sprayer might not be the only thing he's gone after. He made a comment to me that you need to consider carefully before acting. When I said we'd need a scapegoat, he asked me how high I thought we needed to go. I don't know who Coelho reported to directly, but you might have to start there. The other problem is that you'll need someone from your legal department... probably someone with international law experience, to look at every division and subsidiary you have, to find out who the incorporators are in each country. Who are the key personnel in each division?"

"What?" Carroll asked.

"Large companies often find it necessary for tax purposes or other regulatory reasons to incorporate as separate entities in other countries. I'm sure Echo probably does as well." Both men nodded and Karlsson continued. "While the labor forces are typically comprised of indigenous personnel, key positions are often staffed with ex-patriates. I think you need to do a deep dive into all of your foreign holdings and the people who manage them. You've probably got most of this information somewhere already, if you had to fill out an SF-328 for the government; the Foreign Ownership Control and Influence form."

Carroll nodded, "We have. I think Tom Mathers in our Legal Department keeps that information."

"That's probably as good a place to start as any. The other part is to have someone in your Finance section...preferably someone with forensic audit experience, take a look at all of your manufacturing facilities and look for the same kind of trend we found in Shanghai. Start with the facilities that are doing piece work for your government contracts, and then expand your audit to facilities that produce high value, easy-to-sell items."

Arthur Collins quickly processed what he was hearing. "My God, that could take months!"

Karlsson nodded. "Yes, it could. But the benefit is, now you know you have a problem, and you have an idea of how to fix it. That's an internal Echo Aerospace issue that is outside of my scope. Since I am technically a government contractor, my duty is to report my findings to my boss in Washington. I'll let him know that I briefed you on this and that you're undertaking a comprehensive investigation. Is that safe to say?"

Collins picked up the flash drive. "Yes, thank you. That's quite acceptable. If you don't mind, can we load this up on a laptop and you can walk us through the data that our auditors should be looking for?"

Carroll asked, "You said Zhou doesn't know that we know about Rene being a part of his team. How did you come by that information?"

Karlsson thought for a moment. "Let's just say that Echo is not the only organization with counterfeiting problems."

It only took a half-hour to walk them through the data that he had been given in Shanghai. As he headed west on I-90, he glanced at his watch and saw that it was close to 4:00 P.M. He had two hours to rest up before meeting Jackie at the Marble Room. He knew his body. He needed to lie down for a while, even if he didn't fall asleep. Sometimes, this meant nodding off and waking up in an hour with a headache, feeling more tired than before. Nevertheless, he was a walking Zombie. Once back in his room, he stripped down to his shorts, set his alarm for 5:30 and stretched out on the bed.

It seemed like he blinked his eyes once and the alarm was chirping in his ear. It was time to arise, rinse his face and head down the street to meet Jackie. He pulled his gray slacks on again and found a clean dress shirt in his bag. It was no longer dry-cleaner crisp, but with the blue sport coat over it, the wrinkles would be concealed. He gargled and lightly spritzed some expensive cologne before heading to the lobby to hail a cab. He decided that between a shortage of available downtown parking spaces and the possibility of more than two cocktails, he'd let someone else do the driving.

The Marble Room was the most recent renovation and incarnation of Cleveland's first steel skyscraper. Originally built in 1893 by two sons of President James A. Garfield, it went through a series of tenants and updates, and for years had served as a respected banking center. In 2015 a company purchased the building and converted the offices into a hundred twenty residential apartment units and then added retail space. In 2017, the open and opulent first floor lobby was magically transformed into one of Cleveland's finest restaurants utilizing as much of the original bank's appointments as possible to add to the ambiance. Marble and bronze columns rose more than forty feet in the air towards an intricately crafted ceiling with a dining area illuminated by orb lights and a menu reminiscent of some of the finest steakhouses in the world. Even the marble check cashing counters had been converted for high-top seating in the bar area.

The bank's lower-level vaults, rumored to have once held Rockefeller's money, were updated and redecorated to create an exclusive private party space. Bank executives' offices were converted to private dining rooms and cocktail lounges, available for private parties. Antique fixtures and gilded tiles, meticulously restored, accented the eclectic décor.

He arrived five minutes early and found Jackie Biehn waiting by the hostess stand. "Jackie! So good to see you again!" He approached with a smile and gave her the kind of hug that onlookers wouldn't be able to discern if they were friends or something more. She instinctively drew her right elbow down alongside her rib cage, protecting the butt of the Sig 9MM tucked inside her waistband, under the jacket of her blue pantsuit.

"Matt! How was your trip?" She kissed him lightly on the cheek. She was staying in character. It might have meant something, but on the other hand, maybe she had told the Maitre'd she was waiting for her uncle. "How was your flight?"

"Torture! Absolute torture to the point that I need liquid medication right away!"

The bespectacled host introduced them to Tracey, who led them to a cozy table- for-two along the wall on the right side, almost towards the back of the grand lobby. "I'll send Jill, your waitress this evening, right over." She said, handing them each a menu.

They made small talk about Cleveland weather and then complained about the incessant road construction that always seemed necessary due to sewer collapses and sink holes in the city's major arteries. Lane closures were common and usually unanticipated by motorists who changed lanes suddenly and expressed their dissatisfaction with other drivers verbally or through commonly understood and often provocative non-verbal signals.

After their drinks had come, she leaned closer across the table. "Paul said you had a productive visit."

Karlsson sipped his bourbon Old Fashioned and allowed it to find his stomach first and then his bloodstream. "I suppose. I was able to locate the source of the counterfeit part; the Sprayer is what they call it. I met with Collins and Carroll earlier and briefed them." He retraced the conversation he'd had with the two executives two hours earlier, and then added in the elements that Paul had told him to avoid with them.

"As you know, the counterfeiting thing is not confined to Echo Aerospace. The Chinese are counterfeiting anything and everything that is currently produced around the world, automotive parts, appliances, cars, books and even movies. There was a joke making its rounds at the Agency a few years back that the movie Free Willy, *was free in Beijing before it made the cinemas here.*" They both laughed. "Zhou made it sound like they had their own people in most manufacturing operations around the world so that they could duplicate things either by using cheaper materials without any quality control, or by involving local management and producing counterfeit goods in their own factories. He told me that this has been going on for at least fifty years."

She sipped her Cosmopolitan, the discarded lime peel garnish on the napkin in front of her. "Yeah. We have some agents working with the FBI on this. The problem is that many US manufacturers are getting into joint ventures with the Chinese to produce aircraft. Commercial and, well, military aircraft. We have strict regulations about that, but we know it is still being done. The private space program has opened the market up for everyone to work together. But the problem is that the same types of aircraft that can safely transport astronauts to the ISS...the, uh, International Space Station, can also very easily be converted to weapons of war. And our official position on this type of cooperation seems to change with every Presidential administration."

"Which, the Chinese can control." Karlsson said flatly.

"What?" She looked at him.

"Zhou let slip that the Chinese either own or control the Canadian company that makes the US voting system. How do you suppose that happened?" He tossed out rhetorically. "Needless to say, this upcoming election is going to be somewhat chaotic if ballots suddenly appear for one candidate or the other, and no one challenges their authenticity."

She took another sip of her drink and signaled Jill that they would need two more. "That could mean an upset. The current POTUS hasn't said anything good about China since he took office. And there are rumors that Senator Layden's kids are involved on some company boards in China and Russia."

Karlsson nodded pensively. "Yeah. But that's not why we're here. Ultimately, that's going to be the FBI's problem, and I think Paul is going to pursue that with his counterpart at the Bureau."

Jill brought their new drinks over and took their dinner orders. Karlsson was impressed that Jackie ordered a steak, medium rare, along with a loaded baked potato and a salad. He didn't know where she was going to put it on her athletic frame but assumed from her appearance that she'd probably run it off tomorrow morning. She was lean, but feminine. He ordered the same.

"So, let me ask you something, Jackie. How well do you know Paul?"

She smiled, "To be honest, I really don't. Paul started out as an OSI agent years ago, before my time. So, it's my boss that actually knows him. Why?"

"Well, in St. Louis, you asked me if I'd been briefed on Apollo. When I mentioned it to him, he told me not to bring it up again to anyone except him. So, what the hell does this case have to do with a fifty-year-old space program?"

Her eyes darted around the room briefly as if to ensure that the conversation wouldn't be overheard. She used the lime peel to stir her new Cosmopolitan and took a deep breath through her nose. "Well, there was an allegation that surfaced some time ago that the contractors in the program were up against budget and timetable problems and may have ordered components of Apollo...well, the Block One Apollo, from sources outside their companies."

"Block One?"

She took a light sip, "Again, it was before my time, but the Apollo Command Service Module was the spacecraft developed by NASA in the 1960's as the spacecraft that would be used for earth and lunar orbit missions. Originally, Werner Von Braun thought we could take one rocket to the moon, land, and come back. However, one scientist, Dr. John Houbolt, remained convinced that we couldn't do that, and proposed the Lunar Orbit Rendezvous model...which a Ukrainian named Yuri Kondratyuk actually proposed in 1919."

"Anyway, the Block One model lacked forward docking tunnels and hatches and was to be used only for tests in Earth orbit to get us ready to go to the moon. It never flew, crewed anyway, after the fire that killed its occupants on the pad in January 1967. Although there were a couple of unmanned test flights that eventually took place."

She continued stirring her drink. "After the fire, the spacecraft was redesigned with crew safety in mind, and NASA tightened down on many of the sub-contractors to make sure that they were getting quality parts and components."

Karlsson thought back to his childhood. He was young when it had happened, but the event affected most of the kids of his day. Especially the ones who had dreams of becoming an astronaut. "Grissom, White and Chaffee, right?"

"Yes, Gus Grissom, Ed White and Roger Chaffee. Chaffee was actually a replacement for another crew member, Donn Eisele, who'd dislocated his shoulder aboard the KC135 they used for weightlessness training. He was scheduled to undergo surgery that January 27, which coincidentally was the day of the plugs-out test, and the fire. So, the Director of Flight Crew Operations, Deke Slayton, had replaced him with Chaffee."

"Plugs-out?"

She looked down at the table, "Yes. It means that they disconnected the Saturn 1-B from all of the umbilicals and cables to see if the spacecraft could function on its own."

She seemed genuinely saddened as she went on. "The ignition source of the fire was determined to be electrical, something in a wiring harness down by Grissom's left foot, and the fire spread rapidly due to combustible nylon material, and the high pressure, pure oxygen cabin atmosphere. Rescue was prevented by the plug-door hatch, which was poorly designed, and could not be opened against the internal pressure of the cabin. Because the Saturn rocket was unfueled that day, the test had not been considered hazardous, and no one had prepared for any emergencies of this type."

Karlsson looked at her sympathetically. "I don't understand. Does someone think that one of the contractors was using counterfeit parts on it?"

"It's possible." She picked up her drink and took a couple of large swallows. "We're not so much interested in the fire or its cause these days. We've been asked to find LEM 14."

Karlsson was weary from travelling and wanted to learn more but was not able to focus as sharply as he would have liked. "LEM 14? The Lunar Excursion Module?"

She nodded her head up and down a couple of times. "Yes. One of NASA's LEM's is missing, and no one seems to know where it is. You see, from 1962 to 1970 Grumman was contracted to build fifteen functional, fully operational modules and named them LM1 through LM15, at a cost of about a hundred fifty million dollars each at the time. There were other mock-ups made, but they were never intended to fly."

She stopped stirring her drink and dropped the lime on the napkin next to the one she'd discarded earlier. "NASA launched ten of them, and we know that six completed their missions and landed on the moon. Others were used for non-lunar training missions and we know that LEM's two, nine and thirteen are now in museums. We know that LEM 10 was ejected into space, and we didn't track it at the time but in 2019, some astronomer from the UK found it floating around out there, in orbit around the sun."

"This means that there were five of them left on ground, making LEM's fourteen and fifteen unaccounted for. We have Grumman records showing that number fifteen was turned into scrap metal. However, the report we were given by our source said that number fourteen was listed as *not used*, as opposed to *scrapped* like fifteen."

"Documents we got from the contractor listed it as *incomplete* but there was no confirmed disposition as to what happened to it. We checked with NASA and a few museums, but they didn't know, and neither did Northrup Grumman. A document we have dated March 1978 showed the code numbers of all the LEM's in the project, but it was missing the page that would have contained the information relative to LEM 14. We checked with historians at the National Archives, and a journalist who was also interested, but they pretty much reported that they had no additional information. Then, following a later tip we received from the magazine journalist, we located a guy at the University of Houston's space archives that said he still had a copy of the complete document, which included the missing page. But all his copy showed was *mission cancelled* in one column, and in the next column *deleted from program*. Again, it doesn't say where it went."

"One of our investigators interviewed an Apollo program expert who worked at an aviation museum, who said that it probably never got built. He wasn't certain, but he had seen an engineering progress chart that indicated that it had only gotten about five percent complete, and that other engineers thought it might have been scrapped. He suspected that they sent the salvaged materials to the F-14 program. But again, he couldn't guarantee that it wasn't taken by someone in whatever stage of completion that it was in."

Karlsson was intrigued by the story but still couldn't understand what it had to do with him. "So, why is this an issue today?"

"In 2009, the Lunar Reconnaissance Orbiter mapped all of our Apollo landing sites. But one of the LRO's unpublished images might have shown us where LM14 is."

"You have my attention." Karlsson said, eyebrows raised.

"Somewhere between Mare Nubium and the large crater Tycho, we think we might have found it."

"You mean, NASA ran another mission that they never told anyone about?"

She finished her drink. "Nope. We think there are a couple of dead Chinese astronauts on board."

CHAPTER 6

Natalie Richards finished making the lunches for her two kids. Twelve-year old Adrian and thirteen-year-old Kristina preferred their mom's culinary skills to those of the cafeteria workers at their school. Before she sent them off to school, she kissed them both on the cheek and gave them firm, loving hugs and told them that their dad would be waiting for them when they got off the bus in the afternoon.

After getting the package the day before, she had told Thomas, her husband of fifteen years, that she had a meeting in Washington DC with the parent organization for her athletic club. It was a short notice request for her to attend in one of the other officers' places, who was down with some sort of flu. She hated to lie to him but would need more time to fully explain the relationship she had with some of the people from her past. It was not really a lie. It was just a momentary pause from the truth.

She knew she had to tell him something for the time being. The well-dressed, middle-aged man with the short hair had dropped off the package to her receptionist the preceding afternoon, along with an envelope that included instructions and five hundred dollars in cash. It was an errand for her *dyadya*, her uncle. He wasn't her real uncle, more like a close family friend. A man who had worked with her father in the KGB, in the old days. Now he was posted to the Russian Embassy in Washington as some sort of cultural affairs attaché. She had been asked to deliver a birthday gift for a niece that did not really exist.

Born Natalia Talysheva to a mid-level KGB officer, in the Arbat section of Central Moscow, she grew up with the privileged class, not knowing the hard work and hunger suffered by her less fortunate contemporaries throughout the country.

With the help of private instructors, handpicked by her father, she had excelled at sports; particularly martial arts and shooting, and was considered good enough to compete in the Olympics. She was academically gifted as well, and was quite proficient in mathematics, thanks to the collaborative work of the private tutors, also chosen by her father.

The kids whose fathers did not occupy key positions in the Communist Party, or the KGB were not as blessed. They spent their summers in work camps. For almost a month, they spent the days working in the fields, and were rewarded with sport training and a chance to eat fresh fruit that night. They had never seen the kind of decadent excesses that Moscow's elite had enjoyed.

Because of her father's status, they could dine in some of Moscow's finest restaurants, or shop in the state-run retail stores known as Beriozka, which accepted foreign currency as well as Rubles. The Beriozkas sold luxury goods such as chocolate and caviar that were not available to most of their countrymen in traditional Soviet markets and shops. The shops from two different chains allowed the Soviet government to collect foreign currency and to then convert that currency to purchase goods and services from the countries issuing the original currency, at its face value. And only high-ranking government officials were allowed to enter these stores, as the mainstream public was forbidden by law to be in possession of foreign currency in those days.

By 1990, her father had seen the writing on the wall and knew that the collapse of the USSR was imminent. As a more senior-level officer now with the *Komitet Gosudarstvennoy Bezopasnosti*, or Committee for State Security, he was a member of the secret police force that was the main security agency for the Soviet Union from 1954 until they officially dissolved in 1991. And, as much as he loved his country, he wanted more for his only child. Through family connections, he was able to get her sent abroad for college, on a quasi-government scholarship, to George Washington University.

There she majored in Business with a concentration in Accountancy and found herself beginning to enjoy this thing called capitalism.

At five-foot-nine, the striking brunette soon found success with some of the most eligible bachelors around the campus and began to think that contrary to her original beliefs, the United States might not be so bad after all. By her senior year, she was sharing an apartment with Thomas Richards, a third-year law student from Pittsburgh with political aspirations.

She considered herself fortunate. Fortunate to have been so well cared-for in Russia, and now fortunate that she had been able to start a new life with a beautiful family. She frowned at the four-by-four package on her kitchen table. She allowed herself a peek at the contents and grimaced at the weirdly shaped piece of metal. Lighter than any metal she had hefted in the past, it still meant nothing to her. But, if it helped her father and the rest of her family back home, she could take a couple of days out of her life to pass it along.

What was she thinking about? America was her home now. She was naturalized. She was successful in business as well as at home. She was active in local civic organizations. And, as an infallibly enterprising woman, she was often asked to speak at events that promoted females being in key management positions throughout commerce and industry. She was where she wanted to be. Had she not come to this country, there was no way to tell what her life would have been like back in Russia, especially now that the country choked on itself trying to sell capitalism as a new philosophy.

In the basement she found some wrapping paper and a pink bow that would make the package look like a nondescript birthday gift for a child. It was silly, in her mind, that they had not just mailed the damn thing. Nevertheless, she wrapped it with care, and set it aside while she looked at the plain note that had been typed in Ariel font on a blank sheet of paper.

"Omni Shoreham. Call on arrival."

She had stayed there before. It was a beautiful hotel which had served as a backdrop for several movies and was always full during political events. About a mile and a half from the Russian Embassy, it seemed like as good a place as any to spend a night. She would call her uncle, give him the package, and maybe have a nice meal. She would get a good night sleep and be on the road back home by seven the next morning.

When she had examined it, the device seemed quite innocent, and she didn't feel like she was betraying anyone's confidences by taking it from one place to another. It was a favor for family. Nevertheless, before she handled it, she squeezed her hands into the blue Nitrile gloves to ensure that her DNA and fingerprints were not on it. She was perhaps overly cautious, but since she didn't know where the thing was going to end up after she surrendered it, there was no reason for it to be tracked back to her.

Satisfied that the wrapping would delight anyone's child, she packed a bag, tossed the gift into the top of it and put it in the trunk of her car. After shredding the instruction sheet and the envelope, she quickly checked the one hundred-dollar bills to make sure that the serial numbers were not sequential, and then she slid the Kahr CW9 and Kydex holster into her purse and tossed it on the passenger seat of the white Honda Accord. Her concealed carry permit would make this a legal transport through several states, right up until she hit the District. Once there, to remain legal, she'd either have to unload it and put it in her luggage in the trunk or take a small chance of it being discovered. If she got stopped, police would see that she had a concealed handgun license from Ohio when they ran her license plate. But she was a stunning middle class professional woman, driving a middle-class white Honda and knew that she didn't fit the vague profile for any type of criminal. It was not a racial attitude. It was just realistic extrapolation, and she was betting she wouldn't get stopped for anything.

She was beautiful, amiable, and fit. Her male clients took an instant liking to her. The wives, not as fast. She was the type of woman that men were immediately attracted to, with her dark brown hair and emerald eyes. But once the wives got to know her better, they relaxed, knowing that she could have about any man she wanted, and she wouldn't have been satisfied with someone's husband. Their husbands, anyway.

Once she was comfortably seated, she punched the address for the Shoreham into her onboard GPS and headed down the street in search of the on-ramp to Interstate 70. It was only a day out of her life.

———————

The morning light had managed to infiltrate the drapes that had been hastily drawn across the sliding doors. Luckily, the room faced north towards the Lake, and not the east. That would have awakened them several minutes sooner but wouldn't have changed her reaction. Jackie Biehn sat up in bed and put her head in her hands. "Oh my God. What have I done?"

Matt Karlsson rolled over and looked at her form, clothed in one of his white tee shirts, the cotton sheet covering her lap as she sat on the edge of the bed, facing the glass door. "As far as I know, nothing."

She looked over her shoulder at him, the embarrassment obvious. "Matt, I am so sorry. I have never done this before with a colleague. I mean...I've never done this before with anyone!"

Karlsson smiled and tasted the noxious remnants of the previous evening in his mouth. "You still haven't. You didn't do anything. We had too many drinks, and you intelligently left your car at the Marble Room. We came back here, and made an educated, adult decision to share the bed. If you recall, I offered to sleep on the floor, and you said *no.*"

She sat silently for a moment and finally said, "I need to use your shower."

He chuckled. "I'll take that as a routine hygienic necessity, and not infer something personal from you having been close to me all night."

"Very funny, asshole!" She slid out of bed and tugged the t-shirt down around her smooth thighs as she bent to retrieve her clothes and shoes. She tiptoed to the bathroom and slammed and locked the door. In moments, Karlsson could hear the shower running.

Karlsson smiled again as he reached for his cell phone to find any messages. As he tapped the appropriate icons to go from text to email, he noticed Jackie's Sig-Sauer P365 in its holster on the floor next to her nightstand. Evidently, she must have felt comfortable enough with the relationship to leave her gun behind with him.

He slid the phone back onto his nightstand, still attached to the charging cord and reflected on their discussion the night before.

"Dead Chinese astronauts?"

"Yes. The counterfeiting group that you are pursuing has been pinching US technology for many years. As you recall, in the last World War, we were allies. For that matter, we were allied with the Soviets too. We think that the Chinese government arranged to take possession of an unfinished lunar module to pair it up with the modified Block Two Command Module that we later found out they were building, supposedly in secret. They wanted to be a part of the space race but didn't want Russia or the US to know about it. Thus, they were able to construct a functional system that launched, but their use of sub-standard materials and corner-cutting on the specs only got them halfway. Well, let's say, it got them there, but their LEM couldn't get back off the moon."

Karlsson looked at her deep blue eyes, now a bit glazed by Cosmopolitans. "So, what you're saying is that they soft-landed, but they couldn't lift off?"

"Yeah. The LRO cameras supposedly captured footprints and other indications of activity around the landing site, indicating that once there, they were able to exit the craft and do whatever research they had intended. Maybe that just meant planting a Chinese flag or something. But the LEM is still there. All of it. If they had returned, the descent stage would be there by itself, having been used as a platform for the ascent stage to get the astronauts back up to their command module in lunar orbit."

"How did they get their hands on it? I mean, it's not like someone stole a Rolex and passed it to them in a parking lot."

"What we think is that it was dismantled and then shipped, in pieces, to a location in California. And then, at some point, the pieces went overseas. Over the next few years, they re-assembled it and made it fit the command module they were building, and were somehow able to test it on earth, without sending any other significant rockets skyward. We track launches around the world, you know. I guess the motivation was that it would be a significant coup if they could be the second nation to land on the moon, and further embarrass the Russians."

Karlsson had done his best to keep up with the conversation. This type of space-age intrigue was more than he was used to. "Okay, so the Chinese counterfeited one of our spacecraft, tried to land it on the moon, and lost a couple of their guys in the process. I'm still having a hard time understanding how that ties to our investigation of the Sprayer."

It was about then that she had ordered another round of drinks, and Karlsson decided that between jetlag and major alcohol consumption he was now just along for the ride. Nothing concrete was going to happen tonight; academically, spiritually, or physically. His ears were starting to ring, he felt a bit buzzed, and he was no longer the cold, calculating government weapon that he'd thought he was supposed to be. Her lips turned up at the corners, suggesting a smile of some sort. "There are three cameras on the LRO that capture high resolution images: maybe less than a meter...black and white images, and moderate resolution multi-spectral images of the surface of the planet. I, uh..." she looked down at the table. "...uh...saw a couple of the photos of the Chinese landing site."

"And?" Karlsson asked, his curiosity aroused.

"The photos look like they were taken from across the street. Not from an orbit thirty-one miles up."

Karlsson allowed her statement to sink in as he poked at the cherry in his Old Fashioned with a plastic swizzle stick. "What do you mean?"

"What I mean is that whoever or whatever took those photos of the landing site were within a few hundred yards of it. Not thirty-one miles. Matt, to me that means we're already flying Aurora. That's the only way we could have taken those pictures. They got it to the moon and back and we need to make sure that no one else can do that."

———————— ·《()》· ————————

Stan Marchand hiked up his trousers and gently set the face of his Ping driver behind the ball that he'd teed up so precisely that a physicist would have guessed he'd used a micrometer to ensure proper placement. They were on number eighteen, and he was even with the big oil man. He had to make every shot count. A tie was commendable. But a win would restore his ego from the pounding he'd taken from the big Texan the week before.

They were playing the black tees on the King's Course and the hole today was about 437 yards. There was much to think about. Take the club back slow and smooth. Bring it through at the same speed. Straight through. Follow through, facing the target. And, despite the compulsion to see where his shot was going, he had to keep his head down. He didn't want to duff one off the tee and have the Texan laugh at an obvious choke. He brought the club back through the carefully planned arc, and the second that he heard the distinctive sound, he knew he had connected. A split-second later he glanced up to see the brilliant white ball against the cobalt blue sky streaking away, straight down the fairway. He done it! With a good roll, it was going to be at least three hundred fifteen yards, maybe more, straight at the green.

"Not bad." Came the deep gravelly voice from behind him. "I'm fucking impressed. Not bad at all!"

When it was Griffith's turn, he didn't disappoint, but even though his drive was straight, it was still fifty yards short of Marchand's. He returned to the cart. "Skin on this one? A hundred bucks?"

Marchand tapped the pedal on the cart and moved them down the fairway. He knew the oil man was just baiting him to add some stress. But Marchand felt lucky. "Yeah. Okay, a hundred on this one."

They got to Griffith's ball first, and Marchand sat quietly in the cart as his opponent approached the ball and took a couple of loose practice swings. He connected okay but seemed to have pushed his shot off to the left. After a couple of bounces, he was in the fringe and not yet pin high. Marchand was afraid to jinx his own performance, so he remained quiet. When they got to his ball, he took a couple of deep breaths, and told himself it was as if he was at the driving range. No big deal. See the shot, swing smooth and let it happen. He pulled with his left arm and the wedge connected the way it had been designed. The ball went high, but Stan felt good. He watched it hit its apex and begin to fall back to earth. A smile turned into a wide grin as the ball bounced twice and stopped about a foot from the cup.

"Shit! This ain't gonna be my day!" Griffith grunted. "You want to just pick up?"

Marchand's grin was still visible as he shook his head. "No way. You're not going to chip it in from there, so I want the skin and the match!"

"Greedy fucker!" Griffith replied as he lined up his shot. He used a seven iron to get it out of the grass, but he over-stroked and the ball rolled past the pin by at least fifteen feet.

"You left yourself a long putt for par, cowboy!"

Griffith grabbed his putter out of his bag and carefully approached, circling around the hole as if he were a chopper pilot looking for a place to land. It was uphill with a right-left break. He knelt and studied the imaginary trajectory and then got into position. The putter gently came through the ball and continued briefly towards the cup for a smooth follow-through. The two men watched it roll until it ran out of steam one inch away. The big Texan had bogeyed.

Stan walked up and without thinking tapped his shot in for the birdie. He exhaled heavily as he bent to retrieve the ball. "All right then! I've reclaimed my honor!"

Griffith began making notations in their score card. "I guess it's my turn to buy the drinks?"

Stan slid his putter into the bag and came around to the driver's side. "I'd love to George, but I have something I have to do. Can we do it again next week?"

George smirked. "Sure, we can. But, what the hell do you have to do that's more important than gloating about your victory?"

Stan thought about the message he had seen when they'd stopped for a beer after the ninth hole. It was another tasking. Marked urgent. He wondered what was going on in Washington that he'd suddenly received all of these taskings. "Oh, man...I promised a friend of mine I'd help him with a project. It involves power tools, so I have to get there with a clear head."

The Texan laughed. "Then let's load up and get out of here.

Now, thirty minutes later, Marchand looked through his emails and found the one from Emperor Insurance. He clicked on it and read, "I have on the desk in front of me an envelope marked T98823. Please tell me what you can about it."

He grabbed a bottle of water out of the refrigerator and returned to his office. The paper and pens were still out on the desk, where he had left them from the previous day's tasking. He turned the blinds down a bit to darken the room and then relaxed in his chair with his feet up on the desk to listen to some settling, meditative music. He was still excited about the win on the golf course that morning, but knew that like all other earthly pursuits, he would have to sweep that into the imaginary dustbin until he returned from his psychic journey. His mind had to be totally clear.

When he felt that he was physically and mentally relaxed and open, he pulled a blank sheet of paper off the stack and wrote his name and the date in the upper right corner. He inhaled deeply though his nostrils and noted the task reference number below that. Then, on the upper left side of the page, he allowed a doodle to emerge from his subconscious, up through his conscious brain and down his arm; an ideogram that, at a distance, might have passed for a treble clef symbol on a piece of hand-written sheet music.

He sat quietly for a moment and then the pencil in his hand began to move sideways across the page as if he wanted to draw something but wasn't sure what. He was receiving impressions, gestalts. It was life, a person. A female. He made notations along the left side of the paper. She was young, perhaps mid-thirties? Dark hair...straight, black hair. Intelligent. She was short, but fit. Attractive. Intelligent.

He took a sip of water and then his hand resumed the back-and-forth motion across the page. "Foreign". He tapped the ideogram a couple of times and then allowed his pencil to rest on a part of it. One the left side of the page he printed, "Was foreign at some point early in life. Lives here now."

Stan Marchand took a couple of deep breaths and allowed himself to float into the ethereal space that wasn't sleep. Neither was it wakefulness. It wasn't physical, but it was still quite real. It was a place he knew. A place with answers. All answers: past, present and future. Some people called this universal database the Akashic record. Scientists and most theologians denied its existence, but it was there. One just had to be able to tap into it. It was actually quite easy to find. You just had to believe.

He drew a stick-figure, seated at a desk with a device...a laptop. "She works with computers in her job." Telephone. "She uses a phone." Other impressions were coming into his conscious brain now, "Intelligent. Sincere with others, but not necessarily trustworthy." He printed the words on the page quickly as the feelings surfaced.

"Dynamic."

"Articulate."

"Intuitive."

"Calculating."

"Focused." He frowned for a second. "Focused, but also seductive. Cunning."

He felt something and went back up to his notation for Intuitive, "Sensitive? Psychic?"

Marchand pushed the page aside and slid a blank piece in front of him. He sketched another ideogram, similar to the first, in the upper left-hand corner and traced over it lightly.

"Educated abroad...first. Completed education in the United States."

"Seeks power." He crossed it out and wrote, "Seeks information...to give others power."

"Confused...recently. Torn between two masters."

"Suffered abuses as child/young adult."

"Teachers exploited her... sexually, maybe."

"Revenge...she manipulated the system and exploited her abusers to get free."

"Violence."

"Connected to power."

"Wants to be around power...powerful people."

"Working towards a long-range plan."

"National impact."

"Global impact!" He wrote and circled the entry.

"Politics. She is working on a campaign of some kind. Someone's campaign."

"She didn't pick the candidate. Someone else picked it for her and she must make the best of it. She sees, perceives corruption if her candidate gets elected."

Marchand took another swig out of the bottle of water. His heart was starting to beat more rapidly. He was connected to the target and was getting input. "She doesn't really work for the campaign. She is working for someone else – who has an interest in the outcome."

Marchand stared at the paper and tried to draw what he was sensing. He drew a stick-figure of the woman and then drew two lines up to two other circles. Her two bosses. Two interests. Then he drew a dotted line to the right and wrote "Lover."

He circled the word and then thought to himself, "What a mess!"

CHAPTER 7

As she stared at her laptop, trying to come up with a penetrating and persuasive speech for the Senator, the strangest sensation came over Jenny Lu, causing her to sit upright and rigid in her chair. She looked around her comfortable Evanston apartment, fifteen miles north of Chicago. She was alone. But, for one brief moment she was overwhelmed by a feeling that she was being watched.

Born Lu Jingfei in Linyi, a city of more than ten million people in the south of the Shandong province, about seven hours south of Beijing, she had grown up under the standard familial indoctrination of Chairman Mao. As a young girl, she was taught the fundamental principles of communism and could think of nothing finer than to run around liberating the proletariat. There was no need for the private ownership of property. The government would give you what you needed.

At least her parents were honest with her. Quietly honest. In public they had a role to play, and they played it. However, in private, her father had pointed out the reality of their situation. Having been a university professor, he had been given access to things that other Chinese citizens did not have. Less-biased information.

In several of many private talks, her father enlightened her as to the façade that was Mao; that despite being considered a feminist figure by some, and a supporter of women's rights, he was far from it. He was perhaps the quintessential misogynist. It was rumored that in a 1973 meeting with Henry Kissinger, Mao claimed that women were *nonsense*. He went on to suggest that China was a very poor country that had little. However, what they did seem to have a surplus of, was women. He supposedly said to Kissinger, "Let them go to your place. They will create disasters. That way you can lessen our burdens."

She suddenly thought about her home in Linyi. She remembered the stifling summers with heavy rainfall every July and August. During the long summer months, the temperatures could range as high as a hundred degrees with punishing humidity. Still, it was usually several degrees cooler there than in surrounding counties. In the cold and dry winters, the temperature could plummet to near zero for days at a time.

She remembered the smells and the foods. The Linyi pancake was one of the main features eaten during dinner throughout Shandong. Served with green onions, the dish became famous during wartime due to its convenience of preparation and storage. It was even offered by the many street vendors that served their wares on the busy thoroughfares in town.

She remembered walking with her father through Linyi Calligraphy Square, and seeing the Kong Temple. Her mother and father took her to the Yimengshan National Geopark, and YiMeng Mountain where her family had their picture taken by a friend near the large glass bridge overlooking the Guimeng Scenic Area. There, one could find a dichotomy to the large cities, with an abundance of greenery, clear water, fresh air, and friendly people. It was different than Beijing and Shanghai.

With the support of her father, she had been admitted into the Journalism program at Shandong University, in Jinan. They had offered programs in Chemistry and Engineering as well as History and Culture. But while there, she learned that if she focused on a career instead of finding a husband, she would be considered *shengnü*, or left-over, in English, and stigmatized for her unmarried status. The government, her peers, and even her own family would look down on her for being too picky in her choice of a partner. It was there that she met Zhou, the older, successful gentleman from Shanghai, who would help her unlock some doors and kick down others.

The cell phone began to vibrate on the desk next to her laptop and she jumped. After a quick glance, she tapped the button to answer it. "Hi babe! How's it going?"

"Hi, sweetie! I really miss you! How's it going there?" Martin Jeffers said with a touch of anxiety in his voice.

There was no doubt that she had genuine romantic feelings for the forty-six-year-old engineer who had traded his creative genius for promotions to a variety of increasingly responsible management roles with the company. Her grandparents would have said that he was now part of the bourgeoisie. She could tell by his voice that he had bad news. But, she had him hooked. She had created a relationship wherein he would do anything to please her, and when he could not, he would withdraw like the child who didn't get picked by either team for sandlot baseball. "What's the matter? You don't sound good."

Jeffers was silent for a few moments. He needed to please her. She was everything to him and he knew that he would never find anyone else like her. She was beautiful and intelligent and alluring. She was almost fifteen years younger than him, and he knew that if he couldn't be successful at business and give her the things she wanted, she would lose interest in him and find a younger, better looking candidate. "I...uh...I couldn't get it."

Jenny folded the screen of her laptop halfway down so that she could focus on the conversation, without the distraction of the unfinished speech staring her in the face. "What do you mean?"

"My...uh...friend was in Carroll's office last night. He looked everywhere and couldn't find it. He'd been keeping it in a cigar box on his shelf, but it isn't there now."

Jenny Lu considered the range of consequences and tried to think of options that might have been overlooked. "But you said that he had it a week ago, right? Do you think he might have taken it home?"

"No. JJ was always pretty firm about sequestering materials under development. He wouldn't have taken it out of the building."

"What about Collins? Could he have put it somewhere up in his office on the twentieth floor?"

"No, sweetie. I don't think so." Jeffers' voice softened and then trailed off like a scolded child. "Carroll would have kept it close to him. I don't think the security guy even knew about it."

"You mean Hadley?"

"No. The, uh…security director for the company. Hadley was just an investigator of sorts."

"What's his name? What do you know about him?"

"Kendrick? He's not an issue. He's a retired FBI guy. They wouldn't have read him in on this because they'd be worried that he'd tell some of his old friends at the Bureau."

"Dammit Marty! I really need that! You're putting me in a tough place with…you know…our mutual friend in Shanghai. He said the company sent another investigator over there last week and if he can't get the piece back, then all bets are off. That includes our wedding present if you know what I mean!"

Marty tried to sound strong and encouraging but knew she could see through the act. "Oh, we can still get by. You and me, we're a team. We could make it on our salaries."

"I don't know, honey. I really need this to happen. We really need this to happen. It's part of a bigger picture that I'm trying to manage through. I've made commitments to people and if I can't deliver, there will be problems!"

"I hear you." Marty practically sniffled into his phone. "Am I going to see you this weekend?"

Jenny Lu lifted the screen of her laptop again and looked at the document. She shook her head and said truthfully, "Probably not. Layden will be here in Chicago this weekend to do some stumping and since I'm writing one of the speeches, his campaign manager said I could stand on the stage with him. I know, it's all bullshit. They are courting minority votes and they'll want an even distribution of Asian, Hispanic, Black and Native Americans standing up there to make him look genuinely liberal."

Marty was silent for a bit. "Okay. I'll miss you, but you know I'm supportive of your career."

"I know." She replied, knowing that he was really supportive of what she could do for him in the bedroom. Things that no other woman had done. Or, would do. She had worked her way out of communist China using her brains and her body, and despite her genuine feelings of affection for Marty Jeffers, she had to keep him hooked. "Look, they're talking about Milwaukee next weekend. Could you come up then?"

The excitement in his voice was a complete turn-around. "Milwaukee? Yeah! I'll plan on it!"

"I've got to get this done. I'll talk to you later...love you!"

"Love you too!" Said a reborn Marty Jeffers as he hung up.

It was growing more complicated than she had originally calculated. She had to sort things out to un-complicate things before they became overwhelming. It was a Chinese proverb that went something to the effect of "When problems become overwhelming, break each problem down into smaller, more manageable components. Then, just solve each minor component individually until the overall solution presents itself."

She had joined the public relations firm in downtown Chicago, with the hopes of latching onto some candidate's campaign. She was there. Through talent and a bit of luck, her boss had asked her if she wanted to try some speech writing for a US senator who was making a run on the White House. She could not believe it. She said yes immediately and was now being paid to help this philandering hypocrite get elected. He was no different from anyone else. In her mind, she was convinced that all politicians were philandering hypocrites regardless of which party they represented.

But Zhou was impressed. She hated to call the thieving pervert a mentor, but she had learned much from him. She had been introduced to him at a university event and quickly surmised that he was a successful businessman with one foot in government and the other in some capitalistic opportunities that old Mao would have despised. Nevertheless, while he was exploiting her various attributes, she was playing him to ensure that she could get a ticket to the United States.

It was through her US political connections that she had been introduced to business executives supporting various political campaigns, and eventually locked on to Martin Jeffers. And it was her connection to Jeffers that got her added to the Echo Aerospace payroll; a sizeable stipend that made her more than comfortable now.

Breaking her problem down into manageable portions, she considered that Zhou was only interested in something they called the Sprayer. She did not know why, but she didn't care. She just knew he wanted it back and she would be paid handsomely. Her agreement with Echo Aerospace was that they wanted to be close to the Senator's campaign, and she could keep them there. They should be happy. They would see her on stage with him at a major rally this coming weekend. The fact that they might have an internal counterfeiting problem was none of her business and she shouldn't feel obligated to let them know about it. If Marty got arrested or fired, then that was his problem.

She felt a momentary pang as she thought about him. Maybe them together. Maybe if things worked out well, they really could get married and settle down. She could continue working in public relations and he could keep building airplanes. On the other hand, she wondered if she could be happy with that type of life.

The troubling part of her problem was the FBI and the Secret Service. If Layden was nominated and eventually made it to Pennsylvania Avenue, she knew that an in-depth investigation into her background would be undertaken if she were asked to go to Washington with the team. She did not have a criminal record, but the files in Immigration would lead investigators back to her family and friends in China. She wondered how much cooperation the Chinese government would give the US government on something like that. If they linked her to Zhou, would she even be eligible for any type of security clearance having grown up in China?

She tried to shake the thoughts off. She had a speech to write, and she was losing her focus. She had to keep demonstrating her value to all of her benefactors.

Liu Wei parked the van and locked it. He headed up the walk towards the entrance, and once inside nodded at Sam, Zhou's bodyguard. The large man nodded back and continued reading the magazine in which he'd been engrossed. Liu had been anxious around Zhou and his employees, ever since the botched kidnapping attempt the week before. So far, he had not noticed a change in the way any of them regarded him, which was good. Still, being summoned to Zhou's office left him a little apprehensive. He walked down the hall until he could hear the boss speaking to someone on the phone, and so he waited patiently outside in the hall. When he heard the call end, he knocked lightly and then entered.

Zhou was making some notes and looked up. "Yes, come in."

Liu Wei stood across the desk. It would not have been appropriate to seat himself until told to do so. Zhou waved his left hand, indicating that it was now okay to sit. After a moment, he laid his pen down and looked up.

"When I found you, you were penniless, hopeless and didn't know your way around Shanghai. You thought you could come over here, make your own deals with Shanzhai and then return to your homeland a wealthy man. Unfortunately, you did not know China like you thought. But now, you have a place to stay and are making a decent wage. You owe me."

"I owe you." Liu Wei repeated.

"Good." The older Chinese man replied. "Now, I have a way for you to pay me back and return home with some money and goods to distribute when you get there. You will make money."

Liu Wei nodded respectfully. "Thank you. What can I do?"

Zhou regarded the younger man for a moment. "There is someone in the United States that you need to take care of for me. He has ceased being useful and now could be an embarrassment. A problem. Can you do that for me?"

Liu Wei thought quickly. His mission was basically finished. Over the past ten months, he had identified the counterfeiter and many of his accomplices. Now was as good a time as any to get out of town. "Yes, Xiānshēng. What is it you need?"

"I need to make this man disappear. Without it leading back to me." Zhou passed an envelope across the desk.

Liu Wei opened the unsealed manila envelope and slid a paper out that had a name, description, and picture. "Who is he, and where do I find him when I get there?"

"On the back of the picture is a phone number. Call it when you get back to the United States. He will give you this person's whereabouts and will supply you with whatever you need. Your target is a *nobody*. An aircraft engineer from Cleveland. No one will miss him. Just don't get caught." Zhou reached into his center desk drawer and removed a pack of cigarettes. After selecting one and tapping it on his desk, he continued. "It has to be done before next weekend. He will probably travel to Milwaukee for a political event and security will be too tight. Do this for me and I will consider us friends."

————)(◑)(————

Karlsson dropped Jackie Biehn at the departures terminal of Cleveland Hopkins. She had returned her car to the rental agency and they'd had a casual lunch together at a place up the street known as the 100th Bomb Group; a period place that was part of the Specialty Restaurants Corporation. The owner had served as a B-17 co-pilot for the eponymous unit in World War II. He built the restaurant to honor the Group, which had one of the highest casualty records of the war. Inside could be found wall-to-wall memorabilia, and outside, exhibits and replica air and ground vehicles were displayed throughout the property. It was close to the airport, and as Jackie had pointed out, even closer to the NASA Glenn Research Center on Brookpark Road. "You know what they do there, don't you?"

When Karlsson shook his head, she continued. "About three thousand people work on science and technology projects for use in aeronautics and space. They do hypersonic testing here, as well as cryogenics and space power research."

"Is that why you picked this place?" Karlsson looked out the window by their table.

She laughed. "No. I hate airport food, and this is one of the closest places to the airport with decent chow."

Karlsson nodded with a smile. "And where are you off to now?"

"Well, Quantico today for a debriefing. Then, back to Andrews to do my laundry and pay my bills."

Karlsson understood the lifestyle. "So, Andrews is home for now?"

"For now." She stirred her iced tea. "Matt...I...uh..."

Karlsson cut her off. "You're not gonna go all weepy on me, are you Special Agent Biehn?"

She smiled. "No. I was just thinking that maybe sometime, when you and I are in the same city again...you know...maybe..."

Their jobs were not really conducive to homes in the suburbs and white picket fences, but comradery did play a part in maintaining a somewhat normal psychological balance. "Jackie, I would very much like to see you again socially. But, you know, I'm old enough to be your...older brother or something. So, you know the first time some waiter asks if he can get me or my daughter anything else, there's gonna be a fight."

He remembered her smile as she bounced out of the car with the unbridled energy he'd first seen in St. Louis. But before she closed the door, she leaned in and kissed him on the mouth. "There. I wouldn't do that to my older brother!"

Karlsson waved as he put the car in gear and headed back to his hotel. He needed to call Paul and tell him what he had learned and find out if there was something else that needed to be done.

When he got back, he decided that after his conversation with the home office, so to speak, he would need about ten hours of uninterrupted sleep. He did not sleep well when he had guests in his house, and guests in his bed broke up his sleep patterns even more. After the call was answered on the other end, he responded "Prometheus for Paul."

"One moment, sir."

There were some crackles and beeps on the other end of his line, and he wondered how many different sets of ears were tuning in for the day's catch. "Hi, Matt." The use of his first name meant that there were, indeed, other ears on the call.

I just dropped Jackie off at CLE and she is headed back your way to make her report in Quantico. Not sure what her plans are after that."

"What do you have for me?"

"This isn't a secure line."

Paul grunted a laugh. "None of them are. The NSA got embarrassed a few years ago because they couldn't hack some suspect's iPhone. Since then, I'm pretty sure they've been on every call made from every phone in the world. Give it to me."

Karlsson summarized the China trip and his subsequent dinner conversation with Jackie. Paul didn't seem shocked. But then, he never was.

"Confidence is high that the Chinese left a couple of airmen on the moon?"

"Yes, sir." Karlsson was trying to be clear and concise but didn't know how much to say on the open line. "Something besides the LRO is taking pictures up there. Do you know anything about that?"

Somewhat pensively, Paul replied. "Perhaps. I've been hearing stories. She said she saw the pictures?"

"Affirmative."

"I wonder how many people have seen those images, and how many people even have clearance for such things. She is a federal agent. She should be able to take care of herself. Tell me more about the driver in Shanghai."

"Like I said, for an abductor-abductee relationship, we got along pretty well. Some of the things he said made me think he was Secret Service. If so, there's more stuff being counterfeited than aircraft parts."

"Well, back in the seventies, the Shah of Iran was supposedly given the same types of printing presses we use for authentic US currency. It could be that some of his technicians have come up with a means to counterfeit current production US currency. If Iran could do it, so could China."

Karlsson went on. "For what it's worth, he did me a favor in Shanghai, so if you find out that he needs something, we probably owe him one."

Paul could be heard typing into his laptop on the other end. "If that's the case, we'll see what we can do. But that's a Secret Service issue and unless they ask for our help, I'm not sure how we would know about it at this end."

"Well," Karlsson was thinking out loud now. "I was asked to consult with Echo, and I did. I gave them the information they were looking for. Am I back to being officially retired, or do you have something else that you'd like me to look at?"

"I hate to keep you on a string, Matt, but I need to check some other things out. Can you plan on staying in Cleveland this evening, and I'll let you know by 0500 tomorrow if I need you somewhere else?"

Karlsson snorted. "Sure, situation normal."

•《◦》•

Natalie Richards kept one eye on traffic and the other on the historical sights of Washington DC until her GPS announced that she had arrived at her destination. She turned into the driveway at 2500 Calvert Street Northwest and rolled up under the portico to await the valet.

"Good afternoon, Ma'am. Welcome to the Shoreham." The young man smiled as he handed her a ticket. "Can I help you with your luggage?"

"No, thank you." She replied as she pushed the button to raise the trunk lid. She handed the valet a five-dollar bill as she exited the vehicle and moved around to grab her duffel bag out of the trunk.

Once inside the luxurious lobby, she went straight to the counter, surprised that there were not more people in line. It appeared

that most of the people milling around were in suits and had surveillance mics with curly cords leading from their collars to their
ears. "Good afternoon Ma'am. Welcome to the Shoreham. What
name is your reservation under?"

"Richards." She replied locating her wallet in her purse. She
found the credit card she wanted and slid it across the counter. "Big
event coming up?"

The desk clerk nodded. "Yeah. Another rally tomorrow night.
When you see this many people running around you can assume
that the VIP's will be flocking in to see someone."

After clicking away on his computer, the clerk took her credit
card for a quick swipe and then handed it back to her with her room
key in a small folder. "We have you in a traditional king for one
night, and you'll be on the on the seventh floor."

"Thanks." She said innocently and headed towards the elevators. It was fast and efficient, just the way she liked it. She was happy they had put her on the seventh floor and not the eighth. She
had heard rumors that there was some kind of ghost in room 870
and she wanted to avoid the entire floor. She did not know whether to believe or disbelieve in that sort of thing, but she certainly
wasn't willing to take the chance.

When she got to her room, she took out the pant suit that she
intended to wear for dinner, so that the wrinkles would have a
chance to work themselves out. The rest of her things she left in
her bag, primarily due to an obsession about being able to grab her
things and go in case of an emergency. If the fire alarm was blaring
at two in the morning, she didn't want to have to run around while
deciding what she should take with her.

She looked out her window at Rock Creek Park, and on the other
side of the Creek in the distance, the embassies along Massachusetts
Avenue Northwest, which gave it the nickname *Embassy Row*. She
took a deep breath and dialed the number. It rang once before she
heard the gregarious voice of Feodor Golovkin, better known to her
as *Uncle Ted*. In the old KGB, he had been a senior official in the
Foreign Operations Directorate, responsible for foreign espionage.

But after the fall of the Soviet Union, his role transitioned to what had become the Foreign Intelligence Service under the new Russian Federation. And, as times and politics changed, he gratefully accepted a US-posting as the Russian Congressional Affairs Assistant Attache and was enjoying life in the United States as much as her.

"Moya lyubimaya plemyannitsa!" He blared with sincere joy in his voice. "How are you child?"

"Your favorite niece is just fine, Uncle Ted. I am in town and wondered if it would be convenient to have dinner."

"I would enjoy that very much! Where are you staying?"

She wondered if the phones were tapped. He knew bloody well where she was staying, but she would play along. "I'm in a beautiful room at the Shoreham."

"Wonderful! You must be exhausted from your trip. Why don't you just make a reservation for us in the hotel restaurant, and I will meet you there in an hour."

"Lovely! I will meet you in the lobby!"

She used her room phone to call down to make a reservation at the casually elegant Robert's. Table for two. She had an hour to get ready and decided to use as much of the time as she could in a hot bath. It was a luxury she did not often have at home, with two kids and an incessantly needy husband to care for. A half hour later, she was so relaxed she was afraid that she would fall asleep and slip under the bubbles provided by the jar of Almond Coconut Milk Honey Bath that she had stashed in her duffel.

She toweled off and looked at the pantsuit. The wrinkles were gone so she was delighted that she would not have to run an iron over it. She spent the remainder of her time working on her hair and by the time the hour was up, she slipped her bare feet into the black Louboutin pumps, grabbed the package, and headed to the elevator.

When the doors opened, she was greeted by two thirty-something men in suits, with earpieces and iPads. They both smiled instantaneously. With her four-inch heels, she was tall and breathtaking. "Hi there! Which floor?" One offered with a mouthful of perfect teeth.

"Lobby please." She smiled back.

She stood facing the doors, offering them a clear view of her statuesque form, and heard one of them ask, "Birthday party?"

She looked over her shoulder and turned slightly to see him glancing at the four-by-four package with the bow on it. "Yes." She grinned. "Something for my niece."

"How old?" The other man asked.

"She'll be six next week." Natalie grinned, turning to face him.

"Great age. I have a daughter who just turned seven." He added, his nostrils flaring almost imperceptibly as he savored her perfume. "Are you in town for long?"

"No. Just tonight." She replied, recognizing that he was flirting, and wearing a wedding ring. It was time to change the subject. "Big event coming up?"

"Not really. Just another rally, tomorrow night."

The elevator doors opened, and she smiled as she stepped off. "Well, good luck with that."

She found it humorous that she was meeting a top Russian official right under the noses of the US Secret Service and getting ready to pass him something of such significant technological value, that it was too important to have been mailed. Freedom. It was a beautiful thing. She found a comfortable chair that allowed her to see the front doors and relaxed with a copy of the Washington Post that had been left on a nearby table. Only a few minutes passed before she saw the gargantuan frame of Uncle Ted enter the hotel. At six-foot-four and two hundred eighty-five pounds, the loveable, but hairy creature resembled the symbolic Russian Bear as epitomized in literature and cartoons since the 1600's.

She ran up to him with a huge smile. "Uncle Ted!"

"Natalia, my dear! You look wonderful!" He hugged her hard enough that had she not been in top shape, it would have snapped a rib. They kissed each other on both cheeks. "Have you spoken to your otets lately?"

She took him by the hand and led him towards the restaurant. "Just last month. Father said that they are well, but things are very different now."

"Very true!" He squeezed her hand. "The place is crazy. It is very difficult to know who is trustworthy. Will you be going home any time soon? They would love to see you."

"Thomas and I hope to take the kids over this summer if we can get the time off." They spoke quietly in English as they walked through the lobby, and when they got to the host, she gave her name for the reservation.

When they were seated, she innocently placed the small gift on the table in front of her uncle. "Let me give this to you now in case I forget."

The Russian grizzly smiled, his teeth showing signs of too much tea and tobacco. "Oh, thank you! She will love it! Did you have any trouble?"

"Not at all. It was the only one they had in stock, so I hope she likes the color."

Golovkin's smile turned into a broad grin. "You have not lost your touch my dear! Your father would be proud." He dropped the box into the deep pocket of his dark wool overcoat and then draped it across the back of one of the unused chairs at their table.

When the waiter reached them, and noticed the coat, he asked, "May I take that for you sir?"

"Oh, of course! If you don't mind, could you just give it to my secretary? He is the gentleman in the suit by the coat check at the top of the stairs."

"My pleasure, sir." He carefully draped the heavy overcoat over his arm. "And may I get either of you a cocktail?"

Uncle Ted looked at his niece. "I think we should celebrate tonight. We need Vodka! Beluga Gold Line Russian Vodka!"

"Why not?" She grinned. Her package would be in the Russian Embassy in ten minutes, and she was finished working for the day. Besides, it was only one day out of her life.

⸺⸻«◊»⸻⸺

Stan Marchand rolled over and looked at the red glow of the digital clock on his nightstand. It was just after three in the morning. It was too early to get up, but he knew that he would not be able to get back to sleep, with all of the monkeys bouncing around in his brain. Something was bothering him, but he couldn't put his finger on it. He was retired. He had his pension. His house was paid for. The kids were okay. Even his ex-wife was comfortable and quiet. His health was good, and he was enjoying doing things that people everywhere wanted to do in their retirements. His golf game was alive; it was on fire!

He rubbed his bald head and his hand drifted down to the three-day stubble of beard, which on some men was supposed to make them look continental and playfully roguish. While he was looking for a personal change to stimulate his life, he felt like facial hair made him look like a criminal on a fugitive poster.

In an effort to preserve, or rather restore, his sanity, he shaved and brushed his teeth. Now he was really awake. He started a pot of coffee, and wandered in the darkness through his house, trying to identify what it was that was tormenting him. When the comforting aroma signaled him that the coffee was ready, he poured a cup and went to his office. He switched on a desk lamp and twisted the flexible neck so that it shined away from his eyes. There on the desk were the notes from all his taskings that week.

The triangle with four lives. Four deaths. Four. He took a sip of the coffee and felt a sensation akin to amphetamine entering the bloodstream. There was something about coffee that stimulated his senses. It brought him back to life. Earlier in his career when he was working the night shift, assigned to a protective detail, coffee was the only thing that kept him and other agents going. Well, that, and nicotine. In the early days it was okay to take a smoke break because the nicotine was thought to have relieved hunger pains, and helped agents stay alert and focused. Now, in these politically correct days when it was okay for people to smoke marijuana, off duty anyway, smoking tobacco was seen as a character flaw. He had not had a cigarette in years. He paged through his notes until he came to the tasking that was nagging him.

He looked at the triangle with the representative stick figures that represented lives. In the triangle, there were three circles with sticks poking out, indicating they were laying down next to each other, in a supine, or face up position. But, underneath them, along the base of the triangle was another circle. A fourth life. He picked up a pencil and traced the ideogram that he had drawn at the top left side of the page.

On the side of the paper, he began to notate his perceptions, "Fire, Quick."

The triangle had depth. Not a pyramid. It was circular at the bottom and rose to a point. It was conical. The three lives lying next to each other shared a common goal. They were different from the fourth life. The fourth life was an outsider. Someone who had been added at the last minute. It was male. He shared common attributes like sex, age, and training. But he was different. He should not have been there. He wasn't hiding – the other three knew he was there, but they didn't know why, and weren't allowed to acknowledge his presence for some reason.

Marchand was suddenly thirsty but hadn't brought water in from the kitchen. He sipped his coffee, licked his lips, and inhaled deeply through his nose. On the side of the paper, he wrote, "Same training. Similar training. But not one of us." He traced the ideogram again.

"Not dressed the same. Dressed in white. Some sort of uniform, but not theirs. Like a technician, or a surgeon."

Marchand winced as he felt abject fear. Pain. Knowledge. He wrote, "Flash fire. Knew they were going to die. Not the stranger's fault." Marchand's heart beat rapidly and his breathing deepened. "Favor. It was a favor. The fourth life was there to watch. To learn. To observe."

Marchand grabbed another piece of paper from the stack on the corner of his desk and drew the cone, with the three lives next to each other and the fourth on the bottom. Apparently oriented in a different direction. "Agreement. The fourth life was male. He was allowed to be there, but his presence was not to be acknowledged. But power, governments, agreed it was okay for him to watch."

"Spark."

"Fast...flash fire"

The fourth life screams but it can't be heard. No communications. No radio. Pilots?"

"Like, astronauts. In space suits. Their voices can be heard by others because their mics are in their helmets. The fourth life has no helmet. No space suit. No radio. Just white clothing. Burning. Suffocating by toxic smoke."

"Can't get the hatch open. Death."

CHAPTER 8

Karlsson heard the ringtone that alerted him to a new text message. He wanted to ignore it and go back to sleep, but he knew it would just chirp again in a minute if he didn't look at it. He opened one eye and tried to focus on the reddish glow of the digital clock on the nightstand. It was four in the morning.

He reached for the cell phone and used his thumb to unlock it. He stared at the inbound message for a moment before giving up with the realization that he would have to find his glasses. Some doctor had tried to tell him a couple years earlier that he could perform a surgical procedure on one eye that allowed him to read without glasses, while the other eye would be responsible for distant vision. He refused. He did not think his brain was capable of being fed conflicting information and making it somehow appear that he had normal vision. Thus, the surgery he underwent made his distant vision near perfect; sharper than it had ever been, but he still needed glasses to read.

It was from a number in the Washington DC area that he recognized. "DL4653 FROM SEA, ARR CLE 0947. YOUR VAN DRIVER WILL MEET YOU IN THE ARRIVALS AREA"

Karlsson squinted and then sat up in bed to look at the text again. "My van driver?" He sent a simple question mark back as a response. It was too damned early for brevity.

A few seconds later, the reply was sent back. "QUID PRO QUO. HE SHOWED YOU SHANGHAI AND IT IS YOUR TURN TO RECIPROCATE"

Karlsson tried to search the memory banks of his sleepy brain. "Liu Wei? Coming to Cleveland?" He had no idea what was going on, but since he was still obviously on the payroll, he acknowledged. "ROGER THAT".

He tossed the phone back onto his nightstand and rolled over. The flight from Seattle wouldn't arrive for several hours and he was only about thirty minutes away from the airport. He'd had more sleep that night than he'd had in several weeks, but still wanted a couple more hours. Unfortunately, his mind would not let him, and as one thought created a dozen possibilities, it was soon replaced with another. Why would Liu Wei have dropped what he was doing and hopped a plane for Cleveland? What had happened in Shanghai, and why would he be headed here, instead of back to his Secret Service office to make out his report? That is, if he really was Secret Service.

After about ten minutes of pondering all the variables, Karlsson finally gave in, got up and made a cup of coffee. He knew that the individual brews the hotels left for their guests barely passed for coffee and were usually just a grade above hot pond water. Nevertheless, he needed the boost to get going and to get his head straight. After a couple of sips, he headed to the bathroom for a shave and a shower.

Feeling more awake after cleaning up, he packed his belongings and headed downstairs. He didn't check out of the hotel because he wasn't certain if this new development would necessitate another night or two in Cleveland. But, if he had to hit the road fast, he was ready. He stopped in the restaurant on the first floor to breakfast on sausage and eggs. One of the rules of combat operations was for troops to eat when they could, because they never knew when they would have another chance. The legendary Frank Bolz, NYPD's renowned hostage negotiator, often told his students and reporters that before he headed out to a barricade incident, he made sure his team went to the bathroom, for the very same reason.

Karlsson headed to the garage and found his car, backed into the same space in which he'd left it. He let it warm up for a few seconds, before pulling out. The GPS had been programmed earlier for a similar trip with Jackie Biehn, so he simply scrolled through his recent history and selected the route down Interstate 71 that would take him to the airport. He didn't really need it. He'd been there a few times and the destination was pretty well-marked. When he arrived, he decided to find a spot in short-term parking and walk inside to the arrivals area. Liu Wei would not know what kind of car to look for, and if he rolled up to him on the sidewalk, there would be no way to see if there was anyone following him.

He waited near baggage claim in a place that gave him a good view of arriving passengers and sent a quick text back to the number in Washington. "AT CLE, AWAITING ARRIVAL".

A few seconds later, the anonymous response came back, "ON TIME".

Karlsson busied himself checking emails and catching up on the latest news, most of which was about the campaign. Layden was certainly making noise and it seemed to be the opinion of the media that he would be the candidate of choice to face off against the incumbent President in November. He was a career politician, and as such brought the usual baggage that comes with a life in politics. Nevertheless, the mainstream media liked him, and that mattered. The media had gotten away from reporting the news, and now fancied themselves as change agents of one kind or another. Hollywood liked him too. And even though most of them were not qualified to discuss matters of strategic importance, since most celebrities knew nothing about anything outside of their profession, it nevertheless got people's attention, and their votes.

It wasn't long before Karlsson noticed the skinny Asian man in his early thirties walking towards him with a sly smile. He stood, with a bit of a smirk himself, and approached him. "Welcome to the United States, Laowai."

Liu adjusted the bag's sling on his shoulder so he could shake hands. "I guess there will be some explanations in order?"

"Not necessarily." Karlsson replied. "Let's start with your real name, and whether or not you think you're being followed."

He shook his head. "I'm pretty sure I'm solo, but if you see someone taking our picture, all bets are off. My name is Jerry Lee. But my real ID and creds are in a safe in San Francisco right now; Montgomery and Chestnut, across the street from Pier twenty-nine. You'll have to trust me. Where's your car?"

"Short term. Do you have any other luggage?"

"Nope. Let's get out of here and we can talk."

"I'd appreciate it." He said as he directed Liu Wei, or Jerry Lee as he might now be known, to the exit. They walked in silence, and when they got to the car, Lee tossed his bag into the back seat and jumped into the passenger seat.

Lee buckled in, closed his eyes, and exhaled forcefully through tight lips. "God bless America. Home sweet home!"

Karlsson started the car and pulled into the aisle. "Been away for a while, huh?"

"Eighteen months. Secret Service brought me in right out of the Army. Because of my language skills, they squeezed me into the agent class that was literally starting the following month. They had to rush my paperwork and background through to get me qualified in time. Of course, having an uncle who'd been a career agent didn't hurt."

He squinted out the window as the car emerged from the garage. "I was originally assigned to the San Francisco office, but as soon as I reported in, they corralled me and put me on this job. My guess is they'd been looking for an agent with fluency in Mandarin, and some level of comprehension of Cantonese."

Karlsson put on his turn signal and changed lanes. "Where are we headed?"

Lee slid his phone out of the Otter Box belt clip. "Independence." He reached up to the navigation screen and tapped the address in. "You'll want to delete this before you turn the car in."

Karlsson merged into traffic and quickly glanced at the GPS screen. "And? What are we going to do in Independence?"

"We have to pick up a van in the parking lot of a Podiatry college."

Karlsson hated being kept in the dark but had gotten used to it over the years. "What's in the van?"

Lee scratched his head and looked out at the side view mirror. "I'm not sure. My guess is that it contains some plastic sheeting, duct tape, and probably a firearm or two."

Karlsson drove on in silence until he found the on-ramp for Interstate 480 East. "And, what are we going to do with all of that?"

Lee shook his head. "Well, our mutual friend in Shanghai, Mr. Zhou, has provided the van for me with the expectation that I grab an aircraft engineer by the name of Jeffers, kill him and do something with the body that won't leave a trail back to him."

"Martin Jeffers? Echo Aerospace?"

"That's the one. Apparently, Zhou no longer has a use for him and would feel more comfortable if...what did he say...I made him disappear."

"Just for clarification, let me get this straight. You're a federal agent of some kind...Secret Service?" He had to be someone with legitimate federal credentials, or Karlsson would have never gotten the assignment from Paul's cell number.

"Uh huh."

"I'm guessing that you've notified your superiors that you're back in the States, and clued them in as to what you're supposed to be doing now, to further your cover with Zhou?"

"Uh huh."

"And, while I'm not one hundred percent familiar with the job description of an 1811 classification with the US Government, I'm betting that abducting and murdering a US taxpayer on US soil, is nowhere in there?"

"Right."

"And since your boss' boss was able to convince my boss that you needed some sort of non-official support, I'm going to help you?"

"Uh huh."

Karlsson took his eyes off the road for a brief moment to look at his passenger. "Well, not to be insensitive or politically incorrect, but just what the fuck am I supposed to be doing here? You didn't get my name out of the yellow pages."

"I'm told that your specialty is...uh...nullification."

"It's been called that."

"You persuade enemy intelligence agents to repent of their sins and cooperate, or you make them...uh...go away?"

It was Karlsson's turn. "Uh huh."

"We have to grab Martin Jeffers, explain the reality of his position to him and remove his ability to communicate with anyone. In Zhou's words, I have to *make him disappear*. We have to make it look like I killed him."

Karlsson looked at him again. "And, if he resists? If he doesn't want to buy what we're selling?"

Lee pulled down the visor and moved it slightly so that he could use the mirror to see what or who might be behind them. "Well, we can't kill him, if that's what you're thinking."

"I wasn't. What other options are on the table?" Karlsson asked.

"We can't walk up to his door and badge him or arrest him, since I don't have any official ID on me, and I'm guessing, neither do you?" When Karlsson laughed, he went on. "We can't drag him from his house kicking and screaming as that would certainly draw attention. But we have to put him on ice somewhere until we get to the bottom of this. And, we can't let him make any calls, to anyone. All that, and we need to search his place. I don't suppose you can open a safe.

"Yes, with the combination and a couple of tries. Some combinations are tougher to dial than others."

"Seriously?"

"We're not cops. If we had to open someone's safe, my people would simply twist some sort of wire tighter and tighter around his scrotum until he felt like opening it himself before he lost consciousness. But I suppose that would defeat the purpose of a covert search."

"We can't use any of my people on this. Do you know anyone?" Lee mused.

Karlsson thought for a moment. "Yeah. An old Army buddy is a locksmith in Cincinnati. I'm pretty sure he does the occasional safe job for law enforcement agencies serving warrants, or estranged wives trying to see what their husbands keep locked up. I could give him a call, but it would take about five hours to get him here."

"He's cool?'

"Very. But, he'll want cash."

"Cash isn't a problem. How much does he need to know?"

"Well, the location of the safe...any security alarms, video cameras. The actual type of safe might be good, but it's not a showstopper if you don't have it. I doubt that an engineer has anything that can't be manipulated in a few hours."

"Get him!" He glanced at the GPS screen. "South on seventy-seven up here."

"I know. Are you somebody's wife or something?"

"Sorry, man. No sleep and nothing to eat. I think my blood-sugar has bottomed out. After we get the van, can we get something to eat?"

"Sure. Do you have a hotel room yet?"

"No. What's close?'

"There's an Embassy Suites close to the college. Their food isn't half bad. I've stayed there before."

"That'll do.

"So, the trip from Shanghai left you with plenty of time to think. Did you come up with any kind of plan?"

"I think so. Zhou gave me the guy's home address, but if it's a typical US neighborhood, there are probably not many ways we can set up to watch him without being outed on some neighborhood's intranet or neighborhood watch. I know where he works. My first thought was to follow him from work to see where he goes. If he makes a stop, we might be able to take him there. If he doesn't, we'll have to get him at his house."

Karlsson considered what the young agent told him. "Okay then. After lunch, let's drive by his office and his house and see what we're up against."

"Recon?"

"Sure. In civilian parlance, they call it a surveillance or activity check, but I understand reconnaissance."

"Here." He indicated the need to turn left at the stop light on Rockside Road.

Karlsson put on his turn signal and moved into the left turn lane. Satisfied that he had the right-of-way, he turned north and watched his rear-view mirror. No one was following. Less than a mile north, he saw the sign for the Kent State University College of Podiatric Medicine on their left, and turned in.

The parking lot was on the east side of the facility, so after they drove the perimeter of the lot, looking for anything or anyone that might have indicated the van was being watched, they drove down the aisle that had an unmarked white Ford van with no rear windows and a temporary license plate.

"Is this it?" Karlsson asked.

"Must be. They said it would be a Ford van with temp-tags. This is the only one I see."

"I'll wait."

Lee jumped out and approached the van from the driver's side. The door was unlocked, so he jumped in, and after checking above the passenger visor, was able to find the keys and start it up. As he backed out, he pulled up driver-to-driver with Karlsson and rolled down the window. "Where's that hotel?"

"Can't miss it. It's about two hundred yards north of here. When you come out of the driveway, turn left and you'll pretty much dead-end into it."

Karlsson followed his new accomplice up the road and after Lee had parked the van in the far end of the parking lot, he watched as he jumped out and did a quick inspection of the exterior of the vehicle, under the chassis and up inside the wheel wells. He was most likely looking for some sort of transmitter that Zhou, or anyone else, might have placed on it prior to his arrival. Karlsson parked in a space closer to the entrance and went inside.

When Lee joined him, they walked quietly to the restaurant on the first floor. The bartender looked up and said, "Hi guys. Sit anywhere you like."

It was late for breakfast and early for lunch, so they had the place to themselves. Lee didn't bother waiting for a menu. "Cheeseburger with everything and French fries!"

"Just coffee for me, thanks." Karlsson added.

They found a table in the corner and began brainstorming. Lee pulled out his cell phone and began scrolling through his notes. "He works in Beachwood, and lives near a golf course in Moreland Hills. Do you know that area?"

"I live in New Mexico. Ohio is just a vacation destination for me." Karlsson replied with a touch of sarcasm in his voice.

The bartender brought coffee and water to the table. Lee pulled up his mapping application and tapped the two addresses in. The distance between Jeffers' office in Beachwood and his home was only about five miles, straight down Chagrin Boulevard, and then south on Highway 91 to Jackson Road. "There's a police station right there between his house and the country club."

Karlsson sipped his coffee. "I'm thinking we're going to leave the police out of this one."

"Judging from this satellite view, it looks like he lives on a one or two-acre wooded lot, down a two-hundred-foot drive. Reasonably secluded. However, we can't rule out video surveillance cameras at his house. Everyone has them these days. My guys in San Francisco ran a background on him; he's got one car...a silver Lexus SUV, I think. Ohio plates Gulf Edward Alpha something or other."

Karlsson watched the young agent manipulate the screen of his phone. "His office building is likely to have video surveillance as well. If we take him in transit, that might generate a lot of witness reports depending on how we did it. We could rear-end him at a traffic light and take him when he got out to look at the damage. But there would be a mob of people calling 9-1-1 before we got away."

Lee nodded and looked up. "No doubt. We have to get him away from his house and office, and somewhat out of view."

"Once we grab him, what are we going to do with him?"

Lee tapped some more into his phone and then shook his head and started to laugh. "The fucking field office is right here."

"The what?" Karlsson asked.

The bartender brought Lee's lunch over. "Here you go. Will there be anything else?"

Lee smiled. "Thanks. No." He doused the French fries with ketchup.

"The Cleveland Secret Service office is right up the street. We passed it when we turned left off of Rockside to get here. It's less than a mile." Lee sent a quick text and then put his phone aside while he attacked his cheeseburger like a ravenous wolf. "Mmmm...I haven't had a cheeseburger in eighteen months." He choked down a bite before reaching for his water. "I just sent a text to San Francisco. They're gonna call Cleveland and tell them we'll have a prisoner for them sometime tonight. They have a holding cell there that will do until we figure out what we're going to do with him long term."

He took another huge bite and took time to savor it, grease running down the side of his chin. "The only problem is that they lease space in a commercial building. We can't be dragging an unconscious or struggling human across the lobby to the elevators if there are still civilians there working."

Karlsson pulled up the two addresses on his phone while Lee continued to inhale his burger. He looked at the likely route that Jeffers would take from his office to his home, assuming no stops in between. He switched to the satellite view and enlarged the image, dragging it along the route. "I think I've got it."

Lee washed down a mouthful of Angus beef and looked up. "Yeah?"

"You two have never met, but you're certain he knows Zhou?"

Lee thought for a moment and then nodded.

"Let's drive the routes when you're done eating, just to be sure. But I think a possible play would be for you to call him and tell him you're staying at this hotel on Park East Drive, just south of Chagrin Boulevard. Tell him Zhou gave you something to give to him and you'll meet him in the lobby at 5:15. He doesn't know that Zhou wants him out of the way. Zhou never would have tipped his hand that he was going to do something to him. As far as Jeffers knows, everything is A-OK in Shanghai. Right?"

"Yes." Lee nodded again.

"So, when he rolls up, tell him his package is in the van. When he comes over to get it, we'll either tell him that Zhou is concerned for his safety and we need to move him somewhere or something... or force him in and drive off."

"That's if he doesn't get suspicious about the meeting." Lee noted.

"You've been acting for eighteen months. I think you can pull off one more performance."

Lee thought for a moment. "He's an engineer. He's into mechanical stuff. I'm going to tell him that Zhou has just acquired some part off of an aircraft and he needs to know if it's genuine or not, before he pays for it."

Karlsson considered the pros and cons. "That will certainly get him to come to the van. How persuasive can you be? Can you tell him that the part is in Independence, and bullshit him long enough for us to get him back to your offices there?"

After a few more seconds, Lee thought out loud. 'Wait a minute. Our job is to get him off the grid. Once we get him inside the van, why can't we tell him the truth? Or, as much of the truth as he needs to know?"

"Meaning?"

"Once he's in the van, I'm going to tell him who I am and that we have to take him to the Secret Service office for his own protection. We'll tell him that if he resists, we'll have to cuff him because we know what he's been doing and he's subject to arrest for some section of US Code. But, if he wants to avoid prosecution, he can accompany us to the office peacefully where a more thorough explanation would be forthcoming... something like that?"

"Can you handle him if he wants to rabbit on you?"

Lee smiled, "I was a state champ in Kung Fu and Mixed Martial Arts. If it looks like he's kicking my ass, you can pull over and jump in back with us. You never know when you'll need a seventy-year-old to come to your rescue."

Karlsson scowled. "Sixty...ish."

———————⸞«◉»⸟———————

Feodor Golovkin looked at the preliminary report provided by the science officer at the embassy, which noted that until the piece could be better studied, the cursory metallurgical analysis suggested that the sample he submitted was probably made using the same process as a previously submitted sample, known to have produced in the United States. However, the amount and type of Titanium used in the alloy, seemed to be more common in aircraft parts known to have been made in China. And, without knowing the specific function of the sample, or how it was to be assembled or used, it may or may not fail under various laboratory or environmental stresses. The technician was unable to perform Rockwell or Brinell testing, fearing damage to the sample, but ultrasonic and radiographic tests were attached.

He shook his head silently as he stirred his tea. The Chinese had superlative scientists and technicians, but for some reason, just could not avoid cutting corners. Even when it came to counterfeiting other goods and currencies, they were beginning to fall behind the rest of the world due to process deficiencies and quality issues. Now, even Peru had surpassed China in the production and shipment of counterfeit US currency into the United States, controlling more than sixty percent of the market. It made him think of Leonov, his father's schoolmate at the Zhukovskiy Air Force Engineering Academy.

As a young child, even before he first entered school, Nikolay Vasilyevich Leonov had been fascinated by aviation stories and the exploits of heroic pilots. He dreamed of becoming an aviator himself. He joined an aviation club while still at Kharkov's Higher Air Force School, and after his graduation in 1954 he was admitted to the Academy. The following year he was transferred to an Air Force College in Grozny; the Armavir Military Pilot Aviation School, where he graduated near the top of his class in 1957. He married a local office worker early in 1957 and their first child was born later that year. It was the same year that Sputnik I was launched, which fueled his interest in space exploration.

He was commissioned a Second Lieutenant, and served in the Soviet Air Force's Baltic Military District, perfecting his skills and impressing his superiors. He was promoted to Senior Lieutenant in December 1959, and by April 1960, he was chosen to be among the first group of Soviet cosmonauts.

Leonov was one of the youngest members of the cosmonaut team but trained hard for a planned May launch on the Vostok spacecraft. According to his fellow cosmonauts, Leonov was a mild-mannered person with an amiable disposition. Everyone who knew him remembered his great singing voice and demonstrable prowess in a number of competitive sports.

In March 1961 Leonov was involved in a fifteen-day endurance experiment in a low-pressure altitude chamber at the Institute of Biomedical Problems in Moscow. The chamber's pressurized atmosphere was enriched with more than fifty percent oxygen. Having completed his assignment for the day, Leonov removed the monitoring biosensors from his body and washed his skin with an alcohol-soaked cotton ball. When he discarded the cotton ball, it landed on an electric hot plate he had been using to brew a cup of tea. The cotton ball ignited and then he tried to smother the flames with the sleeve of his woolen coveralls, which then caught fire in the chamber's oxygen-rich atmosphere.

Because of the pressure difference, it took the doctor, who was monitoring the experiment, nearly half an hour to open the chamber door. By the time responders could access the tank, Leonov's clothing had fully burned and all the oxygen in the chamber had been depleted. Reports said that he had suffered third-degree burns over most of his body. The attending physician at Botkin Hospital, reported that Leonov was in such bad shape that the only blood vessels he could find for inserting the IV needle were on the soles of his feet, which had been protected by his flight boots. He supposedly died of shock sixteen hours after the accident, and he was cremated.

That was the official report, anyway. The truth was that Leonov had been too valuable. He had already been selected to participate in a highly secret project. Unlike his comrades that were to be heroes of the Soviet people, his astronautical engineering skills combined with his knowledge of English, lit a path all the way to the Kremlin and Premier Khrushchev. There was talk that the new American President wanted to work behind the scenes so that the two countries could share information and journey into space as one people. If the two leaders were able to come to an agreement, Leonov might soon be living in the United States working with American astronauts. It was to be highly secretive, and he could not tell anyone. Not family, not friends. No one. He would build a new family, in a new country.

There were others that would join his team, but after the investment in selection and training, the Soviets had to be careful about who they presented for this unique opportunity, and how they explained their absence from the program. So, it followed that on March 27, 1963, soviet cosmonauts Grigory Nelyubov, Ivan Anikeyev and Valentin Filatyev after a night of drunken revelry, were publicly arrested for disorderly conduct by the military security patrol at Chkalovskaya station. According to reports, the duty officer agreed to dismiss the entire incident and not make an official report if the cosmonauts apologized. A simple request. However, because they refused, the matter was officially reported to the authorities.

Because there had been previous incidents in their backgrounds, despite their exceptional training and performance, all three were dismissed from the cosmonaut corps on April 17, 1963. Pavel Popovich, the secretary of the party organization, tried to resolve the situation by calling a special meeting where Nelyubov was once again encouraged to apologize to the patrol chief and to the other cosmonauts, but he again refused.

Following his dismissal he went back to flying interceptors in the Far East but allegedly began to suffer bouts of alcoholism and depression. His death was reported February 18, 1966. The report said that while drunk, he stepped in front of a train near the Ippolitovka station, northwest of Vladivostok. It was officially ruled a suicide and the severely disfigured body was cremated.

To protect the image of the Soviet space program, efforts were made to cover up the reason for Nelyubov's dismissal and his subsequent suicide. His image was airbrushed out of the *Sochi Six* photo to which showed the top members of the original class of Soviet cosmonauts. After more facts were revealed following the collapse of the Soviet Union, the airbrushing led to speculation about a host of supposedly *lost* cosmonauts. They were being reassigned.

Golovkin sipped his tea and remembered what his father had told him. Leonov hadn't died in an accident in 1961, but on Launch Complex 34 in Cape Canaveral, Florida on January 27, 1967.

⸺⸻◆⸻⸺

Karlsson parked the van on the west end of the hotel parking lot, a hundred yards away from the lobby entrance. He hoped that with the setting sun, the surveillance cameras would not pick up as much activity as they normally would during daylight. "Do you think he'll show?"

Lee smiled. "He'll show. He thinks that by doing this favor for Zhou, he'll be paid handsomely. He needs the money to impress his young girlfriend."

Karlsson thought out loud. "Well, the way you set it up, he's not likely to call her. He's certainly not going to call anyone else to tell them that he needs to meet some unscrupulous characters in a parking lot to look at some illegally obtained aircraft part."

"Yeah, agreed. I need to head to the lobby to make this look good."

"What are you going to tell them?"

"I'm going to ask if they have any rooms available and tell them that I'm meeting someone here. If they say no, I'll act disappointed and tell them I need to wait for my guest. If they say yes, I'll tell them that I might be staying over but don't want to book a room until I'm sure."

"The lobby will be covered by surveillance cameras."

"No worries. We're not going to do anything there. I'm going to introduce myself and then lead him to you."

Karlsson digested the information and recited the plan. "And, when I see you coming out, I'll get out of the van with a huge smile and tell him that I'm so sorry we had to bring him out on a night like this."

"What did your buddy, Fritz say?" Lee asked.

"He's on his way. He'll meet us in the parking lot at the Secret Service office at seven. He'll dump his gear in here and then we'll head to Jeffers' house."

"Okay." He shrugged nonchalantly as he gave a thumbs-up gesture. "What's the old Army adage...*no battle plan survives first contact with the enemy*?"

"Something like that. I always preferred the one that went; *never share a foxhole with someone braver than you*."

He smiled as he got out. "Meaning?"

"Meaning don't hang out with people that draw unnecessary fire."

"Got it. We'll try to keep this calm tonight."

He closed the door softly and walked briskly to the lobby. Karlsson had pulled head-in into the parking space and watched him in the passenger side-view mirror. From the location he'd chosen, it would supply easier access to the side door of the van. Plus, vans that were backed into a parking space often drew more attention.

He looked at his watch and then fiddled with his cell phone so that if anyone looked his direction, he'd look busy, rather than looking like a guy who was technically about to commit a felony abduction. More or less. It would depend on what the Secret Service or FBI ended up charging the guy with. If no charges were filed, then some attorney somewhere might decide that coaxing a guy into a van for a drive to a holding cell without any type of warrant, might be construed as abduction. And since Karlsson was strictly non-official cover, he was on his own.

He didn't know why he did it. Maybe because he was bored, he sent a text to Jackie. "HOW'S THINGS WHEREVER YOU ARE? GETTING YOUR LAUNDRY DONE?"

Less than a minute later, she responded. "STILL WORKING ON IT. THERE WAS A LOT. EVERYTHING OKAY WITH YOU?"

"SO FAR SO GOOD." He clicked. "CALL YOU TOMORROW WITH AN UPDATE"

Seconds later, her reply, "LOOKING FORWARD TO IT."

She was a good kid. Hell, she was a grown woman. A professional woman. She was attractive and sure as hell didn't need some old goat chasing after her. He deleted the text string out of caution in case the phone fell into the wrong hands. The sun had set, but in the side view mirror he could see Lee and his quarry walking towards the van. It was show time. He made sure all the doors were unlocked, and then got out and walked around to the sliding door on the passenger side.

As the pair got closer, he grinned his biggest grin. "Hi guys!"

Jeffers was a short stocky guy with a receding hairline. Even if he hadn't known better, Karlsson and anyone else would have immediately guessed that he was a computer geek or an engineer of sorts. In khaki slacks and a white button-down collar shirt, he would never have passed for a rock star. Lee touched him on his arm congenially. "Marty, this is Matt. He's the guy that has something for Zhou that you need to look at."

Martin Jeffers was apprehensive but forced a smile. "Anything for Mr. Zhou. What do you have?"

Karlsson opened the sliding door on the side of the van. "Well, Marty, it's a bit complicated." By now, the duo was standing next to the van and Karlsson nodded at Lee.

Lee picked up the conversation, his hand on Jeffers' arm right above the elbow. "Everything is fine. But...you need to come with us. We couldn't fit the assembly into the van and Zhou said that if we don't do this tonight, it'll cost him millions and he won't like that."

Jeffers tensed almost imperceptibly. "What do you mean?"

"It's on a pallet at the office...in Independence. It's about a fifteen-minute ride and we'll bring you back."

Jeffers tried to back up, but Lee had a good grip on his arm. "Marty, man, I'm sorry. You can't say no. Believe me, you're going to be okay, but if you don't go with us now, you'll be dead in forty-eight hours."

"What? Who are you people?" Jeffers asked in protest.

Lee applied the necessary pressure and Marty stepped up into the van. "Drive."

Karlsson pushed them inside and then slid the door shut. He ran around and jumped into the driver's seat and fired the Ford up. He cautiously backed out and then slowly drove out of the lot, north on Park East, and then right on Chagrin towards the freeway ramp just yards away. He turned the radio off so that he could hear the conversation in the back seat.

"Marty...Mr. Jeffers, I have a lot to tell you, and it is important that you listen to me. We're headed to the Secret Service office off of Rockside Road. After we have a better chance to brief you, you will be allowed to call your attorney...if you like. You may not want to. If your attorney gets you out of our custody tonight, Zhou will send someone to kill you in the next day or so and your lawyer won't be able to help you. They might also kill your girlfriend. What's her name...Jenny or something?"

Jeffers looked at him quietly. He was weighing his options. He was a pudgy engineer sitting on the floor of a van with two men that he could not hope to over-power. He was trying to make up his mind as to whether or not his abductors were on the level, or if he was being taken to some deserted park somewhere for execution. He could not believe Zhou would do this. "What is it you think I've done?" He asked, a mild trace of fear in his voice.

Lee responded. "Well, for openers, 18 U.S. Code Section 2320, which pertains to trafficking in counterfeit goods or services. If your lawyer needs more stuff to work on, there's also the Espionage series, which is 18 U.S. Code Section 792, and its provisions of Chapter 37, that deal with documents, material, or information, related to our national defense... and Section 793, which applies to activities such as gathering, transmitting to an unauthorized person, or losing, information pertaining to the national defense, and to conspiracies to commit such offenses."

Karlsson had to hand it to him, the kid had a good memory. "Or Section 794 that applies to persons who deliver, or attempt to deliver, information pertaining to the national defense of the United States to agents or subjects of foreign countries, with intent or reason to believe that it is to be used to the injury of the United States or to the advantage of a foreign nation." Lee stopped for a breath and then went on. "But my personal favorite is Section 798 that applies to the willful communication of classified information to foreign powers by greedy engineers with stiff dicks who think that they can fuck hot young Asian girls. Give me your cell phone."

Jeffers complied. Lee took it and turned it off.

Inside, the van was quiet for a while. Outside, life went on. People were on their way home, or somewhere else, their thoughts occupied only by matters of personal importance. No one paid any attention to the white Ford van heading south on Interstate 271. Nevertheless, the sales pitch worked.

Martin Jeffers quietly acquiesced. "What is it you want to know?"

CHAPTER 9

After giving the secret fraternity handshake or muttering the appropriate password, Lee was able to convince the Special Agent in Charge that he was, in fact, a duly appointed Special Agent assigned to the San Francisco field office. Well, that and some electronic support helped. As the three men were admitted to the offices, the SAIC handed him a building access card that already had his picture on it, presumably retrieved from their online personnel files. Karlsson was given a simple green visitor ID and Jeffers, a red one.

The office atmosphere was cordial and friendly, but the office was thinly staffed as most of their agents had been assigned to security details or were busy advancing venues known to be hosting political events in the upcoming months before the election.

They offered up a conference room and gave Lee a list of restaurants that would deliver food for his new charge and depending on the outcome of the interview, could recommend a safe house that was about ten miles away. If the subject was determined to be uncooperative, they had an arrangement with the US Marshal's Service for more austere accommodations, with steel bars and bigger locks. However, it was evident from the start that Jeffers was not a hardened criminal, but rather an opportunist who fell victim to one of the oldest and most successful espionage artifices known in the profession. The honey pot.

The honey pot trap was the practice of using romantic or sexual relationships towards investigative, political, or financial goals. The scheme involved hiring an attractive person, usually a woman, to make contact with an individual who had something that the opposition wanted, and then the trapper would seek to entice the target into a false relationship, usually sexual, in which they could extract information or develop influence over the target.

It had been around since biblical times. As a matter of fact, in 2009, MI-5, the British domestic security service, distributed a lengthy, well-researched document to hundreds of British banks, businesses, and financial institutions, entitled *The Threat from Chinese Espionage*. It described the comprehensive Chinese effort to blackmail Western businesspeople utilizing sexual relationships. The document explicitly warned that Chinese intelligence services were trying to cultivate seemingly long-term relationships and were known to *exploit vulnerabilities such as sexual relationships ... to pressure individuals to co-operate with them.*

Lee brought Jeffers a cup of coffee and sat non-dairy creamer and sugar packets next to the cup. "I wasn't sure how you liked your coffee."

"Black is fine."

"I'm going to level with you. I've been working on this case from the Shanghai side for eighteen months. Other agents have been working on it over here. We know that you have been providing information and materials that are classified and therefore subject to US government regulations. In short, you're screwed."

Jeffers sipped his coffee and stared at the table in front of him. "I don't want to go to prison. I don't want to give up my career. My life."

Lee was a pretty good interrogator, considering his short tenure with the agency. "Uh huh. You should have thought of that before you started helping a Chinese criminal counterfeit parts in your own factory. Echo aerospace is not going to like that. Neither will the US Attorney. She lives for misconduct shit like this. She's going to want to throw you to the media so that she can run for congress."

Jeffers looked up, fear flooding in his eyes. "Wait. What? You said the parts were counterfeited in the Puxi factory?"

Lee scowled at him. "Don't bullshit me. Where did you think they were being made?"

"I don't know. Honestly. I just provided a sample and said that I'd continue to work with them and give them what I could. You have to believe me, that I didn't know that anyone from our company was involved."

"Whatever." Lee replied somewhat condescendingly. "Unless you start talking to me now, I'm not sure that I can even keep you out of Gitmo."

"What?"

Guantanamo. You know...Cuba. Where we send all of the other terrorists."

"Oh, shit, no! I'm not a terrorist!"

"You are to us. You sold military secrets to the Chinese, which will be used to kill Americans everywhere in the world."

"Oh, no! You've got the wrong idea. The information I gave them was for an aircraft that was designed to go into space. It was never to be used as a weapon. I just thought that if we were all working together..."

"Bullshit!" Lee cut him off. "Don't start that whole we're-all-in-this-together speech. I've heard it before and I'm not going to buy it now. How much did you give them, and how much did you get?"

"No. You don't understand. I got a hundred grand for my part. It was just to help them stay on par with our space exploration research. It was not to be used as a weapon."

Lee had the hook in and was not about to let him off of it. "There are two things that can come out of this tonight. One, you give a full statement to our transcriptionist right now and offer to cooperate with the US Attorney, or you are headed to Guantanamo Bay day after tomorrow. No attorney. No farewell speech to your friends and family. You board the plane in handcuffs and hope that the United Nations sends some attorney down to see you in a couple weeks to check on your health and sanity."

A sullen Jeffers pondered his fate. It didn't take a rocket scientist to figure out which way he was going to go. "I'll talk to whoever you want me to talk to. I'll tell them everything I know."

Lee winked at Karlsson. "All right. Let me get an agent in to take your statement. Obviously, you can't go home tonight. We're going to protect you. But you have to keep cooperating. Do you live alone?"

Jeffers nodded slowly.

"Give me your keys."

"My keys?"

"House keys, car keys. You can't go home. I don't know if Zhou has someone watching your house right now, so we'll drive by and take a look. Is there anything in your house that you need for the next couple of days?"

The engineer shook his head. "No."

"Do you have any pets that need cared for?"

Again, he shook his head.

"Okay then. Give me your keys. By the way, do you have an alarm system or anything that we need to know about?"

"Yeah. Alarm...a couple of cameras."

"What's the code?"

"It's...uh...twelve three six and nine. Points of the clock."

"Do you have a safe that anyone will try to break into?"

Jeffers was still trying to consider his options. He paused for a moment, and then replied. "Yes. There's a safe behind my desk in the den. It's behind a picture."

"Is that the only one?"

"Yes."

"I don't suppose you want to give us the combination?"

He shook his head. "If it looks like I need anything in it, I'll have my attorney let you into it. It's just personal stuff and I don't want you going through it."

"No problem. I'm just trying to look out for you."

It was about three minutes until seven when Karlsson's cell phone chimed with an incoming text message. He glanced at it and replied. "Fritz is downstairs. Are you ready?"

Lee nodded and looked at Jeffers. "Mr. Jeffers, you're making the right decision here. I'll send someone in to take your statement. Just for the record, you know you're in some trouble. Do you want your attorney present tonight?"

"No."

"Okay. That's fine. She'll ask you to sign a form that acknowledges that you know your rights under Miranda...Miranda versus Arizona...you've heard it on TV, I'm sure."

Jeffers nodded.

Lee and Karlsson stood. "After they're done with your statement, they will get you something to eat, and a place to sleep if you're tired. When we get back, we'll take you to a comfortable place where you'll stay with us for a couple of days. I'll give you your cell phone back later."

The humiliated engineer nodded almost solemnly, and Lee moved towards the door. "You should look at this as a chance to help your country and repair some of the damage you've done."

On the way out, he handed the phone to the duty agent. "Do me a favor. Find a charger for this and keep it alive, but turned off. We need to check out his calls and activity. My guess is that people will be calling him tonight, but we don't want the GPS to show that he was here."

The agent nodded and went through his desk drawer in search of a charging cord. "No problem."

Lee and Karlsson walked into the brisk, clear night. The white van was easy to spot, with Fritz's company name emblazoned across the sides, Miller Lock and Security Services, Cincinnati Ohio. Originally from Florence, Kentucky, Fritz had entered the Army to become a paratrooper and was honored to have served in the 101st Airborne Division. He'd had a number of overseas deployments in his twenty-four-year career, which had netted him a couple of Bronze Stars and an Army Commendation Medal.

He returned home with a pension and Post 9/11 G.I. Bill money and began studying computers and electronics. But one afternoon, after accidentally locking himself out of his Pleasant Ridge apartment, he gained a sudden desire to study locksmithing. He figured it was in his blood. At a family reunion many years earlier, an elderly uncle told him of the exploits of a distant relative by the name of Harry C. Miller, who had been a famous WWII-era OSS agent and safecracker for the government, who went on to teach courses in safe-cracking and lock-picking for FBI agents and other law enforcement officers. In 1942, Miller started a prestigious security business specializing in safes and combination locks, which consisted almost entirely of government contracts.

During the late 1940's Miller traveled around the world on special assignments to unlock safes and security deposit boxes that local authorities had been unable to open. Among these special junkets were a wartime trip to China, where he opened a gold bullion chest for General Chiang Kai-shek, and a subsequent trip to Cuba, where then-dictator Fulgencio Batista hired him to open several safes that had been captured from Fidel Castro, who was busy planning an overthrow of Batista's government. Fritz was not a hundred percent convinced that he was related to the industry icon, but it made for a good story at parties.

Fritz set up shop in the Cincinnati area, and had decided upon Pleasant Ridge as a domicile, primarily due to its proximity to most of the area's best bars. Now in the fifty-five-and-over age group, with two ex-wives in his past, he was living the carefree existence that many men craved. When he received Karlsson's text, he was elated. His days had grown a bit monotonous, and this project seemed like just the thing to raise his spirits. He called Karlsson immediately. "When do you need me there, and what am I opening?" He asked.

"As soon as you can get here. We're going in tonight, but it may take us a while to find it."

"What's my end on this?" Miller asked, not really caring.

"How much do you need?"

"My usual rate for law enforcement, when they have a warrant, is four hundred. For a black-bag op like this, because we're friends, let's say two thousand plus travel."

"No problem."

"What do you know about the safe?"

"Absolutely nothing. It's supposedly behind a picture. So, the three of us can look for it, and once we find it, it's yours."

Miller was excited to be back in the game. "See you around seven."

Fritz had been on time. Karlsson and Lee approached the van and after introductions, Lee suggested leaving the highly conspicuous locksmith vehicle there and throwing his gear into the van provided by Zhou.

Fritz opened his side doors and handed equipment bags and cases out.

"What is this stuff?" Lee asked.

"In your left hand is the ITL-2000. It's an automatic dialer that you hook onto the dial and then let it figure out the combination."

"You're shitting me! I thought that was just in the movies!" Lee hefted the plastic case.

"Nope." Fritz looked around in the van and tossed some additional tools into a canvas bag and grabbed another plastic case. "The difference between the movies and real life is that depending on the safe, it could take up to twenty-four hours to get into it. And, there are some safes that it won't work on."

"Seriously? How's it work?"

"The device is a stepper motor assembly that clamps onto the front of the dial, held in place on the front of the safe by fairly strong magnets. It then systematically dials all possible combinations that can open that particular safe. But the problem with this approach is time. If I don't know that first number, this rig can run over twenty hours before opening the lock. But, if you can give me the first number of the combination, then the machine manipulation time drops to less than four hours. This is because the time increases exponentially for each additional wheel pack inside the lock that has to be solved."

Lee looked at him as the group walked to the other van. "So, if it doesn't work, then what?"

Fritz went on, "No big deal. If I go for a manual manipulation of the dial, which by the way, is a skill that's been lost by most of today's locksmiths, I will need to work to find the inconsistencies in the wheel packs. Unless you want me to drill it?"

"No. No drilling." Karlsson replied. "We'd like to get in and out without leaving any traces, if we can."

"If it's an older safe, I could manipulate it more easily, but the newer locks are a bit trickier. I only get feedback from the drop point on the dial, and the tolerances on the gates are much tighter now than with the older models."

"Meaning?" Lee asked as he opened the side doors of his van.

"Meaning that until I see what we've got, I can't tell you how long it'll take. Could be an hour...could be ten hours."

Lee jumped into the driver's seat, and Karlsson took his place in the passenger seat. "Got your phone?" He asked Karlsson.

"Yeah."

"Punch in Eighty-Two East Juniper Lane, Moreland Hills." Lee directed as he pulled out of the parking lot.

It was a reasonably secluded two-story red brick home at the end of a two-hundred-foot driveway. Tall evergreens provided privacy but shaded out any opportunity for grass, except in the open landscaped areas. At the end of the driveway was a pole- mounted security light that illuminated the garage area. Inside the house, there was a light on in the front window, probably on a timer.

While Lee had been reviewing his interview plans with the Cleveland SAIC, Karlsson had looked up the house on several real estate websites. It was a 3,260 square foot four-bedroom, four-bathroom place on a little less than two acres. The den was on the first floor overlooking a wooded ravine at the rear. Jeffers had owned the place for about eighteen months.

"Well, here we are." Karlsson whispered. He looked over his shoulder at Fritz, who was organizing his gear. "The alarm code is twelve, three, six, nine. But I'm not sure if there's a panel near the front door."

Fritz slid his hands into the Nitrile thin-walled gloves. "No problem. If there isn't one there, we'll head towards the garage. It's probably on the wall near that entry door." He passed a couple pairs of blue Nitrile gloves up to the men in the front seat. "I always carry extras."

The three men quietly made their way up the paver-stone walk and Lee found the key that looked like it was cut for a residential door lock. The door opened and they could hear the timer on the alarm panel chirping. Fritz smiled, "It's coming from the kitchen." A few seconds later, the chirping stopped, and Fritz came back around the corner smiling. "Got it! Let's go find us a safe!"

"Way ahead of you." Lee returned the smile. "It's in here...in the den. At least, that's the one he wanted us to find."

"Everybody, take your shoes off. No sense tracking footprints around." Karlsson added, looking at the carpets that showed tracks of being recently vacuumed.

The men found their way to the den and Fritz went straight to a large Norman Rockwell reprint that was above a credenza on an inside wall, near the built-in bookshelves. It was a sixteen-inch by twenty-inch color reproduction of the commissioned illustration that was published in the April 20, 1965, issue of *Look magazine*, depicting Gus Grissom and John Young suiting up for the first manned Gemini mission; Gemini 3. He lifted it off the hook and carefully leaned it against the wall, out of the way.

"Gardall WMS912 Fireproof Wall Safe with an S&G 6700 series combo. My guess is there's a bathroom immediately upstairs that runs plumbing inside this wall, because this safe is about sixteen inches deep, and I'm sure he didn't want it poking through the wall into the dining room."

Lee and Karlsson shrugged. "How long?" Lee asked.

Fritz opened his tool bag and found a pad and pencil. "I don't know...hour or two. If it's sooner than that, I'll sound off." He unfolded a towel on the mahogany desk and began to lay out items plucked from the canvas bag; a lock-pick set, a small hammer for tapping on sticky lock mechanisms, a 5mm inspection camera, and a few other assorted tools, including a battery jump box for spiking electronic locks and a stethoscope. Finally, a whisk broom and small plastic dustpan.

He looked at his tools and then at the safe. "First, I'll see if the lock is already close to open...meaning that it's set just off the drop point. Then, I'll check to see if there are any other weakness or inconsistencies in the lock mechanism that can be exploited. I'll manipulate the dial to find the drop point range, and then work the dial around to see if it's going to be easy or not. Then I'll determine the number of wheels by dialing to the right four times, and then turning left until I feel the second, third, and maybe fourth wheel in the lock."

Lee regarded the man, dressed in a nondescript maintenance outfit, khaki pants and shirt, no name tags. He would look like he belonged anywhere. Even in the Secret Service's building. "All right. We're going to check the rest of the house out and leave you to it."

Fritz winked at Karlsson. "Not to tell you your jobs, but you might start in the basement and have a good look at the cable box and punch-down board. It could be that you're not the only team who's on to this guy. Plus, that's usually where most people hide the stuff they don't want found."

Karlsson smiled. "Thanks."

Fritz chuckled. "There's some flashlights in my bag...unless you brought your own?"

Both men looked at each other, somewhat embarrassed. "Thanks." Lee said. He had been undercover for way too long.

After making sure the front door was locked again, the two men did a quick walk around the first floor, and then headed to the second to get an idea of the area they would be searching. "Nice place." Lee commented. "Do you want to split up or double-team it?"

Karlsson bit his lip. "We don't have walkies, so it might be better if we stayed on the same floor. Now that Fritz mentioned it, I'm kind of anxious to take a look at his communications lines."

"Yeah." Lee concurred. "I didn't see any poles outside, so I'm guessing there's a pedestal box somewhere out back, with buried cable into the house. We came in from the south. Did you see a dish on the side of the house?"

"Huh uh."

"Yeah. Basement."

They located the basement door and flipped on the lights. It had obviously been professionally renovated in the recent past. Jeffers had turned one section of it into a cozy theater with a large screen and several leather reclining chairs. The rest of the finished side was made up of a bar, that seated six, and a table that seated an additional four. There was a door on one end that led to the unfinished portion, which looked more like a basement. Bare concrete block, exposed joists and the usual number of cobwebs. He had a sizeable gas water heater, gas furnace and electric sump pump. And there, on one wall was what they were looking for. Next to the electrical breaker box was a cable box and splitter. One of the cables ran from the splitter to a small punch-down board, which distributed dial tone throughout the house.

Lee used his borrowed flashlight to illuminate the equipment. "Geez. He's got eight TV's in here. Cable in...cables out." With his flashlight he followed the lines stapled up in the joists until they disappeared on the other side of the concrete wall that ran down the center of the basement, separating the finished and unfinished sides. "We may need a specialist to run TDR on all this."

"Maybe not." Karlsson said softly as he examined the punch-down block. "Look at this."

Lee moved his flashlight over. "What?"

Karlsson pointed as he spoke. "This is the line that comes from the cable box to the punch-down. This is what gives the phones in the house a dial tone. He's wired for Voice Over IP. This one line goes to the alarm system control box. I'm guessing there's an RJ-31X jack in there that lets you transmit alarm signals out over the telephone lines." He moved his light to the right. "But this one..." He ran his finger down the board, "...is not the same kind of wire and it runs a different direction."

Lee looked at him. "You think it's a tap?"

"Could be. We need to follow it and see where it terminates."

"Okay." Lee agreed. "That's one thing for our list that we need to resolve. Let's keep looking and see what else we can find."

Karlsson turned and stared at the corner of the basement. "This guy has a three-car garage, and only one car, right?"

"Yeah."

"But he stores a step-ladder in the basement." He pointed at the aluminum ladder. "If he was fixing stuff on the first or second floors, this would be a long way to carry a ladder. If it's here, then we'd have to ask ourselves, what is it in the basement that he'd need a ladder for?"

"Let's use it and find out." Lee grabbed the ladder and opened it. He climbed up as far as he could without running his head into the flooring above, or any of the nails poking out. "These joists run north-south. We'll have to look at all of them."

"What? You got dinner plans?" Karlsson remarked. Nothing was ever easy.

Starting on the west end of the basement, the men shined the light down the joists into the finished part of the basement, moved the ladder and then repeated the process. On the sixth attempt, they struck pay-dirt. "Hmmm...I've got something on the other side. We need to go into the other room and move the ceiling tile out of the way."

Once on the finished side, they set up the ladder again when Karlsson halted his partner. "Hold up a minute. Look at that."

Lee looked down on the floor where Karlsson had indicated. Apparently, the maid's chore list didn't include the basement. On the floor, beneath the area they wanted to search, were particles of the foam ceiling tiles used in the finished area. "Uh oh...someone's been up there."

Lee gently moved the tile up and out of the way and then care-fully shined his light on the black cloth bag that had been folded and crammed up against a diagonal cross member. "Would you look at that? I wonder what this could be."

Karlsson moved around so that he could see the item in ques-tion. "Well, I'm not a lawyer, but if it's evidence of something, I'm thinking we'd need a warrant."

Lee used his cell phone to take a picture of it in place and then shined the flashlight around the immediate area before using the sides of two fingers to pull it out. "He's confessing to everything right now. We will agree that we're not charging him with posses-sion of whatever this is...and we're only doing this to ensure his safety. What do you think?"

"I think we could always put it back where we found it if it be-comes an issue. In the meantime, I'm kinda curious."

Lee replaced the ceiling tile in its original position and climbed back down. Karlsson held the flashlight while Lee opened his find. They looked at it for a second before Karlsson spoke. "How many of these fucking things are out there?"

"What?"

"That's the sprayer thing that they sent me to Shanghai to find. Except, this one seems to have more parts on it than the one I saw in...oh shit."

"What's the matter?"

"The one I saw in Bratenahl was supposed to have been coun-terfeit. It didn't have these extra parts on it. It was the one that Collins and Carroll showed me. Jeffers must have snatched a real one off the line at some point."

"What's it do?"

"Fuck, I don't know. It sprays something on the outside of an aircraft that lets it travel at ridiculously high speeds. I'm not an engineer."

"We're taking it." Jerry snorted. "Let's keep looking."

They finished their search above the joists and then walked the basement again. Had they been wearing shoes; they probably would have missed it. Karlsson stopped near the corner of the fin-ished part of the basement, where Jeffers had installed a shelf to store movies in various media. There were DVD's, Blu-ray, VHS and other media stacked or shelved for easy access. "Wait." He ran his foot over the carpet. It was the slightest bit uneven. "We need to pull the carpet back."

Lee got down on his hands and knees and ran his hand over the area that Karlsson had found. Closer inspection revealed that the carpet there only ran up to the base of the wooden shelves, a trim piece holding it in place. Lee removed the trim piece as he fingered his way along and then started to peel it back. There, cut into the basement concrete was a floor safe. "Naughty boy! He didn't tell us about this one."

"He didn't tell us that he had another copy of the sprayer, either."

"Fritz is going to have some overtime tonight!"

When they got upstairs, they found Fritz Miller relaxing, with his feet up on the desk, headphones on, listening to something on a small laptop that he'd had in the bottom of his bag. "Hi guys. I yelled Tally-Ho, but you must not have heard me."

"What?" Karlsson asked.

Fritz dragged the headphones off his head. "It's unlocked but I haven't opened it yet. Care to peek?"

"Absolutely." Lee replied. "In the meantime; northwest corner of the basement. We just found a floor safe."

Fritz grinned excitedly. "Bonus time!" He collected his tools and checked the surroundings for any sign that he had been there. Satisfied, he grabbed his canvas bag and headed towards the basement stairs.

Karlsson looked at the safe. "Well, this is your caper. I guess you get the honors."

Lee took a picture of the outside of the safe with his cell phone. "Here goes nothing!" He opened the door about a half inch at first, to give the edges a quick examination, and then opened it up all the way. He took another picture of the contents to document how they found everything, so that it could be put back the exact same way.

Lee let out a low whistle and activated the voice memo function on his phone. "The inside dimensions of the safe appear to be about nine or ten inches, by about twelve inches. Upon entry, I see two mustard-banded stacks of one-hundred-dollar bills, presumably, at ten thousand bucks per stack."

He gently removed the two stacks from the safe and handed them to Karlsson. "Put these on the desk." He looked at the remainder of the contents. "There's a black thirty-two gig flash drive." He visually examined it before passing it to Karlsson. "And, a nine by eleven manila envelope, sealed."

He passed the manila envelope to Karlsson and then ran his hand around the inside of the safe. "That's it."

Karlsson frowned at the envelope and then picked it up, looking at both sides and the tape used to seal it. There was no writing on it, and it was sealed with standard transparent tape. He returned it to the desk and started going through the drawers in the credenza.

"What are you looking for?" Lee asked.

"More manila envelopes. There's no writing on the outside, so if we can find that he's got some in here that are just like it, we can open it up, photograph the contents and replace and reseal them in another envelope."

"Good idea." Lee began searching some of the other drawers and found the one that contained office supplies. There, stacked neatly along the side of the drawer were four more envelopes identical to the one they found. "Got it!"

Like exuberant schoolkids on Christmas day, they gathered close, and Karlsson used his pocketknife to open it. Inside were found six eight-inch by ten-inch black and white photographs of documents. Karlsson flipped through them and passed them to Lee one at a time. "Cyrillic? They're in Russian."

Only one photo was even partially decipherable by them. It seemed to be a page from an early 1960's personnel file of a Soviet pilot. The man in the photo appeared to be in his early twenties, short blond hair and was wearing the dress uniform of an officer in the Soviet Air Force. He was wearing what appeared to be an aviation qualification badge.

Lee looked up. "I don't suppose you…"

"Not a word." Karlsson replied before his partner could finish the sentence.

Lee shrugged and laid the photos out side by side on the top of the desk. He adjusted a desk lamp to illuminate the images without adding glare, and then carefully photographed each one, flipped them over and took a picture of their reverse sides. When he was finished, he inserted the original photos into the new envelope and sealed it with transparent tape. It might not stand up to laboratory scrutiny but is was close enough for their purposes.

He picked up the flash drive. "I'm no forensics guy, but I think that if we try to read this on Fritz' laptop, we'll leave a trail...alter the hash files or something. We can't take it out of here without some sort of probable cause. But I think in the interest of national security, we should probably look at it anyway."

"Did I hear my name?"

They both looked up to see Fritz standing in the doorway to the office.

"Problem?" Karlsson asked.

"Nope. It wasn't locked. Well, it was kinda locked. Whoever got into it last time didn't spin the dial enough. They mighta' been in a hurry. I told you I always check first to see if I can catch the last number. And I did. What do you need my laptop for?"

Lee held up the flash drive. "We want to take a peek at this."

"Why don't you image it and take it with you?" He asked.

"We can't. We don't want to leave a trace that we downloaded it. We don't have the equipment and don't want to come back in here again if we can avoid it." Lee replied.

Fritz shook his head and smiled. "Wait till you guys get my bill for this."

He walked over to the corner and picked up one of the plastic cases that he'd brought along. "I always bring some Logicube stuff along on these types of visits in case we happen to need a perfect copy of a source drive, without altering the original. This unit is a drive-to-drive duplicator that gives you an exact sector-for-sector copy of the original. This way, you'll have a clone that be used for forensic examination later."

He sat the case up on Jeffers' desk. "I can also run Encase Forensics. It's a Windows based forensics suite that lets you make qualified forensics duplicates. It's easy to use, but it also has some quirks with the Op System recognizing suspect drives and some-times altering their contents. It's not like it actually generates data

– it doesn't. It's just a court thing. Most of my civilian clients just want to know what their husbands have on their computers. Law enforcement clients have their own forensics teams. Either way, no one will ever know we were here."

Lee grinned as he looked at Karlsson. "I sure as hell don't ever want this guy in my house!"

Fritz looked at Jeffers' laptop on the desk. "You want me to do that one too?"

"You can do that?"

"Yeah. The flash drive will take a couple of minutes, but for his laptop, I'll have to take the drive out of the machine. Depending on how much data he has on there, it could take an hour or two."

"Do it." Lee said. "We need to look inside the safe in the basement."

They left Fritz to work his magic on the flash drive and laptop and returned to the basement. They stared at the square piece of steel that had been squeezed into a perfect cut in the concrete. The flat steel lid with the center finger hole had been moved aside and the knob and the handle were ready for them. Lee took a picture of the unit with the door closed, and then opened it up.

Depressing his memo button on his phone, he recited: "The device is labelled as a Hollon B-1500 floor safe and appears to be made of blue quarter-inch steel, about fifteen by thirteen inches, and about twelve inches deep." He took another picture and then hit his memo icon again. "There's what looks like a dark green hand towel or washcloth wrapped around something."

Lee retrieved the terry cloth-wrapped item and laid it out on the carpet. Inside was a small wooden box, which he photographed before opening it. "There is a black and white, four-inch by four-inch photograph of a young blond man in white coveralls and a white hard hat. It appears to be old...maybe from the sixties. And what looks like several pieces of Russian military insignia."

He separated the three items and laid them out left to right. "The first piece appears to be a medal of some sort; red ribbon with gold longitudinal trim. The medal bears a picture of Vladimir Lenin cast in silver, surrounded by gold and red metal with Cyrillic writing and a red star on the left side. Hammer and sickle on the bottom. On the reverse side is found Cyrillic writing around the bottom and across the top is stamped a six-digit number that appears to have been struck-through in an attempt to eradicate it."

Lee took a couple of pictures of the front and back and then moved to the next item. "Number two consists of a red ribbon bar, suspending a one-inch pentagon-shaped medal with Cyrillic writing across the top two sides, CCCP at the bottom, and some kind of oak leaves running up the other two sides. In the center of the medal-lion is a relief of earth...showing the Soviet Union, with some sort of aircraft orbiting north-south around the poles."

"The third piece looks to be a two-inch diamond-shaped badge with a screw post with screw in place, on the back. The front fea-tures a red star, as a separate part that's been glued or soldered on or something. And attached to the center of the star is a gold wreath. Inside the wreath is a globe with a hammer and sickle. At the bottom of the diamond is a small plate attachment with Cyrillic writing."

Lee re-arranged the items again. "Hit those switches over there and see if we can get some more light on this stuff."

Karlsson found the switch on the wall and flipped it up. Track lighting bathed the media case and entertainment center in warm, even lighting. "I don't get it. The guy keeps twenty grand in cash, Russian documents and a flash drive in a safe that's pretty easy to find and buries some old military trinkets in a basement floor safe that most people wouldn't have discovered."

Lee moved around and focused as close as he could on the photograph. After snapping another picture, he flipped it over to get a shot of the reverse. In pencil, someone had written "1966 Cape Kennedy". As he flipped the picture over again, he paused and brought up his photo album on his phone. Silently, he scrolled back to the image he had taken of the Soviet personnel file upstairs. He looked at the photo on the floor again and then passed the phone to Karlsson. "Pretty close, huh?"

Karlsson enlarged the image of the file and compared it to the one just found. "Yeah...pretty close. So, why was a Soviet pilot getting his picture taken in coveralls at the Cape during the height of the space race?"

Lee took another set of individual close-ups of each piece, front and back, and then carefully replaced them in the wooden box and closed the lid. He re-wrapped it the way he'd found it and returned it to the safe.

"Yeah. These must be important to him for some reason." He turned the handle to engage the bolts, and then turned the dial about a quarter turn, before replacing the flat steel covering. He smoothed the carpet back into its original position and winced as his fingers found one of the tacks in the carpet strip. He replaced the wood molding strip and stood up. "That's as good as I can get it without calling a professional carpet installer."

Karlsson began to collapse the ladder so that he could return it to the other room where he had found it. "Relative, maybe?"

Lee shook his head. "No idea. That stuff is old. Could be anyone."

When they got back to the den, they found Fritz in his usual position, feet up on the desk, earphones on his head. He offered them his perpetual grin. "I copied the flash drive onto a file on my laptop. I'm imaging his laptop drive now. I'm guessing it'll take another half hour. It's a relatively new machine, and he doesn't have a lot on here."

Lee nodded. "We need to take another look around the upstairs anyway." Karlsson followed him up the stairs. The three guest rooms were sparsely decorated, probably due to the property settlement with his ex-wife. The closets were empty of everything except hangers. The master suite though had been somewhat redecorated with a king-sized bed, two dressers and a chest, that all seemed upscale and new. The darker bluish-gray paint on the walls seemed more modern and contemporary than the rest of the house. The large walk-in cedar closet contained a nice eight-gun walnut gun case with a glass front; obviously designed more for presentation than for security. And while the clothes were mostly men's, there was a section that had been offered up for high-end ladies clothing and shoes. All of which looked elegant and new.

Lee picked up a couple of pairs of the female's shoes and looked at the bottoms. "No scuff marks. These haven't been worn that much, but we'll have to see if Jenny Lu is a size six." He replaced them where he'd found them and opened the dresser drawers. Again, most were men's clothes, but three of the drawers in one dresser had been filled with women's garments. He shined his light behind the furniture and then under the bed, but nothing of interest caught his eye. He saw Karlsson eyeing the rifles in the gun case.

"Anything interesting?"

"Yeah." Karlsson opened the glass door, which had not been locked. "He's got some pretty nice hunting rifles and a couple of shotguns. You might want to record the descriptions and serial numbers for your report."

Lee joined him in the closet and as Karlsson pulled each rifle out and identified it, he read off the serial number. There were two Remingtons, chambered in 30.06 and .270 respectively, with nice wooden stocks and expensive scopes. There was a Weatherby Mark V with a beautifully crafted wood stock, chambered in .300 Weatherby Magnum. Karlsson knew from experience that the ballistics for the .300 Weatherby were close to that of the 300 Winchester Magnum, used by some sniper teams, but the two rounds weren't interchangeable. He was impressed. The rifle, by itself, was probably worth more than $2,500.00, but with the Leupold 7-42x56mm variable power scope mounted on it, was certainly worth twice that.

There were two Remington 870 twelve-gauge shotguns; one with a shorter eighteen-inch riot barrel, similar to what police officers carried in their cruisers. The other was probably for sport, with a thirty-inch ribbed barrel. After Lee got pictures of both of them, Karlsson reached for the last piece, a Bushmaster M-4 carbine; the shorter version with the five-and-a-half-inch flash suppressor, which brought its overall length into compliance with federal regulations. This copy was decked out with a tactical rail system, tactical light and had a holographic weapon sight built for close-quarter engagements with fast-moving targets in a variety of lighting conditions.

After it was photographed and the serial number recorded, Karlsson started to return it to the cabinet, and as an afterthought, gave the flash suppressor a twist. It was loose. Federal law stated that for the flash suppressor to be counted towards length, it had to be soldered on. "Ooops." He said as he unscrewed it off the end of the barrel and showed it to Lee. "ATF probably wouldn't like this."

"Too short?"

"Yeah. This is the modern copy of Colt's Vietnam era XM177. It has an eleven-and-a-half-inch barrel, but with the flash suppressor permanently mounted, it brings the length to more than the required sixteen inches." Karlsson rolled the metal cylinder around in his hand. "This one's never been soldered or pinned. He couldn't have purchased this from a licensed dealer unless he'd paid a tax stamp for an SBR...a Short-Barreled Rifle."

Karlsson matched up the threads and screwed the suppressor back on. "And, if he wanted to buy a can...a silencer, he'd have to pay a second two-hundred-dollar tax stamp for that as well. You should be able to find out from your ATF guys with a quick computer check."

Karlsson returned the rifle to its place in the cabinet and then opened the bottom drawer. There were a couple of boxes of shotgun rounds, and six boxes of ammunition for the scoped rifles. "No five-five-six ammo, and no magazines."

Lee snapped a picture of the open drawer. "He has an assault rifle with no ammo and no magazines?"

"Doubtful." Karlsson closed the drawer. "It's here somewhere, we just haven't found it yet."

CHAPTER 10

I t was a big day for Jenny Lu. Senator Layden would be arriving in four hours and his team was ecstatic about the speech she had put together for him. This evening, she would be seen on stage with him at a national event that was sure to be picked up by all the networks. That meant that Zhou would see her. It also meant that her benefactors at Echo Aerospace would see her as well. She was excited.

However, she had not heard from Marty for almost forty-eight hours. It was unusual for him to avoid calling when they weren't together. Especially if he knew she had something big going on. She had scolded him pretty harshly the last time they'd spoken. Maybe too harshly? She tried his number again, but it went straight to voicemail, and since she had already left a message for him earlier, she just hung up. She tried his home telephone number as well, but it too went to voicemail. When she called his office earlier that morning, the receptionist said that she had not seen him yet, but since the engineers were all on flexible schedules, it was difficult to say when he would be in.

She wanted a chance to speak with him and get an update before she spoke to Zhou again. Her plan was to contact Zhou after the rally in the hopes that he would be happy with her progress within the campaign. She had also hoped to be able to give him some good news about the sprayer, whatever that was. Nevertheless, she had a job to do and after her shower, she collected her things and headed out to the convention center.

She quickly checked her laptop bag to ensure that she had the special credential that Layden's staffer had given her the evening before. It had a microchip that had been registered to her, and she had been told that if she lost it, she had to notify them immediately so that they, in turn, could notify the Secret Service advance team. She'd had to provide them with her personal information and a copy of her driver's license so that a limited background check could be run, and she'd been told to show up at least two hours early, to go through the metal detectors and bag checks. Once inside, she had been directed to report to the event management office to pick up her pin.

A basic component of the Secret Service's protection plan at special events was the use of special credentials, known as *SARGE* pins to help control who had access to the rings of security around a particular Protectee. The pins served as temporary identification that were to be worn on an individual's lapel, and each pin carried a specific letter and sometimes, a number so that colors and shapes could be changed frequently, ensuring uniqueness at each event: *S* for Staff, *A* for Airport, *R* for Resident, *G* for Guest, and *E* for Enforcement, which included armed law enforcement or properly vetted private security. This program allowed agents to quickly determine if an individual was authorized to be in a specific area or not. Entering a secured area while wearing the wrong pin was a sure way to be detained, interviewed, inconvenienced, and sometimes arrested.

McCormick Place was one of the top convention centers in the United States, with 2.6 million square feet of exhibit space. Connected by pedestrian promenades and a sky bridge across Lake Shore Drive was the Arie Crown Theater, with seating for up to 18,000 people. Both venues, as well as Navy Pier, were owned by the Metropolitan Pier and Exposition Authority, and drew more than fifty-five million visitors into downtown Chicago each year. She had attended conventions and concerts in the complex before and had no trouble finding the underground parking facility. She checked her instructions again and as she donned her event credential, she re-read the instructions given her by the Senator's staffer to make sure she was headed towards the correct entrance. Her friends had asked her if she was concerned for her safety, living in such a big city as Chicago, but she just laughed. There were at least twenty cities in China that had a larger population that Chicago's paltry two and a half million, and most of the world had never heard of them.

She found the entrance designated for event staff and bypassed the line of more than a hundred people, some of whom had been there since dawn. It was a free event and had been heavily advertised throughout Chicagoland, to assure a huge turnout. There were three tables set up near a metal detector and x-ray machine, with men and women in business suits working at laptops, all wearing the characteristic earpieces with curling cords that ran inside their jacket collars.

She walked up to the first table. "Hello. My name is Lu and I'm on the communications team. Am I in the right place?" She smiled innocently.

The agent with the short brown hair and the strapping chest that looked like it would stop a bullet looked up and returned her smile. He quickly glanced at her credential and typed her name in. "Oh, Ms. Lu, nice to meet you. It looks like you're going to be on stage tonight with the Senator. But first, we need to swap out your credential."

She handed him the four by six-inch ticket that she had been wearing around her neck. He removed the paper card from inside the plastic covering and ripped it in half. "You're going to be on the stage tonight, so we have to give you a different pass." He reached under the desk and found another one and inserted it into a printer. When it came out the other side, it had the same red, white and blue logo for the campaign, but instead of indicating EVENT STAFF, in large black letters across the bottom, it said STAGE. He slid it back into the plastic carrier and handed it to her. "Please don't lose this. If you do, grab any one of the agents and let them know as soon as possible. We'll have you follow this agent over here back to the briefing area, but it's important for you to remember that unless the Senator takes you to the podium himself, you can't cross the blue line."

"The blue line?" She asked.

"Yes. On the floor around the podium, about twelve feet out, there's a blue line that's been taped down. Under no circumstances can you step inside that line unless you have a credential that says PODIUM. It's a security thing." He winked at her.

She was impressed with the process but a bit overwhelmed by it all. "And, if I do, you'll shoot me?" She smiled.

The agent forced a smile back at her. "Well, not me, actually. I'll be out here most of the evening. Enjoy your event."

⎯⎯⎯⎯⎯⎯⎯⎯⎯⎯⎯⎯⎯⎯

Stan Marchand inserted his credit card into the reader and keyed in his pin code when prompted. After the clerk handed him his receipt, he pushed his groceries towards the door, but then decided to just carry them to his car and abandon the cart where it was on the sidewalk. His Audi recognized his pocketed key fob and the back door opened easily as his cell phone began ringing. He tossed the four blue plastic bags on the back seat and then looked at the number on the screen. He thought he recognized the number, but with the ridiculously high number of scam telemarketers spoofing calls, he could not be sure.

"Hello, it's Stan."

"How's retirement?" Asked the familiar voice.

"Randy Mifflin?" Marchand guessed. "What are you doing these days? Are you still in the game?"

"Yeah! I'm SES now...Senior Executive Service."

"I know what it means you kiss-ass. I can't believe you made it to ASAIC with all of your stunts. And they kept you on anyway? With a promotion?"

"I guess so. I got remarried and needed the money. It's almost two hundred a year, and it's not like it's a tough job. Which is why I'm calling." He paused for a moment. He had known Stan along time. "Listen, most of our guys are out working digs or advancing venues for the campaign. Is there any chance you could pick up a freelance babysitting job in Cleveland for a few days?"

"Cleveland? In February? Are you shitting me?"

"Oh, man...you know me. If it wasn't absolutely critical, I wouldn't ask, but I have to start pulling retirees in to fill all of the stuff that's coming up. They have us spread too thin and we're not running academies like we used to."

"I'm retired."

"Oh, come on. You must be doing something for somebody because I checked the list and saw that you still have an active clearance. Who are you working for, by the way?"

Marchand screwed up his face as he realized that his work for Paul was compensated through the same federal system as the Secret Service and every other federal agency, and the security clearances were visible to most of them, even if the actual scope or specifics of employment were not. "Oh, it's nothing. An intelligence thing that pops up from time to time. Analysis and shit."

"Come on, man. Help me out. I can get you a thousand a day plus the usual per diem. We'll get you sworn in as a Special Deputy US Marshal when you get there."

Marchand contemplated the offer. "How long?"

"Ten days...two weeks, tops."

The job had been his life for twenty-five years, and his golf clubs would still be there when he got back. He hated to admit it to himself, but he missed the adrenaline rush that came with the work. He needed it again, at least, for a while. "Aw shit. Okay. I need to make a phone call, but...where and when?"

It was a large white colonial home on a one-acre corner lot, about fifteen years old, but with a new roof and an updated kitchen. With four bedrooms and three and a half baths, it made a perfect place to stash a witness who was awaiting trial, or hiding from insolent malfeasants with bad judgement, who were occupying less-fashionable surroundings at any of the country's finer federal penitentiaries. The price had been right. The previous occupant had been convicted of several federal crimes including RICO, narcotics trafficking and counterfeiting, and with a stroke of a pen, a federal judge, citing 18 US Code, section 985, had taken possession of the property, since the US attorney proved that it had been acquired as fruits or elements of a continuing criminal enterprise. In short, it now belonged to the Secret Service, even though the county auditor listed it as being owned by a tech company in Maryland.

The safe house on Country Club Drive in the nearby suburb of Medina had seen many guests come and go. But now, it was the temporary home of Martin Jeffers. It was also the temporary home of Jerry Lee and Matthias Karlsson, who had checked out of their respective hotel rooms and were now guests in the same abode. Though it was a consensus among all the guests that each wished they were somewhere else.

Jeffers had been totally honest about his involvement with Zhou and explained the details as to how he had met the seductive Jenny Lu, at a party hosted by Echo Aerospace some months back. Jeffers was an overweight engineer with fantasies of meeting an alluring woman who would satisfy his most primitive sexual pleasures. A provocateur, or provocatress, in her case, that would help him achieve sexually what had been lacking in his life. He could design high performance aircraft, but he could not attract those radiant A-list women.

Jenny Lu had bridged that gap. She appreciated his brain and loved the attention and gifts he showered upon her. He bought her a wardrobe that she could use now that she was a public relations specialist, travelling around some of the busiest cities in the country. He recognized her potential. And she, his. They were a perfect match. He felt that if he could just keep giving her the things she needed to enhance her career, then she would love him for it, and they could be happy forever.

As for the small obstacle of industrial espionage, in which he found himself involved, he continued to stick to the story that it was all for the right reason. Zhou had explained that the Chinese had fallen behind the Russians and the Americans, and all their country wanted to do was to stay relevant. They did not want to be left out.

"Let me explain this to you…again." Lee looked at him. They were playing rummy, for a thousand dollars a point. Hypothetically. "Zhou wants you dead. He hired me to kill you. Lu also works for Zhou. How can you ever think that she is going to come back to you with love and affection and want to raise a family? When you fall asleep in each other's arms, how will you know if you're going to wake up the next morning?"

"We're in love. I know it. She knows it. Sure, we've probably had our ups and downs like everyone else, but she loves me."

"Well, for what it's worth, I'm guessing you do really love her." Lee took a sip out of the soft drink can. "I bet she has a key to your house."

"Of course."

"So she knows where all of your valuables are kept, right? Guns?"

After a moment he replied. "I suppose so. Why?"

"Well, then. That just goes to demonstrate your sincerity. Why would you give her a key to your house, and show her where all of your guns were if you didn't think she really loved you?"

Jeffers looked at him for a moment. "So, what?"

"You have several guns, don't you, Marty?" Lee quipped as he pulled the three of clubs off the deck, frowned and then tossed it on the pile in the center of the table.

"Of course. I like to shoot. There's nothing wrong with that."

"No, there isn't. I used to do some shooting myself. What kinds of guns do you like to shoot?"

"I've done some hunting. Mostly out west, but my cousin has a farm in western Pennsylvania. I've gone there a few times."

"Yeah? Deer? Elk? Black bear? What do you like to chase, Marty?"

"Deer, mostly. I've never come across a bear when I had a rifle... and permit."

"I know what you mean. What calibers do you like to hunt with?"

The line of questions seemed innocent enough. It sounded like Lee was interested in the topic and just making conversation. "In Ohio? You have to use a shotgun. If you go out west or to Pennsylvania, you can use a rifle."

"What about five-five-six? Did you ever hunt with an M-4?"

"M-4? Huh uh. I got one of those a few months ago, but it's strictly a range gun. Why?"

"I just wondered...you can't really hunt deer with them here. I was just curious if you'd ever shot one before."

"Yeah, a couple of times. I actually got it for her. I keep it at my place. She wanted to learn how to shoot it. But, she lives in Chicago, and they're illegal there. So, when she comes out to visit, we take it out and she gets to feed a magazine or two through it for fun."

"Is she any good?"

"Yeah, I think so. She's getting better."

"So, what was the plan? You and her would get a payoff from Zhou and live happily ever after in some hunting lodge somewhere?"

"It's not like that."

"No? Where is she now?" Lee asked.

Jeffers looked at his watch. "Turn on one of the cable news channels."

"Excuse me?" Karlsson replied taking a card from the deck and tossing the Jack of clubs on the pile.

Jeffers found the remote control and when the TV came on, scrolled through the station guide until he found a news station. "Here."

The men watched Senator Layden addressing a noisy group of supporters from the Arie Crown Theater in downtown Chicago. There was energy in the air as he said the things that they wanted to hear. Clean air. Clean water. No wars, and plenty of money to go around for education and health care. Glaringly absent, of course, was any mention of how much it would cost, and how the bill would get paid. Every once in a while, the camera angle would go wide, and on the stage behind him could be seen some enthusiastic supporters, one of whom was a striking Asian woman about five foot three, wearing a dark blue pant suit.

"There!" Jeffers exclaimed with a grin. "That's her!"

"Attractive." Lee commented quietly. "What did she have to do to get a spot on stage like that?"

"She wrote the speech he's giving." Jeffers went on to explain her work with the public relations firm that led her to the senator's campaign.

Karlsson had not mentioned to Jeffers that his fiancé was also supplying information to key executives at Echo Aerospace, yet. Even though there existed the probability that he knew. That was knowledge that rested strictly with Paul until such time as he was given permission to let him, or anyone else know about it. He had told Lee that snippet a couple of days earlier, when it looked like they were working towards the same goal. Lee had passed the information to the necessary parties at Secret Service, which meant that even though she had passed their background check, they knew who she was.

After a few more rounds of applause for dazzling political rhetoric came the announcement. He led up to it with tales of how the Chinese had been our allies in World War II and given sanctuary to our pilots who'd had to ditch their planes after bombing Japan. "I look forward to a new generation of friendship with our Asian friends and promise that under my administration China and the United States will grow stronger together."

Lee and Karlsson looked at each other and then at Marty Jeffers.

Marty shrugged, a smile forming on the corner of his mouth. "See, guys? If Layden gets elected, we are all going to be working on these projects together. How is what I've done so wrong?"

"If he wins," Lee snickered, "...maybe he'll appoint a US Attorney who's more predisposed to ignoring your actions."

Jeffers momentarily retreated. "I feel stuffy. I've got to get out of here for a minute. Can't we go for a walk or something? Nobody knows us here."

"You know the rules." Lee answered. "You don't exist. At least for now."

"But this is ridiculous. I've got to do something!"

Karlsson reminded him. "There's almost an entire gym in the basement. Why don't you go do some sit-ups or something?"

"Yeah! We could all use some exercise. You could work those abs down and when you see Jenny again, you'll be a stud." Lee added.

"Why can't I call her? She's probably called me a dozen times in the past twenty- four hours. This isn't fair to her, or to my friends and co-workers."

"Marty, we know you love her, but we don't know which side she's on yet. We need to give it a couple of more days to see what she does when she thinks you've dropped off the grid." Karlsson threw his hand in and got up. "Now, I've got cabin fever. I think I'm going downstairs and hit the treadmill."

After Karlsson descended the stairs, Jeffers collected the cards on the table, shuffled them once and sat the deck in the center. He turned to face Lee, his guardian or captor. "So, how will we know?"

"If she's legit, she'll call your office to see if you've been there, and then the police to report you missing. We're betting she'll call Zhou first."

"How will you know who she calls first?"

Lee looked at him. "Marty, we're the Secret Service. We know."

—((O))—

It was after eight by the time Jenny Lu got back to her apartment. The Senator's team was fervently euphoric about the speech and invited her to a private dinner at Smith & Wollensky. Although the Senator was already on the way to his next campaign stop, the local party Chair and a couple of carefully selected journalists were invited to the private dining room overlooking the Chicago River, and the lights of the city, where they could recap the speech and the Senator's plans for a changing America.

Like many in her age group, she was an idealist and liked all good things for all people. But because she was a relative newcomer to politics and could have just as easily been assigned to a candidate representing the opposing party, she shied away from deep philosophical discussions. Especially with reporters. She had a job to do. Several jobs. And she didn't want to be misquoted or pigeon-holed into a political position that made her unfavorable to her employers.

The party was still in full swing at the upscale downtown eatery, but she needed to make some calls and create some space between her and some sixty-year-old party front man who kept inquiring about her relationship status a little too obnoxiously. She tried Marty one more time but hung up the second it went into his voicemail. She was worried. Something was definitely wrong, but she was unsure as to how to find out more. She could not put off the conversation with Zhou any longer.

Later, in her bedroom, she stepped out of her shoes and reached her hand between the mattress and box springs to retrieve the cell phone that she kept for private conversations with her sponsor. She dialed the number from memory and waited for it to ring on the other end. It would be close to nine in the morning in Shanghai.

"Wèi." The female voice answered curtly.

"Wèi. Qǐng wèn Zhou xiān sheng zài ma?" Jenny asked.

"Duì bu qǐ, nǐ dǎ cuò le." The woman replied, advising that the caller had the wrong number. It was part of their communications security protocol, and thirty seconds later, Zhou called her back.

"How are you, child?"

She detested being called child, or any other term of affection, by the lecherous goat. "I am well. Have you seen the news?"

"Yes. The Chicago rally. You looked good! Has there been any talk of more work with his campaign?"

"Yes. I am working on his Milwaukee speech for next week, and one of his senior staff members has suggested that I travel with them to several more functions."

"I am pleased with your success. My confidence is building." After a pause, "And, what of the other matter?"

This was it. The moment she had been dreading. "There's a small problem with that. My friend was unable to acquire the item you requested. He searched where he thought it should be, but it was gone. And now," She inhaled unevenly, genuine concern coming through in her voice. "He is...missing."

"Missing?" Zhou asked, sounding almost amused.

The inflection in his voice was confusing. "Yes. We spoke two days ago, and he was working on another plan to find your item, but I haven't heard from him. He is not answering his cell phone or his home phone. And his office has not heard from him, either."

"I see." The sociopath responded. "It may be time for you to sever your ties with Mr. Jeffers. If he is unable to find my property, then he is of no further use to me."

"What?" She asked.

"He was a tool. I will simply have to make other arrangements to try to get it back."

"What are you telling me to do?"

"Do as you wish. But, if he is not returning your calls, perhaps he has had second thoughts about your relationship. If he is truly infatuated by you, he will call you back. Walk away child."

Zhou hung up, the click causing her to flinch. It was a cold mechanical response, void of any emotion. How could Zhou expect her to go from the role of loving fiancé to icy bitch so quickly? Was he not concerned about how it would look to the people who knew them both? She had created a character. She had met his friends. She had developed genuine feelings for the guy.

She turned off the special cell phone and pushed it back between the mattresses. In the other room, she found her other phone in her purse. She pulled up her contacts and scrolled through them until she found what she was looking for. It was late in Cleveland, but she had to give it a try.

"Spotless Cleveland. This is Jeff."

"Jeff my name is Jenny. I'm Marty Jeffers' fiancé and I'm in

Chicago right now. I haven't been able to reach him for a couple of days and wanted to know if you could go by his house and see if everything is okay."

"Jeffers? He's a residential customer out in Medina, right?"

"Yes. I'm so sorry to bother you, but I don't want to call the police if he's just having phone trouble."

"Sure. I'm on a commercial site right now, but I can head over there in about a half hour. I'll have to catch Bonnie Jo, though. She's got his house key."

"Thank you so very much! Please call me the second you get in the house." She sat the phone down on the kitchen counter. A sudden chill came over her. Something was wrong for sure. Clairsentience. Sometimes, you just know.

———— «(()» ————

The treadmill had taken a beating under Karlsson's two-hundred pound frame and given it right back in the form of sore legs and lower back. As Lee and Jeffers came down to take their turns on the equipment, he decided he needed a shower. He stood under the hot water for several minutes allowing it to pound on his head and cascade over his body. He toweled off and put on clean sweats and then headed back down to the kitchen to see if there was something in the refrigerator that would make a good bedtime snack.

"A little help down here!" It was Lee yelling up from the basement.

"Yeah? What do you need?" Karlsson responded from the top of the basement stairs.

"Get down here! I think we need a medic!"

Karlsson took the steps as fast as he could, without banging his head on the ceiling joist at the bottom. Marty was laid out on the floor. Lee was trying to take his pulse. Martin Jeffers seemed to be conscious but could not speak. "What happened?"

Lee was checking his pulse in his neck and on his wrist. "I don't know. He was on the bench press and suddenly sat up. He got a strange look on his face and fell off the bench. I sat him up again, but he can't talk. I don't know if he had a seizure or a stroke or something."

The left side of Jeffers' face seemed to droop. "Marty, can you hear me, man?"

Jeffers made an incoherent grunting noise. He seemed confused and could not get his mouth to form words.

Karlsson looked at his eyes and noted that the pupils were not the same; one dilated and the other constricted. "We have to get him to a hospital right now." Karlsson said anxiously. "We can wait for EMS and try to explain our relationship, or we can throw him in the car and make a run for Medina General on East Washington."

"Shit!" Lee exclaimed. "He's two hundred pounds of gelatin right now. How do we get him up the stairs?"

Karlsson remembered some of his battlefield first aid training. "Just a minute. I'll get a blanket."

Lee held on to Marty's hand. "Hang in there, dude. We're going to get you to the hospital."

Marty's eyes seemed to stare at a point somewhere above the ceiling.

Karlsson was back with a comforter he'd snatched off of one of the beds. He unfolded it on the basement floor, and the two men maneuvered Marty, as softly as they could, to the middle of it and then wrapped it around him and compressed the ends to serve as a stretcher of sorts. "I'll try to get his head if you can handle his legs."

Together, they worked to get Marty up the steps in his makeshift litter, with as few bumps on the steps as possible. Karlsson gently sat his head down on the kitchen floor and then got the car keys from the counter. He hit the button to raise the garage door and then opened both rear doors on the Ford Explorer that the Secret Service had loaned them. He got back to the kitchen and instructed Lee, "We have to get him to the garage and set him down again. I'll get in the back seat and then pull him up and in."

"Let's try it." The carefully moved Marty out the kitchen door into the garage and it only took a moment for Karlsson to get into position in the back seat, lean out and grab the comforter and pull with all his strength. Lee got Marty's feet in and then closed the door of the black ford SUV. The van would have made a better transport vehicle, but it had been left back at the podiatry school where they had initially acquired it.

Since Karlsson was already holding Marty's head, Lee jumped into the driver's seat and headed towards the hospital. "North on River Styx and West on Route eighteen…seven minutes." Lee said out loud, recalling from his memory. They had advanced, or *reconned*, the routes in and out of the safe house two days earlier, which included routes to the hospital as well as other safe havens like police and fire stations.

Lee spotted the red-letter sign across the portico, EMERGENCY and headed towards it. He came in a bit fast and when he tapped his breaks, Marty and Karlsson were thrown forward. "Sorry guys!"

Lee jumped out and ran inside. When he returned a few seconds later, he was accompanied by an attendant in green scrubs who seemed to know something about emergency medicine. Together, they got Martin Jeffers onto the gurney and pushed him inside.

"Are you guys family?" He asked as they went through the double doors.

"Yes. We're… cousins." Lee replied sheepishly.

They were met in a treatment room by a sturdy nurse who seemed to be in her early forties, wearing a stethoscope over her shoulders like a shawl, a roll of medical tape dangling from one of the earpieces. "What happened?"

Lee regained his composure and allowed his breathing to slow past his heart rate. "We were working out in the basement and he slid off of the bench and became unresponsive."

"Okay. I'm going to have to ask you two to leave for a minute. You'll need to fill out some paperwork for us and we'll send someone out to talk to you when we see what's going on. Is he on any drugs that you know of?"

"No." Lee shook his head.

"Do you know when he last ate something?"

"Probably around six thirty. We had pizza." Lee responded.

"Any history of heart problems?"

"Not that I can think of." He replied.

"All right...out!" She ushered the men out of the treatment rooms, back into the lobby area.

Karlsson looked on as Lee dialed a number on his phone. "It's Lee...I need the SAIC right away." He looked up at Karlsson. "What a clusterfuck."

"We need his wallet and insurance cards, or someone's insurance cards to get him signed in." Karlsson offered softly.

"I know." He rubbed his eyes. Someone answered on the far end. "Hey boss. We're at Medina General. NIGHTENGALE went down...some sort of seizure or something. We need an agent with credentials and the liaison from Medina PD to meet us here to get this guy checked in."

Karlsson was only privy to one side of the rapid-fire conversation. "Don't know...he's in there now. What? We were working out downstairs and he just passed out. No, I don't think it was his heart. Looks more like a stroke. I don't know. Okay, thanks."

Lee pocketed his phone and shook his head. "What do they think I am, a fucking doctor?"

"Take a breath. We need to sort through some scenarios to figure out how we're going to play this." Karlsson looked around to make sure they were out of earshot.

"Did you two bring in the patient in room three?"

They looked over at man in scrubs behind the counter. He was holding a clipboard. "I'm going to need one of you to give us some information."

"Yeah. I will." Lee said as he took the clipboard and walked over to a couch in the waiting area. Karlsson sat down beside him. They were the only ones in the waiting room, besides a teenage girl and presumably, her mother.

"Let's start with his name." Lee said. "He's still Martin Jeffers as far as anyone is concerned. He's off-grid, but he hasn't disappeared yet."

Karlsson thought for a moment. "Let's stay with that for now. Your guys are bringing his wallet over. I say, let's get him booked in under his own name. We'll get him a private room and continue to babysit him until he gets good enough to travel and then we'll move him to another safe house. Unless…"

"Unless what?"

"Unless for some reason, he doesn't make it."

"And then?"

"As far as the Zhou case is concerned, you're still undercover. If he dies, you just cemented your relationship with Zhou tighter than any other UC would be able to do. You could milk this for years."

Lee looked at him blankly. "You're a cold, sick bastard, aren't you?"

"Goes with the job." Karlsson concurred.

Lee started completing the form and listed Jeffers' correct name and address, and then added for occupation, Engineer, Echo Aerospace. He left the medical history section blank, but when it came to the box for next of kin, he looked back up at Karlsson. "Should I put Jenny Lu's contact information in here? It would be staying in character."

"Well, if you put one of us in there, that's where the paper trail will lead back and we'd have some explaining to do to someone, sometime. I think Jenny Lu gets the vote."

Lee took the partially completed document back to the attendant. "I'm sorry that this isn't finished. We have someone bringing his wallet and insurance cards over, but they could be a few minutes away. This will, at least, get him in the system."

"Thanks." He said as he took the clipboard, focusing on his computer screen and not making any eye contact. It was just part of the job.

Karlsson gave him a minute to steady his nerves and get back to the present. "So, walk me through this again before your friends get here."

Lee looked at him, confused. "You were there."

"I was in the shower. I came downstairs and heard you yell from the basement."

Karlsson pursed his lips. "Your agency knows that you were U-C for over a year. You got back to the States on a ticket paid by a suspect. A suspect, who asked that you eliminate a certain problem. Mr. Jeffers. Mr. Jeffers is now on the way to being thus eliminated and it won't be long before one of your inspectors has you on the box asking you if you had something to do with this."

"A polygraph? Seriously?" Lee did not know whether to be angry or concerned at the statement.

"Look, Jerry...you have to understand my role in this. I'm not a federal agent. I'm not a cop. I was asked to look into this to find out who was selling some kind of secret aircraft parts to the Chinese, and I've done that. You helped. I have no idea what your orders were, or how this plays into them. I've got my man, as they say, and I can go back to my retirement. But you...you have another eighteen and a half years before you can retire, and you don't want a blemish like this on your record. You lost a Protectee. Maybe a treasonous douchebag, but a Protectee, nevertheless. I know how you guys get about stuff like that."

Lee nervously picked at his fingernails. "You don't believe that this was just an accident? Something that happened on its own that we couldn't have foreseen?"

"I'm not your problem. I get paid to neutralize threats. And Jeffers gave every indication that he'd done some bad things that threatened our country. If my boss had told me to take him out when I first met him, then we wouldn't be here. It's not my job to question Washington. It's not my job to intervene in someone's life to make them a better person. I'm a soldier. That means; I have to eliminate the enemy, once the enemy is identified to me. I swore an oath forty years ago to support and defend the Constitution of the United States of America. Against all enemies, foreign and domestic. I don't define who the enemy is. The US Government does. I don't define the battlefield. The US Government does. I love my country." He shrugged. "Politicians, on the other hand, can kiss my ass. But, in the end, my vote doesn't count for anything more than yours does."

"What is this, a fucking pep talk?" He looked blankly across the room.

"My job and your job happen to be connected right now. It's like, for the time being, we're running in some parallel universe. In the end though, my goal and your goal might be a little different, but I need you to accomplish your goals so that I can accomplish mine."

Lee was silent.

Karlsson continued. "Did you ever study astronomy, Jerry?"

Lee nodded. "Of course...High School, college."

"Do you know what a black hole is?"

"Sort of." He answered, preoccupied, and somewhat annoyed at the question. "It's a star that has collapsed on itself and could shrink to something the size of a dime but still has an intense mass with the gravitational effect of something a million times that of the sun."

"Excellent! The gravity is so intense, that not even light can escape it. Do you know what an event horizon is?"

"Event...uh...it has something to do with the gravitational effect or something."

"Correct, again! In astrophysics, an event horizon is a boundary beyond which events can no longer affect the observer. The term was coined by a physicist named Wolfgang Rindler, working on something to do with general relativity. Einstein, and all that. Stephen Hawking, great brain, bad teeth, even threw in on the topic and brought up some ideas that baffled the greatest scientific minds of the time. No one is certain, but the consensus was that any object that approaches the horizon from the observer's side appears to slow down and never quite crosses the horizon. Other physicists speculate that if an object gets too close to a black hole, it basically gets elongated and shredded, on its way to being sucked in."

Lee looked at him as if he were trying to read his mind. "Well, Jerry, my job is often to get as close to the event horizon as I can, understand as much of it as I can, and still get back in one piece. The problem is, that much of the time, I can't tell where the true horizon is. It's sometimes illusive. Know what I mean?"

"I'm not sure."

"It means that I need to use the system, your system, like a spaceship, getting closer and closer to that black hole. Once I figure out what's going on, then I do what I have to do, and fire my retro-rockets to get back home."

Karlsson shifted his gaze out the window of the waiting room. "I don't want you to get sucked into that black hole. If you slipped Jeffers something to give him a stroke, I just need to know so that I can get on with my job. On the other hand, if this is just a stroke of misfortune...no pun intended, then I can still do my job and we can help each other."

Jerry looked at him. "Why do I get the feeling you're a sick motherfucker?"

"I'm not, Jerry." Karlsson picked up a magazine off the table in front of them. "I'm a soldier, just like you."

It was after eleven when her phone rang. Jenny Lu didn't recognize the number but picked it up as quickly as she could. "Hello?"

"Hi! Ms. Jeffers?"

She wasn't going to nit-pick at surnames at this hour. "Yes?"

"Ms. Jeffers, this is Bonnie Jo. I'm the housekeeper for your place on Country Club Drive."

"Yes?"

"I'm standing here right now, and it doesn't look like Mr. Jeffers has been here for a few days. Everything is pretty much like I left it when I was in last."

"You're sure? He hasn't been home?" She asked.

"No Ma'am. Everything is like I left it. Ain't nobody been here for a couple days, anyway."

Zhou. She thought for a moment. She knew what she had to do. "Thanks, Bonnie Jo. Please lock up when you leave."

CHAPTER 11

A lieutenant from the Medina Police Department, named Scott, arrived about fifteen minutes after Lee had made his call. Special Agent Franklin T. Jones, from the U.S. Secret Service, was about five minutes behind him. The four men collected in the corner of the waiting room and Lee gave a summary of what was going on.

"We have a federal witness who was taken ill while exercising. His name is Martin Jeffers, male, white, age forty-six, five-foot ten, two hundred twenty pounds. He is currently in exam room number three being evaluated. Symptoms appear to be similar to that of a stroke, but so far, no one with MD after their name, has told us that for sure. We're going to stay with him until he is released."

"Martin Jeffers?" The Medina lieutenant repeated.

"Yes. You know him?" Lee asked.

"No, but Cuyahoga County and Moreland Hills Police just reported him missing. It was on the radio as I was pulling in."

Lee looked at him. "Who made the report?"

"I don't know. To be honest, I wasn't paying that much attention. Give me a minute and I'll find out." The lieutenant stepped outside to use his radio and made some notes on a small pad he pulled from his shirt pocket. When he returned, he said, simply, "Complainant was a Ms. Jenny Lu, the subject's fiancé. Apparently, a housekeeper verified that he hadn't been home in several days."

Since Jones had the badge and the suit, he was elected to meet with the attending physician and staff, when the time came. It was a half an hour later when the doctor emerged from treatment area to give everyone an update.

"Hi. I'm Doctor Nixon. You're here with Mr. Jeffers?"

Jones presented his badge and credentials. "Yes, doctor. US Secret Service. It's a bit complicated. He's a federal witness under our care and we'd like to ask your cooperation in restricting any information about his condition and, naturally, controlling his visitors."

The doctor closed his eyes and nodded. "Your, uh...witness didn't make it. He had another CVA about five minutes ago when we were getting him ready for a CT scan. We were trying to determine if was embolic, meaning that fatty material had clogged a vessel, or thrombotic...a blood clot. Regardless, on the way down, he suffered an intra-cerebral hemorrhage. It's where bleeding occurs from a broken blood vessel within the brain. Hemorrhagic strokes sometimes follow other types of cerebrovascular accidents, so this is not uncommon. We tried to get him into surgery, but it was too late for him. There was nothing we could do. I'm very sorry."

There was a momentary silence. "Well, hell." Jones finally said after an uncomfortable pause. "Not to sound insensitive doctor, but because of the nature of this, we're going to need a detailed autopsy...toxicology and the like." He handed the doctor one of his business cards.

"Certainly. I'll make sure Pathology gets your information. Will you be making notification to his next of kin?"

"Yes. Thank you." Jones nodded as the doctor pocketed the card and departed back through the doors to the treatment area, leaving a discomfited emptiness in the room.

Lee walked away with his head down. Jones turned to Karlsson, "Is he going to be okay?"

Karlsson nodded. "Yeah, give him a minute. We were just playing cards with the guy a couple of hours ago. I think they were starting to grow on each other."

It took Jerry Lee a couple of minutes to understand what had happened and how it might have affected him personally or professionally. When he returned, he was a bit more pensive, but nonetheless professional. "Sorry guys. I uh..."

Karlsson punched him lightly on the shoulder. "No worries. We understand. What's the plan going forward?" Karlsson sensed that the young agent was competent but needed some encouragement.

Lee inhaled deeply though his nose. "I suppose we should go back to the safe house and collect his things. If our team has completed their forensics on his phone and the drives that Fritz gave them, then we can get his phone back with his body, and get the rest of his personal things back to his house."

Karlsson nodded. "I'm okay with that. But, I'll need to let my boss know what's going on. Somebody should probably sit on his house."

Lee pondered the observation. "Yeah. Probably a good idea. Do you want to flip a coin?"

Jones spoke up. "Maybe you could use your guy...uh, Marchand."

Lee looked at him. "Who?"

Jones pulled out his phone and looked through his emails. "Sorry. Things got a little crazy, and I didn't get a chance to tell you. Washington has a contractor flying in. He was supposed to help you with Jeffers. But...you know. Retiree. He's in town, but there's nothing for him to do, now. So, if you need someone to watch the house, maybe he's your guy?"

Lee quickly looked through his emails and saw the note from headquarters telling him they would send someone to take over the Jeffers detail, freeing him up to get on with his case. "Marchand? He's Secret Service?"

"Was." Jones replied. "He's a retiree. We're using them for a lot of support stuff since our people are all tied up on the campaign. The US Marshal from Northern District is supposed to swear him in tomorrow morning."

Lee thought for a moment. "Jeffers' car is still in that hotel parking lot in Beachwood. Let's get his keys and give them to this Marchand guy. He can drive it to Jeffers' house and sit on it for a couple of days to see if anyone shows up."

The lieutenant spoke up. "I know the chief in Moreland Hills. Do you want me to call him? If so, what do you want me to say?"

Lee looked at Karlsson and then at the Lieutenant. "Just tell them that it's a suspicious death and we're going to have a guy inside. Tell them that we don't need anything right now, but if they get a call for assistance, to send the troops."

"Can do." He said and walked outside again.

Lee looked at the email from headquarters and found Marchand's contact number. It was after midnight, but if the guy was on the payroll, then he was probably used to receiving weird messages at even weirder hours. He sent a text. "SORRY TO WAKE YOU. MEET US IN PARKING LOT AT THE DOUBLETREE, BEACHWOOD, 3663 PARK EAST DRIVE. LOOK FOR A SILVER LEXUS IN PARKING LOT."

———)(()(———

Stan Marchand had been drifting in and out of consciousness with the TV on to a classic movie channel that was playing the 1955 film Guys and Dolls, starring Brando, Sinatra, and Jean Simmons. He had seen the movie at least a dozen times. Often enough that he had some of the dialogue memorized. When his phone chimed for the incoming text message, he rolled over and looked at it.

"Beachwood? Where the fuck is that?" He said aloud, as he texted back a thumbs-up icon and then looked up the address. "Seriously?" He said to himself. He had eaten and showered when he got in from the airport, so he was ready to go. It was the job. He had been doing it for thirty years, so he was prepared. He grabbed his bag and headed down to his car. An annoying snowfall had dropped some flurries on his windshield, but it was nothing that couldn't be cleared with a couple of swipes of the windshield wipers. He punched the address into his GPS and shook his head. Cleveland? In February? "I must be nuts."

Within moments, he was headed across the interstate looking for the 271 ramp and followed it north. Having lived in the south for much of his career, he was neither a fan of snow, nor comfortable driving on it. He missed his golf clubs. The temperature in Dallas right now had to be at least thirty degrees warmer.

When he arrived at the hotel, he didn't need inscrutable detective instinct to find the car. It was the silver Lexus next to the Ford Explorer, backed in, with the two men inside, and two shark fin antennas on the back of the roof. He pulled in next to them and rolled down the window. "I'm Marchand. Are you waiting for me?"

The driver, who had rolled his window down as well, replied. "Jerry Lee, Secret Service. This is Matt Karlsson...uh... some other agency."

"Nice to meet you. What's up?"

Lee shut his car off and got out. "Here are the keys to the Lexus. This is the address and the alarm code." He handed Marchand a slip of paper. "I don't know how much they told you, but we need you to sit on this house for a few days to see who might show up. The owner of this car is one Martin Jeffers, now deceased, who lives... lived at this address." Lee gave him as much of a briefing as he could without attracting the hotel security people, who were undoubtedly watching their activity on the surveillance cameras.

"And?" Marchand asked. "If someone shows up, what do I do?"

Lee gave it some thought. "Well, if they ring the bell, don't answer it. If they have a key, let them come in. Tell them who you are and find out what they're doing there. And, then let me know. If it looks like they have some sort of criminal intentions, then, do what you need to do. Moreland Hills police are up to speed on this, so if you call nine-one-one, they'll respond."

"So, what's this about? What's the nexus? The predication?"

"Counterfeiting case, out of Shanghai. Jeffers was selling aircraft parts to the Chinese, but we're pretty sure that other people are involved. Especially his girlfriend, a woman named Jenny Lu. I'll send you the information about her, but, she's in Chicago right now so I wouldn't expect that you'd run into her for a day or two."

"So, this is a lock-in?" Stan asked. "How long?"

Lee tugged on his ear. "I don't really know. Probably three or four days. At least until after the funeral."

"All right. I'll find a grocery store and head over there right after that." He looked at the key ring Lee had given him. "House key, car key...maybe an office key. What are these others?"

"No idea." Lee shrugged.

Marchand used the key fob to remote start the Lexus. "Just so you know, I haven't been sworn in yet, and I don't have a weapon."

"No worries. Check his master bedroom upstairs. He's got a Glock nine-millimeter in his nightstand. There's a rifle case and ammo in the closet, and I'm sure if you look around, you'll probably find another handgun or two stashed somewhere. We gave the place a *once-over* earlier but didn't have time to do a thorough search. So, if you're looking for something to pass the time while you're inside, you can poke around."

Stan moved his bag from his rental car to Jeffers' Lexus and tossed the keys to Lee. "Can one of you get this back to the airport and drop my paperwork?"

"You bet." Lee assured, passing the keys to Karlsson. "We'll drop it on our way back to the safe house in Medina."

The two men watched as the lights of the Lexus receded in the distance. Karlsson finally broke the silence. "You going to be okay, man?"

"Yeah." Lee replied quietly. "He died right in front of me. There was nothing I could do. I've never watched anyone die before."

Karlsson wanted to say something supportive but could not. He had seen several people die. In some cases, he had been the cause. In other cases, his emotional trauma was due to being a bystander as events unfolded. "Do you want to follow me to the airport? We'll drop his rental and then head back to the safe house."

—((•))—

Thirty minutes later, Marchand tapped the garage door opener over the passenger visor in the Lexus and waited for the garage door to fully open before pulling in. The door leading into the house wasn't locked, but as soon as he opened it, he could hear the alarm panel on the adjacent wall chirping to let him know that he needed to disarm it. He punched in the five digits that Lee had given him, and then returned to the car to bring in his groceries. He had stopped briefly to pick up some basic staples with the understanding that he wouldn't be able to leave the place for three or four days.

It was not a bad gig. Early in his career, he had been the junior agent on a case where they'd watched a counterfeiter's house trailer in a park south of St. Louis. It was February and freezing cold. He'd had to bed down in a van for three days waiting for the fellow to return. So, for three days and nights, he had eaten Army MRE's and used a bucket to relieve himself. It was the only vantage point they had been able to use that afforded them an unobstructed view of the suspect's trailer and driveway. If he'd made any noise, he would have given away his position and either jeopardized the case or gotten himself killed.

This place, on the other hand, had heat, plumbing, cable TV and every modern convenience. After a quick walk-around of each floor, he came back to the den and looked at Jeffers' artwork. The recurring theme seemed to be aviation and astronautics. That seemed about right for a career aerospace engineer. He stopped to look at the Rockwell print depicting Gus Grissom and John Young preparing for their Gemini III launch. He felt a momentary uneasiness and looked more closely at the print. It seemed familiar. Something about it touched him, but he felt it was incomplete. There was Grissom, but he didn't imagine him being with John Young. He had a flashback to his earlier viewing of a target given him by the man named Paul in Washington. In his mind, Grissom should be with White and Chaffee.

He was wide awake now. He wandered around the den, appreciating the late Mr. Jeffers' collection of space memorabilia. On one shelf of the bookcase were two professionally built models. One of the Saturn 1B and one of the Saturn V; the rocket that carried the astronauts to the moon. The model of the 1B was almost twenty inches tall, and its big brother, the Saturn V was three inches taller. He wondered if they were built to the same scale and marveled at the engineering that it must have taken to build and launch them. On the shelf behind the models was a three-and-a-half-inch embroidered mission patch. He tilted his head and saw that it was for the ill-fated Apollo 1.

He reached for it and was momentarily light-headed. Something came over him and without thinking, he returned to check the doors one more time to ensure they were locked. Then he re-armed the alarm panel so that if anyone came in, it would immediately alert him to their presence. Satisfied, he returned to the den and looked at the mission patch on the shelf. There were no marks or thread to indicate that it had ever been worn. The US flag in the background, the circular patch showed the service module orbiting the earth. His breathing quickened as he picked it up.

An electrical charge enveloped him, and he could feel the energy flow through his body. He took a deep breath and closed his eyes. He remembered. They were locked in the tight spacecraft with three different hatches inhibiting their escape. An outer hatch that had been designed to protect the service module from the heat during blast-off. A hinged middle hatch, which was part of the spacecraft's heat shield. And the poorly designed inner hatch that was built around the plugged door concept, like a cork in a wine bottle. The inner hatch had to be opened from the inside and pulled inwards to allow emergency egress, which with significantly higher air pressure inside the spacecraft, was next to impossible. The air pressure pushed the hatch into the plug.

He was there psychically. Within seconds of the first report of fire, the capsule basically explodes on the inside, with temperatures that would later be estimated at more than fifteen hundred degrees, as hot as a modern crematory. The hull of the spacecraft ruptures and sends debris through the access doors of the command module that spread across level A8 of the gantry tower. Some technicians immediately retreat, fearing a larger explosion, or thermal activation of the launch escape tower rocket. Those that attempt to remove the outer hatch must take turns on the ratchet since the atmosphere has become toxic and filled with dense smoke. No one predicted this type of accident and they aren't prepared. Papers on a nearby desk are singed as flames lick up the side of the capsule towards the launch escape rocket mounted on top.

Marchand pulled out the leather swivel chair and sat down at the desk. He placed the patch in front of him and rested his fingertips on it. He was receiving feelings, perceptions of the event.

Confusion. Cursing. The astronauts had told NASA how many problems they had found in the spacecraft, but they were up against deadlines. Time and budget. They had pointed out the inferior wiring that had been grouped together in bundles without regard for the potential for fire. Now it was coming true. The worst. Lieutenant Colonel Ed White scrambles to start unlocking the bolts on the hatch. Grissom realizes that he cannot get it done in the ninety seconds that they'd previously stipulated. He drops the bottom of his couch so that he can get around from underneath and help White work on the hatch, but in the process, he steps on the observer and momentarily loses his footing. He glances down, but with his helmet on, he can't see the man who is laying on the floor in the equipment bay. However, as he turns his body, because of the lack of responsiveness, he can tell that the man is unconscious, or worse. Grissom's left leg is on fire, the flammable material of the spacesuit now ablaze in the one hundred percent oxygen environment.

He ignores the pain and tries to focus on the hatch, but he can tell that his oxygen line has been compromised. He takes a breath and knows that he is breathing super-heated fumes from the cabin. He tries to hold his breath, but knows from experience that under these circumstances, he can't last more than a minute. Chaffee with his smaller lung capacity might already be unconscious. Through his helmet, he hears screaming. His microphone and earpieces have poorly performed all day and now he can no longer hear or speak through the communications unit. He pulls himself forward across the belly of the equipment bay and gets to White and begins working on the bolts. But, it's too late. Tunnel vision has begun, his vision is narrowing. He only has seconds left. He loses conscious-ness, at which time his breathing automatically resumes, and he is dead seconds later. As the soul leaves his body, he is no longer aware of the searing pain of the flames upon his flesh. He'll miss his wife and his kids. Maybe they will understand.

White's breathing lines are also compromised, and he succumbs seconds later. Chaffee, trapped by the hatch and his two motionless comrades realizes that Grissom had been right. He remembers the photograph the three of them posed for a few weeks earlier, heads bowed in prayer above a model of the Block I spacecraft. He re-members the lemon that his mentor, Grissom, had earlier hung in the spacecraft as a jab at NASA. Grissom had been right.

It would be five minutes before anguished and exhausted tech-nicians would be able to get the hatch open. It was another ten before other personnel arrived on Level eight to see what had hap-pened. The chief astronaut looked into the smoking caldron of soot and melted materials, all fused together in the inferno. He wanted to wretch at the horror in front of him, unable to tell the exact po-sitions of the bodies. Cloth, Velcro, nylon, plastic, and metal were melted and contorted around what was left of the astronauts.

"We have to get them out of there." Someone said.

"No. They're gone. We must preserve the scene until investiga-tors can photograph the inside."

The bodies would remain inside the charred cabin for four hours, until the right representatives of the various agencies agreed as to how they should be removed and by whom. Two men in suits, who were unknown to the rest of the gantry technicians, arrived and closely supervised the removal of the astronauts and then cleared the gantry. The area was sealed off. Like a crime scene.

Marchand sat upright in his chair. He was shaking. After a cou-ple of deep breaths, he returned the patch to the shelf where he had found it and paused in a moment of solitary remembrance. The fourth life. Who was the fourth person that was in the cabin of the spacecraft? He remembered the event from his history classes.

NASA had never mentioned anything about a fourth person present at the time of the fire. Why not?

In the kitchen, he poured a large glass of water and drank it down in what seemed like two or three gulps. Viewing always made him thirsty. Intense connections like he'd just had left him parched and dehydrated. He looked out the window over the sink but could see nothing. There were woods out there, but it was nighttime, and with the kitchen lights on, he could see no further than the glass. He looked at the bald head, angular jaw and aquiline nose that looked back at him. Who was he? What was he?

He was tired, but not sleepy. He tossed a couple of ice cubes into the glass and refilled it with water before returning to the bedroom. He wandered around and went to the far side of the room. He opened the nightstand and saw the Glock 19 in the Kydex holster. Instinctively, he dropped the magazine out and looked at the holes in the back to see how many rounds he had. At least a dozen. It was loaded with some sort of copper jacketed hollow-point ammunition. Possibly Speer Gold Dot. He did a press check on the slide to see if there was a round chambered. There was. He re-inserted the magazine and smacked it with the palm of his hand to make sure it was seated and locked, before returning it to the drawer.

Jeffers had lived well. Marchand strolled back into the large walk-in closet, greeted by the smell of cedar, and smiled at the guns in the walnut cabinet. On one side of the room were a few dresses and skirts, indicative of an occasional female guest. On the other side were a dozen wool suits of fairly good quality, indicative of a corporate engineering manager who was making money selling secrets to the enemy. Nice material. Nice colors. One by one, he pushed the suits side to side on the hangers and about halfway through, looked between a couple of pinstripe editions and moved them further to the side. In the wall behind them was an electrical outlet that seemed to be installed a little higher than the rest of the outlets the house. It was almost invisible with the suits hanging there. When he squatted down to look at it more closely, it seemed that the receptacles weren't real. More like someone had put black tape on the back side of them.

Curious, he returned to the kitchen to find Jeffers' junk drawer. Everyone had one. Jeffers' was the third drawer down to the right of the sink. And, of course, amid batteries, light bulbs, and tape, he found a variety of screwdrivers. He grabbed the one he wanted and raced back up the stairs. Seconds later, he had the outlet cover off. Sure enough, it was a fake. The outlet cover was actually covering an industrial grade lock with an interchangeable core, made by Best. Something that was rarely used in residential applications. But certainly not something that an engineer wouldn't know about. Marchand studied the installation and realized that the cedar paneling behind the suits was concealing a door of sorts. He lightly pressed along the vertical and horizontal axes until he could make out the panels that outlined a hidden door. To what?

He took a picture of it and sent it to Lee in message form. "DID YOU SEE THIS? MASTER CLOSET." What the heck. They had told him to look around, so he was earning his money.

He reached into his pocket for the key ring that Lee had given him and flipped through the keys. There was only one Best key on the ring; the one that he had guessed earlier that was an office key. He inserted it into the keyway and turned. Nothing. Whatever that key opened, it was not this lock.

Karlsson and Lee were about halfway through the bottle of sixteen year old single malt scotch that someone had left in the cupboard of the safe house at some time before their turn at occupancy. Since their mission was at a temporary standstill and it was after midnight, they decided to have a friendly debriefing as they collected Jeffers' belongings and searched his room to see if he had stashed anything in there prior to his medical collapse. There was nothing to find so they put his personal effects into the canvas duffle that they'd given him and left it by the front door. They were each awaiting instructions from their respective bosses, and really had not much else to do for the remainder of their night.

"Mmmm...real scotch." Lee said as he savored the brew and swirled the ice around in the glass.

"No real scotch in China?" Karlsson asked.

"Probably. In the western hotels. But, when you work for one of the world's largest counterfeiters, you don't take anything for granted, and sometimes you can't tell the real stuff from the fake stuff."

Karlsson smiled. "Have you decided how you're gonna play this?"

"I asked HQ to let me stay UC for a while longer. As you pointed out, Zhou asked me for a favor, and that favor has been delivered." He looked sullen. "So, I might as well play it out and see what else we can get out of it."

"When will they let you know?"

"Probably tomorrow or the next day, at the latest. This is a big deal for them, but I don't know how many other agents they have on it, and what the US Attorney is looking for."

Karlsson held up his glass to the light and studied the color and consistency of the expensive cocktail. "I guess I'll hear something from my boss tomorrow as well."

"So. Back to retirement for you?"

"I guess."

"Just out of curiosity, what did they really expect of you?"

"Pardon?"

"I mean, when you found the counterfeiter, what were you supposed to do? *Neutralize* them?"

"No. It's not like that." Lee was almost drunk and Karlsson could tell that the agent's inhibitions and vocal filter were down. "They asked me to meet with the people at Echo Aerospace and find out where their leak was."

"Then what?"

Karlsson regarded him quietly for a moment. "Then report." He took a sip of his drink. "It's not my job to run around the world whacking Chinese counterfeiters at the whim of a couple of corporate flunkies. The agency wanted to use me because I was retired and off their books. Whatever their rationale was, someone in Washington decided that using a washed-up old goat like me was better than putting one of their current people on it."

"I'm not a killer. I joined the Secret Service because I wanted to protect people." Lee said quietly and evenly.

"That's pretty much how I got into this too, about forty years ago. I wanted to protect the US of A; defend the weak, lead the blind, wave the flag. It's why most of us get into it." Karlsson reminisced.

Lee took another sip of his drink. "I wanted to be an Army officer. That's it. Then, at some point, I wanted to be an international businessman or something. Then...shit happens, life changes, and I thought the Secret Service would make a good career."

"You're, what...twenty-eight?"

"Twenty-nine. I'll be thirty in two months." Lee corrected.

"Fuck you. My kids are older than you. Just fucking relax and enjoy the ride, will ya? You've got your whole life in front of you, so do what they tell you to do. For as long as you can. When you don't think you can do the job anymore, then get out and do something else that brings happiness to you and your family."

"You make it all sound so...normal."

Karlsson raised his eyebrows and smiled. "Normal?"

"Yeah." Lee sighed.

"Do you know what normal is? I had a college psychology professor who told me that *normal is what other people are until you get to know them better.* She was right!"

"Psychology?" Lee rubbed his head and forced a smile. "I wonder what she'd say if she knew what you..." The text on his cell phone cut short the rest of an obvious sentence. He looked at it quickly and then passed the phone over to Karlsson. "Can you get your buddy Fritz back up here? It looks like Marchand found another hiding place at Jeffers' house."

Karlsson looked at the lock in the cedar paneling and forwarded the photograph to Fritz Miller's phone with, "CAN YOU COME BACK UP? BRING YOUR PICKS."

He tossed the phone back to Lee. "I wonder what this guy has in here, and how much we haven't found. He was one strange character!"

═══》《◍》《═══

In the lower level of a building near the White House, the US Secret Service maintains the world's most elaborate twenty-four-hour operations center, tracking, among other things, the current whereabouts of an undisclosed number of individuals of importance. Some office holders such as the President, the Vice President, and their immediate families, are considered permanent Protectees, and their protection is mandatory under 18 US Code, Section 3056. Other stipulated Protectees, depending on their personal lifestyles and preferences, may refuse protection if they so desire. So-called *temporary* Protectees may include candidates for high office or other visiting dignitaries for a pre-determined period of time.

Specifically, how they track each individual is a closely guarded secret but is rumored to include transmitters concealed in clothing, software added to their cell phones and even voluntary surgical placement of a microchip. However, thanks to software and various programs that enable *Geo-fencing*, when Protectees or suspects move outside of a masked area, an alert can be triggered, and their pattern of activity analyzed.

Such had been the case at 0210 hours Eastern Standard Time, when Donnie Walters' screen suddenly changed from the report he had been working on, to a map of the Midwest, and a small flashing circle that appeared on Interstate 80, just east of Gary, Indiana. He clicked on the circle and read the comments, "Cleveland three sixty-eight." There was a security notification box that popped up to the right, indicating that the information should be forwarded to Special Agent Franklin Jones, in the Cleveland field office. There was also a code that indicated a headquarters telephone number to call after making notification to the agent assigned. This usually meant that while Special Agent Jones had requested the geotagging, it was part of a much larger investigation being managed through Washington.

Walters clicked on the *Forward* tab and selected *Send Notifications*. About thirty seconds later, he saw the reply from Jones, indicating that the message had been received.

In Westlake, Ohio, Jones sat up in bed and rubbed the sleep from his eyes. He would have to log in to the US Government system to track his suspect and provide Lee with her current location and direction of travel. Still in his underwear, he went downstairs to the kitchen and took his laptop out of his briefcase.

After credentialing into the system he was able to find his blip, still moving east on I-80, near the Portage, Indiana exit, travelling about seventy five miles an hour. He opened a new screen to check on the weather and saw that the area was still receiving light snow. She was in a hurry. At two-fifteen in the morning.

He reached for his cell phone and found Lee's number in the directory.

"Lee." He answered on the second ring.

"Good morning. You asked to be notified if your suspect left her area?"

"Yeah?" Lee asked with interest, trying to sound more sober than he was.

"Right now, she's heading East on I-80 at about 75 miles per hour...just passed the Portage, Indiana exit."

"Interstate eighty?" Lee drew a mental map in his mind. "If she's headed towards us, that could put her in Cleveland in about four and a half to five hours?"

"Sounds about right." Jones agreed. "You want me have a troop from ISP stop her?"

Lee thought for a moment. "No. Let her come. I'll let Marchand know to expect her at the house sometime after zero six hundred. Let me know if she changes course. Thanks!"

"Will do! I'll let Operations know to keep tracking her. In the meantime, I'm going back to bed."

━━━━━(((●)))━━━━━

When his eyes opened, Feodor Golovkin could not determine if he awoke due to the need to urinate, or the vibration of his phone with the incoming text message. Since he was close to seventy years old now, he decided to visit the bathroom first. The message would still be there when he returned.

Afterwards, he turned out the light in the bathroom before opening the door to allow his eyes a moment to adjust to the darkness. As he traipsed quietly back across the carpet, he could hear Valentina snoring. Neither the text nor his trip to the vannaya had disturbed his wife's sleep. He slipped his reading glasses on and looked at his message, knowing that, at this hour, it could not possibly be good news. "PROSTAK PRESUMED DEAD. POLICE ASKING QUESTIONS"

The Russian word for a simpleton or a sucker, PROSTAK was the code name given to the American aerospace engineer who had volunteered to provide valuable project data, as well as an occasional favor, in exchange for cash. Naturally, the FSB had done their research on him and learned that even though he was a highly competent engineer, he was an absolute sucker for women and financial schemes of one kind or another. The naïve man's wife had kept a lover for two years before using his own tryst with the young Chinese woman as grounds for divorce, and a large cash settlement. Thus, the code name had been aptly chosen.

Engineers and scientists had proven to be valuable intelligence sources for the Soviets, and later the Russians, from the standpoint that they had access to new technology, before it entered government hands. And even though they went through a rigorous background check in order to obtain their security clearances, many of them were never subject to polygraph examinations. They could be managed without fear of discovery during the government's frequent internal investigations into leaks of information within classified programs.

He had been negotiating with PROSTACK through an intermediary for the first two years. The use of a go-between, or *cut-out*, as they were sometimes known, would prevent an investigation from leading back to the Russian government. A cut-out could be an occasional tennis partner at the club. It could be an attorney or accountant that conducted the transactions in a confidential setting. Or, cut-outs could be quite elaborate. For instance, if they knew their target would not want to share information with Russia, they could put together a false flag scenario and convince the target they were actually working for Israel or some other country. Sometimes, as in this case, the intermediary could be a family member.

PROSTACK was not the only asset that Golovkin's department had been working. There were others across the country, in other companies. There were, undoubtedly, more like him in other companies around the world. Golovkin's interests focused only on the United States. After all, Russian intelligence, like US intelligence, was highly compartmentalized to reduce the amount of damage he could do if he ever decided to cross over. Nevertheless, they had already paid for an original copy of a fuel system component and had expected to take delivery the following week. They needed the opportunity to evaluate the differences between the genuine article and the Chinese knock-off that they had already received from another source within Echo Aerospace. It was a minor setback.

On a personal note, however, Golovkin was saddened. He knew something more about their choice for exploitation, than most of the other operatives in the Directorate. The engineer, Martin Jeffers, actually had Russian blood in his veins. As the FSB had discovered, even though the US government probably had not known from their own security clearance investigation, Jeffers' great uncle had been a Soviet test pilot and later a part of their space program. With his command of the English language, he was a natural for the assignment that President Kennedy had secretly proposed to Nikita

Khrushchev to assure the peaceful exploration of space. And so, in August 1961, five months after his supposed fatal accident, and two years before the assassination of the young president, Nikolay Vasilyevich Leonov underwent a name change and was sent to join one of the largest defense and space contractors of the era, as Nicholas Jeffers, and was assigned to NASA's Apollo program.

During the next few months, the senior Jeffers integrated into western society. He made new friends. He took a wife who bore him a son. His relationships with the astronauts in the US space program improved as they got to know him as a competent astronautical scientist. They would never know the true reason for his presence but grew to accept his participation in their training exercises as a concerned contractor who was ensuring the smooth operation of the equipment. He had established himself in American society so well, that by 1965, the Soviets were able to supply him with an extended family to further strengthen his cover; an older brother who already had a wife and twelve-year-old son. And, because of their British citizenship, they were rapidly granted naturalization.

PROSTAK may have been gullible in matters of the heart, but he had been honest in matters of the soul. Loyal and relatively ethical, he had served them in several capacities. He had been quite trustworthy. Golovkin frowned. There was nothing that could be done about it at 3:30 in the morning. He replied, "LUNCH TOMORROW – NOON – USUAL PLACE".

CHAPTER 12

Marchand managed to grab a couple of hours of light sleep before the alarm on his cell phone buzzed at 5:00. He showered and shaved in the darkened house, and by 5:30 was ready to meet the day, as well as anyone who decided to visit the house in Moreland Hills.

He dressed in jeans and his University of Cincinnati sweatshirt and then fluffed the pillows and arranged them under the rumpled sheets and comforter to create a form of someone sleeping. After a quick look outside the second-floor window, he stuffed Jeffers' Glock in its Kydex holster into his waist band and covered the butt with his shirt. Downstairs, he walked around to make sure the doors were locked, and the burglar alarm was still armed, and then looked out the living room window at the driveway. The dusting of snow had adequately covered the tracks the car had made the night before. Good. He was prepared to sacrifice his life for his country, but he drew the line at shoveling snow.

Satisfied that the stage had been set, he returned upstairs, opened the blinds on the window that overlooked the driveway and stretched out on the floor in the cedar closet to wait. He sipped the cold coffee that he had made the night before. He needed the coffee but did not want anyone walking into the house to smell it. For the same reason, he had avoided using cologne or after-shave following his shower. Scent carries, and depending on the olfactory sensitivity of a person, it could alert the visitor to his presence. He was expecting Ms. Lu to arrive sometime after six and he needed the place to look, and smell, like Martin Jeffers was there by himself.

At 6:15, he could see the reflection of headlights on the tree branches and could hear a car rolling slowly up the driveway, the tires making a soft compacting sound on the snow. Moments later, he could hear the garage door opening. His breathing slowed and deepened, and he stood behind the open closet door and listened. He could hear the kitchen door opening, followed immediately by the chirp of the alarm panel.

Seconds later, the four quick beeps signaled that the panel downstairs had been disarmed. He looked across the room at the duplicate panel next to the bed and saw that the red light had changed to green. Holding his breath, he turned his ear towards the room and could hear the sound of keys being tossed on the granite kitchen counter. It was not long before he could hear the light steps of someone climbing the stairs. Marchand sent the pre-arranged signal of a thumbs-up icon to Jerry Lee, indicating that contact had been made, and then shut his cell phone off.

"Marty?" A female voice softly called from the upstairs landing. The bedroom light came on, and from his vantage point, Marchand could see her approaching the bed. Nearly five-foot-four, a hundred twenty-five, black hair and a fantastic figure. It was her.

"Marty?" She stood at the end of the bed, afraid of what she might find under the sheets. She put her knee on the bed and leaned over to touch his shoulder.

"Federal agent!" Marchand stepped out of the closet. "Please don't move!"

Jenny Lu shrieked and started to spring out of the bed. Marchand stepped between her and the bedroom door, and her eyes quickly darted to see if there was another way out of the second-floor room. Other than crashing through a window, the only way out was through Marchand. Her hands came up defensively. "Whoever you are, I don't want any trouble."

Marchand had spent twenty-five years reading behavior and responding appropriately. He raised his hands up to waist level, palms up. "I don't want any trouble either. Marty isn't here."

If the man had been there to kill her, she knew she would already be dead. He obviously wanted something from her. Jenny

Lu edged away from him around the foot of the bed, not taking her eyes off the six-foot tall man with the bald head and muscular frame. She got to the other side of the bed and tore the covers off the pillows. "Where is he?"

"I'm sorry, Ms. Lu. He died yesterday."

"You know my name?" She asked, surprised.

"Yes, Ma'am. Your name is Jenny Lu, and you were engaged to Martin Jeffers, age forty-six. He was an engineer at an aerospace company downtown."

"How did he die?"

Marchand continued to observe her but did not move any closer. "I wasn't there, but I understand he had a stroke. They took him to the hospital, but he expired a short time later."

"When?" There was suspicion in her voice.

"Yesterday afternoon."

"Liar!" She stepped away from the bed and backed up against the wall. "He hasn't answered his phone in three days!"

"Ms. Lu, I can explain that, but I need you to trust me."

"You said you were a federal agent. What, FBI?"

"No, Ma'am. Secret Service."

"Let me see your badge and ID."

Stan thought quickly, then reached into his back pocket for his wallet. He carefully opened it and extracted the small, laminated ID they had given him for LEOSA; the Law Enforcement Officer Safety Act. It basically served as a concealed carry permit in all fifty states, for any law enforcement officer who had retired in good standing. "Here." He tossed it on the bed.

She carefully moved forward and picked up the ID. "What is this? This says you're retired."

"Yes, Ma'am. I am retired. But I am working in a consulting capacity and can prove my identity if you'll let me call the office."

She studied the card, and Marchand detected her gradual movement to her left. She was inching towards the nightstand. Marchand kept his position, his hands still just above waist level.

"How would I know who you're calling?" She asked as she

laid his ID card on the nightstand. Her hand paused at the drawer handle.

"The gun's not in there, Ms. Lu. I have it." She checked her movement and reached for the ID again. She flipped it over and looked at the reverse as she moved back around the bed towards Marchand.

"It looks genuine. Let's say I believe you. What do you want?" She was four feet away and reached out to hand the card back to Marchand.

He was rusty, and she was apparently a skilled martial artist. He thought she had acquiesced a bit too soon, and he should have been ready. As he reached to take his ID card back, she snap-kicked him in the groin with lightning speed. He dropped to a knee in agony as her next kick caught him on the side of the head. He rolled with it to dissipate some of the energy, but it gave her the time she needed to get out the bedroom door and down the stairs.

Like a panicked animal with honed survival instincts, she knew that she would never get the garage door up and the car started in the brief amount of time she had. She raced towards the front door, threw it opened and as she looked back over her shoulder towards the stairs, she slammed hard into the sinewy frame of an incredibly surprised Fritz Miller.

She tried to knee him in the groin but missed the target and ended up catching him on the inside of his upper thigh. Far from disabling him, it brought him to boil, and instinctively in this close-quarter combat, he defaulted back to his training. He dropped his bag and immediately his right hand went to her hair and his left hand went under her chin. With a controlled twist, she was on the ground. Although stunned, she still had an ample amount of fight left in her. While on her back she kicked hard at the now slightly bent Fritz, catching him in his left shoulder near his neck.

In an instant, Miller knew that if he didn't change his hold on her, she'd keep kicking him, so maintaining his hold of her hair, he stepped across and dropped his knee across her neck and lower jaw. "What the fuck, lady?" He yelled at her.

Her eyes were wide in fear and the way hear head was turned, she could see another man making his way up the sidewalk. An Asian man in his late twenties or early thirties. It would not be long before the man upstairs recovered enough to join the fray. Whoever they were, they had her. "Okay, okay! That's it. I'm done."

"US Secret Service! Roll over on your stomach and put your hands out to your sides!"

Fritz Miller kept his grip on her hair but lifted his knee off of her as she rolled compliantly to her right onto her stomach. Jerry Lee brought her wrists together behind her back and handcuffed her. The two men carefully stood her up and walked her back inside.

"You okay?" Lee asked her.

She was still breathing hard from the fight but nodded her head. "Yes."

"I'm okay, too." Fritz added. "Just in case you need to know."

An injured and somewhat demoralized Stan Marchand limped his way down the stairs and motioned for them to bring her into the kitchen. "I need some fucking coffee."

Lee pulled out a chair from the kitchen table and helped her sit down as Marchand filled the coffee maker with water and guessed at how much coffee to pour into the basket.

"Ms. Lu, we don't want to arrest you. We just want to talk." Lee began.

"About what?"

"About your involvement with Martin Jeffers and your connection to a Presidential candidate."

Lu considered her options. She was fairly certain that her life had just changed, and she needed time to sort through what was happening. "All right. But first, I want to know what happened to Marty."

"We were exercising yesterday, and he collapsed. We took him to the hospital in Medina where they told us he'd had some kind of stroke. He had a second stroke while in the emergency room and didn't recover."

"Yesterday? Where was he for the two days before that?"

"He was with us. We had him in a safe house pending discussions with the United States Attorney as to which direction his case would take."

"A safe house? Why didn't he answer phone?"

Lee pursed his lips. "Because someone wanted him dead, and we thought it best to make them think that the assassin had succeeded."

She exhaled and slumped in her chair. "Zhou."

"Yes, Zhou." Lee felt that he had gotten through to her. "Ms. Lu, if I take these cuffs off of you, will you relax and talk to us?"

She nodded and Jerry Lee rotated the small handcuff key in the lock to open them.

She rubbed her wrists over the marks left by the cold steel. "I suppose *you* have an ID?

Lee looked quickly at Marchand and grimaced, "Well, uh..." He pulled his electronic access card from his top pocket. "It's a long story but...no. I have this."

She looked at both sides of the generic plastic card containing a microchip. "What is this?"

"Uhm...it's my card that gets me into the office in Independence."

She turned her gaze to Miller. "You?"

"Huh uh. I'm just a locksmith."

"Seriously? None of you fuckers have any kind of official government identification and you want me to believe that you're all federal agents?"

"Not me. I'm just a locksmith." Fritz Miller reminded her flippantly.

She scowled at him as she rubbed her neck. "Yeah. Yeah, I know about you."

They all looked towards the front door as Matt Karlsson entered and stomped the snow off his shoes. "Sorry. I parked down the street so that no one would see the car in the driveway."

Jenny Lu regarded the tall skinny man in his sixties. "What about you? Are you Secret Service or a locksmith? Do you have any kind of identification?"

Karlsson looked at the group assembled around the table. "No, no and no."

Lee interjected. "He's another retiree who's helping us on this case."

"You're kidding. Right?" Her shoulder-length hair had fallen over an eye and she brushed it back. "Is there anyone here, who's not retired from something, who can tell me what's going on?"

Jerry Lee pulled out the chair next to hers. "I'd like to try. I can't tell you everything, because I'm not sure I know everything. And I understand you've just lost someone very close to you. So..." He looked up at Marchand. "Can you show Fritz the...uh...thing?"

Marchand nodded and followed Fritz out of the kitchen towards the stairs. Karlsson slid a chair away from the table and moved it out a few feet so that he could block the door if she decided to make another run for it.

"I'm afraid we have as many questions about you as you have about us. We know nothing about you before you were naturalized ten years ago, and we'll need to be completely honest with each other if we're going to help each other."

"Help each other? Is that government slang for squeezing me until I'm of no more use to you?"

Lee nodded. "Yeah. I guess I would have suspected the same thing if the roles were reversed, and you were asking me questions." He spoke carefully. "A lot depends on what your true assignment was with regard to Martin Jeffers and to Senator Layden. It may mean the difference between your value to us as a foreign agent, or just another American opportunist who got caught up in more than she wanted."

Jenny Lu looked at Karlsson. "You're not a cop. You don't have the eyes. You have killer's eyes. What's your interest in this?"

Karlsson looked at her somewhat sympathetically, but noncommittally. "I'd rather not say just yet. For what it's worth, I think you have value. But I don't make the decisions here. He does."

"I see." She nodded with a smirk. "So, if I don't cooperate, are you the one that's going to make me disappear?"

Karlsson was silent. Lee answered her. "Ms. Lu, it's not like that. Right now, you're in federal custody. Custody of the US Secret Service. I don't know what you've been told about our methods in the past, but we don't make people...uh, disappear."

"Uh huh. So, what kinds of questions do you have for me, and what will I get in return?"

Lee leaned forward and folded his hands on the table in front of him. "You've been an American citizen for ten years. From what we can tell, you have been pursuing legal employment in the communications business and now find yourself assigned to a Presidential campaign. I need to know if that was your original assignment from day-one, or were you a sleeper that just got activated?"

"A sleeper?" She asked as if she had been programmed to respond that way.

"Yes, Ma'am." Lee leaned a little closer. "An agent who was brought to the United States in some unofficial capacity years before and asked to blend into society, knowing that one day, someone from their home country would call them and ask them to complete a mission."

"Did you see that in a spy movie or something?" She responded, a waver in her voice.

Lee continued. "The Soviets used to call them *legends.* Individuals who were supplanted with authentic and verifiable covers that were so solid even counter-intelligence professionals couldn't identify them."

She shot a quick glance at Karlsson, who hadn't taken his eyes off of her. "I'm a victim."

"Excuse me?" Lee asked.

"A victim. I was born in the wrong place and time. I was born in communist China to loving, educated parents, who taught me that there was more to life on the other side of the ocean. They gave me the tools to think for myself. I used them to make a better life." She glanced at the coffee maker on the counter. "Could I get a cup of coffee? It was a long drive."

"Sure." Karlsson rose. "How do you take it?"

"Black. It smells good."

Karlsson opened a couple of the cabinets above the counter until he found the cups. "Lee...you too?"

Lee nodded and Karlsson pulled three cups down and filled them with the brew. He placed a cup in front of both of them and then returned to grab his own and came back to his seat.

She took a thoughtful sip. "I met Zhou in college. He was supposedly some sort of businessman, but he was a little too successful, if you know what I mean. I knew he had to be connected to the government in some way. He was welcome in different social circles; government, academic, business. So, I listened and learned."

"Learned what?"

"How to be western. How to succeed. How to enjoy capitalism."

"What else?"

"How to use my...assets in order to get what I wanted."

"Did he ask you to sleep with anyone?"

"Is that a man-type question? Is that really what you want to know for your investigation?"

"Asked and answered." Lee took a sip of his coffee. "Anyone that you would think was powerful or influential in, or for, the Chinese government?"

"No. They were all crack heads." She frowned. "What do you think?"

"Like, who?"

"They didn't wear name tags."

Lee nodded sympathetically. "You're an intelligent woman. You must have had some idea who you were...uhm...assigned to."

"He had a system. He would rate their importance on a scale of one to five. If I was sent on a date with a five, it was more of a courtesy thing for a visiting guest. I was to find out about their interests, be cordial, but be professional. He wanted to know more about them, but I was not under any pressure to sleep with them."

She took a sip of her coffee. "Some were Chinese, but most were foreign visitors. Businessmen. European, American. They were people that I wouldn't see in the news, but I might have heard of their respective companies in conversations or on TV. Sometimes, the visits were regarded or portrayed as exploratory interviews by corporate executives looking to recruit Asian talent for internships. That was the story anyway. It was intended to make them feel better about getting hooked up, so to speak. Some of the corporate people went to the parties with the specific goal of getting laid. If it cost them an internship, then so be it. Zhou had many of the rooms bugged. So, there was usually video of their activity filed away for future use."

Karlsson watched as Lee moved his iPad closer to the center of the table, ostensibly to make additional room for his coffee cup. He was recording the conversation. "And this was successful?"

"Are you kidding? We live in a world where diversity has become a cult. Companies are falling all over themselves to recruit Asians for their workplace so that they can continue to get all those lucrative government contracts by demonstrating their embrace of equal opportunity."

Lu shook her head and then continued softly. "Listen, I don't want to give the impression that I was a full-time slut. In the year or so that I worked for him, I was only with...maybe a dozen men. I was a college student with a job on the weekends. That was it."

"So, what does he have on you that made you want to jump on the Senator's band wagon after all these years?" Lee asked.

"Nothing. I made a promise that if he could get me connected with a decent job over here, I would owe him. If he wanted, I would occasionally supply information. He didn't place me with Layden. It just happened that way. Zhou only got me the job at the PR firm."

"How did he do that?"

"He knows the owner. The owner knows a number of high-level political candidates across the country. Zhou also knows the owner of Pinnacle, one of their clients. I think it's actually Zhou's cousin."

Karlsson and Lee looked at each other. "What's Pinnacle?" Lee asked lifting his coffee cup to his lips, nonchalantly.

"Pinnacle Voting Systems. It's a Canadian company that provides the voting systems for US elections."

"Did you ever meet the cousin? The one that owns the voting machines?"

"Yes. But it wasn't a date. It was at a party with some other VIP's."

"Did you meet any US politicians at this party?"

She hesitated. "Uh, technically, no."

"What does that mean?" Lee asked a little more pointedly.

"No political candidates per se, but I once met someone's son." She answered cautiously. "He was there as an unofficial guest. A new kid in the corporate law department for a defense contractor. He wouldn't remember me."

"Yeah? Who?" Lee inquired.

"Don't go there."

"I'm going there." Lee pushed.

"He's one of what Zhou calls the Teflon Dons. You can't touch him, and you'll only wreck your career trying."

"I'm still going there. Who?"

She looked down at her hands in front of her for a moment. "Forrest Layden."

"Who?" Lee had never heard of him. "You said Layden? Senator Layden's son?"

She nodded. "That's the one."

"Did you sleep with him?"

"No." She almost giggled. "He's the kind the ladies love. Rich, tall and good looking. He could have had any woman he wanted in the room, so Zhou knew better than to try to hook him up with one of his girls."

Lee opened his iPad and made some notes. When he was finished, he closed the vinyl cover and looked across the table. "So, who actually was your...romantic target for the evening?"

"A guy from Guoanbu. One of Geng's senior deputies." She looked down, embarrassed.

Lee looked up, stunned. Guoanbu was the Chinese reference to their Ministry for State Security. The MSS, though technically a civilian agency, had a broad mission with far-reaching authority, to ensure the security of their country through whatever measures were deemed necessary. Their charter was against enemy agents, spies, and any rebellious or revolutionary ideology that threatened to sabotage, destabilize, or overthrow China's socialist system. The MSS had the same authority to arrest or detain people as regular police for crimes involving state security. Chinese law granted them broad powers to conduct many types of espionage activity both domestically and abroad and allowed them to administratively detain those who were suspected of being involved in intelligence work for up to fifteen days.

The MSS had been established in July 1983 as a result of the merger of the Central Investigation Department and the counter-intelligence elements of the Ministry of Public Security of the People's Republic of China. In recent times, economic espionage had become a prime directive of the group, with the FBI estimating that more than three thousand companies in the United States were covers for MSS activity.

"Who is Geng?" Lee noted the name in his iPad.

"He was the head guy. He was the Minister of State Security."

Lee remembered the name now. After coming up through the ranks, Geng Huichang had begun to integrate himself into international politics. One of Lee's Secret Service instructors at Beltsville had mentioned the name in context around the security planning for the 2008 Olympics. Geng had actually traveled to Athens in 2006 to meet with Greek officials to see how they had planned for the 2004 Olympic Games there.

He was the first Minister of State Security with a background in international relations rather than internal security, and thus his international prowess proved beneficial. As a result, in August 2007, he was promoted to the top position; Minister of State Security, succeeding Xu Yongyue. Many in intelligence circles suspected that this was so former Party General Secretary Hu Jintao could consolidate his own power. Nevertheless, Geng was an international relations specialist and an expert on the United States, Japan and, of course, industrial espionage. It was an interesting development.

Lee tried to sound as calm as he could. "How many times did you meet with Geng's people?"

"Not many. There were three or four parties that I was asked to attend as window dressing. So, if any of the other State Security guys were there, I wouldn't have known."

"How about other *number ones or twos?*" Lee pressed.

"Like I said, they were never introduced to me by name. Well, at least not by their real names. They all had families and important jobs, and the last thing that Zhou would want would be to have college girls running around spreading idle gossip. They were clean. They treated me well, and they tipped handsomely."

Lee considered her information and candor and could not be certain if she was just what she said she was or was in fact, better at her job than he was at his. He knew from his experience and what he had read, that Chinese intelligence played a variety of games with the West. He knew that they controlled their media and the internet. It had been their biggest priority in establishing the subservience of their people. It was necessary to maintain the rule of the Communist Party. If only one side of a story made the evening news, then that was the truth.

He recalled the 2010 case wherein the Shanghai State Security Bureau of the MSS attempted to recruit foreign agents. It was publicized that they directed a US citizen on a study-abroad program, Glenn Duffie Shriver, to apply for a position in the National Clandestine Service Directorate of the CIA. He had been approached by a woman, who called herself Amanda, after writing a school paper on American-Chinese relations. She gave him one hundred twenty dollars.

And, in 2017, SSSB case workers were implicated in the recruitment of a US Department of State employee named Candace Marie Claiborne, who was subsequently charged with obstruction of justice and drew a forty-month prison sentence and $40,000 fine.

But the case that stood out most prominently in Lee's mind, because it had been discussed in the Secret Service academy, was the 2013 incident involving a Chinese agent who was employed by

Senator Dianne Feinstein as an office generalist, and as her chauffer when she was at home in San Francisco.

Once the activity had been discovered by the Bureau, the Senator was notified that the driver was being investigated for possible espionage activity. The FBI told her that he had probably begun employment with her innocently enough, but at some point, he had visited China and had been recruited by China's MSS. However, even though he had worked for Senator Feinstein for nearly twenty years, the FBI concluded that the driver had not revealed anything of substance to the Chinese government.

"Okay. Let's talk about Marty. You said Zhou got you the job with the PR firm in Chicago. How did you meet Martin Jeffers?"

"It was a cocktail party that the firm had thrown for some of their clients. Largely political in nature, but several larger companies; particularly companies with government contracts, had people in attendance with the goal of establishing PAC's. Corporate political-action committees."

She took a healthy sip of her coffee. "As you probably know, Corporations often establish federal PACs to support the election of officials who are aligned with their businesses' financial goals. This is necessary because the Federal Election Campaign Act prohibits using corporate treasury funds to support federal candidates or political parties. A PAC is a separate entity of a corporation, but still managed by it."

"The corporation and its PAC may solicit voluntary contributions of up to $5,000 per year per individual from their salaried employees, shareholders, and their respective families. The PAC can make contributions to candidates for federal office of up to $5,000 per election with the funds it raises, once it qualifies as a multicandidate PAC. In the last few years, it seems like they've also been used by candidates and their parties for matters not necessarily relating to a particular campaign. I've no doubt that much of our revenue at the firm comes from money raised through these outlets."

"Corporations can also sponsor lobbyists and their activities, which covers efforts to influence politicians and political candidates.

Lobbying dollars are most often spent on legislators, but the outcomes of congressional decisions and the loyalties of legislators can impact presidential elections too."

"So, you met him at this party? Do you remember when and where the party was, and who all was there?"

"Not the specific date, but I could probably look it up. And the guest list is probably on the office computer somewhere." She looked towards the hallway.

"Sorry to interrupt. Can I talk to you for a minute?" Fritz Miller asked Lee.

Lee went around the corner and the two men spoke in an excited whisper. Karlsson decided to occupy the time. "How's your coffee, Ms. Lu?

Jenny Lu looked at the near-empty cup. "I could use another one if you don't mind. Thanks."

Matt Karlsson filled their two cups and returned to the kitchen table.

"Thanks." She said as she warmed her hands around the edge of the cup. "I don't know your name."

"It's Matt."

"Matt, what?"

He smiled. "Let's stay on a first-name basis for now. Believe me, it won't make a bit of difference. Your attorneys will never have to track me down, and you're not going to sue me. For what it's worth, I want to believe that you loved the guy. I understand the circumstances that got you together, but we all know that circumstances change."

"Yeah? Did that ever happen to you?"

Karlsson nodded. "Yeah. And it wasn't a story book ending for me."

"What was her name?" Jenny Lu asked, lifting the cup to her lips.

Lee returned to the kitchen before a contrived lie was about to cross Karlsson's lips. "Ms. Lu, I need to ask you about the deal. What did you get from Zhou to get Jeffers interested in you, and what was Marty's end in all this?"

"As I already mentioned, Zhou got me the job at the firm, and when I got selected to work for Senator Layden, I let him know. He basically said keep in touch. But when I told him I'd met a guy from Echo Aerospace, he seemed more interested in Marty than he was in the candidate. He told me to get to know him better."

"How much did he pay you for that?"

"It wasn't initially about the money. It was more about Róngyù... actually Duìxiàn."

"Honor?" Lee translated.

"You speak Mandarin?"

"A little. Enough to know the difference between the two words. You owed him a debt for getting you into the country and you wanted to repay him so that you could wipe the slate clean?"

"Exactly." She replied.

"So, what you're saying is that you weren't assigned a specific task, but knew that someday you'd have to do him a favor to pay him back?"

"Yes."

"Okay, back to my earlier question, how much was he giving you to return his favor? What did you get for bringing him Marty and getting Marty to play ball?"

"I got a hundred thousand, US dollars." She paused. "Which Marty and I split."

"And did Zhou ask Marty for something that was being made by his company?"

"Yes. Something called the sprayer."

"Did Marty deliver it?"

"Yes."

"To whom? Did he give it to you or to Zhou?"

"Not a clue. It was something they were making for an aircraft... a part of it was made in their plant in Shanghai. Marty was able to get a copy of it and give it to Zhou. Either directly, or through a third party. Why?"

"Was the payment in cash or electronic transfer, or what?"

"It was cash. I was given instructions to meet a person at the mall in Tower City Center. I was told to look for a large, older woman wearing a red coat and blue jeans on a bench. She had a shopping bag on the floor next to her and when I sat down, she got up and left. The money was in the bag."

"A hundred thousand?"

"Yes. Do you need me to write a statement or something?"

"No, Ma'am. But I need to ask you some questions on the record. First, we found women's clothing in the master bedroom. Is it yours?"

"Yes."

"And, in light of your engagement...your relationship with Martin Jeffers, did you consider this your domicile?"

"My what?"

"Did you consider this house to be your residence? Your shared residence?"

"Yes. We'd planned on my moving in here after the wedding. Why? What's..."

"Would you give the United States Secret Service permission to search the residence you shared with Martin Jeffers?"

"Well, I suppose. Yes."

"You need to come upstairs with me for just a minute."

She shrugged. "Sure. I've been driving for six hours before I got here and was brutally assaulted by your locksmith. I could use the exercise."

Lee rolled his eyes, and he headed towards the stairs with Jenny behind, and Karlsson in the rear.

When they got to the top of stairs, Marchand was leaning up against a dresser in the master suite, and Fritz Miller was relaxing on the bed, with his feet still on the floor.

Stan motioned to the cedar closet. "In there."

Lee entered the closet and noted that all of Jeffers' suits had been removed from the rail and stacked in a corner. A portion of the cedar wall was open, exposing about an eight-inch-deep false compartment that was about five feet wide, and six feet tall. The cedar wall of the closet had been built eight inches out from the original wall, so that no one could tell there was a compartment there. Inside the compartment, at the top, there was a fluorescent light, illuminating the stacks of banded US currency. On one side there was also a stack of gold ingots that seemed to be the size of thick credit cards. They were labelled *10 oz TROY*, with individual serial numbers, and the stamp of the smelter.

When Lee turned to look at him, Marchand casually replied, "Near as we can tell on first count...we didn't touch anything, and we really can't see how far the compartment goes...he's got ten ingots at about twenty grand apiece. As for the cash stacks, we counted fifteen up and seven over, which would give us a hundred five stacks of hundreds at ten grand apiece. My math probably sucks, but we're guessing there's about a million fifty thousand in cash and at today's rate, two hundred thousand in gold."

Lee looked quickly at Jenny Lu, who stood transfixed in the doorway, genuine shock on her face. "Did you know about this?"

She shook her head slowly from side to side.

"A hundred grand? Really?" Lee was angry.

Jenny Lu backed carefully out of the closet. "I'm serious. I had no idea. I thought he kept everything in his safe down in the den."

"She didn't have a key for it on her key ring." Fritz added. "I scooped them up from the counter where she dropped them on her way in."

Fritz handed Lee a flashlight, which he shined along the inside of the secret compartment. "Holy shit!" there were some other stacks of currency, which had fallen over, or been tossed in hastily, as well as some rumpled canvas duffle bags, which, presumably might have been used for transport.

"If this place had caught fire, he'd have lost a fortune." Lee observed.

"Knock test." Fritz said. "If he'd lined it with steel or concrete, and a burglar or...well, us, came in and knocked on the wall, they'd have noticed the difference in touch and noise if the wall was reinforced."

Jenny stood quietly in the bedroom, a tear forming at the edge of her eye. "The last thing he said to me was that we didn't need Zhou's wedding present. We could get by on our own. I had no idea."

"Wedding present?" Lee asked.

She nodded. "Zhou told me that if we got him the sprayer, and I still wanted to marry the guy, he'd give us two hundred fifty thousand as a gift."

She rubbed the tear away. "Marty told me that we wouldn't need it."

Karlsson started thinking about his work on the case and finally spoke. "You said Zhou already had a copy. What exactly did he want with another one?"

"Zhou made a copy...a counterfeit copy of it that somehow ended up over here. He wanted to get it back. That's what the two hundred fifty thousand was for. He needed his counterfeit part back."

"A counterfeit sprayer was over here?" Karlsson asked, already knowing the answer.

"Yes. But Marty said that he couldn't get it back. The guy that had it, had moved it. It wasn't where he thought it would be."

"You tried to recover a counterfeit sprayer in Cleveland Ohio? Where from?"

She sniffled and tried to choke back more tears. "Echo. The guy at Echo had been keeping it in his office. Marty paid one of their cleaning people to try to find it, but it wasn't in the guy's office anymore."

"Which guy?" Karlsson's heart was beating a bit faster.

"Carroll. His ex-boss. A guy named JJ Carroll."

———— ◈ ————

Feodor Golovkin showered and dressed, and descended the staircase to the smell of breakfast. Valentina had prepared syrniki; dumplings made with cottage cheese, eggs, some flour and just the right amount of salt and sugar. Fried to perfection, they made a nutritious and high-protein breakfast, with less calories than pan-cakes. She brought his black tea over to the table and joined him as he sat down and immediately reached for the jam and sour cream to liberally apply to the dumplings.

"Do you know what you would like for dinner tonight? I have a dentist appointment at three and can stop at the store on my way home." Valentina proposed as she used her fork to split a syrniki cake.

"I have a lunch appointment at noon today, so I am not sure yet. What are you having done at the dentist?"

"Nothing much. I hope." She smiled. "Just my annual check-up."

He smiled back at her as he chewed. "Why don't we see how my noon meeting goes, and perhaps we will dine out this evening."

Valentina smiled back as the annoying cellphone on the table began to buzz. "Excuse me. I must take this." He quickly wiped his mouth.

"Allo?"

"The missing-persons bulletin on that individual you inquired about has been cancelled by the Sheriff's Department."

"He has been located?" Golovkin asked.

"More or less. His body is at the morgue in Medina. Apparently, he suffered a stroke while at the emergency room, but they weren't able to save him."

"Has anyone made arrangements to claim the body?"

"His girlfriend. Rather, his fiancé. Her name is Jenny Lu. Apparently, she lives in Chicago and will be in later today to begin making the necessary arrangements."

"Was an autopsy conducted?" Golovkin sipped his tea.

"Yes. It was basically supportive of a CVA diagnosis; a stroke of some sort. But toxicology won't be back on blood and tissue for several days. Do you suspect something?"

Golovkin contemplated recent events. "Not really. We all have bosses though, and I am certain that mine will want to know if there was anything suspicious about his death. I am assuming that Ms. Lu will be responsible for collecting his personal effects and making notification to any living family members. Having mentioned that, I am missing a small piece of equipment that was supposedly in his possession. I am trying to think of a way for you to get someone inside his home to look for it."

"If you're not in a hurry, we could wait two or three days for the funeral and send a team in to look around during the services."

"Possibly. But we would run the risk that a family member, or perhaps friends from out of town might also be in the house. I do not wish to rush you, but I feel the sooner, the better in this case."

The line was silent for a moment. "The Bureau keeps a marked cable television van in their garage. They use it to set up taps pursuant to federal wiretap warrants, and occasionally loan it out to other state and federal agencies for surveillance, when requested. Let me see if I can get it, and then I'll find some contractors to go in under the guise of changing out older analog cable equipment for digital fiber. That would give them the ability to enter with tools and move freely about the house, without arousing too much suspicion."

"You have worked with these people before?" Golovkin was reluctant to take any action that might draw unwanted attention to the embassy.

"Oh yes. Many times. This request will seem quite commonplace."

"Cable TV?" Golovkin smiled. "If you are going to do that, might I ask another favor of them while they are there?"

CHAPTER 13

Karlsson sat in his car in the parking lot of the grocery store. He dialed the Washington number and briefly wondered who would pick it up. Paul answered on the second ring. "Good morning. I was beginning to think you had been kidnapped or disabled by depraved barbarians." The sarcasm evident.

"Sorry." Karlsson replied. "Things are moving quickly. Although, I don't know if they're moving in the direction you'd intended. How condensed do you want it?"

"Concise and logical." Paul replied, little emotion in his voice.

"As you recall from our last discussion, Mr. Jeffers dropped dead on us a couple of days ago while exercising at a Secret Service safe house. They had a guy sitting on his residence, and his fiancé showed up earlier this morning. Her name is Jenny Lu. I think you're familiar with her. I think she is favorable to cutting a deal to work with the Secret Service, but as we speak, they are working with the Assistant US Attorney to try and figure out what, if any, US laws have been broken, that they can charge Zhou with."

Karlsson paused for a breath. "A consent search of Mr. Jeffers' home has resulted in the discovery of one shit-pot full of money. Close to a million five in cash and gold ingot. This tells us that Marty wasn't just selling stuff to the Chinese but had another client as well. At least one. None of us think that his company's competitors would have ponied up that kind of cash, so we are suspecting Russian involvement. Therefore, we're pretty sure we have Echo's counterfeiter and thief, but I'm still not sure how far you want me to take this?"

Paul didn't respond, so Karlsson moved on. "Jenny Lu is being highly cooperative with the Secret Service and is attempting to name some of the companies and individuals with whom she shared her pleasures at the request of Mr. Zhou. However, earlier this morning, she did mention that he has a cousin who owns the Canadian company who supplies the US voting systems. This being an election season, I thought you'd like to know."

After a lengthy silence, Paul spoke. "She's prepared to say that under oath?"

"Hard to say, sir. Right now, she's being cooperative in an intelligence capacity, but I think she has some funds at her disposal that will get her out of the country in a hurry if we start pressing her to testify in open court."

"Do you think she has been honest with you up to this point?"

"I suppose. I think she's a smart operator. She's intelligent and thinks fast on her feet. I'd rather have her on our side than someone else's. Right now, I think our hook is that she was actually in love with Jeffers and holds Zhou responsible for his demise. That could play well in our favor when the time comes along."

"Indeed." Paul spoke carefully. "Have you received the translations back from the documents you found in Mr. Jeffers' safe?"

"Not yet. What should I be looking for?"

"We have learned that there was more to Mr. Jeffers than what came up in his background investigation for his Defense Department clearance. Our sources found that his grandparents were not British subjects as had been reported to immigration when they entered the country in the sixties. Upon closer scrutiny, their covers didn't hold. They were probably sleeper Soviets, who never got activated. But, in all likelihood, Jeffers never knew. Nevertheless, if we consider them to have had fabricated identities when they entered, we would need to question if they were really related to a Nicholas Jeffers from Cocoa Beach Florida, who died in a boating accident in 1967."

Karlsson tried to read between the lines but found nothing. "Who was Nick Jeffers and why do we care about his boating skills?"

"Nicholas Jeffers was an astronautical engineer working for a contractor at NASA. For reasons that I can't disclose at the moment, we had cause to look into his past, and therefore the accident that claimed his life. Supposedly, during the evening of January 27th, he was out in the Atlantic, about five miles east of Cocoa Beach when his boat exploded. It was a horrific fire. He was burned almost beyond recognition."

"And you suspect foul play?" Karlsson asked.

"We do. He was involved in a variety of systems tests at the Cape, and then sometime that evening, was overcome by a desire to do some late-night fishing by himself. The cause of the fire was never established, and a limited autopsy failed to reveal any cause of death beyond smoke inhalation and severe burns. The body was cremated, and the ashes given to his wife."

"And the wife would like to re-open the investigation?"

"No. She died in 1997."

"His kids?" Karlsson guessed.

"One son, born 1964. An attorney. A Yale grad living somewhere down south. He has no interest in the case either, as far as we know."

"Then what is the connection to our guy?"

"Nicholas Jeffers had a brother by the name of Frederick, who supposedly emigrated from England in 1965, with his wife and twelve-year old son, Peter. According to the documents we found, Peter was Martin Jeffers' father. In the family's immigration paperwork, they listed Nicholas as Frederick's brother."

"We think Martin Jeffers' great-uncle was working at Cape Kennedy in the sixties?"

"As was his grandfather. The records show that Frederick became a naturalized citizen thirteen months after arrival in the States."

"Occupation?"

"Aerospace engineer. He had apparently been working with British Aircraft Corporation on the TSR-2 until the project was cancelled in 1965. In search of lucrative employment, he headed west to the land of opportunity. Of course, that was the same year that the MiG-25 was unveiled in the Soviet Union."

The monotone voice on the other end took a breath and continued. "Known as the FOXBAT, it was capable of flying in excess of Mach-three, at altitudes very few aircraft could reach. There was some question as to the Soviet's originality in some of their systems and component designs, but an official inquiry by the Brits was never publicized."

"Do we think that the Russians snatched some British technology to help build their own aircraft?" Karlsson asked.

"That's one opinion. That would open the door for speculation about Frederick's role on the British project and the real reason why he left. Was he, in fact, working for the Soviets while employed at British Aircraft?"

"You mean, as a deep cover agent?"

"Precisely. Back in the sixties, there were no computer databases to connect people with their pasts. Rarely were photographs or fingerprints collected on anyone who wasn't a government employee or criminal. Driver's licenses didn't even contain photographs back then. It was relatively easy to print and file false birth certificates, and from those a person could obtain a driver's license, enter school, or buy a car, just like any other legitimate citizen."

Karlsson thought out loud. "So, if Fred was a legend, then it's doubtful that Nick was really his brother. And if Nick was bogus, then we'd have to question his real activities at the Cape."

"And why he happened to die in a fire on the twenty-seventh." Paul completed the thought.

Karlsson was curious about yet another reference to the date. "Was there something significant about the twenty-seventh?"

"At eighteen thirty hours that date, a fire broke out in the Apollo 1 spacecraft on launch pad 34, killing the three US astronauts on board."

Karlsson remembered his recent discussion with Jackie Biehn. "You think there's some connection between the fire on the pad and Jeffers' boat blowing up?"

"We are starting to. Nicholas Malcolm Jeffers was born in Brewster Hospital, Jacksonville, Florida on July 12, 1935, but had no official records until 1961. No driver's license, no Social Security card, no school records, and no property ownership, until 1961. Almost overnight, he magically appeared with a college degree, a lucrative job and a security clearance."

Karlsson listened intently. "And?"

Paul could be heard clicking his mouse as he presumably paged through an online report. "Our research indicates that another Nicholas Malcom Jeffers died of scarlet fever in Brewster Hospital, Jacksonville, Florida on October 20, 1936. So, one might conclude that while the Defense Department exercised its due diligence in confirming Jeffers' citizenship and eligibility for employment, it might have dropped the ball when it came to assuring that he was, in fact, alive. There was no computerized system to match birth and death records at that time."

Karlsson had undergone several background checks while in the Army, and a couple more as a civilian. "How is that possible? I don't know what the clearance process was like back then, but I'm sure they would have spoken with people who knew him; previous employers, college professors, neighbors...someone."

"Yes. Any normal clearance process would have included those references. However, Jeffers' background investigation was fast-tracked and approved by an individual named Francis Wake, who at the time was on the staff of the Assistant Secretary of Defense for International Security Affairs."

"Don't tell me...dead?"

"Of course. Retired from the Air Force in 1959 and went to work for Grumman in their Government Relations department. Kennedy brought him in to be on McNamara's staff in 1961. He died in 1995 at the ripe old age of eighty-one."

"You said Brewster hospital. I don't know Jacksonville that well, but could we go back through their records and..."

Paul cut him off. "I'm afraid not. Brewster was closed in 1966. As a matter of fact, the city of Jacksonville has been working to get it on the list of historical places because of its social significance."

"Social significance? What social significance is that?"

"It was the first hospital in the region for African Americans. Established at the turn of the last century, after a large fire that resulted in numerous casualties. In eight hours, the so-called Great Fire of 1901 burned a hundred forty-six city blocks, destroyed more than 2,300 buildings, and left about ten thousand residents homeless. Reports indicated that flames could be seen as far away as Savannah, Georgia, and the smoke, as far as Raleigh. At the time, the Black fire fighters who were injured weren't accepted in White hospitals, even though they were injured trying to keep the fire from spreading to White neighborhoods."

Karlsson frowned at his phone. "Shit. Jeffers was White, right?"

"Yes."

"So it's unlikely, that prior to the Civil Rights Act of 1964, that White parents were having their White babies delivered at Black hospitals?" Karlsson thought out loud.

"I think you grasp the puzzling elements of the story." He was quiet for a few moments. When he resumed, he was more sober than usual. "A little over a year ago, I came into possession of some information regarding President Kennedy's plans for the exploration of space. He didn't trust the Soviets, and he knew that we would be enemies and technological rivals far into the future. However, he also understood, as did his Russian counterparts, that we needed to be somewhat transparent when launching crewed vehicles into orbit. From Moscow, a launch could easily be perceived as a deliberate act of war unless the true intent of the mission was known to everyone. He didn't want a manned spacecraft shot down because someone thought it was a spy satellite, and he didn't want any of NASA's test rockets mistaken for ICBM's."

"Two weeks before he was assassinated, he directed NASA and the CIA to share information relating to our interests in space, with the Soviet Union. Needless to say, the Agency and the Joint Chiefs were livid. They tried to talk him out of it, but he was firmly convinced of the utility of such an act and remained steadfast in his belief. He had already been in talks with Khrushchev, and they had worked out a plan to embed qualified astronauts into each other's programs, to serve as observers, or monitors, if you will."

"This information was so highly classified that there were only two or three people within his administration who knew that the talks were occurring. By the time he issued his official directive in November 1963, we had already sent two of our astronauts to Tyuratam, and the Soviets had sent two to Cape Canaveral. So as to maintain the necessary level of secrecy with this transaction, the astronauts were given realistic covers that would allow them to integrate into their new roles. Their true identities were known to only two or three people in Washington and an equal number in Moscow."

"Wait." Karlsson's brain was analyzing the data it was taking in. "Do you think that the senior Jeffers was actually on the pad during the fire, in some sort of covert monitoring capacity?"

"Possibly. But the technicians who raced to put out the fire, despite their varying levels of exposure to heat and toxic gases, were all accounted for. The problem is that the bodies were left in the capsule for four hours, and unidentified government agents in plainclothes cleared everyone from the gantry. This fact pattern would indicate that if Nicholas Jeffers died in the fire at Pad 34 that day, he wasn't in the white room or the gantry on level eight. He was actually inside the Apollo spacecraft."

Karlsson had grown up in an era where astronauts were considered cultural icons and role models. Every kid wanted to be an astronaut, and every science geek wanted to work for NASA. "In the spacecraft? Where? There's no room in there. I remember seeing the pictures at the time."

Paul explained. "It was not uncommon for technicians or other astronauts to observe the testing activities from the equipment bay; basically, the floor of the spacecraft when it sits atop the rocket on the pad. As a matter of fact, there was one design that was passed around NASA early on that enabled the Apollo capsule to serve as a rescue vehicle, with two additional seats down there. My thought is that Mr. Jeffers was monitoring the plugs-out test from that position."

"But, wouldn't other technicians have known about it? Wouldn't they have seen the fourth body when they removed the astronauts?"

"Looking at the official transcripts of the investigation, they couldn't see anything. The chief astronaut commented that he couldn't distinguish whose body was whose. The severe heat had melted wires, cable, hoses, and everything else together and it was all covered in soot. Pictures released to the public were shot from an angle outside the spacecraft looking in, giving the impression that there was nothing below the astronauts' couches. With all of the debris, it might have been difficult to identify an additional human body in the mess at first glance. Plus, the time lapse that occurred from the fire until the bodies were removed, and the presence of unidentified civilians who had taken charge of the scene, leads to speculation as to the potential for alteration of the fire scene before NASA investigators took over."

Paul summarized his thoughts. "Thus, NASA, or the Agency, or other persons unknown, now had a burned-up corpse on their hands that they had to do something with. A boat fire, five miles off the coast, would have created a convenient means to resolve it to reasonable satisfaction."

Karlsson was pensive. "So, the presence of these so-called monitors was intended to assure that our space program was both legitimate and peaceful?"

"That is the speculation."

"Jackie Biehn said that there was no LEM included in the Block 1 design package. How do you think this is connected to her investigation into the whereabouts of LEM fourteen?"

"An event that has pretty much been lost in history occurred in the early 1960's. The Soviets had been proudly exhibiting their Lunik spacecraft at venues around the world, and since we perceived them to be ahead of us in the space race, we wanted to see how it worked. Because they had their own security personnel guarding it at the exhibitions, an elaborate hijack was planned to take place while it was enroute from one exhibit venue to the next. It called for the driver to be pulled over for some traffic infraction and escorted to a motel for the evening. A substitute driver took the trailer containing the spacecraft to a local salvage yard that they had acquired for the night, and a team opened the crate, disassembled the craft and photographed it inside and out. When they were finished, they put it back together, put the lid back on the crate and applied a counterfeit seal that they'd made. By the next morning, the original driver was reunited with his cargo and he dropped it at the rail station, with no one the wiser."

"Cute." Karlsson nodded at the phone. "And? The moral of this story?"

Paul completed his cogitation. "If they took a lesson from us, and already had people embedded in our program, then it's possible that while the Chinese were in the process of hijacking our LEM, that the Soviets pulled a similar stunt on them, and were reverse-engineering it before it ever got to Chinese soil."

"The Soviets built a LEM? If that's the case, then Air Force OSI can't really be sure that those are Chinese astronauts in the LEM they photographed on the moon?"

"Correct. I don't know how accurate all of my information is, but I think we could say that at this point, we just don't know."

—————««(»)»—————

Marchand, Karlsson and now Jenny Lu had adopted the Moreland Hills house as their new residence. Until they got to know her better, there was no sense letting Jenny know where the other safe house was, and their stay there would also give the appearance of family gathering to settle the affairs of the late Martin Jeffers. Besides, it would just be in bad taste to have her staying where her fiancé had died.

As a prelude to looking as normal as possible, they cancelled the cleaning contract with Spotless Cleveland, and began a regimen of running the vacuum and dusting each room every morning.

This was not so much for cleanliness as it was supportive of sur-veillance. Reverting back to Karlsson's training in tactical tracking, he and Marchand decided that the frequently vacuumed thick-pile carpets would show footsteps of anyone who entered the rooms, making it easier to see where they went and in what areas they might have had a particular interest. That, of course, and the sys-tem of covert wireless cameras that had been quickly installed by the Secret Service to focus on specific areas inside the home as well as the outside perimeter. The cameras were concealed in house-hold appliances and furniture in a manner to make detection quite difficult.

No one was certain how long they would have to operate in this social configuration, but they agreed they needed some sort of plan. Jerry and Jenny Lu would be travelling back and forth to the US Secret Service office in Independence throughout the days, with Marchand and Karlsson alternating watches on the residence. Karlsson had made a run to the store for groceries and personal items around 11:30 leaving Stan to catch up on daytime TV.

Around noon, Stan was making a sandwich when his cell phone buzzed, indicating that one of the cameras had picked up activity. He had enough time to wipe his hands and look at the image to see the white cable TV van pull into the driveway. Moments later, the doorbell rang.

Stan opened the door to find one man and one woman, dressed in the brown service attire of a local cable company. The man was in his early thirties, carrying a tool bag. The woman was probably in her late twenties, carrying a brown corrugated box that was clearly labelled *Fiber Optic*. The earlier kick in the testicles had awakened his dormant agent training and experience, and he was immediate-ly alert to their suspicious nature. Despite temperatures in the mid-twenties, the attractive woman was wearing a dark blue down vest, zipped only halfway, over her uniform shirt with the top button left open, proudly displaying the cleavage of her breasts. It seemed an obvious distraction.

"Hi. Mr. Jeffers?" The man asked.

"No." Stan replied, admiring the woman's chest as was probably intended. "Mr. Jeffers is gone. We're family. What can we do for you?"

"Mr. Jeffers arranged to have us come in and upgrade the old cable lines with fiber so that he could improve his Wi-Fi and internet services."

Stan glanced passed them at the cable TV van in the driveway. He did not know anything about cable television, but he knew the system in the residence had been installed by a different company than what was indicated on the side of the van. "Uh...can you come back later?"

"Not really. Mr. Jeffers set this appointment up two weeks ago. It could be two or three more weeks before we can get it re-scheduled."

"How long will it take?"

"A couple of hours. We might need to pull fiber through the same routes that cable is in now. We'll try not to bother you."

Stan suspicions grew, but he wanted the chance to find out more about them, and he couldn't do that if he sent them away. "Do you have to drill a bunch of holes?"

The man smiled. "No. Hopefully not. Fiber is more flexible than cable so we should be able to get in and out without any mess. If we have to, we'll pull the new fiber through using the existing cable as a pull-wire."

"Well, I was watching something in the kitchen. Do you have to shut the cable off?"

"Not just yet. We will for a couple of minutes when we make the switch over, but you should be fine for the next hour or so."

The woman installer's scent reached his nostrils. Her perfume was clean and exciting. She smiled as he looked towards her. "Oh, okay. I suppose now is as good a time as any. Just don't track anything in from outside."

"We won't." The man smiled back as he and his female associate stepped out of their shoes and entered past him.

Stan was suddenly excited. In his experience with contractors of various sorts, they had always brought with them paper booties that they slipped over their shoes to prevent tracking mud or other dirt in. Further, most cable TV technicians wore work boots of one kind or another. The ones that worked around industrial environments even wore steel-toed boots for safety. This pair was wearing sneakers. "Great! What do you need from me?"

"Well, if you can show us where the cable comes in, we can start from there."

Stan nodded with a grin. "Basement. Follow me."

He led them down the stairs and around to the back of the basement where the utilities came into the house. Pointing at the various boxes near the breakers he said, "One of these must look familiar?"

The blond man smiled again. "Yes. That's what we need."

Stan smiled again. His senses were stirred. He was in the game once more. "Well, if you don't need me for anything else, I guess I'll finish watching my show upstairs."

Marchand returned to the kitchen, unable to suppress the grin stretching his cheeks. He turned up the volume on the TV, so that the audio of the classic movie might conceal any other noises and reached for his cell phone. He scrolled through the camera options and found one of the wireless cameras that had been hidden in the basement. He turned the volume up just enough that he could hear their conversation, but not loud enough that either of them could tell what he was doing if they suddenly came upstairs.

The blond man opened the cable TV box on the basement wall and looked at the inputs and outputs. Finding the one he wanted, he pointed at it silently and the woman began to trace the line to its termination. It was the bug that Marchand and Karlsson had found the evening of their first walk through of the house. It was connected such that it could record and re-transmit conversations on the VOIP portion of the network. Once Karlsson had photographed it, they simply left it in place so as not to let anyone know it had been discovered. The woman was out of view of the covert camera for three or four minutes as blondie began walking the other direction, inspecting the walls and rafters.

Stan Marchand stifled his laugh as he saw the young blond man eye the ladder in the corner and walk out of view momentarily before returning and setting it up at the far end of the basement. "Been there." He said out loud as he watched the man set up the ladder and begin shining his light down the space between the floor joists, just as Karlsson and he had done. Their search had started at the opposite end of the basement, but everyone has their own style.

The woman returned into view and showed blondie a small device with a severed piece of coax cable protruding from one end. From his view, he could tell that the cable had been hastily, but neatly cut. She placed it into the tool bag and then the blond man gestured with his head towards the stairs. As she rounded the corner, Marchand switched to a different camera angle and saw her as she mounted the basement steps. He switched his cell phone back to an app for an online auction site. A few seconds later, she emerged at the corner of the hall and came into the kitchen.

"How's the reception up here?" She asked, slightly flushed.

"Pretty good. I'm not sure I could tell the difference between a coax cable signal and a fiber one." He smiled.

She moved her way around the island as if she was on a dance floor in a club, approaching a stranger to gauge his interest. "What are you watching?"

"Oh, I like old movies. This is something with David Niven and Doris Day from 1960. I think it's called, *Please Don't Eat the Daisies*."

"You're kidding?" She smiled seductively. "Isn't that before your time? You don't look that old."

Stan immediately recalled one of his instructors at Beltsville, many years before, lecturing them on the consequences of inattention and distraction. "Men…" He preached, "If you're standing a post and some voluptuous babe sidles up to you and makes you think you're the most important man on the earth, then you should be very alarmed. Let me tell you right now, you ain't. If some woman is making you think she likes you, it's a sure sign she's either trying to distract you from an imminent threat, or she wants through the door you're guarding. Don't fall for it." Despite the warning, during the many practical exercises that took place there during their seventeen-week stay, several agents still fell for the ruse. And, of course, failed the assignment. The Secret Service often hired attractive models and actresses to role-play. Their only job was to quickly seduce and distract agents as an object lesson. However, the same con didn't work on female agent trainees.

Marchand chuckled. "I'm not. I was a Theatre and Drama major in college, and I've always had a soft spot for these old films."

"Really? I thought you kind of looked like the actor type. Where did you go to school?" She asked, just a little too smoothly to be believable.

"University of South Florida." He lied. He had a general knowledge of the campus because early in his career, he'd been assigned to guard the daughter of a foreign head of state who had attended the Tampa school for six months. Unfortunately, an extra-marital tryst with a female agent on the detail, necessitated a transfer of Marchand and the other agent. To different parts of the country.

"Oh? You still live down there?"

"As a matter of fact, yes. How did you know that?"

"Your tan. You didn't get that in a salon up here."

He laughed. "You're sweet. It helps having Middle Eastern ancestors. What about you? Where did you go to school?"

She shrugged. "A couple of semesters at Cleveland State, four years in the Air Force, and now I'm here in your kitchen."

"Air Force?" Stan replied, playing along. "You don't look like the military type. What did you do in the Air Force?"

"Communications Technician." She kept her smile. She was probably being honest about that.

"Well then, I think it's customary these days to say thank you for your service."

She looked down at the counter briefly before returning his gaze. She was slightly embarrassed. "Thank you. Were you in the military?"

"Me? No way. Stuck-up rich kid from Ft. Lauderdale. Played golf for a year on scholarship and then coasted through college without any real goals."

She pretended to frown. "I doubt that. What do you do now?"

Stan was enjoying himself. "I sell golf clubs. I call on pro-shops and retail outlets and get them to sell our line of clubs."

"Wow. You must be really good." She inched closer. She wanted to make sure that he was getting the right signals. "I've always wanted to learn golf. But I hear it's really tough!"

She wanted to *play*, he mused. "I'd love to teach you, but I'm only in town for a few days, uh...I didn't catch your name."

"Tricia." She seemed genuinely interested. "What are you doing up here in the winter?"

"Burying my cousin."

She looked at him for a moment but tried to stay in character. "Your cousin? What happened? If you don't mind me asking?"

"Stroke. A few days ago."

"Were you close?"

"Not as close as I wished we'd been. This is...was his house."

"Mr. Jeffers?"

"Yeah."

"Oh, I'm sorry." She reached forward to gently touch his hand, resting on the counter. "I didn't know."

He shrugged. "Why would you? Your work order came in weeks ago. This just happened. It was pretty sudden." Marchand reached for his phone. "Can you hold on for a minute? You just reminded me of something."

Marchand sent a text through to Karlsson, "STAY AWAY, BUT GET LICENSE PLATE ON VAN IN DRIVEWAY"

"Sorry." He looked at the young woman. "I was supposed to be somewhere, but I need to stay here until you're done."

"Oh, that's okay. We're bonded. A lot of people let us in to work and then go run errands. If you have something to do, please don't let us keep you from it. We're going to be here for a couple of hours."

Stan smiled at her as he looked into her piercing blue eyes. They were really quite blue. Like a young Paul Newman. "If it was my house, I'd let ya, but Marty was always funny about having strangers in his home."

"No problem. Hey, do you think I could get a bottle of water?"

"Absolutely." He gestured. "Refrigerator behind you. Take all you want. You can take one to your partner, too, if you think he's thirsty. Are you hungry?"

"No. Not right now, but maybe later?" She reached inside and grabbed two bottles of water off the top shelf. "Let me take one of these to Jared before he starts wondering where I've gone."

"Oh, we mustn't forget Jared." He chided with a grin.

"Thanks!" She whispered as she left the kitchen, making sure that Stan was watching her captivating behind in the tight jeans. Her job was to distract him, so he felt not the slightest bit of guilt in accommodating her. He stared long enough to make sure she saw him.

As she returned to the basement, he switched his cell phone back to the app that allowed him to track the duo's progress around the area. They were as thorough as they could be, given the circumstances. But even though they checked above the ceiling tiles, they missed the floor safe in the corner near the entertainment center.

About ten minutes later, Jared returned to the main floor and stuck his head in the kitchen. "Excuse me...can you show me where all of the TV's are?"

"He had one in the den over there, and one in the family room, back this way." Stan walked past the stairs. "There are four bedrooms upstairs and I think there were outlets in each of them."

"Thanks, man!" He said as they entered the first bedroom. Jared knelt and began to unscrew the plastic cover. "I just need to check signal strength on these ports. The system is newer than I thought, so we might be able to get by with adding some converters."

Marchand nodded. "Whatever you like. I'll be in the kitchen if you need me."

As he returned to the kitchen, he calculated that their process would move rapidly, since three of the bedrooms were empty. But, considering the master suite had full dressers and an intriguing closet, they would want more time. He had to hand it to them. They worked well together as a team. As Jared quickly searched the cedar closet, Tricia busied herself doing something unnecessary with an electrical outlet near the door. Even though it had nothing to do with cable television, it positioned her where she could intercept Marchand if he were about to enter the room.

Jared carefully examined the walnut gun cabinet, removing the drawers at the bottom so that he could see if anything had been concealed behind or beneath them. He patted down all of Marty's suits to see if anything had been left in the pockets. But he missed the outlet behind the suits. They were good, but not perfect. He checked the pillowcases and ran his hand between the mattress and box springs, and then smoothed everything back out. After checking the drawers of the two nightstands, he looked under the bed. Tricia screwed the outlet cover back over the receptacle. It was not long after that they returned to the kitchen.

"You know, your signal strength looks really good upstairs." Jared said as he took a swig of his water. "Did you say you had some outlets down here as well?"

Stan smiled and nodded. He was enjoying himself. "Yeah, in the den." He pointed. "There may be other outlets, but I wouldn't know where they are. I'm just a guest this week."

"Thanks!" Jared took another sip out of the bottle and left it on the island.

As if it had been scripted, Tricia stayed behind in the kitchen. When her partner had gone, she looked at Marchand. "See? It's not going to be as bad as you thought."

She was flirting, so he flirted back. "So, tell me Tricia, where's a good place for an out-of-towner to go for a nice meal tonight?"

"It depends. What are you in the mood for?" She winked.

"I'm flexible. You're not a vegan or anything like that, are you?"

"Me? After four years in the Air Force, I'll eat anything that didn't just come out of a plastic bag that was packaged while I was still in High School!" They both laughed.

"Okay. How about tonight?"

She tilted her head and looked at him out the corner of her eyes. "How about tonight, what?"

"Just dinner." He proposed quietly. "And, you know, a couple drinks."

"Hmmm…" She purred. "I live on the other side of town. It's probably better if I meet you somewhere." She finished her water and screwed the cap back on the empty bottle. "Trash can?"

"Under the sink." He said opening the cabinet door for her. "So, that's a yes?"

She tossed the bottle in the trash can and he tapped the door shut. "Sure, why not? North of here, about a half hour up two-seventy-one, is a town called Eastlake. Across the street from the American-Croatian Lodge is a nice little place called Soprek's. You should be able to find it on your GPS. Six o'clock?"

"Six is good." Stan smiled back.

She winked at him again as she turned. "I better go check on my partner or we'll be here all day."

Stan nodded eagerly, but as soon as she left the room, with smooth precision, he went to the refrigerator and pulled out two more bottles of water. He dumped the entire contents of one down the drain, screwed the cap back on and set it aside. The other he poured about half of it out, and then positioned it next to the bottle that Jared had left on the island. The perfectionist that he was, he dumped another half inch of water out and then screwed the cap back on it.

In the drawers next to the sink, he found the gallon-size zip-lock bags and carefully placed an open bag over the top of Jared's bottle, flipped it upside down and zipped it shut. He took the second bag and performed a similar maneuver to pick Tricia's bottle up out of the trash can under the sink. Then he tossed the bottle he had emptied into the receptacle in its place. He found a black marker in the top drawer and wrote *M* and *F* on the bags so that he could distinguish them later on, and then tossed both bags into the salad crisper in the refrigerator and covered them with an assortment of vegetables. He took a deep breath as his heart rate normalized. It was exhilarating, like the old days.

On his surveillance app, he watched Jared and Tricia make their way around the den. In keeping with their practice, she focused on searching the filing cabinet and shelves nearer to the door so that she could keep running sexual interference. With the volume down, he could not hear their whispers, but could see him lift the print of the Gemini astronauts and point at the wall safe. Marchand was content. All the activity was being recorded and he was sure that the audio would pick up their conversations when they were retrieved from the system at the offices in Independence.

Fifteen minutes later, Jared stuck his head in the kitchen again. "Hey, I'm having trouble locating an outlet. Did your cousin have one out in the garage?"

Marchand shook his head. "Beats me. You're welcome to have a look."

"Thanks!" Jared replied, noticing his water on the island. "There it is. I couldn't remember where I left it." He snatched up the bottle and headed out the door to the garage.

Marchand grinned again. Being psychic had its benefits.

———— ««◊»» ————

Feodor Golovkin took a couple of bites of cheesecake and then pushed it towards the center of the table with his gregarious laugh. "This is too much for me! I am not a health food advocate, but this is entirely too rich and too fattening for me!"

Peter Pasternak pushed his dessert towards the center of the table at the same time. "I know what you mean, Uncle Ted. There is something about dining out that makes us all think that we are immune from calories and cholesterol!"

Golovkin sipped his tea as the waiter came to the table and removed the plates. When he had departed with a carefully balanced stack of dishes, Golovkin smiled at the young man across the table. "So how are things in your office?"

Pasternak quickly glanced over his shoulder in a furtive way and lowered his voice. "They are searching the house, even as we speak. But, I am told that the man has relatives staying there, as you had suspected." He looked at the slender Cartier watch with the leather strap on his similarly slender wrist. "I should be hearing back from them in an hour. I hope that is satisfactory?"

"Nothing is perfect." Golovkin beamed. "It is enough to know that we did our best to secure that which was, technically, ours. Whom did you use?"

"They were DHS, Department of Homeland Security contractors. People who were right for the job but were not employees of our department. Anyone's department, for that matter. They were told that it was a national security investigation. They were given a vehicle that came from the FBI pool for such purposes. The license plates are dead, and if anyone tries to run them, the Highway Patrol will let the FBI know, who will in turn, let me know. It is the best we could do on short notice. You said urgency was…"

"Important." Golovkin interrupted. "Yes. Urgency is always important. But it is also important that you do not…uh…over-extend yourself. This is an election year, and I would not want to jeopardize your position by doing such a … favor."

"No." Pasternak said. "It's not like that at all. I am happy to help you on matters of mutual importance. It is just that, until the administration changes in November, I have to be very careful about being too obvious about any particular case. This year, every matter has political consequences of one kind or another."

Golovkin stirred his tea and appreciated the view, overlooking East Ninth Street and the Celebreeze Federal Building; named for Anthony Celebreeze, a former Mayor of Cleveland who had served in both JFK's and Johnson's cabinets.

He had taken the embassy's private jet into Burke Lakefront Airport to meet his protégé, who was now an Assistant United States Attorney specializing in foreign intelligence investigations in

the forty northern counties of Ohio. Pasternak's office was responsible for enforcing federal criminal law, including matters pertaining
to national security, public corruption, civil rights, and other high-
profile cases, from their offices on West Superior Avenue. He was
a progressive liberal at heart, with Russian blood flowing through
his veins.

"I understand. Are you comfortable that any internal investigations will not point towards you?"

"Absolutely." Pasternak sipped his coffee. "US Attorneys and
Federal judges don't get polygraphed. Therefore, if we continue to
meet or speak in ways that do not leave an audit trail, then we are
fine."

"Thank you." Golovkin said quietly. "And the vehicle they used?"

"Verbal request. I contacted my source who oversees the equipment for the Cleveland Field Office. He and I have built a solid relationship over the past three years and he did not think it out of
the ordinary. The van will be returned later today, with a full tank of
gas, and the inside cleaned thoroughly."

"Excellent." Golovkin glanced down and the man's right
hand and admired his class ring. A graduate of Yale Law School,
Pasternak's father had been a roommate of Nicholas Jeffers' son,
Anthony. The two men had taken an instant liking to each other as
both had similar interests in politics, religion, and the law. Neither
were avowed communists but understood and often preferred
the introduction of more socialist ideology into modern political
thought. This ideology was supported in Yale's culture, which was
known for its scholarly orientation and interest in human rights.
The famed institution had produced numerous federal judges and
Supreme Court justices as well as presidents and senior cabinet
members and encouraged all of its graduates to spend a few years
in government service. Thus, the Jeffers and Pasternak families had
a long history, and it seemed a natural progression that Peter and
Anthony Jr., would also go through Yale together.

"And the items you inquired about?" Pasternak sipped his
coffee.

Golovkin frowned for the first time in their meeting. "There are too many places in which it could have been concealed. I do not think there is much chance of finding it in the time your people will have onsite. That is, if he even hid it in his home. As for the other device, once it is removed, if I could intrude on your time, I would like you to deliver it to someone in Columbus. She will be able to get it to me."

It had been a long day and Jerry Lee was exhausted. He looked at the photograph of the white van parked in the driveway of the Moreland Hills house, and enlarged the area of the license plate. He passed the phone across the desk to the Special Agent in Charge of the Cleveland office. "Can you run this plate for me?"

Dennis Ostroski was an eighteen-year veteran who had risen through the ranks of the Secret Service via a strong commitment to duty, and an uncanny ability to keep his nose clean and not screw up in any way visible to persons of importance. He looked at the phone and began entering the license number into the computer on his desk. Then he stopped. "Wait a minute. Where was this taken?"

"The Jeffers house in Moreland Hills. A couple hours ago." Lee responded.

Ostroski passed the phone back across the desk. "I don't need to run that plate. I know that van. As a matter of fact, we've used it."

"What?" Lee asked, looking again at the photograph that Karlsson had texted. "What do you mean?"

"That van is part of the FBI's vehicle pool. We use it when we're installing wiretaps."

Lee's surprise was evident. "The FBI? The cable guys at the house this morning were FBI?"

Ostroski shrugged, "They didn't have to be FBI, but they were law enforcement of some kind. Probably federal, but possibly state. You want me to call over there and see what they've got?"

Lee quickly shook his head. "No. Not yet. Washington was supposedly coordinating this case with other agencies, so I need to check with them before we make any local contact. Why in the world would the Bureau...or whoever, have sent a team in without telling us?"

Ostroski smirked. "Who knows? I quit trying to rationalize the workings of Washington years ago. I suppose you'll learn that too, in time."

CHAPTER 14

S tan Marchand slowed when he saw the elaborate red and white neon art proclaiming Soprek's, *An American-Croatian Experience*. The brilliant sign illuminated the front of the red brick, two story place that had probably served as a large residence in a previous incarnation. Possibly commercial offices or even a small school at one time. The parking lot was towards the rear, and when he backed into his space he noticed that there were only five other cars in the lot. Naturally, he recognized the white Honda with Illinois plates.

Being an acclaimed old-movie buff, once inside, Marchand found Soprek's to be a modern Eastern European version of Rick's, from the classic 1942 Warner Brothers film, Casablanca. Despite being in a working-class neighborhood, it exuded subtle elegance without arrogance, music, drink, food and dancing that appealed to a wide cross-section of the community. It was still early and not yet close to being busy; four men seated together at the bar, and three couples seated at tables in the center dining room. There was additional dining on the second floor, but the gold rope across the bottom of the stairs indicated that those stations were closed for the time being. He estimated that the main floor and bar area occupied close to twenty-five hundred square feet. Bathrooms were down a front hallway. There was a second hallway at the other end of the bar, but he couldn't see where it went. There was an emergency exit located near the bandstand, and a fire extinguisher mounted on the wall next to the door.

It was a Secret Service thing. Agents could not walk into a place and simply appreciate its aesthetics. They had been indoctrinated to memorize floorplans and always be able to find their way back out, even if the room was filling with dense smoke or flying lead. They had to quickly find alternate exits in case their main egress was blocked, for any reason.

The hostess told him that his waiter would be with him in a moment, so he selected a chair that allowed him to see Jerry's table, as well as the front door and relaxed to people-watch. Some patrons were dressed in suits and some were more casual, in jeans and sweaters. He expected to see a Bogie-like character in a white dinner jacket before the night was over. As planned, Jerry Lee and Jenny Lu were one of the couples, but paid him no more attention than anyone else had when he entered. They were seemingly deep in a romantic conversation, with Jerry facing the door.

He looked at the bandstand in the corner of the room, on the other side of a modest dance floor. Permanently built on a six-inch riser, it was on the opposite side of the room as the bar and situated so that some of the tables could be moved out of the way for additional dancing space, or additional seating brought in and arranged for concerts. Void of musicians thus far, it was dominated by a six-foot Yamaha grand piano, an elaborate drum kit complete with three rack toms, two floor toms, and cymbals galore. There were also stands for guitars, horns, and microphones, but no instruments or mics. If the band were going to play tonight, it wouldn't be until later.

People at the bar were dressed for a casual evening and involved in a conversation that suggested that they were together. But he'd noted as he was being seated, that a fashionably attired couple walked through the lounge area towards a door down the hallway on the far end of the bar. The door they entered was electronically access-controlled, and brightly marked *Private Residence*. A separate street address was printed below the bold notice in gold letters. At first, it seemed odd to have a residence door off the main floor of the club, but then it hit him. Parts of the club were considered *members-only*. Obviously, the members had been given individual access cards, but still had to pass by the large chap in the black tux who cordially greeted each one by name, and briefly stepped aside to allow them entry.

Gambling. The separate private entrance had to be the way that the owner was bending the Ohio laws relating to gaming. Limited gambling might skate the system if conducted in a private residence, and if the house didn't rake the pot. Besides, he had learned earlier the establishment was owned by a retired police officer, who would certainly know the nuances of the applicable statutes. For all anyone knew, on any given night, the gaming was being conducted by a bonafide *fraternal organization*, further shielding it from prosecution. Even though the set-up might follow the law as closely as possible, with the six-foot-five penguin standing in front of the door, there was no one going into that area who was not known to them. That included the vice squad and other state investigators.

Karlsson remembered the briefing that Ostroski had given them earlier. Dubravko Soprek had done well for himself. His mother was two months pregnant with him when they had emigrated from Pula, Yugoslavia. Once settled in their new country, he would welcome two younger brothers and experience a relatively normal childhood, with both Croatian and English spoken in their new home. In an effort to facilitate the family's Americanization, his mother changed Dubravko's name to Robert before he entered the first grade. But it wasn't until he was halfway through the second grade that the young lad finally started dreaming in English.

He had performed well in sports and academics and after two years in junior college, joined the Sheriff's Office. He loved the work and with his linebacker build, was eminently suited for it. Over the years, he was cited numerous times for bravery and professionalism and served with distinction on several of the department's special teams. But after twenty-five years, the politics drove him nuts and propelled him to take his pension and open his signature restaurant.

Now in its fifth year, it drew an eclectic clientele and was a frequent stop for affluent Eastern Europeans passing through town. It was also adored by many Italian families in the area due to the two cultures' rich history together. Soprek had been seen as a mediator of sorts and had offered upstairs meeting rooms to families and organizations that were sometimes at-odds, in order that they might have a safe space to work through their differences. There was talk that some US and foreign agencies wanted to plant listening devices in the upper rooms, due to the sensitivity of some of the conversations, but he said no to all. Soprek did not bug the rooms and he wouldn't let anyone else bug them either. Rumor had it that he employed a sweep team periodically to ensure its technical purity.

Marchand glanced again at Jerry's table. The couple seemed to be enjoying each other's company and he wondered if they were keeping the relationship strictly business, or if his young associate was about to make some of the same mistakes that many of their peers had made over the years, destroying careers and marriages. Jenny Lu was, admittedly, a gifted actress who was capable of using her body to get what she wanted. And Jerry might literally be her stay-out-of-jail card. On the other hand, Lee had just come off an eighteen-month undercover assignment and was probably a fairly good actor as well. An experienced observer might have a difficult time trying to determine who was playing whom at that table. But one never knew; perhaps sincerity reigned and neither party was playing the other. Maybe they were just finding common ground.

The middle-aged man in the white waistcoat approached his table, notebook in hand and a small white towel draped across his forearm. "Something from the bar, sir?"

Marchand glanced across the room at the ornate bar of granite and brass, and the assortment of liquor bottles backlit on the glass shelves. "What types of single malts do you have?"

"I think we keep about a dozen back there. Personally, I like the eighteen-year-old Oban. Do you have a particular brand in mind?"

Marchand smiled and nodded. "That sounds great. And two waters if you don't mind?"

"My pleasure, sir."

Marchand was not certain that Tricia would show. As a matter of fact, he gave it about a fifty-fifty chance. Nevertheless, when he'd explained the plan to Jerry, the team agreed that Jerry and Jenny should show up at 5:45 to provide cover and be an extra set of eyes and ears, just in case Tricia didn't come by herself. Karlsson had been elected to stay home in the dark to see if anyone came in to look in the safe. There were a lot of *maybes* in the equation, but as John Heywood proposed in 1546, *nothing ventured, nothing gained*.

"You're going to what?" Karlsson asked surprised as the four of them gathered around the kitchen table earlier that evening.

"I'm going to call her bluff. I want to see if she shows. I want to find out who they are and who sent them." Marchand explained.

"Well, we know they're not Secret Service. But they have to be LE of some sort or they couldn't have gotten the van." Jerry noted. "It will be a while before we get any kind of information back on their prints and DNA."

Jenny Lu looked at Jerry. "I know I'm not a voting member of the group, but might I propose that you and I go along, as if on a date, and we could watch the restaurant to see who else is watching them?"

Jenny Lu had spent the day at the Secret Service office in Independence, naming names and describing dates and activities. Her information was determined to have significant value and Washington had authorized her to come on to the case as a Confidential Informant. She had demonstrated her sincerity and veracity by agreeing to sit for a polygraph, which the examiner concluded, showed no signs of deception. For the time being, she had earned the right to keep her freedom and work through her personal loathing for Zhou, the man who, in her opinion, had taken her fiancé from her.

"You really think she'll show up? What would be the benefit for her?" Lee asked.

"If she's a true professional, then she'll be as curious about me as I am about her." Marchand speculated. "She's the younger agent of the two of them...probably the least experienced. That means she'll be more eager to make a name for herself, and more likely to try to rope me in than her partner or the people she works for."

Karlsson concurred. "Yep. They were low-level talent, with high-level Intel. They were sent here to look for something important. They found the bug. They found the safe. They just didn't have time to get into it with Stan here. My guess is that she'll show up at the bar to draw him out of here, and that they'll try to send someone else back in here to manipulate the safe tonight."

Marchand nodded. "And her partner came back for the bottle in the trash. They didn't want to leave any evidence of their visit, even though they left fingerprints throughout the house."

And now it was five minutes after six and the waiter was returning with Marchand's scotch. As he artfully arranged the drink on the bar napkin placed in front of him, the waiter looked up with an insuppressible smile. "And, for you Ma'am?"

Stan looked up to his right and was momentarily stunned by the transformation. Form fitting black slacks and a pink cashmere sweater had morphed the attractive cable TV technician into a winsome and mesmerizing angel who was sure to turn heads. Her blond hair was down, but back far enough to spotlight the diamond earrings. The sweater was fitted such that her curves were obvious but not in bad taste. As he rose to greet her, he immediately recognized the difference in their ages and if he had not been suspicious of the contact before, he certainly would have been now. He reminded himself that he was sixty and she was probably not yet thirty. If he made it through dinner without the waiter referring to her as his daughter, he would be content.

"Wow!" He said, extending his hand. "Ya clean up well!"

She lightly took his hand and sat down. "Well, thank you." She whispered shyly. "It's been a while since I wore civilian clothes. I wasn't sure this would still be in style for a...you know, date."

Stan was working now. "If you're wearing it, it's in style."

She glanced up at the waiter and offered him a smile that an actress would have died for. "Could I get a gin and tonic?"

"Bombay, Beefeater's or Tanqueray?"

She thought for a moment. "Tanqueray is fine. Thank you."

In the subdued lighting of the restaurant, her blue eyes took on the color and luster of sapphire. When he looked at her, she looked back, and held his gaze when she spoke. "I wasn't sure if you'd show up or not."

"Really?" Marchand sipped his drink and grinned. "What guy in his right mind would stand you up?" He allowed his focus to shift briefly to the table across the room. Jerry was sending a text; no doubt letting Karlsson know that she had arrived.

"You'd be surprised." She glanced quickly around the room. "I just thought with your...you know, situation with your cousin, if you'd have family things going on tonight."

She tossed the bait out, so he decided to play along. "Not really. My cousin's fiancé is with her family tonight and I didn't have anything going on. There's not a lot of golf in Cleveland this time of year."

She laughed. "So, you're up here by yourself? No girlfriend?"

"No girlfriend." He shook his head. "At least not up here." He added coyly.

"What about you?" He thought he'd call out the difference in their ages to see how she worked around it. "We're in Cleveland. You must have a couple of young football or baseball players after you."

She shook her head and rolled her eyes. "They're a bunch of big babies. Arrogant jerks who think they can get in your pants because of who they are."

Stan's confidence was returning. He was wearing a dark blue wool sweater that highlighted his muscular forty-four-inch chest and flat thirty-four-inch waist. He was in top shape and thought he could well pass for forty. Okay, fifty something. He was trying to think of something witty when the waiter returned with her drink. It gave him a moment to collect his thoughts and decide how best to play it.

"So, what about you? Air Force. Cable TV. Who is Tricia, and what does she want in the civilian chapter of her life? Why'd you leave the Air Force, if that's not too personal?"

"Most of my friends were getting married and having babies,

and I decided that I'd like to be normal again. That's not going to happen at Kandahar Airfield or any of the other places I've been stuck." She sipped her drink and with a shrug, gave it an acceptable evaluation. "Not bad."

"You're originally from here?"

"Yeah. Sheffield Lake. It's way west of here, as you're headed towards Sandusky. You? Were you always a Florida boy?"

"For the most part." He'd used the cover before, so he felt comfortable dropping into it whenever it was necessary. For work or for pleasure. "I've travelled a lot on the job and had the opportunity to see different places. But each time I get somewhere, it's like I can't wait to get home." At least he was being partially honest with her.

A moment later, the waiter returned with two large brown leatherette folios that could have been used as street signs. *Soprek's* was embossed in gold letters on the outside, and when opened, the left page proudly displayed a transparent blue lithograph of the Arch of the Sergii in Pula, Croatia with the restaurant's logo above it. The right page listed the menu, which was quite diverse and featured European and American specialties. They were large enough that when opened, one would have to lower the menu into their lap to see their dinner partner.

They ordered, and when the waiter had retired, she mentioned sheepishly, "I'm sorry. I need to use the ladies' room. It was a long drive."

He gestured down the front hallway and then rose partially as she stood and pushed her chair in. It could have been as innocent as she'd intended. Or she could be leaving to send a message. He looked at Jerry's table and, without any prompting, noted that Jenny Lu also excused herself and headed in the same direction. As both men watched, they determined that no one else was making a bathroom trip at that particular time, so if anyone was covering the lovely Tricia, they weren't ready to reveal themselves just yet.

After she returned, and through most of the dinner, Tricia excitedly absorbed the world of golf. Marchand lectured on the way to select the proper clubs; taking one's time and not rushing to buy something because one of their favorite pros used the club on tour. Everyone was different and therefore, everyone had to find the club that fit them uniquely. He spoke of grip size and shaft flexibility and they both laughed.

"Did you mean that to be sexual, or did it just sound that way?"

"Who knows?" He laughed. "Is that how you took it?"

She answered in a way that left him guessing, as many attractive women would have responded, even if they were not assigned to keep him busy for the evening. By eight, they noticed that musicians were starting to arrive to begin setting up on the bandstand.

"I hope you brought your dancing shoes." Marchand said as he sipped a cup of coffee.

"Are you kidding? I could dance you off the floor!" She challenged boastfully.

"We'll see about that." He countered. "I still have a couple of moves left in me!"

⸺ ◦((◐))◦ ⸺

Karlsson peeked at his cell phone. He had been able to load the app that allowed him to watch the surveillance cameras installed at the Moreland Hills house and wanted one last nervous glance to confirm it was all working properly. He'd left the front room light on since it was on a timer but ensured the rest of the house was dark. He wanted the target to look empty and inviting if anyone was struggling to decide as to whether or not to break in. He sat quietly in the darkness of the formal dining room, his back against the wall in the corner, so that he could hear the approach of anyone deciding to come through the woods behind the house. Even though most burglaries were through the front doors, he knew that this could be different. He knew he'd 'be dealing with a professional safecracker who did not want his car seen in the driveway.

He dozed off a couple of times, but his body position prevented him from getting too comfortable and therefore sleeping through the event. It was after 8:15 when he heard the crunching of footsteps on snow and frozen ground, on the end of the house that was closest to the tree line. He steadied his breathing and listened carefully so that he could adequately determine if it were a human or a deer making their way around the end of the house. The steps seemed to stop at the window above his head, and then move on to the windows in the front room. He quickly sent a text to Lee. "FOOTSTEPS OUTSIDE, WEST END. STANDING BY"

He strained to discern every noise that was not ambient in the cold Cleveland evening. There were two of them. They walked carefully, the second man perhaps trying to walk in the first man's footprints so as to throw off investigators later. When the doorbell rang, he jumped. It was the adrenalin. He knew they would attempt to see if anyone was home. He should have expected it. A full minute later, the doorbell rang a second time, but he was mentally prepared and sat calmly and quietly in the dark.

They waited for another thirty seconds before the silence was broken by the sound of cracking wood. They were forcing a pry-bar between the door and the jam. His buddy Fritz would have been mortified at this lack of sophistication and professionalism. Seconds later, they were through the front door and heading straight to the den. He could hear the alarm panel chirping but knew from their earlier inspection that the ersatz cable TV crew had disconnected the audible alarm siren and the digital dialer when they were in earlier. The burglars obviously knew it as they quickly moved with flashlights and found the room they were looking for. He could hear them clearly as one took the print off the wall and handed it to the second person. Then the silence of the house was disrupted by a noise that at first sounded like a large drill. But within seconds, Karlsson recognized the sound of the circular saw.

They were going for the smash-and-grab. No covert manipulation tonight. They were using battery operated tools to cut the entire safe out of the wall. Apparently, whoever sent them in did not care about the crime being discovered, or else they wanted it to look like local thugs at work. Little did they know that they were stealing a safe that was, for the most part, empty. The Secret Service already had the documents, and the flash drive had been substituted for one that had some kid's term paper on Medieval courtship or something. They had left one stack of the hundreds in there, just to make it look good. Regardless, whoever was involved was now guilty of felony burglary, but the only thing they were getting was a mere ten thousand dollars in cash.

Karlsson remained silent and professional, fighting the overwhelming urge to burst in on them, shoot one and then slowly garrote the other. But tonight, he wasn't being paid to produce a body count. He was being paid to simply observe and report. So, he sat quietly on the floor, his back against the wall, trying to steady his breathing and heart rate.

Four minutes and eleven seconds later, they had taken what they came for, and left the same way they had come in. Off in the distance, he could hear a car start up and drive casually away, out of the neighborhood. When he was certain they were not coming back, he went to the front door and took a picture of it. There was enough flex in the frame that the jam had not really provided any protection, and he found that he could still close the door and lock it. Some carpenter could easily repair the minor damage at some point in the future. He moved to the den and turned the lights on.

The Rockwell print rested neatly on the floor against an outer wall, and the cavity left by the safe would be repaired with a piece of drywall and some paint. He smiled and opened the refrigerator. He wanted a beer before sending the text and the photos back to Lee. "TWO PERPS. CUT THE SAFE OUT AND LEFT. MINOR DAMAGE TO FRONT DOOR."

The music changed to a slow dance number and Marchand pulled Tricia close to him. He knew he was on the job but couldn't deny that she still felt good. She was firm and warm and seemed to move up against him as if she were genuinely interested in him. They had each had a couple of drinks and a fantastic meal, and he couldn't help wondering how far she was prepared to go to keep him occupied. It had been a while since he'd been with anyone, and now at his age, the likelihood of him dating an attractive woman, young enough to be his daughter, was growing more and more remote. They moved intuitively together, and her perfume was hypnotic.

"You dance well." she cooed. "And you're in really good shape."

"Thanks." He grunted. "In all honesty, it's been a while for me, and you feel really good. Too good."

"Too good for what?" she whispered in his ear.

He pushed her away only far enough that he could focus on those sapphire eyes.

"You know," He spoke just loudly enough to be heard over the band, but yet remain intimate. "I'm only in town for a couple of days."

"I know."

"You're young enough to be my...uh, niece."

"I know."

He regarded the sapphire eyes with bewilderment. He knew she was baiting him, but it seemed so real. So genuine. "So, how far is Sheffield Lake from here?"

"Too far. What time is your cousin's fiancé coming home?"

"I don't know. Probably pretty soon." He twisted their hands to glance at his watch. "It's a little after nine. By the time we get there, she'll probably be there too."

"There's a Sheraton down by the freeway. Why don't we have one more dance, finish our drinks and we'll get out of here?"

He smiled at her. Even though it was work, he was enjoying himself. "Awesome idea!"

They danced closely, his cheek near her ear. At the right time, he gently kissed her neck. When the music stopped, they returned to the table and sat down.

Her phone was flashing. "Excuse me." She spoke innocently. "This might be my grandmother. She had a fall last week and I told her to text me if she needed anything." She thumbed a response back and put the phone in her purse.

Karlsson took the opportunity to look across the room. Jerry had paid their check and they were putting their coats on. They would move to the parking lot and be ready to follow her as she left the restaurant.

"Trouble?" He asked her as she looked across the table at him. The mission was complete, and she had obviously just received the message telling her to break it off and go home.

"Yes. It's probably nothing, but I really should check on her. I hate to break the mood, but could we do this again tomorrow?"

In a way, he was relieved. If she had slept with him, he always would have wondered if it was because she had wanted to or been told to. He was much too proud for that. "Here, at six? Yeah, that sounds great. I need to attend Marty's memorial service at three, but we should be done by then."

Marchand walked her to the parking lot and gave her the appropriate kiss goodnight. He watched her Ford turn right on Lakeshore and head east down the street. He had memorized her license number but knew that Jerry would get it as he followed her out of the lot a few seconds later. It didn't matter. The barcode on the left rear window told him that it was a rental. They would have to do an inquiry with the rental agency in the morning to get a copy of her driver's license. He shook his head soulfully as he got into his rental and sat quietly for a minute allowing the engine to warm up. If only he were twenty years younger, and they'd met under different circumstances.

He texted Karlsson. "HEADED BACK. JERRY IN TAIL"

A few seconds later, the reply came back to him. "SUCCESS HERE – THE BAR WILL BE OPEN"

A light snow had begun to fall again, and Marchand drove a bit slower than he normally would have. The salt trucks were out, and he felt it unsafe and unlucky to try to pass one. His winter driving skills were rusty, and it just seemed like bad luck to push it. Forty minutes later, he was in the driveway at Moreland Hills.

Karlsson was in the kitchen, seated at a bar stool at the island, watching something on the small television that was mounted under one of the cabinets. When Marchand entered, he grinned and used his thumb to point at the den.

"Geezuss!" Marchand exclaimed, as he looked at the gaping hole where the wall safe had been. "I guess they were interested more in speed than stealth!" He inspected it at a distance so as not to step in the powdered drywall that covered the credenza and floor below. "They cut through the drywall and the metal brackets too. What the hell did they use?"

"Some sort of battery-operated saws. It only took them about four minutes, and they were gone. They came and went through the woods back there. We can track them in the morning, but I'm pretty sure the footprints go to the next street over. I could hear a car start up a few minutes after they'd gone."

Marchand grabbed a beer out of the refrigerator and joined his associate. He unscrewed the cap and tossed it on the counter by the sink. "Two of them?"

"Yeah. Pretty sure it was two men, but I couldn't tell for certain by their voices. I took a peek outside afterwards, and it looks like both sets of prints were man-size. But I really don't think they were outdoorsy kinds of guys. It looks like they both wore sneakers."

"Sneakers?" Marchand smiled, remembering the footwear the cable crew had slipped off at the front door. "That sounds like our guys."

Twenty minutes later they were joined by an exhausted but otherwise energized Jerry and Jenny who made a brief report. "We followed her west on ninety until the seventy-one split. She was driving so slowly that we couldn't tell if she was just being safe or watching for a tail. So, when we saw the signs for seventy-one south, we took it."

Everyone had reviewed the damage to the den and considered the evening a success. Celebration was in order. Seizing the moment, Karlsson spoke up. "Some of us didn't have the chance to dine in a four-star restaurant tonight. I'm ordering pizza! Anyone else in?"

"I could eat something." Jenny Lu replied. "Some of us were too nervous to eat, and only had a salad."

Jerry added, "Yeah. I need to check my inbox to see if DC sent me anything. So, we may be up for a while. Something greasy for me...pepperoni and sausage."

Jerry opened the laptop that Ostroski had provided and logged in to his Secret Service account. After entering his credentials and password, his box opened. Karlsson was on his cell phone ordering a couple of pizzas, but Marchand looked over Jerry's shoulder at the pdf's that had been sent to him, and with childish exuberance told him, "Open the ID's first."

Lee clicked on the file labelled *Suspect Identification*, and read the highlights of the report, "The fingerprints off the bottles show suspect number one as Farmington, Jared M., United States Army, eight years, MOS 35 Lima; Counter-Intelligence. Clearance: Top Secret...Army Commendation, Iraq Campaign medal, Iraq Commitment Medal, Army Commendation again...blah, blah blah."

He paged down and continued. "Discharged as E-6 Staff Sergeant three years ago...no criminal history."

"Yeah, what about the girl?" Stan asked.

"Knight, Patricia R...E-6, Tech Sergeant, United States Air Force, MOS two Alpha six X-ray two; Communications. Her awards include Air Force Commendation, Afghanistan Campaign, Air Force Good Conduct, Bronze Star, and Presidential Unit Citation. She's clean too."

"No, her date of birth." Stan pushed.

The group looked at him in unison with their eyebrows raised. Jerry looked at her personal history form. "Well, if my math is right, she's thirty-one."

"Yes!" He shouted, raising his fist in the air, before realizing that he was not appearing as objective as he should have at that moment. "I just...uh, you know. I was curious."

Karlsson returned from the other room after ordering two pizzas. "What do you have on the translations and the medals?"

Jerry Lee exited the one file and clicked on another one labeled *Medals/Photo*.

The files opened and the group looked at the summary as Lee read the descriptions next to the color photographs of each.

"Medals recovered from basement safe. Item number one appears to be the Order of Lenin. Until the dissolution of the USSR, it was the highest civilian decoration bestowed by the Soviet Union. The order was awarded to four principal groups: civilians for outstanding services rendered to the State, members of the armed forces for exemplary service, individuals who promoted friendship and cooperation between peoples or strengthening global peace, and individuals who performed meritorious services to the Soviet state and society. They were issued with individual serial numbers on the reverse, but the number has been eradicated on the sample submitted."

"Grab me one of those beers." Jerry asked of no one in particular, as he moved to the next item on the list. "Item number two as described and photographed, appears to be a red ribbon bar with a gold and black pentagon shaped medallion. The Pilot-Cosmonaut of the USSR medal. Instituted in April 14, 1961 and awarded by the Presidium of the Supreme Soviet to all cosmonauts who flew for the Soviet Space Agency. It was sometimes accompanied by a certificate for being a Hero of the Soviet Union."

Karlsson handed the beer over Jerry's shoulder while he was reading. "Medal number three, a diamond shaped badge with a screw post on the reverse appears to be a Zhukovskiy Academy Graduation badge. Most of the Soviet Union's cosmonauts graduated from this prestigious Academy and received these badges with identification cards during their graduation ceremony. The Zhukovskiy Air Force Engineering Academy is a military educational institution for training of engineers for the Russian Air Force. It is the world's largest and oldest scientific school of aeronautics, having been established in November 1920. This particular badge was issued in the early 1960's."

"Item four is a black and white, four-inch by four-inch photograph of a young blond man in white coveralls and a white hard hat. This appears to have been taken with a Polaroid-Land,

self-developing camera in the early 1960's. In this process, the photo was snapped, and an emulsion packet was pulled through rollers
that allowed an image to develop after a minute. Once the photo
was produced, the negative side was discarded. There is no way to
scientifically determine the exact date or location where or when
the photo was taken."

"So, Marty was keeping some old Soviet cosmonaut awards in
a safe that was concealed in the basement?" Karlsson asked, thinking out loud. "They must have been important to him. I mean, they
might have value on the curio trading market, but even if they were
worth a couple of grand, why did he keep them isolated down
there? If they were that valuable, why not keep them..." His voice
trailed off.

"What about the flash drive?" Marchand inquired.

Lee backed out of the file and moved back to the one labelled
Flash Drive. There was a forensic analysis of *gigabytage* and hash
information and other technical jargon that no one cared about,
which Lee skipped over. "It appears to be largely financial data.
Money in and money out. The summary page indicates that the file
was started three years earlier and that over that time has seen more
than thirteen million dollars flow through it. There's a second tab
to the spreadsheet that lists incoming funds and disbursements."

Lee clicked on the embedded icon and opened the report.
Marchand let out a low whistle, and Jenny suddenly sat upright and
gasped. Obvious signs that she was not prepared for what she saw.

The sheet opened and the group looked at it for a couple of
seconds. Lee read out the obvious entries. "He was getting regular
deposits...somewhere, from an account he called Bear, that came
every month and ranged from a few hundred thousand to a million each. It looks like he distributed to several accounts, but the
one he called ARCHER, seems to be the biggest recipient. He's paid
ARCHER close to ten million over the last three years. And, according to this, he paid SEMPER another million or so."

"Wait a minute." Marchand jumped in. "This is an aircraft engineer who made a hundred fifty grand a year?"

"Yeah." Lee confirmed. "Someone's been paying him for three years. This isn't about a sprayer thing. This is something more. This guy's a banker for someone."

Jenny Lu wilted into her chair and put her head in her hands. "I'm sorry, Jerry. I had no idea." She wouldn't look up, but it was evident she had genuine tears in her eyes. "I truly had no idea."

Jerry looked across the table at her. "I believe you." He started to reach for her hand and then checked himself. "This is for the finance guys to figure out. Let's see what the translations are of those docs."

He opened the file and skimmed the high points. "Complete translations are currently underway. Initial review by our Russian linguist follows:"

"Photograph number one depicts a certificate or letter from Zhukovskiy Air Force Engineering Academy issued to Nikolay Vasilyevich Leonov, who graduated first in his class in June 1957. Photograph number two is a commission as a second lieutenant in the Soviet Air Force for above-captioned individual, June 1957. The photographs submitted as samples three and four are part of a Soviet Air Force personnel file indicating Leonov's commission and assignments. He was promoted to senior lieutenant October 1959 and transferred to the Baltic Military District. In 1960, he was reassigned to cosmonaut training. Analysts believe the photograph of Leonov matches the Polaroid shot of white male in hard hat referenced in the other report."

"The fifth photograph in the series appears to be a death certificate for Leonov dated 10 March 1961. Cause of death was due to asphyxia occurring as a result of a fire while on a training exercise. Remains were cremated and returned to widow."

"The sixth photograph is a copy of a marriage certificate to bride Sofia Astakhova issued through ZAGS, the local vital statistics bureau, with a propiska stamp for Moscow, dated Wednesday June 12, 1957."

"It's a file for a dead cosmonaut?" Karlsson observed out loud.

"So, the question is, what was this guy to Marty?" Marchand added. "A relative? If this cosmonaut died in a fire in Moscow in 1961, then what was he doing at Cape Kennedy in 1966?"

"Headquarters must be mistaken." Jerry replied, re-reading the investigative report. "That doesn't make sense. It can't be the same guy."

Something was bothering Marchand. "Unless..."

Karlsson remembered his earlier conversation with Paul. "Unless he had been resurrected and given a new identity, courtesy of our Defense Department."

"What?" Jerry Lee turned in his seat.

Karlsson closed his eyes so hard it wrinkled his nose. "Uh...occasionally I'm given the discretion to take fellow professionals into my confidence and reveal certain information that may be relative to the mission, and has not, by itself, been classified. In this case because it's never been proven."

Marchand felt a mild wave of anxiety. In the back of his mind, his recent taskings suddenly became clear. "And?"

Karlsson continued. "For all official purposes, Leonov did die in that fire in 1961. It was shortly after that, that Nicholas Malcom Jeffers, Marty's great-uncle, suddenly appeared at the Cape, working on the Apollo program."

An electrical chill cascaded through Marchand's body. It made sense now. "The fourth man."

———— «(()» ————

It was after eleven when Feodor Golovkin's phone began to vibrate. He had finished brushing his teeth and was preparing for bed when his caller ID indicated that Peter Pasternak was calling.

"Allo, Peter." He said quietly. "It is late. Are you okay?"

"I'm sorry. I hope I didn't wake you." The voice replied delicately. "I think I have what you were looking for."

Golovkin frowned at his reflection in the mirror. "You think?"

"Yes. There was only one place that our team was not able to search the first time through. A safe, in the wall in the den. So, I sent another team in earlier tonight."

"You broke into the safe?" Golovkin asked, concerned about the obvious risk versus any possible reward.

"No. The crew would not have had time for that. They cut the safe out of the wall and are holding it for us. We have not opened it yet."

Golovkin tried to remain calm as his face began to redden. The problem with using non-professionals in these types of situations was the risk that they would try to be something they were not. Their entire breadth of training and experience in espionage tradecraft came from watching ridiculous western movies. He had entrusted a simple covert search to his young protégé after thoroughly discussing it with him and assuring that he was clear as to the objectives of the assignment. Get in, look around and get out without anyone knowing that you were ever there. Now Golovkin was complicit in a felony burglary, along with an Assistant US Attorney. If this were to leak out, there would be severe consequences for everyone.

"Let me understand correctly. Your team broke in, cut the safe from the wall, and took it out?"

"Yes, Uncle Ted." I thought you said it was a matter of urgency. We made it look like a burglary."

Golovkin thought carefully about the repercussions of a police investigation into a simple burglary, which once linked to PROSTAK, could bring the entire resources of the FBI down on him. The publicity, during an election year, would be catastrophic. "Yes. You did the best you could. Unfortunately, I will need you to do two more things for me. The electronic device...you still have it?"

"Yes."

"Good. I will text an address to you. You will need to deliver it sometime tomorrow. Second, how did you select the two individuals you used in today's operation?"

"They were both ex-military operators. They are under contract to Homeland Security, so they are available to do work for several different agencies. They were blind, for the most part."

"They are both local to your area?"

"Yes, of course. Why?" Pasternak asked.

"They spoke to no one?"

"Of course not." Pasternak replied humbly but concerned.

"I need their names and home addresses. This will be most important. It is also important that you do not have any trail that leads back to you."

Pasternak was quiet for a moment. "Wait. What are you planning to do?"

"Through perhaps my own negligence, I have allowed a situation to suddenly blossom into a much more visible problem. I need to fix it. But I need you to be in Columbus tomorrow. Find something to do in the state capital. See a show. Visit a museum. Do not come back to Cleveland until tomorrow evening."

Even though he was inexperienced in espionage operations, Pasternak was nevertheless educated. "What are you going to do?" His voice was weak with anxiety.

"Not to worry. I am going to schedule a drop. I want your two contractors to bring the safe to one of my representatives tomorrow afternoon. Perhaps after rush hour. Let's say six. I will text you the address. It is a warehouse just east of downtown."

"Certainly." Pasternak replied. Maybe Uncle Ted was being cautious and just did not want him around for the exchange in case police happened by.

"Remember. Both of them." Golovkin directed coldly.

"Of course." Pasternak said humbly. Whether it was fate, or karma, or just a miscommunication uttered under stress, he assumed that Golovkin had meant the two operators who had boosted the safe. So, after ending the call, he quickly complied and texted the names and addresses for Jared M. Farmington and his evening associate, Terry A. Consterdine.

———— »«(()»« ————

The pizzas arrived by 11:30 and the group was somewhere between an open and intelligent discussion of the information they'd learned, and a quest to see what the late Martin Jeffers had kept in his liquor cabinet. The conversation, for the most part, had been focused on what Marty had done with the millions of dollars that had flowed through his hands, and what that might have had to do with a possible covert agent who had been placed in NASA before half of those present were born. When the house line rang, it caused everyone to stop talking and look at each other.

Jerry looked at Jenny. "Well, you're the only one of us who's actually supposed to be here."

Jenny shrugged and wiped her hands on a napkin before picking up the wireless phone from the wall-mounted cradle near the sink. "Hello?"

She listened to the caller and then grinned before replying, "Sure, just a minute." She handed the phone to Marchand. "It's for you."

Marchand took it, keenly aware of the eyes that were suddenly focused on him. "Hello?"

The voice on the other end seemed anxious. "Hi Stan. I am so sorry to call so late. I hope I didn't wake you."

"Tricia?" He asked, moderately embarrassed. "How did you get this number?"

"Sorry. It was on the...uh...work order from earlier. We didn't exchange numbers tonight and I didn't know if that was because we already planned to see each other tomorrow, or if..." She paused. "Or if you just didn't want me to have your number. I'm laying here, tossing and turning and I thought I won't be able to get to sleep until I explain some things to you."

"No, that's okay. Jenny's back with some of Marty's relatives, and we just ordered pizza. What's up?"

It was obvious that she was distressed about something. "I really enjoyed meeting you tonight. But I wasn't totally honest with you and I want you to know that I'm usually pretty sincere. I...uh, I've been involved with...someone and it's sort of coming to a close, but if I acted a bit strange, I wanted you to know that I thought you were a really nice guy. Yeah, you're older, but that doesn't matter to me. I just wanted you to know..." Her voice trailed off.

Marchand stepped out of the kitchen as he was uncomfortable playing to an audience of sorts. "What's the matter?"

"It's just...uhm...sometimes people get caught up in things and they don't see where it's leading until they're in too far."

"What are you talking about? We had a great dinner and I thought we got along just fine. Are you having second thoughts about getting together tomorrow?"

"No." she said softly. "Not at all. I just need to tell you some things about me and I don't want it to interfere with our evening."

"Like what? You're married? A lesbian?"

"No." she tried to laugh. "Nothing like that. I'll tell you all about it tomorrow."

Marchand had spent a career as a Secret Service agent and had supplemented his income as a government psychic. It didn't take much intuition or experience to know that she was stressed about something but being quite sincere now. She wanted to talk. "Listen, I'm looking forward to tomorrow. But I want you to do me a favor, without asking any questions."

"What's that?"

"I want you to call off sick tomorrow, and not answer your phone. Don't talk to anyone until I see you at six tomorrow. Can you do that for me?"

"You're not some sort of weirdo or a fugitive, are you?"

"Well, the jury is still out on that." He laughed. "In all serious-ness, I can tell you're a little stressed, and I'd really love it if you wouldn't answer your phone for any reason until I see you."

Jared was the only one who knew about her liaison at Soprek's. And, as a contractor, they didn't really have regular hours or an of-fice from which to work. Her foray into Moreland Hills was business, and Stan certainly wasn't any kind of suspect in anything. Besides, she had already made up her mind not to speak to Jared for a while. She felt their personal relationship had gone farther than it should have, and she needed to get it back to being strictly professional. She needed a change. "Yeah, I can do that. See you tomorrow!"

CHAPTER 15

As the sun peaked in the bedroom window, Karlsson rolled over and pulled the blanket up over his head. His iliac crests were sore from having slept on the floor for two nights. Out of a sense of archaic chivalry or antiquated propriety, not to mention the need to maintain official appearances, Jenny Lu had been given the master suite and the men had made-do on sofas and floors. It was okay. He had slept in far worse conditions.

He surmised that she had probably been the first to rise. The smell of coffee wafted up the stairs into his room, and he could hear the shower running in the master suite. The rest of the house was quiet.

It was after two in the morning when they had begun to disperse from the kitchen table. They unanimously agreed that there had been more to the late Marty than any of his co-workers or friends would ever have known. Jerry Lee would now have a major financial investigation on his hands and would need the support of his headquarters group to ensure that another agency like the FBI or IRS didn't rush in, sweep it out from under him and destroy all of the work that had been done thus far. He needed the home office's resources to sort through the financial transactions and see if they could isolate accounts or wire transfers that might correlate to the payments they found in the spreadsheets.

The only tangible suspect he had though, was Zhou. That is where his case had started, and that's where some or most of it still pointed. Undoubtedly though, there had to be other sources for the funds. Zhou seemed to be a player who could be counted on for a couple hundred thousand here and there, but unless he'd had an interest in more of Echo's components than the sprayer, that wouldn't explain the cash and gold in Marty's wall. It certainly would not add up to thirteen million dollars. The Secret Service was fully engaged now and believed that Lee had done an admirable job. Thus far. They wanted Zhou, in a big way. But they needed to have something concrete on him.

Once the group had been able to sift through the document translations and try to determine their significance, Jerry had dispatched an email to his boss a little after midnight. His boss had responded to him twenty minutes later, with two priorities. The first being to have the Cleveland Office pick up the cash and the gold. While the Moreland Hills house was still available as a temporary command post or bivouac, the US Government felt it would be better if they hung on to the cash and gold at a more suitable location. If it turned out later that Marty's heirs could prove that the wealth had not been acquired as an instrument or element of a crime, then they could always petition the court to have it returned. That is, if any heirs, other than Jenny Lu, would ever find out about it. So far, she was guilty of nothing more than ambition and maintaining questionable associations with questionable characters. Just like most of the politicians in Washington.

The second priority was to have a conference call with a half dozen senior agents and case managers in Washington to decide if it made more sense to keep Jerry undercover as they looked for ways to get Zhou indicted and extradited. He was to be in the Field Office by nine, with Jenny Lu, for a lengthy conference call. So far, she was just a person of interest, and with Jerry's recommendation, was considered somewhat trustworthy. Besides, she could see on both sides of the horizon.

She had a personal relationship with Zhou. And, if she had not troubled him by going to Cleveland to oversee Marty's memorial service, he would want to keep her in place. She had value to him. She was strategically placed in the Layden campaign and would be a good communications conduit. However, she might have some fences to mend with him and his organization. She had left her special cell phone at her apartment in Evanston. She would not be able to tell if he was suspicious of her or not until she got back home and had a chance to review any messages.

Her real boss, at the public relations firm, had given her a week off for bereavement. Upon her return, she would be back on the Layden account and would be able to give it her all. In addition to the information and access she was providing for Echo Aerospace, she was suddenly valuable to the Secret Service as well. It seemed that Ms. Lu was becoming extremely popular indeed.

Karlsson looked at the Omega Seamaster on his wrist. It was almost eight and if he wanted coffee and a shower, he might have to wait in line if he slept too late. The Secret Service was sending a truck over for the loot at eight thirty, and he was not sure if they'd want his help or not. Having had years of experience with US Government operations, he figured they would probably tell him to stay out of the way. Never mind the fact that he had been sleeping thirty feet away from it for the past two nights and had hired the locksmith that got them in there in the first place. If he had wanted to steal something, he would have already done it by now.

He grabbed his toilet kit and wandered across the hall to the empty bathroom. Twenty minutes later he was a new man, although, other than a change of underwear, he was wearing the same sweats he'd had on the evening before. He would have to change into something more presentable to run to the airport after the memorial service. Jackie Biehn had responded to his text with a flight itinerary.

He was looking forward to seeing her. On one hand, he felt as if her case had gotten sidetracked by the Secret Service investigation and he wanted to bring her up to speed and see if their findings were paralleling her interests. On the other hand, she was an attractive woman who seemed to find him interesting. They were both adults and could certainly be counted upon to keep it professional through dinner, since they were providing the back-up that evening for Stan and his new friend Tricia. Jenny and Jerry were expected to return to the Secret Service office after the memorial service, and there was no sense in taking the chance that Tricia might recognize them from the previous evening.

Refreshed by his shower and revitalized by his cup of coffee, Karlsson watched the large box truck back down the driveway, the obnoxious beeping sound letting everyone from blocks around know that something was backing up. This was Jerry's show, so he let him and Stan greet the two men who carefully stepped down out of the cab. One was the large African American gent he had met at the hospital, Franklin Jones. The other fellow looked like any other government employee one might run into somewhere, dressed in a suit, and looking quite out of place in his current role as a truck driver. Nevertheless, after the outdoor greetings were completed, they all entered, and kicked the snow off their shoes on the front mat.

The group made it to the kitchen where Jerry made some hasty introductions. "Franklin, you met Matt at the hospital the other day. Matt this is Todd Lange."

Karlsson shook hands with both men. "Coffee, gentlemen?"

Both men nodded eagerly and Karlsson poured the last of the pot into their cups and began to make another. "Will you be needing me for anything? I owe my boss a quick call to let him know what's going on."

"No, I think we've got this. We have some evidence boxes on the truck that we'll load up and seal." Jones sat his cup down and picked up his folio. "I do need you to fill out one of these witness forms for me if you could. I need to send it in with the evidence package."

Karlsson nodded and quickly looked over the form. Pretty basic stuff: it asked for who he was, and what he saw. "No problem."

Jones sipped his coffee and lowered his voice. "Since this is technically a Secret Service crime scene now, can you keep Ms. Lu occupied down here while we load the boxes upstairs?"

Karlsson smiled. "Sure. She's a witness as well, so why don't you leave me an extra copy of your form and I'll see that she fills hers out while I'm doing mine. It will keep her mind off the fact that you're taking her inheritance out of her new home."

Jones' face contorted with an air of regret. "Well, you never know!"

"I'll see if she's done upstairs." Jerry added and then disappeared around the corner.

Karlsson looked across the island at Jones. "We never did find a key for it. Are you going to pick it?"

The young blond man who had been introduced as Lange replied. "We won't have to. We have a core key from the manufacturer. We'll take lock core out, and put one of ours back in. When we're done in there, we'll put the original core back in, and leave it locked."

Karlsson nodded. He started to say something when he heard Jerry and Jenny coming back down the stairs. Jerry introduced Jenny to the group and then told her that she would need to work on yet another statement for their office; this one dealing specifically with the discovery of the cash and gold hidden in Marty's closet.

"Fine." She said noncommittally as she looked at the coffee pot. "That went fast. I'm glad to see that someone else knows how to make coffee around here!"

Karlsson smiled and then took the report forms over to the kitchen table and sat down. Jenny poured herself another cup of coffee and then joined him. "Is this their idea of busy-work to keep us out of the way?"

Karlsson chuckled. "Of course, it is! I figure it'll take them an hour and a half to get it all boxed up and on the truck. If you don't mind, I need to call my office before I start on it. Do you mind if I step out?"

"Not at all." She said as she looked over the form with a frown. "I'll let you know if I decide to steal the family silver."

Karlsson walked into the living room where he could speak as privately as possible with a house full of federal agents and a budding Mata Hari.

He sat comfortably on the couch in the corner of the formal living room, looking out the windows that allowed him to see the box truck in the driveway, and the woods behind the house, from which the safe crackers had emerged the previous evening. He could still see their tracks.

Paul picked up on the second ring. "Good morning, Matthias."

The use of his formal name told him that Paul was concerned that others who considered themselves powerful, might be listening. "Good morning, Paul." He replied in acknowledgement. "I have a couple of moments and wanted to update you. Is this a good time?"

"Yes. What do you have?"

Karlsson gave him a rundown of the previous evening, including the translations Jerry had received from the Secret Service. "So, as you hinted, it looks like our guy Jeffers, whether he knew it or not, was a descendent of a possible Soviet agent. An agent who had been brought into our space program by JFK under some kind of agreement to assure the safe exploration of space. This, of course, would make us question what ever happened to the individuals we sent over there?"

"I don't have that information right now, but I'm not sure it's germane to your mission."

"Well, sir, not to be a problem child, but I'm really not sure what my mission is any more. You wanted a counterfeiter, and I gave him to you. The US Secret Service is now tracking his known associates and the source of the funds we recovered. Which, by the way, are at this moment, being carted out of here to destinations unknown."

"I don't wish to sound deliberately vague, Matt, but your mission is still developing. I need to keep you in play there for a little while longer. Have you given this information to Ms. Biehn yet?"

"I will tonight. We have a memorial service for Marty at three, and her flight gets in at four thirty. I thought it would be better to speak to her in person and allow her to ask the questions that are important to her."

"That's a sound approach." He paused. "How are you getting along with Mr. Marchand?"

Karlsson paused for a moment. He could not remember if he'd mentioned the name to Paul before or not. He must have. "Aces, sir. We've been roommates for several nights and seem to be getting along. However, other than being an extra set of hands for an understaffed Service during the campaign, I don't think he knows any more about this assignment than I do."

There was a long pause. "At some point, when it makes sense to do so, I will need you to sit down with him and discuss in depth his perceptions about this case. Marchand is one of ours."

Karlsson was taken aback. "Excuse me? I thought he was brought in by the Secret Service. I mean, they are swearing him in as a US Marshal this afternoon and keeping him on the job. At least, for a while."

"I know." He paused again. "Mr. Marchand has been a special kind of...intelligence analyst with us since he retired from active service. I cannot tell you at this point, the specifics of his contributions. Needless to say, he may be able to provide additional support for Ms. Biehn's OSI investigation as the situation requires."

"Wait. They know each other?" Karlsson asked.

"No. I am fairly confident they have never met."

"Well, my understanding was that he was hired in as a contractor by the Secret Service to help support the protective mission of a witness; whom we're burying today at three o'clock. I'm gonna need more."

"Marchand is a very capable and trustworthy operative. My interest is in his handler. At some point, I would like to know why, and by whom he was selected for this particular assignment."

Karlsson was now genuinely confused. "What do you mean?"

"The Secret Service is pulling dozens of retirees in for the campaign, as are a number of other federal agencies who are trying to support their ranks in the absence of full-time agents to help them fulfill their respective roles. Marchand spent a career in protection, all the way to the White House. So why, with all of the experienced professionals available to them for this type of work, would someone send him to protect a witness, whose potential contribution was nothing more than background on a counterfeiting case?"

"Why don't you ask him?"

"I already have. He identified the person who recalled him to active service and asked for my permission before he took the job. I saw no reason to say no, considering he is a retiree and can do as he pleases, so long as he maintains security over any information he might have developed for our group. So, to answer your question, I could ask him again, but he would not know. My reason for telling you now is that sooner or later, you will find it appropriate to tell him about your investigation with Special Agent Biehn and ask for his input. As I explained to you earlier, Washington is a different place now. Agencies and key personnel are being manipulated for political gain."

"Well, that explains his comment last night."

"What comment?"

"We were looking through the translations and for no apparent reason, he said, *the fourth man*. It was as if he'd known something about the fire before we started sorting through all of the paperwork."

"It sounds like Mr. Marchand has started to piece it together." Paul was silent for a moment before adding. "When the time is right, please quietly ask him to call me."

With that, he was gone. Karlsson pondered the conversation for a moment and then returned to the kitchen to write his report. It asked for basic information, so that was what he gave them; succinctly stating that during a search of the residence, several safes were discovered and surreptitiously opened, in the presence of other government personnel. The contents of the safes were reported to the US Secret Service, who arranged for their evidentiary collection. End of report.

Jenny Lu looked up from her coffee. "How much should I put in this?"

"Keep it simple." Karlsson responded truthfully. "The people that need to know this stuff, already know it, so keep it simple. Tell them what you saw in the closet and who was with you when you saw it. You're a communications professional. That's the message."

Pasternak headed south on interstate seventy-one, mildly anxious about his cargo, but nonetheless determined to get it to a woman named Natalie Richards, who owned an athletic club on the east side of Columbus. He didn't know who she was and didn't want to know. Pursuant to his instructions, he had gift-wrapped the device in the kind of paper that would look like it was intended for a young child. It was electronic, so he felt safe. If it had been some sort of narcotics, he would have been afraid that an unexpected stop by the Highway Patrol would have prompted a canine search and it might have been discovered.

What was he worried about? He had his credential that identified him as an Assistant United States Attorney. No trooper would detain him once they saw his credential. Still, he knew he was skirting the lines of his personal and professional ethics. What had begun as a discretionary incursion into his personal political beliefs had now evolved into him making clandestine deliveries for a Russian diplomat. He was in over his head. In the beginning, he had simply wanted to align himself with the new liberal movement towards a quasi-socialism, as did many of his friends and colleagues. All in the interest of world peace, of course.

Two hours later, his GPS told him to take the two-seventy east beltway exit. He was headed towards the suburb of Gahanna, not far from the Port Columbus International Airport. A town of about 35,000, it was demographically mixed. There were rich people and poor people, just like the rest of America. However, there tended to be more people on the rich end than the poor end, with an excellent school system and high-priced suburban residences throughout the city. If you worked in Columbus, it was a nice place to live. Every bit as comfortable as Dublin, but not nearly as arrogant.

He drove under the highway and took the ramp that circled back east. Columbus had not received as much snow as Cleveland, and the roads had been clear. The morning traffic had subsided, and he cruised along at just over sixty-five. He was in a hurry but did not want to get stopped for speeding. He needed to relax. This would be easy. He would simply enter, drop the gift off and then be on his way. On his way to somewhere. He had to find something to do for four or five hours to keep him out of Cleveland. He was not certain what Golovkin had in mind, but he wanted to make sure that he could prove that he was nowhere near Cleveland when it happened. Whatever it was.

Richards' Fitness was located in a small commercial park, not far from the Mt. Carmel Hospital and several small strip malls. Inside, there was a spacious room for the weight machines and two other rooms for fitness classes of one kind or another. He glanced about at the typical signs and banners that attested to the benefits of a healthy body. They offered several programs tailored for the affluent, such as Pilates, Zumba and even martial arts classes, two nights a week. And when he entered, he was greeted by a sweet twenty-something brunette in a tight athletic outfit, who would certainly have captured the heart of any heterosexual man, including his, if he had been one. She was wearing a well-fitting short-sleeve golf shirt with the name *Krista*, in script lettering.

"Hello. I wondered if Natalie was available. I have something for her."

"Oh. Did you have an appointment?"

"No. My name is Peter. I just wanted to leave this for her." He said as he gently placed the wrapped package on the counter.

"No problem." She smiled graciously. "I'll see if she's free."

She picked up the phone and punched in a sequence of numbers. "Hi, Natalie, there's a man here who has a gift or something for you. He says his name is Peter." She smiled at him. "Okay, thanks."

Krista hung the phone up. "If you don't mind, just leave it with me and she said she'd pick it up after her meeting."

Pasternak paused before answering. If it were that important, why wouldn't she have come out to accept it personally? She knew he was coming. Uncle Ted Golovkin must have notified her of his visit. On the other hand, he didn't want to call too much attention to his presence. "Yes. Thank you." He said meekly, and then turned and walked out.

Karlsson hadn't packed any formal clothing but had been able to stop and pick up a dark gray sweater and black sport coat that would serve the purpose. It wasn't like he was going to run into any old friends at Jeffers' memorial service. He arrived at Garber and Sons and parked in the rear. It was a stately older white home with the high pillars in front. It could have been a mansion at one time, and later repurposed for funerals and cremations, probably sometime in the late seventies.

One of the chapels had been set aside for Marty's family and friends, soft reflective music piped in from somewhere. The smell of flowers, or aerosol deodorizers designed to smell like flowers, was in the air, and from the hallway, Karlsson could hear whispers emanating from within as he signed the guest book on the small podium. He was by himself. Everyone would be by themselves today because no one was certain who would be in attendance. However, there was no need for anyone from Marty's work or social circles to know that Jerry, Jenny, Stan, or he knew each other.

As he entered, he noted Jenny down by the urn that rested atop an altar of sorts, surrounded by flowers. She was the grieving fiancé, so it fell to her to organize the service and handle most of the details. Marty was an only child, whose parents had preceded him in death. He had no children of his own, but it was interesting to see that Marty's ex-wife seemed to be getting along well with Jenny.

The two women greeted the mourners and one-by-one, the former Mrs. Jeffers introduced them to Jenny. Karlsson joined the cue and noticed that two people ahead of him was Arthur Collins, the CEO of Echo Aerospace. He quickly looked around but did not see Carroll in the room. Karlsson got as close as he could, without crowding the person in front of him. He wanted to hear this introduction.

When it was his turn, Collins looked sheepishly at Jenny Lu. "Hi. You must be Ms. Lu. I'm Arthur Collins." He shook hands quickly before turning to the former Ms. Jeffers. "Kathryn, I'm so sorry about this. It seems like such a long time since we last saw you. May I present my wife, Adele?"

Adele and Kathryn shook hands warmly and then Adele took Jenny's hand in both of hers. "Ms. Lu, I'm Adele Collins. I am so sorry for your loss. Please let us know if there is anything you need." She looked at Kathryn Jeffers. "Either of you. Please don't hesitate to ask."

When it was Karlsson's turn, he kept it sincere, but brief, greeting Jenny first. "Hello. I'm Matt Karlsson. I worked briefly with Marty, and just wanted to say how much we'll miss him."

He moved on to Kathryn and shook hands. "Matt Karlsson. So sorry for your loss."

After pausing for a moment in front of the urn, he turned to find a seat near the back of the room. He passed the Collins' and nodded briefly at Arthur. They weren't really supposed to know each other, so it wasn't the time for hugs and commiserations. Within a few minutes, he saw Jerry in line, and a couple of minutes after that, Stan could be seen signing the guest book. But rather than stand in line, he took a seat in the rear, on the opposite side of the room from Karlsson. *Overlapping fields of view*, he thought.

A thin, sixtyish bald man in a dark blue suit was one of the last in line before the service started. As he greeted Jenny Lu, he bent slightly and gave her a business card. He whispered something to her and then shook hands cordially with Kathryn before leaving the room. The man had *attorney* written all over him.

It was evident that the pastor who delivered the touching eulogy was good at his job but had never met Marty. The template was a pretty standard assortment of references to *a life well lived, cut off in the prime* and related passages intended to give the mourners a chance to remember the deceased in their own way. When he was finished with his part, he asked the assembly if anyone would like to rise and say a few words about Marty. No one did. He folded his notes, led the group in a brief prayer, and then said simply, "This concludes the services for Martin Jeffers. You are encouraged to pay your final respects and then leave at your leisure. Go in peace."

He left the podium and spoke quietly to Jenny Lu and Kathryn Jeffers for a moment and then soberly walked out into the hall.

Some of the guests wandered around the room, looking at the floral arrangements, and others met in small groups. Karlsson remained seated and watched respectfully until Collins and his wife left the chapel. The two men nodded to each other again. Karlsson would probably need to call him at some point, but it could wait. He looked at his watch and decided it was time to head to the airport to pick up the lovely Special Agent Biehn. It had been a gloomy day; in the morning, they had taken away his fortune and now he was saying goodbye to someone. He paused on the way out and turned to offer one last farewell to a guy he barely knew. "Ashes to ashes, amigo."

Once again, he found the airport without the need for the GPS. He had been there enough to start offering a shuttle service. She was coming in on a Delta Airlines flight and since the police were not allowing anyone to stop who wasn't loading or off-loading passengers, he found a space in the garage and walked to the arrivals area. If the flight was on time, he still had ten minutes to wait. Local meteorologists were betting on a cold front moving in over the next twelve hours and O'Hare was promising delays in flights. When Chicago or New York airports began reporting delays, it generally meant that everything else across the country would be impacted as well.

When he saw her, his face lit up with an irrepressible grin. Her blond hair bouncing as she strode across the concourse dragging her carry-on bag. She had on jeans and a dark blue sweater, and a shiny maroon coat with a hood that was outlined in faux fur. She looked like she had just come from a ski slope somewhere. She smiled back at him and as she approached, the smile turned to a beam. "Uncle Matt!"

He hugged her close and whispered in her ear. "Uncle Matt? Are you shitting me?"

She laughed and whispered back. "The guy sitting next to me asked if I was meeting anyone and I told him I was staying with my uncle."

"Uh huh. Very funny! Did you check anything through or is this it?"

"This is it. I can only stay for a couple of days. I'm lucky they let me out of the office without an official escort. We're starting to get political interest in this case, and I don't think anyone trusts anyone." She lowered her voice as she passed off the handle for her roller bag to him and took his arm. "The rumor is that the Bureau is choosing up sides before the election because the mud is about to get slung. Some people are worried that their jobs may be on the line if they don't support the right... uh, check that, the correct political party."

"Meaning, the opposite of right?" He asked innocently.

"Uh huh." She nodded. "Your text said that you were taking me someplace nice tonight for Valentine's Day."

"Valentine's Day?" He looked at her. "That was last week some time, wasn't it?"

She grinned. "Yeah, but we never got a chance to celebrate, and I don't have a boyfriend. Don't worry, I'm not expecting flowers or chocolates."

"I'm glad. It was all I could do to find an outfit for today."

"You look nice. I was going to ask you if I needed to change for dinner."

"Not at all. You look perfect! We had Marty Jeffers' memorial service today and I really hadn't packed anything suitable for the event."

"Jeffers? The guy from Echo that you fingered for the counterfeit operation?"

"That's him." They got to Karlsson's rental and he tossed her bag on the back seat before opening her door for her. When they were seated inside and the heater was running again, he continued. "Strange turnout. There were about thirty people, none of whom wanted to stand up and say anything nice about him when the reverend asked. Me, and three others were there because it was part of the assignment: The two Secret Service guys and Jenny. Collins was there with his wife, representing Echo, but I don't know who else was there from the company. Other than his ex-wife, I don't think he had much in the way of family or friends."

She put her seatbelt on. "What do you say that we forget about funerals for a while and concentrate on relaxing?"

Karlsson smiled broadly. "I like that. But, there's one small caveat that I need to update you on regarding dinner."

"It's okay. I'm on an expense account."

He laughed. "No. It's a...working dinner. We're dining at a place called Soprek's, but while we're eating, we're providing security for one of the Secret Service guys and a supposed cable technician who bugged, or rather debugged, Marty's house."

She turned in her seat to look at him as he headed towards the exit. "Say that again?"

Karlsson explained the events of the previous twenty-four hours, trying as best as he could to make them both chronological and fathomable. "Suffice to say that there's no guarantee she'll show, but either way, you and I are going to have dinner!"

"And you're sure I'm dressed okay for this place?"

"Got your gun?"

"Of course."

"Then you're dressed just fine." He confirmed.

By the time they pulled into the parking lot behind Soprek's, a wintry mix had begun to fall. At least, that's what the weather people called it when it was a combination of rain, sleet and snow, and they didn't want to go too far out on a ledge to define which would be more plentiful. "I should have asked earlier, but do you have a hotel?"

"Yes. Same one as last time."

He nodded and looked at her playfully. "You mean the one you booked or the one you slept in last time?"

"The one I slept in. Aren't you staying there too?"

"No. I've been at Marty's place out in Moreland Hills, but to be honest, sleeping on the floor has gotten a little painful."

"Well, if you play your cards right, I might give you a new floor to sleep on."

They parked and entered. Like the previous evening, the place was relatively empty. It would not start to fill up until eight, and Karlsson was hoping that they'd be done with whatever it was they were supposed to be doing by then. Marchand's reservation was for six, so they were a bit early. It would give them time to look around and see who looked like they were there for dinner, and who looked like they were there to watch Stan and his date.

⸻ ⟪◉⟫ ⸻

Rolando *Rollie* Mendocino parked his black Ford Explorer near the entrance to the abandoned warehouse off Euclid Avenue. The dilapidated railroad tracks were overgrown and had not been used in years. The gate attached to the eight-foot chain link fence desperately needed repairs, but since the warehouse had been vacant for five years, no one cared. As such the lot had not been plowed, and there was more than a foot of snow on the ground, making it difficult for him to back his vehicle into the loading dock on the west side of the building.

He frowned at the tracks he had made, but figured it was a necessary risk. The sun was still up so he took advantage of the remaining daylight to heft the plastic gasoline cans out of the back and stage them inside. He pushed them into a corner that was already littered with garbage and human waste. The place had obviously been frequented by thrill-seeking juveniles or gangs that needed a place to enrich their spirituality with crystal meth or heroin. No coke in this neighborhood unless it was stolen.

He returned to his truck and started the engine. It was cold, and he had no interest in freezing until the two targets showed up. Besides, he did not want it to look like an ambush. It was just an out-of-the-way place that had been selected to take possession of a safe that had been cut from a wall. His instructions were simple. Look bored, accept the safe, and ask if they would put it in the back of the Ford.

Pretty simple. It was not the type of job that he specialized in, but he had run the same scenario before. The fat Russian guy paid well. But there was no way he was French, like he told everyone. Mendocino wasn't an expert on foreign accents, but having grown up in the streets, he was pretty good at telling the difference between French and Russian. Nevertheless, he had chosen the Explorer because it looked like every other unmarked police vehicle in the area, and when backed in, would give the impression that he was with a law enforcement agency.

He removed the dealer plates his brother-in-law had given him when he borrowed it from his used car lot and affixed the stolen US Government license plates over the brackets with the magnetic attachments. He wouldn't need them for long. They had been snatched six months earlier and even though they were still listed in the system as being stolen, cops in the area had long since quit looking for them. For the two supposed Homeland Security agents, it would look as if they were handing off their item to a government official in order to close out their case. Evidence delivered.

He wanted a cigarette but knew that if they drove up and saw him smoking in a government vehicle; a G-Ride as they were known, then it might tip them off to a possible set-up. So, he just sat and waited.

About ten minutes after six, the sun was setting, and he could see the reflection of their headlights before their Jeep Safari came around the back of the building. He inserted a rubber earplug into each ear and then pulled his knit cap down to cover them up. He did his best to continue looking bored. That was the only way this would work.

There were two of them as promised. The young blond man pulled head-in next to the Explorer and rolled down his window. "Are you Dave?" He asked, somewhat suspiciously.

Mendocino had already lowered his window on their approach. "Yeah. You have something for me?"

The blond driver turned to the occupant and whispered

something that Mendocino couldn't hear, and then replied. "Yes. But why are we here? This seems like a stupid place to meet for this."

Mendocino shrugged. "Who knows? I just go where they tell me to go and do what they tell me to do. How heavy is it?"

After conferring with his partner, the blond replied, "Not bad. Maybe twenty pounds."

Mendocino nodded as he pushed the button under the dash to release the hatch. "Do me a favor, and just throw it in the back."

There were some additional whispers and accompanying shrug. "Yeah. Okay. Just a minute." The blond man hit a button and opened his rear hatch. His passenger got out and walked to the back of the Jeep and then, with a groan, emerged with a bulky item that had been wrapped in a sheet. He walked it around to the back of the Explorer. When he got to the rear and started to set it down, Mendocino lifted the Glock off the seat and fired once into the man's left eye socket. Inside the Explorer, he could feel the concussive effects of the muzzle blast on his face. Rollie was left-handed, so it was an easy shot from the driver's seat. Before the man's surprised partner could respond, he turned and thrust the muzzle of the weapon out the driver's side door and fired a second time, striking Jared M. Farmington in the temple above his left eye.

He was not worried about the noise of the shots. Even if they had been heard by anyone, there were so many shootings each night in this part of town, that residents quit reporting them. He looked at the snow between the vehicles to see where the brass shell casing had been ejected. He could see only one slot in the snow caused when the hot brass casing touched down. The other one must have stayed in the Explorer and could be recovered later. He got out and after reaching into the snow to find it, stuck it in his pants pocket and closed the hatch on the Explorer. He quickly checked on the two men. Satisfied that they were dead, he pulled his car out into the yard in the large tracks made by his now-deceased visitors, before returning to their Jeep. He pulled the driver's body out of the car and then backed it around into the space he had just vacated at the loading dock.

With some effort, he dragged both bodies up the ramp into the warehouse and doused them with the gasoline that he had staged earlier. He placed the Glock in Jared's limp hand, and a gas can in Consterdine's. He reached into his pocket and retrieved the spent shell casing and tossed it between the bodies. When he returned outside, he grabbed the snow shovel out of the back of his Explorer and began to shovel the ramp and the tracks on the dock that he'd left earlier by backing in.

After a half hour, he was tired and decided that he had done as much as he could to temporarily confuse the homicide investigators that would show up later. He couldn't erase all of his tire impressions, but he would get the footprints and drag marks anyway. He was on a flight to Barbados in the morning. The Explorer would be back on his brother-in-law's lot with a *For Sale* sign on it. The murder weapon would be found in Jared's hand, and the gas can would be found gripped in Consterdine's, so detectives would have their hands full trying to determine if it was a murder-suicide or if someone else had staged an elaborate and complex scene.

He went back inside the warehouse and after finding a piece of newspaper in the corner, lit it, and then tossed the makeshift torch onto the bodies. With a seismic *whoosh*, the bodies were engulfed, and the gasoline trail he'd left throughout the first floor immediately caught. Within five minutes, the entire building would be ablaze, and the two bodies would be sufficiently incinerated.

Mendocino walked back to his car and calmly removed the Government license plates. He replaced the dealer tag and carefully drove through the Jeep's tracks into the night. He had been paid a thousand dollars in cash and was told that when he got the safe cut open, he could have any cash or other items of value contained therein. They just wanted the documents and data. He did not know what he would find, but it was going to be a profitable evening any way one looked at it.

Marchand sat at the same table he'd been at the night before and looked across the room to see Karlsson and his date seated one table away from where Jerry and Jenny had been the previous evening. He was fidgety, but not necessarily nervous. If she didn't show, it was no big deal. Officially. They knew who she was, and they could always find her later. But, on a personal note, he wanted her to be there. It would be a confirmation that he could still read people accurately, and that his perceptions of her interest in him were not that far off base.

His brief wait was rewarded. She bounced in like a teenager, dressed in tight blue jeans, high-heeled boots, and a dark cherry turtleneck of a soft wool that accentuated every curve of her athletic body. Her hair was pulled back, providing a glimpse of the simple pearl earrings that spotlighted her smooth skin and angular jawline without being ostentatious in any way.

She was a bit tense, but nonetheless engaging. "Hi! Am I late?"

"Not at all. I just got here myself and haven't even seen a waiter yet."

As if he had been reading their minds, or had the table bugged, the same waiter in the white waistcoat from the previous evening, materialized by their table. "Welcome back folks! I'm glad to see I didn't scare you away last night. Would you like a cocktail, or something from the happy-hour menu to snack on until you decide about dinner?"

Marchand smiled at her. "What do you feel like tonight?"

She smiled at Stan and then the waiter. "I don't know. What do you recommend for confession?"

Ted grinned. "I'm not that good a Catholic, I'm afraid. I am tempted to say a fine bottle of Cabernet; bold and efficacious, and in the right circumstance, tranquilizing and de-inhibiting. On the other hand, if you're trying to quiet the demons of unpardonable sin, there's nothing like one of our martinis."

"I think you talked me into it, Ted." She raised her eyebrows just a bit. "How about a very large, very dry Martini with two olives?" She looked across the table like someone who had just wrecked someone's car. "Stan?"

Stan grinned. "Oh. It's going to be one of *those* kinds of evenings! I guess I'll have the same."

After Ted departed, Stan leaned in close to her. "So, what's got you wrapped tighter than a guitar string?"

She exhaled through tight lips. "Let's wait until we get our drinks. How was the...uh...how did your cousin's service go today?"

Stan was intrigued by her. "It was okay. You know how those things are. People that you haven't seen in years get together and talk about where the time has gone. Everyone wonders why it takes a funeral to being families together. That sort of thing. But thanks for asking. Marty was a strange bird at times, and I guess you never really start to appreciate someone until after they're gone."

"Much of a turnout?"

"I suppose. About thirty people, but I didn't know any of them."

She looked surprised. "You didn't? Your family's not that close?"

Stan fumbled. "Well, yeah. Some of the other cousins, but many of the people were coworkers or friends, and since I don't live in the area, I just said hello and moved on."

"My family has always been a little closer. Sometimes too close if you know what I mean. My parents, aunts and uncles and cousins are all between here and Toledo."

He smiled at her. "Sometimes that's good. But, sometimes, when you're trying to break out of that kid-like role that your elders always put you in, it's better just to put some distance between you."

She nodded. "Yes. There have been a lot of times when I just wanted to be myself, but couldn't get past being someone's daughter, or niece. I worked hard to get where I am, and I sort of resent it when everyone at family gatherings thinks of me as that gangly teenager who couldn't get a date for Homecoming."

"Uh huh." He looked at her sideways with a fake frown. "I don't believe you were ever gangly, or that you couldn't get a date."

"You're sweet, but that's what I left behind."

Ted wandered back to the table and sat the drinks down. "Unless you're in a hurry, I'll give you a minute to work on those and I'll be back to check on you after that."

They toasted and then Tricia took a healthy gulp of the martini and closed her eyes. Marchand wasn't going to rush her. He knew she would open up when she was ready. It didn't take long.

"Listen, we don't know each other that well, and I know that you'll be leaving soon, but I wanted to set the record straight about something. If it is not too much to ask, if I tell you something, can you promise to keep it a secret between us?"

Stan took a savoring sip of the martini and nodded his approval. "Sure. What's up?"

She closed her eyes again as if she was waiting for some type of sign from the universe. "I'm not really a cable installer. I am a...a contractor."

"You build houses?" Stan replied, feigning surprise.

"Not that kind of contractor. When I left the Air Force, I wasn't sure what I wanted to do and Jared, the guy I was with at your cousin's house, mentioned that he was doing contract work for Homeland Security. Several of us had clearances and needed work after leaving the military, so we signed up."

"You mean, the US Government? The Department of Homeland Security?"

"Yes."

"That's a pretty big group. Coast Guard, Customs...US Secret Service. Aren't they all part of Homeland Security?"

"Yes, but we started out in NCS...the, uh, old National Communications System office. In 2012, Obama merged the group into the Office of Emergency Communications. Anyway, we'd get called in for different jobs relating to communications and it seemed like we were working for a variety of agencies at any given time."

She took another sip of her drink. "It was fun for a while, but then it started getting weird."

"Weird? In what way?" Stan probed.

"I can't go there right now. Stuff that would blow your mind!" She took another sip. "We started out helping federal agencies with wiretaps...you know, with warrants. Then it just, sort of escalated into some bizarre network intrusions that left me wondering what we were doing. Anyway, I want to get out of that. I want to get back to living a normal life and meeting someone, y'know, more normal." She looked up questioningly. "I know. This probably doesn't make any sense."

Stan tried his best to sound open and objective. "Okay, but what does that have to do with us?"

She looked at him as if she was slightly flustered that she had to spell it out. "Stan, I wasn't at your cousin's house to work on his cable. Your cousin was involved in something that had national security implications, and we were looking for something."

Stan hadn't felt this alive in years. He missed this type of intrigue. "You were looking for something in Marty's house? What?"

She downed her drink and closed her eyes again. "Evidence that he might have been doing business with a foreign power."

Stand regarded her for a moment and believed that she was being as truthful as she dared. But he needed to string her along a bit more. What she was saying made perfect sense to him, but as far as he knew, the Secret Service had the lead on this case, and he couldn't help but wonder where she or her group could be fitting in. If it was the Secret Service making the request, someone would have told Jerry Lee or him by now. They were too far into the investigation. He smiled compassionately. "You think my cousin was a spy or something? What kind of evidence did you have of that? The family would be absolutely shocked if that were true."

Ted was at their table again. "Have you had enough time to look at the menu, or could I get you another cocktail?"

"Definitely another cocktail." She replied. "And a steak, medium rare. Baked potato and some mushrooms on the side."

Stan was impressed with her purposiveness. "I guess, I'll have the same. Medium rare."

Ted nodded and moved swiftly away. He seemed to be a good judge of non-verbal communication. When he was out of earshot, Stan pushed for more information, but offered the appearance of being naïve to such things. "So, you were working for the FBI?"

She shook her head. "No. This assignment came from the US Attorney's Office."

"The US…" As a golf club salesman, he wasn't supposed to know about such things as the federal legal system. "The what?"

"The US Attorney. They are the ones who prosecute matters of foreign espionage and apparently, they had reason to believe that Marty was somehow involved in something. They must have had a warrant, or we wouldn't have gotten the assignment."

He didn't have Jerry's depth of knowledge about the case, but he was certain that between the Washington Headquarters and the Cleveland Field Office of the United States Secret Service, someone in the US Attorney's Office, other than the AUSA who was already assigned out of Washington, would have to have known about their investigation, and would have told them if they were going to run a wiretap at the Moreland Hills residence. And, if that were the case, who wanted the wiretap, and for what reason. Even though the integrity of the FISA Courts had been widely criticized, there still had to be some level of coordination between agencies and offices.

"Which US Attorney?" Stan spouted, unable to control his interest.

She brought the glass to her lips and stopped, as she looked across the table at him without expression. "Why? Do you know someone down there?"

Stan quickly recovered. "Uh…no. Of course not. But if someone is bugging my conversations, I'd like to know why." He tried to sound as nonchalant as possible. "I mean, Marty's been dead for several days. Why bug his house now?"

"We weren't really bugging it. We were…" She finally moved the glass to her lips. "We were taking one out."

Stan looked at her warmly. The woman was trying to be as honest as she could with him. That meant, if her sincerity was to be believed, that she was really interested in him on a personal level. He knew that there was more to get from her, but there was no sense rushing it and shutting her down. He needed time.

"You know, last night was the first time I danced with anyone in twenty years."

She grinned. "Well, me too. I didn't know there were places like this that still had dance floors."

He raised his glass to her. "Then, I'll tell you what. If you're not planning to arrest me on some charge of selling illegal golf clubs, maybe we could have a quiet dinner and a dance or two?"

"Then what?" She smiled somewhat seductively.

He smiled back. "Then we'll go back to Marty's house, find a blanket, and see if his cable TV still works. Or if I'll have to call another technician."

<hr />

Forty feet away, Karlsson and Biehn were on their second round of drinks and had just ordered an eastern European version of Coq au vin, a chicken in wine sauce recipe that their waiter said was the best in the Midwest. Made with chickens so tender that one would think they jumped into the pan voluntarily.

Jackie stirred her Cosmopolitan with the piece of lime, an indication that she was deep in thought. "So, Lu is driving back to Chicago tonight to resume her job, and Jerry is headed back to China to pick up where he left off with Zhou?"

Karlsson nodded. "Yep. Jerry's riding with her as far as Chicago and flying out of O'Hare."

She looked at her drink, a load on her mind. "And based upon what you found in the safe, you think that Jeffers' father and uncle were lawfully employed at NASA in some sort of exchange program with the Soviets? And, that the uncle might have actually been inside the Apollo one spacecraft when it blew?"

"Yep. That's our speculation so far."

"But, until we find our missing LEM for sure, or a living witness, we won't know who landed one on the moon."

"That's about the size of it, near as we can tell." Karlsson conceded.

"How much have you told Collins?"

"None of this. I assumed it's classified, and he certainly doesn't have a need to know. I told them who their counterfeiter was and walked them through what was going on inside their company. I offered them some insight into who might be involved. Unless something of national security importance pops up that implicates more of their people, then that's that."

Karlsson lifted his Old Fashioned and softly swirled the contents around. "Zhou is into a lot of western industry. Not just Echo. Jerry is going to try to bait him into several deals that will help us identify who some of his partners are over here. But, even if we shut them down, I'm afraid that there'll be dozens more taking their place by the next business day."

"And, as you said, that's just part of the Chinese problem. We don't know for certain yet if the Russians are also involved. Or to what extent."

He was surprised that she was talking business this openly in a public place and nodded as the waiter approached with their dinner. If it tasted as good as it smelled, they were in for a treat. But, in deference to her usual reluctance to discuss ultra-secret matters in an open area, they kept their remaining dinner conversation simple, and confined their discussion to more light-hearted fare such as loves lost, opportunities missed and what people do with their lives after government service. As they finished dinner, they saw Marchand and Tricia get up to dance.

"When was the last time you danced?" Karlsson asked her.

"Hell. I don't remember. It's been a while!"

"Care to give it a try?"

She hesitated for just a moment before he added, "Oh come on. It's business. We're supposed to be providing security for a teammate. If we look stupid, we'll just have another drink afterwards and agree not to talk about it."

She rolled her eyes and stood. Karlsson took her hand as they walked to the dance floor and then easily fell into the beat of the song. It was surprisingly fun. Both of them smiled naturally and an observer might have thought they were perfect for each other. When the band switched to a slower number, it took them a moment to figure out where hands and bodies should connect. Karlsson was six-foot-four, almost a foot taller than his partner.

She moved in closer and rested her head on his chest. "Don't get the wrong idea. I'm just doing this to get a better view of our surroundings. You're so damn tall, I can't see around you."

"Very funny." He said as he stepped back and raised her right arm so that she could spin underneath. At the end of the turn, he brought her back closer and kissed her ear. "Just staying in character."

The song ended and the band moved right into *Someone to Watch Over Me*, a 1926 song by George and Ira Gershwin that had been performed by dozens of different artists over many decades. She looked up into his eyes. "Cute! Is this going to be our song?"

Karlsson laughed. "It's certainly appropriate tonight." Whether it was the alcohol or the carefree ambiance, they twirled around the dance floor to the point that they almost forgot what they were doing there. At the end of the song, they applauded the band and then Karlsson saw Tricia head for the restroom as Stan returned to the table. "Well, there she goes. You're up!"

Karlsson returned to his table and sat down, just as the text from Marchand came across his screen. "I NEED THE HOUSE TONIGHT. CAN YOU FIND A ROOM AND CALL ME IN THE MORNING?"

Karlsson could not keep from glancing over at Stan, who was trying to restrain a grin, and nodded with a polite smirk. He texted back, "NO WORRIES. CALL ME IF U NEED ME."

He finished his drink and listened to the band do a reasonable rendition of a movie love theme about a sinking ship and had it on his mind when Jackie returned from the ladies room.

After seating herself, she spoke softly. "She peed, she wiped, she washed her hands. If she did anything else, I didn't see it."

"Fair enough." He smiled and gestured at the band. "I liked this movie. Great film score by James Horner." He slid his cell phone across the table to Jackie, with the text from Marchand still up. "It reminds me of the Law of the Sea."

Jackie read the text and then pushed the phone back to him. "The law of the sea?"

He grinned. "Yeah. The 1982 United Nations Convention. It says that the master of a ship is required to render assistance to any person found at sea who is in danger of being lost."

"What?" She looked at him with mock disdain, as an elementary school teacher might, confronting a student who just brought a dead frog to class for a science project.

"Stan needs the house for official business tonight, and I don't have a place to stay. I could freeze out there if you leave me."

CHAPTER 16

K arlsson and Biehn paid their check and started for the parking lot when they saw Marchand paying his. He started his car up to let it run for a while. The temperature had dropped, and light flurries were falling. "We might as well sit for a moment and see if they take one car or two." He suggested.

"Why do I feel like a high school girl on a date with a guy who has a bad reputation?" She leaned over towards him.

A smile formed on the corner of his mouth. "Maybe because you haven't met a really bad guy before." He kissed her lightly and then she opened her mouth and they moved closer towards each other. They stayed in the passionate embrace, touching, and kissing until he saw Marchand and Tricia walk towards their cars.

"Damn. Show time again." He said, unafraid to hide his frustration.

She looked at the dashboard and punched through the options on the environmental controls until she found the button to switch from heat to defrost. "The windows are starting to steam, Mr. Karlsson. I'd hate to miss something important." She smoothed her hair and added, "Out there."

Karlsson could tell that Marchand's practiced skills or innate magnetism were working. They both got into their cars and she followed him out. If they were saying goodnight, they would have lingered longer at her door. Both cars turned out of the parking lot the same direction and seemed to be heading back to Interstate seventy-seven south, where Karlsson let them go.

"You think he'll be all right?" She asked watching the cars move out of view.

"Seriously?" He grinned at her. "He protected presidents and other heads of state for twenty-five years. I'm guessing he can take care of himself if it comes to that."

"What about you?" She asked softly. "What were you doing for twenty-five years?"

He didn't want to take his eyes off the road but risked a quick glance in her direction. It was the conversation he had been dreading. "Just the opposite."

Her eyes stayed on him. "The opposite? What's the opposite of protection?

It seemed like they covered a mile or two before he finally answered her. "I really like you, Jackie. I don't want to lie to you, but for obvious reasons I can't tell you the whole truth. I'm a soldier. I get paid to fight wars, not to keep other people alive. Your boss must have understood that distinction when he spoke to my boss about putting me on this assignment. I'm not the guy they send in to deliver food or provide first aid to the oppressed and downtrodden. I'm the guy they send in when all other means of stabilizing a situation have failed."

She stared at him silently. When she didn't speak, he continued. "Look at it this way: when the police show up at a house during a hostage situation, some officers are assigned to talk the bad guy out. Others are assigned to take the bad guy out if he refuses to cooperate, and he represents a continuing threat of harm to other persons. The same rules apply to civilians who carry concealed weapons. They're only allowed to use those weapons in defense of their own lives or in defense of another life, if serious physical harm becomes imminent."

He saw his exit approaching and flipped down his turn signal. "The same rules apply to me. I don't have some fictional James-Bond-license-to-kill status. When the US government, usually the Defense Department, sees an imminent threat to our country, or specific persons within our country or our allies, they dispatch the military if it's going to be a public action. If they don't want an official use of force broadcast in the media, they use one of us."

"You kill people?"

He nodded. "I have. Yeah."

"In combat."

"Yes, depending on how you define combat. Sometimes, the President needs to use force of some kind; flex his military muscle for one reason or another. He calls the Pentagon, and the Joint Chiefs mull it over and decide what kind of plan makes sense. They issue orders to one or more of the armed services to achieve the objective and that gets communicated to generals, who order colonels to send majors and captains into battle with their troops. Based on an approved battle plan, someone gets bombed, someone might get extracted...and sometimes, someone gets shot."

She was still silent, so he kept talking. "To the private or corporal taking the shot, it doesn't matter how he or she got the job, or whether or not the United States exhausted all other possible resolutions to the crisis of the day. When the time comes, he or she pulls the trigger, and the unit moves on. In my case, it's the same battles, but the middlemen have been removed. I work for a guy in Washington who gets his orders from the President. Sometimes he gets his orders from Congress. But, regardless, it's not up to me to ask any questions that aren't germane to my assignment. I don't run the government. I just get a paycheck from them."

They exited the freeway and turned onto the street where her hotel was located. She looked out the side window at the lights of downtown Cleveland. "How many...uh, where..."

"I've been defending my country in one capacity or another for almost forty years. The where's, when's and how-many's aren't important anymore."

She nodded slowly as they turned into the parking lot and headed for the garage. After he backed into a parking space, he put the car in park and asked. "Well, Ms. Biehn, have I worn out my welcome?"

She shivered briefly, and then smiled at him. "Not at all, Mr. Karlsson. Besides, the Law of the Sea. I can't leave a comrade-in-arms stranded in the middle of Cleveland on a freezing night!"

Stan pressed the button on his garage door opener but parked outside in the driveway on the same side as Marty's Lexus. Perhaps it was his experience taking over or some sort of obsessive-compulsive symptom, but he did not want to be blocked in if he had to leave in a hurry. He got out of his car and locked it and then waved her in. "You can park on that side if you want. I don't know how much snow we're getting tonight, and it would be easier on both of us if we didn't have to scrape it off later."

She laughed as she slowly and carefully pulled in and shut the car off. "I've heard about you guys. You trap young girls in your garage and then force them into a pit in your basement."

"Yeah." He opened her door for her, as the garage door whirred its way back down. "You were in my basement yesterday. If there was a pit, you'd have found it!"

She stood and looked at him with a smile. He took the opportunity to kiss her lightly on the cheek, and then moved around to her mouth. She reciprocated and moved close against him. It had been a while for him, and he wanted to put business behind them and just spend an evening wrapped in her arms. Even if it did not result in sex, he knew that it would fill a void in his soul that had been developing for months. Years.

"Are you going to invite me in, or are we going to spend the night in your garage?"

He smiled. "Yeah. Come on in and I'll...."

"Give me the tour?" She laughed. "Been there!"

"Yeah, okay. I can at least show you where Marty kept his liquor. I bet you didn't spend much time in there on your search!"

He followed her inside and watched her move in the tight blue jeans. It reminded him of a trip to the zoo with his kids many years earlier. He watched the leopards and panthers move across their confines and marveled at the impressive musculature beneath their smooth skin. So powerful, yet seemingly docile on the surface.

When they got into the kitchen, he looked at her face in the bright light. She was beautiful. He had thought that even before the drinks at Soprek's. She was divine. "Another martini?"

"Hmmm..." She tilted her head. "Did your cousin have any wines?"

"Oh yeah." He replied and led her into the den where a small wine rack contained a variety of reds, whites and blushes.

"It's too cold for a chilled white tonight. Might I recommend something in a Cabernet or perhaps a red Zinfandel?"

She looked around briefly at Marty's office and focused momentarily on the print that until recently, had concealed the safe. The picture had been re-hung over the hole and the drywall mess had been cleaned up. They knelt down on the plush carpet and looked at the wines in the rack. She pulled out a couple and then saw one that she liked, simply because of the design of the label. "How about a Malbec?"

"Okay." He said and took it to the island in the kitchen. He found the corkscrew in the second drawer that he searched. "Look up there and find some glasses." He gestured at one of the cupboards near the sink.

"Wow! Your cousin must've known wine. There are all kinds of glasses up here. Which one goes with Malbec?"

"No fucking idea." Stan replied instinctively. "I don't know anything about wines, but I'm guessing it's the fatter ones there."

She stood on her tiptoes and started to pull two of the glasses in the back around from behind two others. After the martinis, she wasn't quite as agile as she might have liked and moved the white wine glasses out of the way before sliding the other ones forward. When she did, a key slid out and clanged across the granite counter. Stan's reflexes were razor sharp and he snagged it before it slid off the counter.

"Extra house key?" she asked as she took the glasses and sat them on the island near the bottle he had just opened.

Stan quickly looked at the key and noted the *Best* name stamped in it. It was for the same type of lock that was installed in the secret compartment in the cedar closet. "Yeah, must be." He certainly did not want to draw any attention to it at this point and knew that he would have plenty of time later to find out for sure. He tossed it back up in the cupboard. "It ain't mine and I don't care." He laughed. "The only thing I want to open up tonight is about three feet away from me."

"Are you a pig?" she giggled.

"It depends on who you ask. Do you like Florida?" He poured the Malbec into the two glasses and twisted the cork back into the bottle.

She took the proffered glass and toasted him. "Yeah, I kinda do. Are you inviting me down to see your golf course?"

A momentary pang of guilt came over him and he wondered if she would like Texas instead. "Golf courses are the same everywhere you go. Some are challenging and some aren't. But if you play the game right and know your clubs and your swing, you can play any of them."

"You'll teach me?" Her nostrils flared slightly as she sniffed her wine.

"Absolutely. I don't know if you'll end up liking the game or not, but I can assure you that you'll learn the right way to swing."

"Oh God! Does everything about golf have to have some sexual connotation?"

He smiled at her and moved closer. "You should know that my driver has a long offset and a relatively stiff shaft."

She took another sip of her wine and shook her head. "You are so full of shit!"

"I'm glad you recognized it. Grab your drink and follow me." He led her into the family room and flipped on the TV.

"You're a cable girl. What would you like to watch?"

"I'm a fake cable girl, and I don't care what we watch. Find a music channel and throw a blanket on the floor. I'm not an easy lay, but I wouldn't mind just kicking back and relaxing for a few minutes. We have something called snuggling up here."

"I'm familiar with it. We do it in the south, but we don't wear as much clothing as you do up here."

Stan turned the lights down and tossed some cushions onto the floor next to her. She had taken her boots off, and looked innocently seductive, lying on her side, her head resting in one hand and the other holding up the edge of the blanket for him to crawl under. He slid in next to her and put his arms around her. She kissed him once and then rolled on top of him and rested her head on his chest.

"Not that it changes anything for us tonight, but were you being honest when you said you weren't married?"

"Divorced. About fifteen years now." He answered honestly. "You? Have you ever been married?"

"I was once. It didn't last long. He was a nice guy, but he couldn't deal with my deployments. It seemed like we were apart more than we were together, and he eventually lost interest or something."

"Or something?"

She sighed pensively. "He married a friend of mine, if you must know."

"Sorry." He gave her a small hug and kissed her neck. Her fragrance was stimulating and with the closeness of their bodies, he was immediately excited.

Their hands maneuvered around the various ridges, bumps, and valleys of each other's beings and before long they were out of their clothes and were sweating profusely. After a long while, when their vital resigns returned to normal, Stan remarked, "That's how we snuggle in the south."

She laughed. "In the north too. I just didn't want you to think I was being forward."

He grabbed their wine glasses from the coffee table, which had been moved out of the way to make room for the play area. After each had managed a sip or two, he returned them and then slid under the blanket with her again. The held each other quietly for a few minutes and then Stan glanced at his watch. "Hey, would you mind if we caught the news? I'd like to see basketball scores."

"You've just had hot steamy sex with the woman of your dreams, and you want to see basketball scores?"

Stan grinned widely. "Yeah, when you put it that way, it does seem kind of insensitive and shallow." He found the remote and switched over to a local network broadcast. "But what if I hold you tenderly while they're..."

"Our lead story this hour is a four-alarm warehouse fire off of Euclid Avenue that has left two men dead, and homicide detectives baffled."

Tricia sat up so quickly that the blanket slid off, exposing her breasts. Transfixed by the report, she subconsciously reached down to pull it back up around her.

Marchand looked at the screen and then back at her. She had grown suddenly pale. "What's the matter?"

"Jared."

"Farmington?" He responded impulsively.

"Yes." She waved her hand at him. "Shhh..."

"We take you now to Channel Nine's Melinda Macarthur for more." The coverage shifted to the location feed from Euclid Avenue, and the young reporter in mittens and a dark parka with the station's logo over the left breast. "Thanks Bob. What we know so far from Battalion Chief Thad Wiggins is that at approximately six thirty this evening the fire department responded to a call of smoke billowing from this address. On arrival, they found the first floor of this two-story warehouse fully involved. Second and third alarms were sent, and firefighters say that it took them nearly an hour to bring this blaze under control."

She gestured over her right shoulder. "Once the building was safe to enter, their search uncovered the bodies of two males, who had apparently been shot at some point before the fire. Police are not speculating as to whether or not these two men were involved in starting the fire and are considering the possibility that the arsonist may have fled the scene in a second vehicle. One detective, who asked not to be identified indicated that the fire may have been started to conceal the murders or other criminal activity, because this warehouse has been vacant for nearly five years."

"The bodies have not yet been positively identified, but police say they did find an electronic access card for the Celebreeze

Federal building in the glove compartment of a car left at the scene and will be interviewing state and federal officials to see who the ID card belonged to."

The anchor seemed as interested as the viewers. "Any idea, Melinda, who these two men were? Do we know anything else about them?"

"Not at this time. Although police are fairly certain that robbery was not a motive. Both men's wallets were found on them at the time of discovery. However, names are being withheld pending no-tifications of family members. Back to you."

"Well, there you have it. Fire in a warehouse on the east side that police are still investigating. We'll stay on this folks and update you if we learn anything else during our broadcast. In Washington today..."

"I have to make a call." Tricia said, looking for her underwear.

"What's going on?" Stan found his shorts and slipped into them.

"Hold on just a sec." She found Jared's contact file and dialed his number. It rang through to his voicemail and she hung up. "No, no, no!"

"Talk to me. What's the matter?"

"It's Jared. I know it is!"

"How do you know that? What would he be doing at an abandoned warehouse on a shit side of town? This time of day?"

She put her head in her hands and began to weep. "What have I done? Oh God, what have I done?"

Stan had a good idea as to what had gripped her but needed to hear it from her. "Okay, stop for a minute. Take a deep breath and then tell me what's going on."

"Oh my God." She shook her head. "I am so fucked."

"Tricia! Talk to me!"

She was shaking, so Stan put his arm around her. Her reaction was genuine. It took a while for her to muster the courage to say what had been on her mind.

"I told you that I really liked you. I'd really like the opportunity to get to know you better. You believe that don't you?" She looked up.

"Yeah. Of course. Why wouldn't I?"

After a while she spoke softly. "Jared got another call from that US Attorney. He said that we had to come back for the safe. It was the only part of the house that we couldn't search. He said how important it was, and that it couldn't wait. So...Jared came back in here last night while I was with you. He's the one who took your safe. Marty's safe."

Stan was not sure how to respond. She knew they had taken the safe out of the wall, and she'd obviously seen that the den had been cleaned up. She would have known that he was aware of the theft. "The US Attorney told you guys to break in here, and steal the safe?"

"Yes. I didn't want to be a part of it. I told Jared that I was going to be seeing you, and that I didn't want any part of it. He said that it was probably a good idea to keep you busy for the evening so they could get in and out. But Stan," She looked at him again, "I wasn't on the job with you last night. Or, tonight for that matter. I'm with you because I wanted to be with you. Jared knew that and that's why he used a different guy to help him break in."

He hugged her close to him but was at a temporary loss for the right words. "Which US Attorney? I can't help you if I don't have a name."

Whether it was the words he chose, or the way he uttered them, it brought about a reaction. There was an eerie silence before she began to add things up. "You said Farmington."

"What?" His brow furrowed.

"When I said Jared, you said Farmington. I never told you Jared's last name."

She backed away from him slowly. "I never told you Jared's last name. How did you know?"

She had him. It was going to come out one way or the other this evening, but he had to try to keep it together for a moment longer. "Uh...they said it on the news broadcast."

"No, they didn't. They said the bodies hadn't been positively identified. Just that they found their wallets and an access card for the Federal Building. How did you know his last name?"

"I need the name of the US Attorney!" Stan repeated sternly, ignoring her question.

She seemed to look through him. Beyond him. The beautiful sapphire eyes were suddenly cold. "Who are you? You're not a fucking golf club salesman from Florida."

He shook his head. "US Secret Service."

Her lip quivered as she backed away from him and tried to think of something to say.

Stan continued with compassion in his voice. "Look, whether you're remembered as a dedicated professional who did what she had to do to defend her country, or an inmate in a federal penitentiary; serving time for involvement in a break-in, two murders and unspecified acts of foreign espionage, depends on you giving me the name of the fucking US Attorney who assigned you to this case."

"You fucking asshole!" It was not rage in her eyes. Or fear. They were more like the eyes of the cat being backed into a corner by the homeowner's Labrador retriever. She wasn't sure of her next move. Her brain was working in high-speed overtime, but logic told her she had to cooperate. "I don't know. I never met him."

Stan held his ground. "Bullshit! Tell me his name."

"Jared used to call him the *puny peepee*. A small, frail guy. It was Peter something."

"That's not the US Attorney that's been assigned to our case. Where is he from? Cleveland?"

"Yes. We got our instructions locally. He's the one that got us the cable van."

"Try harder!" He commanded.

"Peter something...uh...Pennington...wait...Pasternak! Peter Pasternak!"

Jerry had driven most of the way from Cleveland, but they had stopped in Merrillville, Indiana for a bite to eat and to change their wrist watches to Central time. Jenny Lu took over the driving chore for the last hour of the trip to O'Hare and even though it was well before midnight, she was exhausted. So much had happened in the previous week, and she was fatigued by thoughts of what the upcoming weeks would bring.

She was scheduled to return to work the next morning, but she couldn't focus on that until she had a chance to check her private cell phone for messages from Zhou. Something inside her head told her that everything would work out satisfactorily, but the intuitive part of her brain kept recalling a Robert Frost poem about having miles to go. She had to keep breaking her problems down into individual elements so that she could solve each one independently and move on. Call Zhou first, re-acclimate herself to work tomorrow, and then contact Echo when she had something of interest to report to them. Easy peezy.

They were northbound on I-294, just past the Fashion Outlet, and she slowed when she saw the signs for O'Hare. On the dashboard, the outside temperature read 11 degrees. It had dropped two degrees since they left Merrillville. Jerry seemed deep in thought and stared out the passenger side window.

With her EZ-Pass device she was able to roll through the toll booth and merge into the O'Hare lane. "What time is your flight?" she asked to break the silence.

"Twelve forty." He said as his brain snapped back to the present. "Straight through to Shanghai. Fifteen and a half hours. I'm going to be tired and smelly by the time I land."

"Zhou knows you're coming?" She asked.

"Yeah. As a matter of fact, he is going to have someone meet me at the airport and make sure I get through Customs with his two hundred grand."

"And he bought the story that you worked up?"

"Yeah. Apparently. He promised me product if I'd do a favor for him, and now that he thinks I'm trustworthy, and paying cash, he's eager to help me build my business."

"Aren't you a little frightened?"

Jerry looked back out the window before answering. "I have the normal anxiety you get any time you work a case like this. But I was there for eighteen months and have a pretty good idea of when they're being straight with me. My biggest concern is if the two hundred grand US, that I'm giving him, are the same bills that he paid Marty with. That would get me killed. But we're banking on the hope that the bulk of the money we found in Marty's closet came from elsewhere. Someone other than Zhou."

"What are you getting shipped?" She was naturally curious and had not been admitted to the Secret Service discussion that centered on what would be in the shipments and where they would be directed.

Jerry trusted her, at least more than the government did. "Most of it is everyday consumer products. But there are several large shipments of computer motherboards. For some reason, he's anxious to get these into the US economy, and my idea of having them shipped into several different ports seemed to appeal to him."

"They're not all going to San Francisco?"

"No. Some will. We want the shipments to go to Miami, New York, LA, and Houston so that we can get a better idea of his contacts over here. By breaking them into smaller loads from China, it'll be easier to track who handles them in different parts of the country. He's fixing me up with the middlemen in each location. We look at it as a chance to bring down more of his network, rather than just him."

She nodded. "You know I'll do my part when the time comes?"

Jerry looked at her. "I do. Thank you. A lot of this project hinges on your ability to get him over here for a meeting. Your work on Layden's campaign may be just the thing we need. Without presenting him an opportunity to meet face-to-face with a presidential candidate, I'm not sure we can get him out of China."

She saw the sign for O'Hare Departures, and changed lanes. "Do you know when you'll be back in the States?"

"Huh uh. Could be a week or so. Maybe more. Are you going to be okay?"

She smiled. "Yes. I need to work through some things, but I think I'm going to be all right."

She got behind a line of cars that were dropping passengers off in front of various airline gates at the International terminal. "Listen, I just wanted to thank you again for all you did to help me... you know."

"I know." He touched her arm with his left hand as his right reached down to release his seat belt. "For what it's worth, the Service will go to bat for you. There won't be any criminal charges, and I'm pretty sure your name will never come up again publically in connection with the case."

She pulled to the curb and put her flashers on. "Uhmm...the lawyer told me that I'm the sole heir to his estate. So, depending on how this ends, you always have an open invitation back at my new house in Moreland Hills. I'm supposed to go back to Cleveland when my schedule permits and meet him for the official reading of Marty's will. I'll be arranging to have someone keep the place clean and get the snow shoveled, but you're welcome to use it when you like."

Jerry leaned across and kissed her lightly on the lips. "I'd like that. I think we should make a date. Say, six weeks from now, after this blows over."

"Yeah." She squeezed his thigh. "I'll look forward to that."

Jerry opened the door and momentarily shivered as the cold air and brisk wind sent a shock through his body. He grabbed his duffel off the back seat and closed the door. He leaned back in the front. "I'll see you in six weeks." He closed the door and headed towards the terminal entrance, feeling a sense of loneliness and loss. But there were miles to go, and he needed to focus on his mission. As he got to the automatic doors of the terminal, he watched her drive out of sight into the cold, windy night, flurries bouncing off the trunk of her car.

In ancient Egypt, it was rumored that a Pharaoh wanted to bury the body of an adversary in a place that would never again be found. He assigned a team of slaves to take the body into the desert, and once the remains had been disposed of, soldiers then killed the slaves. Upon their return to the court, the soldiers who slayed the slaves were themselves killed to assure that the location of the grave would be forever hidden.

It was after midnight when Rollie Mendocino looked out the window of his brother-in-law's garage to see the white Honda Accord drive onto the lot. The single male occupant alighted from the vehicle and walked towards the door. With the bright shop lights on in the garage, and only a few lights illuminating the lot, Rollie was not able to discern the man's face, but knew he had to be the one that the fat Russian was sending for the material he'd recovered. He opened the door, and then quickly looked past him to see if there was anyone else watching from the street.

The man was in his fifties, older than what he had expected for someone making late-night pickups of stolen material. His face was hard. His hands were rough. "I am expected?" He said in heavily accented English.

Rollie let him in and looked once more into the night. He was excited about what he had found in the safe. It would make the trip to Barbados that much more pleasant.

The man was not that tall, barely six feet, but solidly built as if he'd earned a living as a laborer of some sort. He walked to the work bench at the far end of the garage as Rollie closed the door behind them.

"This is it?" He quietly asked as he looked at the metal filings scattered around the work surface and adjacent floor area. The circular saw had generated quite a mess.

"That's it." Rollie replied. "Ten thousand in cash, a manila envelope that's still sealed, and that flash drive."

The stranger handed Rollie a white business envelope, and Rollie quickly opened it and counted out the ten one-hundred-dollar bills.

He stuffed it in his inside jacket pocket. "You get the papers and I get the cash, right?"

"Right. I take documents and safe. You keep cash." He leaned closer to examine the two halves of the safe, which lay open on their sides. "Any trouble?"

"No trouble. Just like you planned it."

"Where is gun? He inquired looking around the bench.

"They told me to leave it with the bodies. No fingerprints."

"What about ammunition?"

"I wore gloves when I loaded the magazine." He said, a bit annoyed that someone would challenge his professionalism.

"Good. You have box?"

"Box?" Rollie looked at the safe and back up. "Yeah. There has to be something around here that you can fit it into."

Rollie looked around the shop and found a corrugate box that had originally contained a shipment of auto parts and returned to the bench.

"Thank you." The man said as he hefted the two halves of the safe into the empty container and stuffed the large manila envelope in along one of the sides. "You..." the foreigner suddenly looked up towards the ceiling. "What is..."

As Rollie involuntarily looked up, the man's fist smashed deep into Rollie's windpipe. Rollie collapsed to his knees in pain and surprise, as the visitor somewhat mechanically picked up the hammer off the bench and smashed it into the top of his head. Rollie fell backwards, his legs under him. And as he lay in the filth on the garage floor, semi-consciously gasping his last breath, he could feel the man reach inside his jacket and retrieve the envelope. He could sense the man walk towards the door, with the box in his hands. And, with his eyes closed in unconscious confusion, he knew at that instant that this must have been a bigger deal than he had imagined, and that he wouldn't be on the plane to Barbados.

The powerful stranger sat the box on the floor and donned his gloves before opening the door. He used his body to hold the door open against the wind, as he moved through it and carried the box and contents back to his car. With the thousand dollars he had been given and the ten thousand he'd recovered, still in the mustard-colored bank band, it was truly a profitable evening, indeed.

〜〜〜《《①》》〜〜〜

Jenny got back to her apartment well after midnight. She checked her mailbox in the lobby and yanked out the volume of junk mail that had arrived in her absence. An electric bill and some other nonsense, but everything could wait until the next morning. She had to check her other phone to see how many times Zhou had called.

When she got inside, she turned on the lights and looked around. Things were as she had left them a week earlier when she'd headed out in haste towards Cleveland. She threw her suitcase down on the floor at the foot of her bed and reached between the mattress and box springs to find her phone. She turned it on and looked for a charging cable. She knew the battery had to be low and wanted to make sure the call did not drop out when she was speaking to Zhou.

When it had booted up, she looked in relief at the screen when she noted that no one had left any messages for her. The only in-bound calls had been robo-spam calls that she knew were nothing more than feeble attempts to talk her out of credit card or other personal information. Following the protocol, she dialed the number that she knew would be answered by a subordinate and left a message. As she waited for the call back, she busied herself dumping her dirty clothes into the hamper by the washer and then checking the refrigerator to see what had spoiled in her absence. It was only ten minutes later when she got her call back.

"You are back from Cleveland, my dear?" Said the sickening voice, seven thousand miles away.

"Yes. It needed to be done." He wasn't offering any human concern in his voice, so she decided to reciprocate with the same lack of emotion.

After a moment, Zhou asked, "Was it a big attendance?"

"Excuse me? You mean Marty's funeral?"

"Of course. Did you see anyone that you knew?"

She could not tell if he was baiting her or if he might have known someone else who would be there. "No, but I met his ex-wife. We got on quite well if you want to know the truth."

"Of course. That is why you and I work so well together. You get on well with everyone. Will you be returning to Cleveland any time soon?"

"I doubt it. Not for a few weeks. I have work to do at the agency. Marty's attorney has some papers for me to sign, but there's no hurry. It would seem that he didn't have any other relatives."

"Ah. Yes." She could tell that he was smoking, the exhalation occurring over the mouthpiece of the phone. "So, you are prepared to pick up where you left off?"

"Of course." She mustered all of the personal strength she could find in her after the long drive. "The plans have not changed. I will let you know what his schedule is, and keep you updated as often as seems appropriate. Unless you would like to speak more frequently?"

"No. That is fine. This is important to us both, so let me know when you have something to report."

"There is a possibility of a meeting with him, or someone high up on his staff, soon. They are looking for sizeable campaign donations from a variety of sources and want to develop key contacts in foreign governments. At some point, there could be a way to introduce you and open the channels of communications you spoke of."

Zhou was silent for a moment. "Will he be travelling to China before the election?"

"I probably won't know until after the convention. Once I see the schedule tomorrow, I can be more specific as to possible dates and locations. If you find a date or a city that is convenient for you, I will work to make that happen. You will need some sort of official trade cover."

Zhou took another draw on his cigarette and exhaled a plume

of smoke towards the ceiling. "That is not a problem. I will begin working on that from this end. We will talk again soon."

She ended the call and made sure the phone charger was secure. The bait was in the trap. Now it was up to Jerry to set the trap properly. The Secret Service needed Zhou in the United States so they could arrest him. As she began sorting her laundry, she thought about how well that would work out for her too.

Golovkin heard his cell phone buzz on the nightstand. It was close to one o'clock in the morning and he sincerely hoped that it was good news. He squinted to see a fuzzy text from a number in the 216-area code. He put his glasses on and looked at the simple message. "IT IS DONE. NO PROBLEMS." His contact in Cleveland was communicating on an untraceable, prepaid *burn phone*, as they were known.

He replied an even simpler "SPASIB" and then deleted the message. He returned his phone to the nightstand next to his bed and placed his folded reading glasses next to it. He stared at the ceiling in the darkness of his home, his wife snoring peacefully beside him. Once the Americans identified the bodies in the warehouse, it would not be long before the trail led back to his protégé. Hopefully, the government attorney had found something to do outside of the city. And, hopefully, he had some sort of official spin to tell the authorities when they knocked on his door in the next day or two. He was important to the operation in his current position and was worth far more alive than dead. Regardless, he knew that if Pasternak were questioned, he would maintain his silence and tell him of the interview as soon as it was possible, and safe to speak.

Other than some leftist ideologies, Pasternak had never really been given anything of value. He had not been given any information about PROSTAK when he was alive, and if questioned, or offered some sort of deal, he had no information about the payoffs that had been taking place over the past three years. Pasternak was not some sleazy informant, but rather a well-placed professional who would prove incredibly useful as he matured in his career. However, due to the requirements of his position with the US Attorney, could not be a part of any wrongdoing. Who knew, Pasternak might even make a run for state or federal office himself in the next few years. Others like him had already done so successfully.

Golovkin rolled over and fell immediately asleep. All was well. The documents would be back in Washington in eight hours.

CHAPTER 17

Karlsson stirred as daylight broke through the crack in the drapes. His bedmate was still sleeping, and he used the opportunity to collect his things and get through the bathroom first. He had packed a suitcase before leaving for the funeral home, because he wasn't sure where he would be spending the night. He guessed that the odds were better than fifty-fifty that he wouldn't be sleeping in Moreland Hills. Jackie frowned and shook her head when she saw him take it out of the trunk the night before.

"Really?" She asked jokingly perturbed. "You were that sure of yourself?"

He shrugged politely. "Actually, no. I knew that there was a strong likelihood that Stan would need the house tonight, and I planned accordingly. For all I know, you're going to make me sleep on the balcony." He winked.

"The jury is still out on that. We'll have to see how you plead your case."

After they had checked in and found her room, she placed her suitcase on a folding stand near the television. Karlsson put his duffel on the floor in the corner near the chair. When he turned around, she was there. She was standing closer than two coworkers would or should. He read the signals and took her in his arms. He kissed her and she opened her mouth, inviting his tongue.

"I need a minute."

"For what, calisthenics?" She looked up into his eyes.

"No, medication. If I'm going to perform this next magical act, I need to excuse myself and take a pill."

She grinned back at him. "Don't tell me. Delay of game for thirty minutes to let the blue pill work?"

"Something like that." He opened his toilet kit and went through the contents. "Not to seem presumptuous, but they're twenty bucks apiece. If you were advising me as to a course of action, would you tell me to take the pill and deal with the physiological results, or save my money?"

Her eyes were wide. "My, my, my. You certainly know how to smooth-talk a girl out of her pants. Take the fucking pill. No pun intended. We'll find something to do until you're ready."

Sometime around three in the morning, they were both awakened by the howl of the wind outside. She had fallen asleep with her head on his chest and his arm draped over her shoulder. He extricated his arm to restore blood flow and normal sensation and she rolled slightly to accommodate him. When their eyes met in the darkness, she said, "Not bad for an old guy. Thinking of running away?"

He moved his arm and tried to make a fist. "Hardly. I wouldn't have anywhere to run. I'm afraid I'm a captive tonight."

"Tonight? It's already tomorrow." She scratched her nose and brushed her hair away. "Thank you."

"For what?" Karlsson asked.

"For being warm and kind and not making this seem like some reckless, drunken encounter between coworkers. For a minute, I felt like we were just two people who needed each other at the end of a long day. A long week, actually."

"Is that what it was?" He continued flexing his hand, the feeling returning.

"I'm not sure what it was. You're the first man I've been with since my divorce, and I wasn't sure what to expect. You get used to doing something a certain way, perhaps out of habit. Then something new comes along and you have to reconsider everything you thought about experiencing love."

"Wait..." He sat up on the elbow that was just starting to feel normal again. "Are you saying I've wrecked you for other men?"

She laughed. "I doubt it! It was good, but it wasn't that good." She put her index finger on his cheek. "It was fun, but, since I wasn't sure what to expect, I wasn't sure how I'd feel about it afterwards. Let's just say that for a man of such a lethal reputation, that when you're between the sheets, you are a very sweet and sensitive guy."

Karlsson kissed her hard on the mouth. "I should be thanking you. I haven't been with anyone in a while, either. This was...cathartic, if that's not too clinical a term for this situation."

She laughed. "You sure know how to say the right things, Mr. Karlsson." She adjusted her pillow and sat up. "Now what? It's too early to get up, and I don't think I can get right back to sleep. You know what might be good?"

He smiled. "I think I still have some time left on that four-hour pill."

She smacked his arm. "Maybe later. Right now, I was thinking that I could really use a cup of coffee."

"Me too." He nodded. "Let's see what the hotel left for us in the way of emergency coffee rations."

Karlsson found his shorts and made his way to the desk and the coffee pot. It was designed to make two cups of coffee, which would probably meet their needs for the time being. He filled the carafe and then stuffed the pre-made pouch into the basket and poured the water in. Almost immediately the brew began to flow, and the invigorating aroma of coffee filled the room.

"I don't know what's better, the smell or the taste." She said from the darkness.

Even though the room temperature was within the acceptable range, the howling wind outside made him feel cold, and he slipped back under the covers with her to await the finished product. "Both. Just the smell of it wakes me up."

She yelped as his cold hands found her rib cage. "Geez! Did you use ice cubes?"

"Sorry." He manipulated the sheet between his hand and her thigh as he massaged the muscles in her glutes and upper legs. "I didn't look outside, but I think it was very decent of you to invite me to stay. It sounds like it's really cold out there and I'm not sure I would have survived the balcony."

She turned her back to him and slid in closer. "So?" She whispered.

He wrapped his arm around her and pulled her tight. "What time do you have to get up? I mean, really up."

"I told my boss that I'd call in around nine or so. You?"

"Paul doesn't have me on any kind of fixed schedule. Once you and I have a chance to talk more, I thought I'd check with Stan and see what he learned last night, before I call in."

Outside, the gusts blowing in off Lake Erie seemed vengeful. She was reflective for a moment. "Who do you trust?" She asked, her voice still low.

Karlsson carefully regarded her comment before speaking. "Are you talking about the people on this case, or my boss, or what?"

"Everyone. This case has me concerned. I told you that I've never seen such politics played out in a criminal investigation like I'm seeing now. I think my people are being pressured, but I don't know by whom, or why."

"Interesting. Paul told me the exact same thing two weeks ago. I understand the counterfeiting angle as being a political device of sorts, but why does the Air Force suddenly care about a missing LEM from the nineteen-seventies? Are you, or they, saying that with all the other intelligence assets and technology we have, we didn't know it was there before your orbital fly-by? Or that over the last fifty years, none of our intelligence agencies knew that some other country was trying to get to the moon?"

"I'm not sure, but I've been trying to piece it together."

Karlsson sat up. "Well, now that we've seen each other naked, I think it's time that we start laying our cards on the table. What have you got? Start from the beginning. Why were you in St. Louis? I could have met you anywhere. Why was it important for you to be at the Personnel Center, in person?"

He could feel her tense, almost imperceptibly. "I had to do a hand search of military personnel records. What I found online when I looked, didn't seem to make sense, and I wanted to visit the repository to examine the old paper files."

"What were you looking for?"

"Pilot records. Actually, servicemen that had been accepted into the US astronaut program and who suddenly disappeared."

"Disappeared?" Karlsson involuntarily missed a breath.

"Yes. Some were killed in training accidents. Some died of supposed natural causes. But, in all cases, there was no body. Either the service member was cremated, or the body was mangled beyond recognition, or it was never found."

Karlsson thought he had heard this story before. "Wait a minute. You're tracking US military personnel that are presumed or declared dead, and you think they actually aren't?"

"Yes. This case came in from an informant, anonymously mailed in, and after we looked at what he had to offer, we thought we just had a simple whistle-blower case of espionage; secret information leaking to the Russians. Then we began to see connections to manufacturers that were selling critical parts for special aircraft to buyers, other than the United States Government. It was then that I began to realize that there was more to the story than a couple of people trying to line their pockets. I think we uncovered an organized operation of significant scope that indicates that we've been trading technology with the Russians, under the table, for fifty years. I think there's another space program that we really don't have a handle on. That only a very few people know about."

Suddenly, the calls with Paul seemed to make more sense. "So, if we found evidence of Soviet cosmonauts being placed with NASA in the nineteen sixties, then that would confirm your theory of a covert exchange program?"

"Yes."

"Don't tell me. You think that due to budget constraints in congress and the need to cloud transparency, this program was actually being funded through private corporations?"

"I think so."

"So, if a certain dead aerospace engineer with questionable

loyalties was found to have about thirteen million dollars in a fake wall, then that might warrant further investigation as to the origination and distribution of the funds."

"Marty Jeffers." She whispered. "Echo is a major sub-contractor on a number of NASA and private *new-space* projects. It would take a lot of Marty's, placed in several different companies, to fund a program like this. But it's certainly possible that we might have stumbled on to one. Add to that the suspicion that if the various Marty's out there were trying to cut corners and save money by introducing counterfeit parts, then who knows how many people would benefit from it? There could be billions of dollars on the table, with almost no government oversight."

Karlsson tried to get his head around what she was saying. "By this logic then, if we were in bed with the Russians in some sort of secret space program, but someone...let's say several someone's in various companies, decided to go to the Chinese for cheaper parts in order to make a few extra bucks, then sooner or later, the Chinese would have to know what we were doing, and want a piece of the action."

"Possibly. Do you remember the SR-71 Blackbird?"

Karlsson nodded. "Yeah. A high-altitude reconnaissance aircraft that replaced the U-2."

"Originally designated the A-12 and known as ARCHANGEL, the aircraft was made almost entirely of titanium, inside and out. During initial development and construction, the United States didn't have sources of rutile ore; the mineral needed to make titanium. It's only found in very few parts of the world, and ironically, the major supplier of the ore was the Soviet Union. So, the CIA put together fictitious companies in several different third-world countries. Through these bogus operations, they were able to get the rutile ore shipped to the United States to build the SR-71. And so, the Soviets never knew, at the time, how much they contributed to build the aircraft we created to spy on them."

Karlsson grimaced. "Interesting. I hadn't heard that before."

"Then there was the case of Buran, the Soviet space shuttle."

She continued. "Some people think they stole it from us. The truth was that we had so much information publically available, they took our designs and then improved on them. The Buran looked much the same as our shuttle on the outside but could carry several additional tons of cargo. It was also lighter due to a different propulsion system, and safer, due to ejection seats for all of the cosmonauts."

"The Russians were driven to compete by the belief that we created our shuttle program to militarize space; to be able to recover their satellites, bring them back to earth and study them. Or plant our own military satellites in space. Their shuttle program would have eventually been better than ours except for one thing."

"What's that?"

"The breakup of the Soviet Union. When the Soviet Union fell and the new Russia took its place, there was no money remaining to fund Buran. The shuttles and one of the Energia booster rockets sat idle and rusted in Baikonur until a roof caved in on the hangar and killed twenty-nine people. From there, the shuttles fell into disrepair and weren't even good enough to move to a museum. So, they say."

"Meaning?" Karlsson asked, studying her form in the darkness.

"Meaning that we have to question the official report that claims they obtained their specs from open sources. Knowing what we know now, was it possible that we quietly helped them with the design and construction to keep us all on a level playing field?"

She continued. "My office thinks it's highly probable. When we announced a second shuttle launch facility was being built in Vandenberg, the Russians probably went into chaos mode. A launch from southern California over the North Pole would put us in a position over their heads in a half hour. But they wouldn't even know it was an attack until five minutes before impact."

Karlsson was following her logic. "Or, with our help, they faked the destruction of some of their Buran prototypes, so that we might have one or two additional spacecraft that the public, on either side of the ocean, didn't know about?" He theorized. "But, if this has been going on since the sixties, how many people would have had to be in on it? How could it be managed without it ever leaking out?"

"It would be difficult. But we know it could be done. Look at Roswell."

"Roswell? The reported flying saucer crash in 1947?" Karlsson slid out from under the covers and poured two cups of coffee. "Is black okay? I don't see any cream or sugar over here."

"Black is fine, thanks." She adjusted her pillow and sat up. "Something crashed during a thunderstorm and it wasn't a Mogul balloon or something with crash test dummies onboard. The Air Force stuck to its story and even though the media pointed out the inconsistencies in their superficial investigation, they never wavered."

"Those stories were true?" He handed her a cup and went around to the other side of the bed to set his on the nightstand.

"Yeah." She took a sip with her eyes closed. "Mmmm...hotel coffee. Yuck."

She brought the covers back up around her and rolled to face him. "It was 1947. It wasn't a kite, and it certainly wasn't ours. It wasn't the Russians', or the Nazi's. Today's high-tech magnates weren't born yet so we know it wasn't theirs, either. I don't know if it came from another planet or another dimension, but wherever it was from, the Air Force was able to contain the information, despite intense media interest and dozens of books about it."

"Thinking out loud," Karlsson frowned, "How could your case have gotten this far along? Someone within the Air Force, especially in OSI, must have been aware of any joint US-Russia operations and could have derailed your investigation at any point."

"I thought about that." She agreed. "I'm wondering if some of the decision-makers might be interested in finally seeing this all become public. Or, if they were curious to see just how much could be uncovered in our investigation; checking the water-tight seals, so to speak, before the ship leaves port."

"Uh huh. With a presidential election coming up in November, one or both of the candidates want to better understand the covert program so they can maximize its value in the media." Karlsson took a sip and put his coffee back on the nightstand. "And, depending on which side of the fence they're on, can exploit either the folly or benefits of the covert space program, and either blast the Chinese for their unofficial support of the counterfeiting industry, or announce a strategic partnership with them to eliminate counterfeit parts from the market."

"Spin." She concurred. "It's all about spin. It's not important that the truth comes out. It's only important how you use the information and publicize only those facts that support your claims."

He could still smell the remnants of her perfume from the previous night. "Paul told me that my assignment would become clearer after meeting with you. I think I'm starting to see some options, but I'm still in the dark. I'm supposed to take my lead from you. Do you have a plan?"

She rolled to face him again and ran her hand up the crease of his legs. "Yeah. I think I have a plan."

————))((————

It had been a rough night in Moreland Hills. There had been much soul-purging and some tear-soaked discussions before Tricia and Marchand had finally retired to the bedroom. When she rolled out of bed in the master suite, the first night for both of them in the big bed, he sent a quick text to Karlsson. "MEET AT USSS – INDEPENDENCE 0900. NEW PLAYER ON OUR SIDE."

After an incredibly fattening breakfast of pancakes, eggs and sausage at a nearby restaurant, they jumped back on I-271 south and joined the last wave of rush hour traffic headed to Rockside Road in Independence. Franklin Jones met them at the main door to the office suite and made sure that Tricia was appropriately disarmed, signed-in and badged. Marchand no longer had to go through the daily visitor process since he'd finally been credentialed as a Special

Deputy US Marshal. As a retired Secret Service agent, he was already comfortable with office protocols, and the local agents were astutely aware of his professional status.

Jones had reserved a teleconference room where everyone could meet for the nine o'clock briefing with Headquarters. The meeting was to be led by Deputy Director Vince Catalogna, a man with whom Marchand had worked only briefly in his career, so both men knew each other more by reputation than by shared experience. When Karlsson and Biehn arrived at 8:50, Jones escorted them back to the conference room where fresh coffee was waiting. Brief introductions were made with the understanding that each person would have to give a more in-depth biography to Deputy Director Catalogna when he opened the call.

The large screen on the far wall of the room came alive and Jones made sure that the microphones were suitably spaced to capture the discussion. Catalogna was a fairly large man in his late fifties. He still had a mop of dark wavy hair, accented with gray around the temples. He took his seat, somewhere in Washington DC, and looked at the case file in front of him.

His opening remarks were not so much brusque as they were business-like and to the point. He had a large case on his hands, with serious political ramifications, and he was too close to retirement to let it mess up his pension or a Special Executive Service waiver after he turned fifty-seven, mandatory retirement age for agents. "Good morning everyone! Before we get into this, I need to remind you that this is a classified briefing being conducted over a secure network. No recordings of any kind are permitted, and no materials can be removed from your SCIF without authorization from Special Agent Jones. Please sign the SF-312 forms in front of you and pass them to Franklin. Thanks!"

"Stan, nice to see you again. I heard they called you out of retirement for a protection gig and it looks like it's mushroomed into something bigger than any of us might have expected. Are you okay with that?"

Stan nodded and moved the flat microphone closer to a place

equidistantly spaced between his chair and Tricia's. "Absolutely. Nice to see you again too, Vince."

"For obvious reasons, Jerry won't be joining us on these calls... at least for the foreseeable future. At his request, Stan, we would like you to sort of take point on this in his absence, and work with Franklin as your liaison. I understand from your email that you've got some guests with you today. Can we do a quick round of introductions? No campaign speeches...just who you are and what are you doing here."

Stan pushed the microphone a bit closer to Tricia and began her introduction for her. "To my right is Patricia Knight, former Tech Sergeant, United States Air Force. Now a DHS contractor, her background is in technical communications, and we'll be spending more time on her involvement with this case later on. She'll be playing an integral role when we explain the problem that we're going to have with a local AUSA."

"Pasternak?" Catalogna replied looking at the file.

"Yes." Marchand replied.

"Good morning." She added.

"Right. Nice to meet you, Patricia. We'll come back to you. Keep going around the table."

Marchand gestured across the table. "Across from me is Matt... Matthias Karlsson. Matt is a former US Army Special Operations..."

Catalogna cut him off. "I already know about Mr. Karlsson. I spoke to Paul Scheller this morning and he explained your interests in this matter. Welcome to the team. Who's with you?"

Karlsson reached across the table and moved the microphone closer. "Good morning. On my left is Special Agent Jackie Biehn, United States Air Force Office of Special Investigations."

"Good morning." Jackie waved at the screen.

"Good morning." Catalogna looked up into the camera.

"I understand from talking to Mr. Scheller that your office's investigation is what kicked off this mess?"

"You might say that, yes."

"And Scheller's office teamed you up with Major Karlsson?"

She had not known his military rank before that moment. It had never come up in conversation. "That's correct."

"Well, ladies and gentlemen, I need to come up to speed on this really quickly. I have to brief the Director at ten, and I'd like to sound like I know what I'm talking about. Let's start with Special Agent Biehn. Ms. Biehn, how and when did you pick this case up, what have you got so far, and where do you need to be with it to make a final report?"

Jackie moved the microphone towards her. "A month ago, our office got the first of a series of unsigned, word-processed documents in the mail, post-marked from Des Moines, alleging that persons-unknown in a Cleveland company known as Echo Aerospace, were using counterfeit parts in some of their aviation components and that they had been engaged in fraud relevant to some of their Air Force contracts. At the bottom of the letter were three names; Steven MacPherson, Douglas Ritter and James Rinehart."

She took a quick sip of coffee and continued. "We first checked J-PAS, the Joint Personnel Adjudication System, to see if they were cleared employees of Echo. They were not. We were also able to determine that they were not current or former employees of Echo Aerospace in any un-cleared capacity. But we were able to find service records for all three. MacPherson and Ritter were Air Force officers and Rinehart had been a Navy officer. All three were pilots. All three died in accidents, in different parts of the country, and all three had been cremated. Their death certificates were all filed within the same week, in the counties where they supposedly died."

Catalogna was about to speak but looked up and away from the camera. "Hi, Carter. Come on in." He was joined by a forty-ish man with dark hair and some rather exotic, red-framed glasses. "Everyone, this is Carter Lembeck. Carter is second-in-command in the United States Attorney's Office for the Eastern District of Virginia. For the present, he is the only AUSA who is involved in this case. To make that clear, he's the only AUSA assigned."

"Good morning." Lembeck said as he took a seat.

Catalogna continued. "Sorry, Ms. Biehn. So, what's the connection between the deceased pilots?"

"None. Other than they were all candidates for our astronaut program."

"They didn't know each other?"

"As far as we can tell, they did not. They never served together. They trained at different bases at different times. Their clearance files don't share any of the same personal references."

"Cell phone records?"

"They all died before cell phones."

"Excuse me?" Catalogna looked up from his note pad.

"Mr. Catalogna, these men all died in the nineteen seventies."

"Go on." Catalogna said, returning to his notes.

"Our audit department looked at Echo's programs and didn't see anything unusual on the financial side. We had our technicians pull a couple of their components for laboratory analysis and didn't see anything out-of-scope with their products, either. We were ready to close the case as being attributed to a disgruntled employee who had no real evidence of misconduct. Then we received a second letter from the same informant, a week later. It was more like a sentence than a letter. It simply said, and I quote; *Find LEM 14, forward slash...and the name Parker McAdams.*"

"It took us a while to locate McAdams; a retired engineer living in Pittsburgh. He was one of the quality control technicians on the LEM project, and maybe one of the last surviving team members to have been inside it. His memory is now a little sketchy; he's ninety years old." Jackie repeated the investigative narrative that she'd given Karlsson at dinner the previous week, and discussed the locations of each Lunar Excursion Module, insofar as the US Government knew, as well as their investigation into how one could have been heisted from the manufacturer without their knowledge. Catalogna listened intently and then asked, "Interesting stuff. You have no idea who the informant could be?"

"No. But we think that it was someone who either had first-hand knowledge about the material or is related to someone who did."

"Do you have the originals on you?"

"No. The originals are locked up in our offices in Quantico, with my boss. I work out of Andrews. I have some copies I could send you."

"Please. Is Kemper still in charge out at OSI?"

"Yes. Don Kemper is in charge of the civilian program. Brigadier General Scott is the overall commander."

"Yeah, I think I've met Kemper. Go on. What else?"

Biehn went on to explain some of the things that she and Karlsson had discussed and then sat silently awaiting his comments or direction of some sort.

Catalogna nodded. And then turned to Lembeck. "Do you know anyone at DARPA that we can talk to without making them curious as to why we're asking?"

Lembeck nodded. "Yes. One of their attorneys. He worked on some matters tied to their Adaptive Vehicle programs. He might be a good starting place."

"Make it quiet. Over drinks or something if you can."

He looked back at the camera. "Jackie, let me ask you a question. With your knowledge of the Air Force organization, if they actually were doing some sort of secret program with the Russians, who would likely be involved?"

"I'm not sure it's really the Air Force. NASA has always had a small portion of their program that only they knew about. This might run further up the chain-of-command to the Defense Department. After all, it was a senior DOD guy that signed off on the Soviets' backgrounds. My thought is that there's an element of the Defense Department that is operating without oversight. It would have to be a small number of people, but they'd all be highly placed."

Catalogna appeared to doodle on his pad for a moment. "Ms. Knight, should I address you as Tech Sergeant, or Patricia?"

"Just Tricia." She replied.

"Tell me about how you got this gig. And tell me more about the relationship you had with Mr. Pasternak."

"As Stan mentioned, I worked in technical communications in the Air Force. When I got out I joined a couple of online groups that offered both short-term and permanent work for cleared personnel. Most of it was for the Defense Department. Some was from the Department of Justice, which is how Jared met Pasternak. He had us doing wiretaps for DHS organizations; Customs, ICE...other government clients."

"How many jobs over the last two years?"

"For Pasternak? Five, counting the one on Moreland Hills."

"How were you paid?"

"It was a flat day-rate of one thousand dollars. They were direct deposits from a government account."

"You never met him?"

"No. In each case, he set up the job through Jared Farmington. Jared then called whoever he wanted on the team and we did the job."

"So, you wouldn't know him if you saw him?"

"No."

"Do you think he's seen a picture of you?"

"Probably. I think they had our military personnel files. There are head and body shots in there."

Catalogna muted and had a brief conversation with Lembeck, before returning to the call. "Tricia, have you ever worked undercover?"

She seemed a bit surprised by the question. "Me? No. I'm a techie."

Catalogna shrugged. "Ever do any acting as a kid?"

"Why?"

"We're going to take a closer look at Mr. Pasternak, but there'll probably come a time when we need you to get him on tape. And I think you're the best choice for that."

"Franklin, get with Biehn and get the death certificates of the deceased pilots she mentioned. Get on to the field office guys and ask them to quietly look into the cause of death in each case and review any investigative reports they can find." He turned to Lembeck. "See what you can find out about Pasternak. See what cases he's been working. How he got the job. You know."

He looked back into the camera. "Major, do you want to be sworn in as a US Marshal for this?"

Karlsson leaned forward towards the mic, "That may not be the best way to go on this."

Catalogna muted his microphone again and leaned over towards Lembeck to whisper something in his ear. There was a moment when Lembeck's eyebrows raised and then he shook his head. Catalogna unmuted. "The government agrees."

"For the time being, we're going to call this Project TRAPDOOR. Secret Service will take the lead. All information will flow through my office, and from me to the Director, and obviously, to the White House. We're going through the Eastern District of Virginia on this since the DC US Attorney actually reports to Congress. I don't want them involved just yet."

"I'll need detailed, written investigative plans with dates from each of you, with the exception of Major Karlsson, who will continue to report to Mr. Scheller. It is critical that no information collected or evaluated on this assignment goes anywhere outside of the team sitting in your conference room in Cleveland right now. We'll try to run this as expeditiously as possible without Agency involvement, but as you all know, sooner or later, they'll hear about it, and want to take it over themselves. If that happens, or rather, when that happens, I can't promise you which direction it will take after that."

Catalogna paused to take a drink of water from the bottle on his table, the crackle of the plastic, briefly over-modulating his mic. "It seems to me that there are a lot of players in this and some of them need to go to jail, but at this point, I can't speculate as to who, if any of them, will do time. Any questions?"

Hearing none, he resumed his remarks. "Stan, we'll need you to stay behind for a minute. We have some information about the late

Mr. Jeffers' financial transactions. The ones coded ARCHER were distributed to two different political front companies. One of which we know to be making payments to the son of a certain Presidential candidate. But, we can't move on it until we are one hundred percent certain that we have all the facts."

Stan nodded. "Got it."

Catalogna further explained. "For everyone else's benefit, we have to move fast on this. Our policy under US Code says that we have to start protecting families of presidential candidates within one hundred twenty days from the election. If we're protecting a suspect, that could prove embarrassing for all of us involved. Last chance for questions."

He paused for a few seconds. "All right then. You all have stuff to do so I'll leave you to it. Please keep me in the loop as information surfaces. Tricia, can you join the call with Stan in a few minutes? We have some ideas that we'd like to run past you."

He tapped a button on his table and the meeting ended.

———— ((•)) ————

Peter Pasternak looked at the front page of the Cleveland newspaper on his desk. "Two men dead in warehouse fire." He shook his head slowly and closed his eyes. What had he done? His stomach turned as he thought about the potential repercussions of his actions. He paced anxiously back and forth in the small office overlooking the Cleveland skyline and tried to think of his options.

It was about nine-thirty when his phone rang. "Hi. Mr. Pasternak? It's Jeff, in the lobby. There are a couple guys here to see you from the Arson Squad."

He took a deep breath and tried to compose himself. "Arson? Oh my. Tell them I'll be right down."

He tried to control his breathing as he waited for the elevator car. When the doors opened, he nodded at some of the familiar faces and instinctively pressed the button for the ground floor, even though it was already lit. When the doors opened on the first floor, he turned and walked to the front desk where the duty officer, retired Cleveland cop Jeff Wolensky, could be seen joking with the two men in suits. As he approached, Jeff smiled and nodded. "Guys, this is Mr. Pasternak."

The younger of the two turned and extended his hand. "Hi. Mr. Pasternak, I'm Denny Philbin with the fire department Arson Squad, and this is detective Dwight Parks with Cleveland PD. Sorry we couldn't call ahead. Do you have a couple of minutes?"

"Yes. I think so." Pasternak replied. His handshake was weaker than usual, and he could not control the sweat on his palms. "What's this about?"

"Good morning. Dwight Parks." Said the other man. He was in his forties and his suit looked like it had been picked off the rack at a department store. Slightly large for him, and ill-fitting, no doubt due to the need to conceal assorted holsters, magazines, radios, and handcuffs.

The two men shook hands. "Why don't we go up to my office?"

They returned to the elevator and then made their way to the eighth floor, making small talk about current political happenings in the area. When they got to the office, Pasternak gestured for them to have a seat in the two chairs facing his desk. It was a standard interview tactic, with the morning sun behind him, and in their eyes. It might help keep them from seeing through any of his facial or non-verbal tells if he was not able to adequately control his anxiety.

"Would either of you like coffee or water?" He asked, to set the stage.

Both men shook their heads and then the younger Denny Philbin innocently asked, "I suppose you saw the papers this morning?" Looking at the copy of the Plain-Dealer on Pasternak's desk.

"About the fire?" He replied since it was on the front page.

"Yeah. We're following up on some leads about it. As you might know, one of the men; a Mr. Jared Farmington, had a pass for this building, and when we checked with the guard, his records indicated that you had authorized the pass. May I ask what these two men did for you?"

"Oh my." He said, looking at the headline. "The newspaper didn't indicate a name. Yes, I remember Mr. Farmer. He was one of our contractors; one of our telecommunications specialists."

Philbin opened his notebook and began to jot down the date and time of the interview, as well as the first comments made by the witness. "Farmington." He corrected. "What exactly does a *contract telecommunications specialist* do for the US Attorney's office?"

Pasternak shrugged lightly and dropped the newspaper into the trash can. "Well, whenever one of the federal agencies has a warrant for a wiretap, they work with the cable companies or service providers to install the necessary equipment and make sure it works."

"They bug phones?" Parks asked pointedly.

"Much of the time, yes. Phones, internet...other communications systems. It depends on what the warrant calls for."

Philbin nodded. "How did you meet Mr. Farmington?"

Pasternak had attempted to rehearse answers to the likely questions he would receive. "It was a couple of years ago, if I remember correctly. We needed some technical specialists and recruited through a website that helps pair military veterans with jobs that require security clearances. He applied, along with several others, and his background checked out, so he was brought on as a contractor whenever we needed one."

"How many times was that?" Parks asked.

Pasternak recognized that they were firing general questions at him. They did not know anything. Yet. "Oh, I suppose three or four times in the last couple of years."

"When was the first time?" It was Philbin's turn.

Pasternak entered a password into his computer and read. "The first time was on a Treasury warrant almost two years ago."

"What was the case about?"

Pasternak smirked a bit as he read from his screen. "A

counterfeiting charge. The IRS filed on the defendant because he had tampered with a tax refund check. Nothing major."

Parks made a notation and then looked up. "What was the most recent case about?"

"Excuse me?"

"What was the most recent case about, that you used him on?"

"It was..." Pasternak stalled as he went through his case files. He had to think quickly. "Uhmmm... it was a national security matter."

"What is that?" Philbin raised his eyebrows.

"It was..." Pasternak could feel his face flushing slightly. "It was something that is currently classified. An intelligence matter, so to speak."

Dwight Parks looked at him sourly. "An intelligence matter?" He looked out the office window and then back at the Assistant US Attorney. "Are you going to tell me that it'll take an act of congress for you to release any details about this case? A case in which two local men were killed?"

A small bead of sweat began to form over Pasternak's eyebrows. "No. Nothing so sinister. It'll just take me a couple of days to get you the necessary permissions...you know, from Washington, to be able to share that information."

Both investigators noted the change in the man's behavior and his speech patterns. For some reason, he seemed to be stressed over the questions. Parks switched his pattern. "How about Platt Company, Limited?"

Pasternak was momentarily caught off guard. "Excuse me?"

"The Platt Company. It's a holding company that owned the Lake Erie Container Company on Euclid Avenue."

Pasternak felt slightly relieved. The name meant nothing, but he went through the act of running the name through his computer to please his guests. "Nothing. Who is Platt?"

"It's the warehouse where the fire was last night. I thought maybe Mr. Farmington was on business for your office when he was killed?"

"No. No way." Pasternak said, a bit too quickly. "He wasn't doing anything for us last night."

"How about Nikolay Antropov?"

"No." He shook his head. "Who is this...uh, Antropov?"

Parks responded. "He was the President of Lake Erie Container, until it was taken over by the holding company. The name doesn't mean anything to you?"

Pasternak searched his memory, but although the name sounded familiar, he could not place it. "No. Nothing."

"Okay, no problem. Tell us about Terry Consterdine."

Pasternak was just getting his vital signs back to normal when the name was mentioned. "Consterdine?"

"Yeah." Parks replied. "That was the guy who was found with Farmington in the warehouse. Was he a contractor too?"

Pasternak fidgeted with his computer keyboard. His hands were shaking. He should have been better prepared, at least, emotionally. He knew that someone would be coming at some point. "Uh, I don't see a Consterdine listed in here." He knew that Consterdine was the other man that Farmington had brought in to help boost the safe. "I'm sorry."

"No problem." Denny Philbin closed his notebook and pocketed his pen. "We're just back-tracking where these guys could have been before they went to the warehouse last night. If they weren't working on something for you, it would appear that they were up to something on their own."

"Sorry I couldn't be more help." Pasternak said. "Can I walk you back down?"

"You might have to." Parks observed. "We didn't get visitor badges from the guard and I wouldn't want to get in trouble with the Fed, if you know what I mean?"

Everyone laughed and Pasternak held the door for them as they left the office and headed back to the elevator. "You'll be okay from here to the lobby." He said with a smile.

Back in his office, he leaned back in his leather chair and tried to regulate his breathing. His heart was whizzing near tachycardia and he exhaustively went over the interview in his mind. Had he been convincing? Had he told them the things that an innocent person would have told them? Did he react the way an innocent person would have reacted?

Through the remainder of the morning, he tried to concentrate on some of his workload, but it was just not possible. His mind was whirring in random directions, contemplating the myriad of scenarios that could emerge from his visit. He owed Golovkin a call but knew that he could not call from the building. He would wait until lunch.

At 11:40, his concentration was further disrupted when another call came in from the lobby. "Hi Jeff."

"Mr. Pasternak, I'm sorry to bother you again, but there's a woman here to see you."

"A woman?" He checked his calendar. He didn't have any appointments until two that afternoon. "Who is she and what does she want?"

"She says her name is Patricia Knight and she needs to talk to you about her timesheet. She says her supervisor was just killed, and she doesn't know who to give her timesheet to."

"Patricia Knight?" The name suddenly struck him. "I see. Please ask her to come up."

Pasternak gazed out his window. He'd had such a good life. He had such plans. He could not allow anyone or anything to intrude on that. He could manage this. He got up from his desk and stepped through the office lobby into the hallway and waited. Within a couple of minutes, the striking blond woman in blue jeans stepped off the elevator and towards his direction.

"Patricia?"

"Mr. Pasternak?"

"Yes. Please come with me." She followed him back to his office and closed the door behind her. As he took his chair, he asked, "What can I do for you?"

She began innocently enough. "My supervisor, Jared Farmington, was killed last night and I need to know how to bill for my time."

He was stunned that she had been notified so quickly. "What *time* are you talking about?" He asked as if he did not already know.

"The time for the job you sent us on. The time for us to search a residence in Moreland Hills, and the time for us to retrieve a listening device, which Jared gave to you."

Pasternak typed her name into his computer. "Oh. I see." He had to think quickly. She was Farmington's partner during the original search. "And how many hours did you want to bill us for? How much do we owe you?"

"Well, let's see. We had four hours on the initial entry and search, and then I had some other work to do relative to the case. So, let's say fifty thousand."

Pasternak paused. He was not sure he heard exactly what she said. "Fifty thousand dollars for four hours' worth of work? I thought you were paid at a rate of a thousand a day."

"That was before you killed my partner. I need to get out of town before you decide to do me as well."

Pasternak looked at her for a moment before speaking. His hands trembled in his lap. "First, fifty thousand dollars is a lot of money for one day's work. Secondly, why on earth would you think I had something to do with killing your partner? Or anyone for that matter?"

"I don't know, and I don't care. This case stinks, and you're the only person I know who was involved in it. I need to get out and I need to get out fast, and for a long time."

Pasternak's brain worked at high-speed trying to figure out her angle. "You're way out of line. I should throw you out right now. You're attempting to extort money from a federal official."

She calmly reached into her purse and pulled out her cell phone. As she brought up her pictures, she said, "These are pictures we took of Martin Jeffers' safe on Moreland Hills Drive, the day after he died, and a day before you killed my partner." She showed him pictures that they had taken on the afternoon of their search. "The police will be extremely interested in seeing these. It will help them clear a burglary off their sheets and indict a US Attorney."

Pasternak looked at the photos, stone-faced, but stayed to his original plan. "All these pictures demonstrate is that you broke into a house in Moreland Hills, and then later robbed the place. I don't see my name anywhere on this."

"How long will it take the FBI to tell the local cops, that the van we used came from you? Well, from them, but with your authorization?"

She had him. Or, at least, she could cause enough trouble that it would ruin him. "I don't have that kind of money on me right now." He looked at her file on his screen. Do you still live in Westlake?"

"No. That was my boyfriend's house. I live on Country Club Drive in Medina, now. Why?"

He was quiet as the scenarios flashed through his mind. "Okay. If you're leaving town, and I'll never hear from you again, I'll bring you the money tonight. Have you told anyone about this yet?"

"Maybe." She replied with a wink, and then stood and turned towards the door. "The address is 6620 Country Club. Be there at seven...and come alone. As you can tell from my file, I have a fire-arm, and I'm not afraid to use it. Cash, please. If I see anyone but you, it will get ugly."

CHAPTER 18

Peter Pasternak left his building and walked towards the lake, with no particular destination in mind. He dialed his mentor's cell phone number with a level of fear and anxiety that he had never before experienced. The wind had died down a bit since morning, but he still had to call from the shelter of a building to keep it from affecting the conversation.

"Da, moy yunyy drug?" Golovkin answered playfully, prepared for the young attorney's uneasy retort about the previous night's events.

"I, uh..." He paused as two men in overcoats and sunglasses walked past him. "I am so very sorry to have to call you this morning, but I am afraid I have made a terrible mistake."

"You are concerned that the details of the fire will lead the police back to you?" Golovkin remarked casually, as he flipped through an unrelated report that required his immediate attention.

"It already has. I had a visit today from the detective and the arson investigator who were looking into Farmington's role in our operations. They know that he worked for us and that I approved his access badge."

"It is nothing." Golovkin replied. "It was to be expected."

"I am afraid that I did not share the entire story with you when we last spoke. There was a woman."

"There usually is." Golovkin joked.

"No. You don't understand. When you asked me for their names, I assumed you meant the two men who took the safe. But..." he took a breath. "The two people I sent in for the initial search were a man and a woman. Farmington and a female associate named Knight."

Golovkin stopped reading and listened intently. "Yes."

"The woman contacted me today. She has pictures of the house and the safe. She wants money. Tonight. At seven."

"Money for what?"

"To keep silent. She wants to leave town. She suspects that the mission I sent them on was not officially sanctioned, and she fears that someone will come after her. I am afraid that I have really botched this."

Golovkin was thoughtful and silent for a moment. It was a scenario that he had already considered. "Not to worry. I can fix this. How much money does the woman want?"

"Fifty thousand dollars, US."

"Do you have it?"

"I can get it, yes. But I cannot guarantee her silence. I am not sure who she might have spoken with."

Golovkin weighed the consequences of the potential responses. Finally, he said, "Good. Take it to her at seven. I'll have it back for you by eight."

"Wait, Uncle Ted..." He licked his lips, which were dry and chapped from the Lake Erie wind. "Please don't hurt her. Isn't there a way to ...to just scare her?"

"It's a minor problem. Something we should have handled last night, but we did not have her name. Piotr, this is bigger than both of us. To ensure the peace and stability of the planet, this needs to be done. You will be fine. You must believe that."

In the back of his professional legal mind, he knew full well the implications of what was being discussed. He knew what his role had been. And he knew that he was taking part in something to which he was adamantly opposed. Nevertheless, he was up against a wall, and heard himself acquiesce. "Yes. Of course."

"Be smart, my friend." Golovkin said softly. "As you know, your cell phone can be tracked. So, tonight, leave your personal cell at home and take this one with you. We will be able to tell when you are away and safe."

"Of course, Uncle Ted."

Matt Karlsson and Jackie Biehn decided it was quicker to drive to Pittsburgh than to find a flight, rent a car and then look for the home of Parker McAdams, the witness who had told Biehn that he might have been one of the last engineers to have worked on LEM number fourteen. Before leaving Cleveland, they checked several websites and reviewed the references to his home off Hillsdale Avenue near the Harmony Ridge Golf Club. He'd been living there since the late 1970's and was probably the second owner. It was a three-bedroom ranch home built in the early 1970's with a two-car garage. The online picture made it look nice and clean. But then, that's what realtors do.

The GPS got them to the driveway on time, but somewhere enroute they had already decided that Jackie would take the lead, since she had been the one to make contact with him the month before. The neighborhood was quiet and peaceful with the homes far enough apart that one could keep a sense of privacy and enjoy their property without having to watch their neighbors doing yard work or shoveling snow. Surrounded by tall trees, it reminded Karlsson of a smaller version of the Moreland Hills place that Marty had picked out. Maybe engineers liked trees, after all.

Jackie rang the doorbell. It was a minute before Mr. McAdams could make it to the door. Still spry and emotionally energetic he didn't move as fast as he did when he was younger. He was about five foot seven, but slender and somewhat stooped in posture.

"Yes?" He said when he opened the door. "You must be Jacqueline. I told you that my wife's name was Jacqueline." He looked her up and down with a sly smile. "You remind me of her too. Well, back in the day, if you know what I mean. Please come in."

Karlsson and Biehn entered, and the first thing that they noticed was the smell of stale cigarette smoke in the air. It was not intense, but it was there. She smiled as she lightly shook his hand.

"Mr. McAdams? I'm Jackie Biehn, and this is my associate, Matt Karlsson."

Karlsson stepped forwards and shook hands with him. "Matt, to my friends."

"Please come in!" He moved carefully, but without assistance, and headed for the lounger in the living room, which seemed like it was his place of operations. There were end tables with stacks of aircraft magazines on either side of his throne, and a coffee table not far away that was for guests to use when they sat on the leather sofa, which appeared expensive, but well broken-in.

"When you called earlier, I remembered that you and I spoke a couple of weeks ago, didn't we? Or months?"

"Yes, sir. We did. We wanted to talk to you about your work on the LEM project; the Lunar Excursion Modules."

He gestured at his collection of models of assorted scales that rested on tables, shelves and even a couple that were suspended from the ceiling by dark thread. "Yes. Not many people remember the old LEM these days. The LEM's, like me, have become a part of history as the new generation pushes us further out into space." He smiled. "Please sit down. Can I get you a soft drink? Coffee?"

"No, sir. But thank you!" She sat down on the sofa. "It is so nice of you to meet us today. I want you to know that what you tell us will be kept confidential."

"Confidential?" He chuckled. "I'm ninety years old. What the hell can anyone do to me that nature hasn't already started?" He looked at Karlsson. "Would you like a beer or something?"

"No." Matt smiled. "I'm okay for now. Thanks!"

"So, what do you want to know?" He asked as he yanked a lever on the side of his chair lowering the back and bringing the leg rest up.

"Well, sir, we'd like to hear about your work on the LEM. To the best of your recollection, how long were you on the project?"

"I joined Grumman at Aircraft Plant Number Five in Beth Page, New York, in the fall of 1965. You see, I was really interested in aviation as a kid, and wanted to be a pilot. But when I joined the

Air Force in fifty-two, I couldn't pass the flight physical, and they wouldn't let me fly. So, after my commission, I ended up moving around the country on some minor projects and eventually got assigned to the Atlas Missile program. That was Convair's project, y'know, and it took four of the Mercury astronauts into space. Redstone, if you'll recall, took the first two up."

"Anyway, at the time, Jaqueline was pressuring me to get out of the Air Force and find a real job, so I resigned my commission in sixty-two and went to work for Convair's parent company, General Dynamics."

"They treated us okay there, but eventually, I got bored. I'd been fascinated by World War II aircraft and knew that Grumman had built some very nice bombers, so I applied there and got hired. As for the LEM project, it really started in July 1962. Eleven different companies were invited to submit proposals for the LEM. Nine companies responded in September of that year, answering a twenty-question document released by NASA in a huge technical proposal. Sixty pages or so. Grumman was awarded the contract two months later. They had actually begun lunar orbit rendezvous studies in the late 1950s and again in 1961, and the contract cost was expected to be around $350 million. That was a lot back then."

"In the early days, there were initially four major subcontractors, like Bell Aerosystems, for the ascent engine, Hamilton Standard, for environmental control systems, Marquardt, who made the reaction control system, and of course, Rocketdyne, who made the descent engine."

The elderly engineer still had a mind as sharp as a tack. "The Primary Guidance, Navigation and Control System was developed by the MIT Instrumentation Laboratory, and the Apollo Guidance Computer was manufactured by Raytheon. Oh yeah, there was a backup navigation piece, called the Abort Guidance System that was developed by TRW."

Jackie Biehn wrote as fast as he talked. "That sounds like a pretty complex program."

"You ain't kidding." He nodded. "You know, up until 1962,

most engineers, including Wernher von Braun, thought we could get to the moon and back in one rocket. But a guy named John Houbolt stuck to his guns and showed them, on paper anyway, that it wouldn't work. He claimed that the only way we could get men there and back was with the lunar orbit model. Von Braun publicly thanked him in 1969 after Armstrong and Aldrin landed and made it back. So, the fact that we really needed a LEM was his brainchild."

"Tell me more about the project." Jackie asked.

"You have to understand the climate at the time. We loved what we did. Really loved it. We were going into space, and, of course, we were competing with the Russians. It was a feeling, you know?"

"Yes. Keep going. "She urged.

The Saturn V was going to get us there, but it was our spacecraft that was going to get American men on the moon and bring them back. We had a significant amount of pride in everything we did. We had parts of this thing being built at more than five thousand locations around the country. We even built models, mock-ups, to practice every element of the flight. The descent stage had a propulsion and pressurization system, and all the propellant for landing. All this stuff we left behind on the moon. Our plan was to leave what we didn't need. There was an adapter stage that held the LEM while it was being transported and explosive bolts to kick out the legs. We designed equipment bays for experiments; seismological, atmospheric, magnetic fields. There were geological experiments, and a means to collect specimens in sealed containers. We had to allow for TV cameras and cables and had to have a throttle-able engine so we could control thrust, because the moon only had about one-sixth of the gravity that we have here on Earth."

"We designed a thermal shielding application to insulate the spacecraft against temperature extremes and buffer against any tiny meteoroids. But there was no way to fly it on earth, so we could only design simulations. The first time those engines fired, they were in space. There was no way to practice with them. They either worked the first time, or people died. It was something." He paused as he remembered those days.

"There was a lot of input needed from the pilot too. The computer could only fly it to about two hundred fifty feet, and then there was a manual take-over. And even with that, once they got to about twenty feet or so they had to shut down and let it drop the last few feet."

He was quiet for a moment of reflection. "I still remember when Sputnik was launched. It was a rude awakening for our country. It gave us a kick in the ass to really get the program going. It was a PR disaster for us, but by 1961 JFK said that we were going to the moon. And I don't know if you were born yet, but Gagarin orbiting the earth took us in to high gear."

"Higher, faster and farther. That was our motto." He added, almost solemnly.

Biehn thought she saw a tear in the old man's eye as he went on. "Even the design of landing gear. Geez, we didn't even know what surface of the moon was made of. We didn't know if it was light powder that we'd sink into, or even ice; y'know, slippery and hard. There were proposal models and operational models built for different purposes. The project was our lives."

Karlsson looked around the room at McAdams' collection of photographs, memories of friends, family and coworkers through the years. His gaze paused on a black and white photo taken in front of a launch pad at NASA. There were a dozen men in white short-sleeve shirts, wearing hard hats and smiles. He got up from the sofa and went to the shelf. "When was this taken?"

McAdams dropped his footrest and leapt out of his easy-chair with pride. He picked up the old photograph and reminisced as he handed it to Karlsson. "That had to be around 1966. The company sent a bunch of us down to the Cape as something of a reward for our hard work. They wanted us to get the feel of the overall program, so that we all knew what we were working towards."

He pursed his lips. "Yeah, I'm the last of that group."

Karlsson studied the faces. "But I bet you remember most of these guys."

"Of course!" He rattled off several names as he pointed to them and explained what each man did on the project.

Karlsson nodded at Jackie, who pulled the two photos out of her folio. "Mr. McAdams, would you have a look at these? Do you remember this man?" She handed him the copies of the two photos they had found in Martin Jeffers' home. The one from the personnel file had been cropped and the cosmonaut uniform had been digitally altered to look like he was wearing a civilian suit of clothes.

McAdams found his glasses on top of one of the piles of magazines and slipped them on with one hand as he studied the images. "I remember this guy. I met him in a couple of meetings when we discussed system operability between the Command Module and the LEM. He wasn't one of ours. He was with one of the sub-contractors working on the Command Module side. What the devil was that guy's name?"

He looked up at the ceiling in the corner of the room. "It was Nick something. I remember he had a weird accent. You couldn't tell if he was English or Slavic...you know...Eastern Europe or Russian, maybe. As I recall though, he wasn't on the program long. When we got back down there in October 1968, he wasn't there anymore."

"We were there for a week in preparation for Apollo Seven. Wally Schirra, one of the original Mercury astronauts was on that one. We all hung out together that week. You know, I think that's the guy that blew himself up in his boat."

Karlsson glanced at Jackie before speaking. "Blew himself up?"

"Yeah. The scuttlebutt at the time was that he was shaken up about the fire on Pad 34. You know, Apollo One. I don't think anyone knew for sure, but some of the people he worked with said he probably took his boat out and drank himself silly. He either did something stupid that caused it to blow, or...you know, suicide."

"Did he have any close friends that you knew of?" Jackie asked sympathetically.

"Oh, I don't know. We were on different projects and he was gantry-cleared. Whenever there was a test, he was up on the gantry with the crews."

"Did you ever get to know any of the other gantry folks?"

"No. They were all a friendly bunch, though. Committed to the project. But we didn't socialize with them. Maybe saw them in one or two meetings over the years."

Jackie changed the subject. "Please, tell me more about LEM fourteen. When was the last time you saw it?"

He nodded, a big smile coming to his face as he returned his group photo to its place and moved to the corner of the room. There was a four-by-six inch black and white photograph of McAdams and another man. In the background, the looming presence of a Lunar Module could be seen.

"This is a shot of me and Ted Daimler standing in front of it. Ted was my manager at the time, and I think this was taken just about a week before the Air Force came in and told us to take it apart and ship it to the Navy in San Francisco."

"The Navy?" Karlsson asked.

"Yeah. I think they were going to use it in an exhibit. We had gotten a stop-work order on it sometime in 1970, and so I know that it wasn't completed."

"How *completed* was it?" Jackie asked.

"Pretty close." McAdams replied. The ascent and descent stages were complete, but there weren't any engines." His finger went to his lips. "You know what? I think I've got something here that will improve my memory." He slowly dropped to a knee and opened a cabinet door beneath his bookshelves. He pulled a stack of file folders and loose papers out to the floor and began to go through them. Suddenly the old man broke into a grin as he pulled a folder out and held it up. "Here you go!"

Karlsson opened the folder and asked, "What am I looking for?"

McAdams rose and took the folder from him and opened it up on the dining room table. He went through the top few pages and then found the one he was looking for. "For this!"

Karlsson looked at the aged document. In small type across the top of the page was printed Grumman Aircraft Engineering Corporation, and immediately below it in larger block letters: LOG.

McAdams explained. "This was back in the day before we had computers and spread sheets. We had a hundred people on this project working twenty-four hours a day and the only way we could accurately track progress was to keep written logs. This is my original from..." He squinted to read his handwriting in the space allotted for the date. "September 18, 1970."

Karlsson looked at the form. As far as he could tell, it appeared genuine. To the right of the LOG title, was a space for page number, and in it had been stamped *No. 94530* in a Roman typestyle. Underneath, in handwriting that McAdams attested was his, was his name, the *Project: LM14*, and the *Location: Plant 5*.

On the line below that, he noted the *Time* as *Day Shift*, the *Title* as *Dismantle/Ship*, and the *Date* as *September 18, 1970*.

Karlsson read the man's handwritten remarks in the space below. "Ted Daimler advised that LM 14 is to be broken down and crated for shipment. AF supplied a dozen personnel under the supervision of Lt. Col. Borchardt. Crate numbers: 57550, 57551, 57552. AF took custody of crates at 5:15 PM."

McAdams nodded. "Yeah. It's coming back to me. They came in on Friday morning. Ted told me to take off at 5:15, and when I came back in on Monday, it was gone."

Biehn looked at the document. "This is an original. Why didn't it go into the official log?"

"Ted said that the Air Force didn't want anything in the log and for me to get rid of the entry. So, I stuck it in my personal folder and forgot about it."

"No notations as to destination?" Karlsson asked.

"Huh uh. I supervised the packing and crating, but I didn't see any of the shipping paperwork. I thought I heard one of them say something about San Francisco, in conversation. Come to think of it, that's how I knew it was going to the Navy."

Jackie looked at the form. "Who was this Lieutenant Colonel Borchardt?"

McAdams shook his head. "No idea. We were civilians, as you know, but we still had government security clearances. There was a lot of stuff on the project, that even though Apollo was public knowledge, certain parts of it were classified. We did what we were supposed to do, and only asked questions when they related to our own piece of the project."

"Had you ever met Borchardt before?" Jackie asked as she took out her phone.

"Huh uh. I don't think so." He shrugged.

"Would you mind if I took a quick picture of this?"

"Not at all. You're the first person to see it in fifty years."

It was almost three thirty in the afternoon when the box truck backed into a driveway on Country Club Drive in Medina. There were very few people who might have recognized that it was the same box truck that had backed into a driveway in Moreland Hills a day before and departed with several million dollars' worth of US currency and gold ingots. To the rest of the casual observers in the upper-middle class neighborhood, it would look like nothing more than a delivery of something. Perhaps, new furniture. Maybe, a washer and dryer.

However, on this day, the cargo was eight highly trained and well-equipped tactical agents of the US Secret Service. Several had spent time on the impressive, and sometimes mysterious, Counter Assault Team. Franklin Jones finished the delivery, slammed the rear door shut and secured it before parking the truck two streets over and walking back. Six more agents, dressed in dark clothing and full body armor, sat quietly in a Chevrolet Suburban two blocks away. Their mission was to roll on signal.

The newly named Assistant Special Agent in Charge of the Cleveland Regional Office, Franklin Jones, looked at his watch and at six forty in the evening, took out his cell phone and notified the chief of Medina Police Department that they were about to serve a federal warrant, and respectfully requested that they keep their cruisers out of the area until further advised.

Peter Pasternak followed the commands of his GPS system and

found the location. His palms were still sweaty, and he feared he'd lost several pounds, and years off of his life, throughout the day. He tapped the attaché case on the seat beside him. It had been a gift from his parents upon his college graduation. He had tried to get the money into a paper bag, but it seemed lopsided and unsecure, and so he tossed the cash into the only other conveyance he could find on short notice. To say that he was nervous would have been an understatement. He knew he wasn't going to be there that long, and so he parked in the driveway and grabbed the case. He looked quickly about to see if he could spot anyone who might see him, and when he got to the door, he knocked lightly.

Patricia Knight opened the door. She looked briefly past him and then out towards the driveway and his car. "Come in. I'd like to count it."

His trepidation was overwhelming, and his heart rate was higher than anything he'd ever experienced. "Okay." He entered and handed her the case. "If it's possible, I'd like to keep my briefcase. It was a gift."

"What?" She said, looking at the rainwater-worn leather briefcase. It looked old, but expensive, and he seemed something of a prig. "Yeah. I don't care." She took the case from him and handed him her cell phone. Or rather a model that looked like the one that she had shown him earlier in his office. "This is what you want. I got a new one today and won't need it anymore." She dumped the cash, unceremoniously, on the couch and flipped through the bundles of currency. "This is close enough."

Pasternak gently slid the phone into his jacket pocket and turned to leave.

She stopped him in his tracks. "Just curious. Why? Why did you have to kill him?"

"What? Why?" He looked down, ashamed. "I'm sorry. It was a mistake. I never meant it to happen."

She had something on her mind, and she wanted him to hear it. "Jared and I were more than coworkers. I need to know something; did you know the man who killed him?"

The black Suburban had started to roll towards the Country Club Drive address as soon as Pasternak had been seen by the surveillance team. They were around the corner, about three driveways away, when the radio chirped. "SPITFIRE ONE, hold your position! Hold your position! We have an unknown heading up the walk to the house. But be ready to move fast if we go hot!"

Pasternak wanted to bare his soul. He wanted the opportunity to tell her things. How sorry he was. He knew that she would be dead in minutes. "I can't say any more." He stopped-short his soliloquy and then reached for the doorknob as the doorbell rang. He quickly looked through the peephole at the large frame of the man on the porch.

"Friend of yours?" He asked wondering if she had a boyfriend coming over.

"Not mine." She shook her head. This was not how the apprehension had been planned. They were going to wait and take him when he opened the door.

She stepped cautiously forward to the door. "Who is it?" She asked, genuinely curious.

The door exploded open, showering the living room in wooden splinters. Tricia fell backwards to the floor; Pasternak was frozen in fright. Something was wrong.

The hulking Antropov burst through the front door, his hand with a secure hold on the pistol grip of the Mossberg 500 as he raised the muzzle towards Pasternak. It was the logical target. It was his training. The man was still standing and represented either a threat or a flight risk. Either way, Antropov knew that he could follow up on the woman after the first target was neutralized. As he began to bring his left hand up to the forend, and the index finger of his right hand began to apply pressure to the trigger, he was momentarily blinded by an intense red-light beam in his eye and he cocked his head out of the way to clear his vision and get a better site picture on Pasternak. Suddenly, there were more red lights coming from the darkness and he was disoriented and bewildered by the activity occurring in his periphery.

Whether or not he heard the command to drop his weapon was now irrelevant. An agent in the darkened hallway fired a three-round burst from the SR-16 CQB carbine, so quickly that the third shot has found its mark in his chest before the first shell casing hit the floor. Another agent simultaneously fired a single shot into the bridge of Antropov's nose, the bullet traversing the sinus cavity and destroying the brain stem. Antropov felt nothing more than a brief punching sensation on his head and chest and then he collapsed to the ground. He no longer existed.

The black Suburban rolled into the driveway and the tactical team jumped out as men in helmets and armor poured in from the adjacent rooms inside the house. Pasternak frozen in shock, had not moved since the onset of the assault. He was pushed to the floor, searched and cuffed, a Velcro strap was fastened around his ankles and he was carried by two agents to the darkened kitchen "Stay down! We don't know who else is out there." An anonymous voice bellowed.

It was like a film scene moving at high speed, which had been slowed down to give the audience an idea of what was transpiring. One of the agents threw Pasternak's and Tricia's phones into a heavy lead-lined steel container and then searched the lifeless Antropov for his. It was thrown into the container as well and was placed in the back of the Suburban. Antropov's and Pasternak's car keys were handed to Franklin Jones by a nebulous form in a helmet and black balaclava. There was too much to take in. It was too fast for Pasternak's mind to keep up.

Jones made the anticipated call to Medina police. "Special Agent Jones here. Warrant served, one down and one in custody. Roll EMS and a coroner."

One team scoured the outside of the house and surrounding area as the surveillance team drove the neighborhood. Within minutes, the all-clear signal was given, and they departed, leaving the indoor team to tidy up.

An agent walked back to get the truck and return for the remaining tactical team members, who were then driven into the night.

They passed an arriving Medina police cruiser and an EMS squad on their way out of the neighborhood. It had happened just that fast.

Jones met the local police at the front door and waved them inside. Paramedics followed and checked the vitals on Antropov. The medic shook her head. Jones explained the incident to Medina PD officer who took copious notes and then started taking photos and video of the crime scene. It was fast and surreal.

Marchand was already in the kitchen with Pasternak. "You're a US Attorney, so I can Mirandize you if you like or you can waive it for now. Either way, we're going to talk. And, just to make sure we start from a level playing field, you know that Mr. Antropov in there was going to kill you. He was raising that shotgun in your direction, and if we hadn't stepped in, you'd be dead, and we might be having this conversation with him."

Marchand un-cuffed him and then cuffed his hands in front of him so that he could drink from a bottle of water. "So, what's going on? Why did Mr. Antropov want to kill you?"

It was the second time that day he'd heard the name Antropov. An Antropov had been the president of the warehousing company where Farmington and Consterdine were killed. The name sounded familiar at the time, but he could not place it. "I don't know. I've never met him." Pasternak replied quietly.

"So, if neither Ms. Knight nor you ever heard of him, never met him, then I wonder who sent him here. Do you think he showed up by chance? He wasn't walking a dog or anything. He doesn't live in this neighborhood."

"I don't know." Pasternak was still in shock and needed time to process what had just taken place.

Marchand continued. "Jealous boyfriend, you think?"

Pasternak seized the opening. "Boyfriend. Yes, of course. He had to have been someone that was involved with Ms. Knight. He saw me come in and was struck by a jealous rage."

"Ah. So, you think they had a thing and he'd been here before?"

"Yes. That must be it."

"But he didn't have a key."

"What?" Pasternak looked up.

"He kicked the front door in. If he'd wanted to surprise you two, why wouldn't he have used a key, or waited for you two to get cozy?"

"Uh..."

Marchand cut him off. "No. The smart money is on the fact that he tailed you here. He was following you, not her."

"I...I don't know what..."

"Come on counselor. That guy wanted to kill you. If he just wanted her, he would have waited until you left. Why have an extra witness? Why kill two people if you only really wanted one of them?"

Pasternak unscrewed the cap on the bottle and took several healthy swallows as he tried to find rational answers.

"Look, you might as well be honest with me now. Your career in federal service is finished. Knight is willing to testify that you hired her and Jared Farmington to search a residence in Moreland Hills, even though no such criminal case exists in the federal system. We checked. The people that you brought back in to grab a safe, are now dead. Probably killed by the guy in the living room who is gradually assuming room temperature. When the US Attorney hears about this, you'll be fired. A lengthy and comprehensive investigation will follow and there's a good likelihood that you'll be imprisoned, or at the very least, disbarred. We have you on a wire, consenting to pay Ms. Knight fifty thousand dollars for her silence. It's the same fifty grand you showed up with tonight. Do you want to talk?"

"I am an Assistant US Attorney..."

"Not anymore. Not now. The real US attorney on this case is trying to decide whether to charge you as a terrorist or not. That means no phone calls...no free shower. You're on the next plain to Guantanamo Bay. I bet you don't speak Arabic, do you?"

"You don't understand." Pasternak murmured.

"I don't have to understand shit! You showed up tonight with fifty grand in hush money! Who sent you?"

"What?"

"Oh, come on! US attorneys don't have people killed. US attorneys don't pay people off. Who sent you? Who told you that it was a good idea to show up at this house tonight and pay off a woman you sent to rob a house and collect the evidence?"

Pasternak was adamant. "It's not like you think!"

Marchand leaned closer to the man. "It ain't about what I think, Counselor. It's about what I can prove. Do you know what a Faraday Cage is?"

"A what?" Pasternak had heard the term but couldn't figure out what bearing it had on his predicament.

"A Faraday Cage. A shielded environment where radio waves can't penetrate."

Pasternak was genuinely confused. "No...I..."

"Right now, your phone, and Antropov's phone are on their way to a lab that is shielded. You know why? Because we're going to take those phones, image their guts, and we're going to find out who you and Antropov called this month. What do you think we'll find?"

"What?" The former public servant was still in shock from the events of the evening. He had brought the phone that Uncle Ted had told him to bring. "What are you saying?"

"In a half hour, we're going to know who you called. We're going to know who Antropov called. It's going to lead us to someone. It will lead us to the guy who wanted to kill you tonight. Does that make sense to you? And by then, the person with whom you've been having these calls will see that both phones went dead, right here in this house at the same time. That means he or she will be burning their phones, emails and everything that ever had your name on it. You'll be on your own."

"But..." Pasternak struggled to collect his thoughts. "You'll need a warrant."

"Oh." Marchand said, somewhat surprised. "Did I forget to mention that we had one? We have an arrest warrant for you for espionage, and a search warrant for your house, your person, your car, your phone...about everything you own."

His hands were shaking uncontrollably. "There's been a terrible mistake." Pasternak said has he tried to take another drink of his water.

It was almost nine that evening when Golovkin's phone rang. He recognized the number and answered in Russian. "Allo."

The voice replied, also in Russian. "We've lost both phones."

"When?"

"Almost two hours ago."

"Where?"

"The address in Medina, Ohio. The one that you asked us to mask." The voice replied, referring to the software that allowed them to isolate texts, emails and conversations occurring around a given address.

Golovkin collected his thoughts as he looked at his wife, snoring peacefully on the couch. "Did you capture anything else?"

"There was some cell-phone traffic, but we also picked up encrypted RF, before and after."

Golovkin wilted. Civilians didn't use encrypted communications. Neither did local law enforcement agencies. The US government had them. He had misjudged the Americans and would now have to remediate the situation before it got out of control. If it hadn't already. "Very well." He tried to clear his thoughts and searched his brain. What was the name of the non-official cutout in New York? "Alert SARDIUS. Tell him I will be there in the morning." He paused. "And have him activate OBVAL."

"OBVAL?" The voice on the other end spelled the word to make sure he had it correctly.

"Da. Bystro!" He answered and tossed the phone onto the coffee table with a clatter.

He touched his wife gently on the shoulder. "Razbudit' moyu lyubov'."

She stirred and smiled. "I thought we only spoke English in America?"

"We are going home, moyu lyubov. It is time to pack."

CHAPTER 19

S am, the giant with the scar across his cheek, placed the computer tower on the floor beside Zhou's desk. Liu Wei gestured at the shell containing two hundred thousand dollars; twenty stacks of hundreds with one hundred bills per stack. The tower had been hollowed out and converted for use as a travelling deposit box.

Zhou looked at it as he lit a cigarette. "Is that the full amount?"

"Yes. As we discussed."

"Where did you get the cash?" He asked as he exhaled a plume of smoke through his nostrils. The billows hit the desk surface and rolled like clouds during a gathering storm.

"From the bank." Liu Wei snorted. "Where else?"

Zhou nodded thoughtfully. "It would seem that my associate was able to get you through Customs without issue?"

"Yes, thank you."

Zhou smiled. "Very well. So, you are back and ready to do some more business. As we discussed, I will help you build your own market if you will help supply my existing ones. Mostly computer parts."

Liu Wei shrugged. "I'm not an IT guy...a computer guy. If we can make money, I don't mind bringing them in, but I have no outlet for them."

"That is not a problem. I will arrange their distribution once you get them ashore. I want you to incorporate. Create a legitimate company."

"I can do that, but I don't know if the State of California is the best place to do that. If we are going to create a legitimate enterprise, if we are going to approach this as a legitimate business, I can think of other US states that have better tax regulations."

Zhou smiled. "We have developed an element of trust between us. You may incorporate wherever you think it is most beneficial. We will import our products through the cities you mentioned. I have people who can accept the goods and move them throughout your country. However, speed is essential."

Liu Wei nodded. "Of course. But how much speed? When do you want to have these goods go to market?"

"It is very important to me that these enter commerce before September. As a matter of fact, I think that July or August would be even better."

"I am ready to go now. I want the money, so I am happy to do whatever it takes to meet your timetable."

Zhou smiled. "I know you will." He paused as he straightened the papers on his desk. "I usually do not concern myself with minor details, but how did you induce the stroke?"

Jerry Lee, now Liu Wei, waited before answering. He had been briefed by a physician who was on the support team for the Secret Service. "It just fell into place. I was going to make it look like a slip and fall down the stairs after a night of drinking, but the events just unfolded, and I took advantage of it. Jeffers was already predisposed to a bad health condition due to his weight, age and level of fitness. When we met, I told him that I was an associate of yours and we ended up going out for drinks. I used an escort service to send an appropriate woman to meet us. She insisted on drinking Vodka mixed with some energy drink and convinced him that it would lead to...uh...sexual arousal."

"By one o'clock in the morning, his heart was racing, so I offered to drive him home. The woman came with us and did what she was paid to do. Afterwards, I gave her cash and she left. Her fingerprints were everywhere, and others saw her leave the bar with us. Anyway, I was going to snap his neck, and make it look like a fall down the stairs, but he collapsed. He went numb on one side, and I used a pillow to smother him."

Zhou looked at him for a moment. "And the police believed it was natural causes?"

"Yes. I was concerned about the presentation of petechial hemorrhage, but that could be explained away by the stroke. I was careful not to apply too much pressure on the pillow to cause an indentation of the teeth on the inside of his lips, so I rolled him onto his stomach and face to make it appear more natural."

Zhou surveyed the man's body language but could find nothing to make him think he was being less than honest. "You seem to be well-informed in the field of forensic medicine." He paused for a moment. "Obviously, you have watched too much western television. Did he have a family?"

Wei Liu gave the impression of curiosity. "I don't know. I only met him that one time, and after it was done, I wiped my prints off everything I touched, and headed back to my hotel."

"How was the body discovered?"

Liu Wei returned Zhou's stare with realistic confusion. "I don't know that, either. I assume a maid or someone. I really didn't think about it. Does it matter?"

Zhou studied the young man intently. "It does not."

Zhou lit another cigarette. "I have another favor. You live in San Francisco, yes?"

"Yes."

"Very expensive place in which to live, yes?"

Liu Wei nodded. "Yes, very much so."

"I have been thinking about investing in real estate in the area and I wonder if I could get you to represent me?"

"Represent you? I'm not a licensed realtor."

"That does not matter. I would like you to find a suitable piece of property that I could purchase as an investment. I would only need it two or three weeks a year. When I am not there, you would be welcome to stay there. Perhaps you could oversee that the property is maintained, and services are kept up?"

"Free rent?" Liu Wei asked.

Zhou smiled. "We are business partners. We will say that this house is owned by the business."

"So, you want me to buy you a house, but keep your name out of it."

"That is correct. Would that be possible?"

"Of course. What kind of house would you like?"

"Nothing...uh...ostentatious. Something large enough that I can bring guests or entertain. I will need a garage."

"Do you need to be in the city, or would something more private, outside of town be acceptable?"

Zhou drew on his cigarette. "Privacy is important to me."

Liu Wei thought about the request. He could not guess as to what Zhou had in mind, but he was intrigued that he was going to be a part of helping him select a place that the government would have plenty of time to wire before it was ever occupied. "Why San Francisco? That is one of the most expensive places in the country to live. I assume your main need would be proximity to an international airport. Are you open to other cities?"

Zhou thought about his plan. "I would consider Seattle. Or Chicago."

Liu Wei frowned. "Why those two cities? Why not the south?"

"It is quite simple. If I need to be out of the country in a hurry and do not feel safe in an airport, both of those cities have water access, and are also close to the Canadian border. Your Border Patrol watches the southern borders more closely, and Asians seem to stand out there."

"Okay, but none of our business will be running through those cities. Is that a problem?"

"All the better." Zhou stubbed his cigarette out in the brass ashtray. "I need a presence in your country. I need...what is the phrase? I want to be a solid citizen. I am a global businessman and want to be regarded as such."

Liu Wei shrugged. "San Francisco is nice. I don't know Seattle, but I could find you a place north of Chicago. By boat, you would follow Lake Michigan north through to Mackinaw, and then you're five or ten miles from the Canadian shore. You could drive it, but you'd have to drive through Wisconsin."

Zhou smiled. "Chicago. I have an associate in Chicago. It would be nice to see her again."

———·«(»)»·———

Stan Marchand frowned at the stack of documents resting beside the laptop that had been loaned to him by the Secret Service. He looked back at his screen to see the notes and attachments sent from the financial investigator in Washington. He knew that it would take some time to review the information and if it were as dry as he anticipated, he figured it would be better to start the morning with something a little more stimulating. A Deputy had dropped off a copy of Antropov's autopsy report earlier, and even though he did not expect to see anything surprising in it, he felt that it would still be more intriguing than looking at data fields and dashboards.

Tricia had been moderately traumatized by the event, and all concerned decided that a couple of days in the sun would be a great way to put it behind her. She had a cousin in Siesta Key, so she locked up her apartment, traded cell phones with one from the Secret Service cache and headed south. The task force was unsure if anyone might be tracking her personal cell, and did not want anyone knowing where she was, besides them.

Stan promised her that when it was all over, he would teach her how to play golf. But in the meantime, it would be sensible for her to relax and take a couple of private lessons from a local pro in Florida. They joked that there were some things, like hanging wallpaper, or giving lessons for something, which should not be undertaken by spouses or significant others. Some years earlier, a prospective girlfriend had asked him to teach her how to shoot a gun. He was well-qualified, and it was a fun experiment, but eventually both realized that it would be better to take lessons from a third-party, who had no intention of sleeping with either one of them.

The autopsy didn't tell him anything that he hadn't witnessed firsthand. It began with a description of how the body was received in the Medical Examiner's Office and included the usual notations such as date, time, and description.

"The body is that of a normally developed white male measuring seventy-three inches and weighing two hundred twelve pounds and appearing generally consistent with the stated age of forty-six years. The body is cold and un-embalmed. Lividity is fixed in the distal portions of the limbs. The eyes are open. The irises are brown, and the pupils measure 0.4 cm. The hair is brown and approximately two inches in length. The ears are unremarkable, but the nose has a wound of entrance. The teeth are natural. The chest is symmetrical, and the abdomen is flat. The upper and lower extremities show no deformities. There are abrasions and contusions to the right cheek area. The hands and the nails are clean and evidence no injury."

"There appears a short-range gunshot wound of the facial area of the head with extensive Cranio-cerebral injuries. Entrance point is through the top of the nasal bone and measures approximately six millimeters. The missile perforated the skin and subcutaneous tissue. It passed through the soft tissues of the nose, nasal cavity and into the base of the skull. It appears to have tumbled as it transected the brain stem. It then passed along the left base of the skull and left cerebellar hemisphere, creating a gutter type defect along the anterior edge. It exited from the skull in the upper left portion of the occipital bone. It created a defect here that measures approximately 1.2 cm at the inner-table and shows up to 0.7cm of outward beveling. This is a fatal wound."

Stan read through the report describing the other three rounds that Antropov had taken in his chest and flipped through the photographs made during the procedure. In lay terms, they shot him in the nose, aiming for the brainstem. Simultaneous follow-up shots to the chest went through his heart, aorta and left lung. He was, as they said in the business, *DRT*. Dead Right There.

As he closed the folder, his mind took him back to that night in Medina. He could not recall if Antropov had at all responded to voice commands to drop his weapon. Had there even been any commands? It was a blur now. He had been through the drill so many times himself that he could not distinguish between how he had been trained, and what had actually been said as the event transpired. He remembered his training in Beltsville years before, using simulated munitions. "Federal agent! Drop your weapon!" He had learned to divide his brain. He could call out commands at the same time he was readying the shot. He had even been trained to take the shot while he was mid-sentence. For some reason, perhaps due to cinematic portrayals, *bad guys* thought they were safe as long as responders kept talking.

Had they said it, or did he just think they'd said it? He had run countless repetitions of the same drill. The Special Operations community coined a slogan that the Secret Service CAT Team had adopted years earlier, *speed, surprise, violence of action*. It was inconsequential now. He shivered briefly and shook his head. It was a good shoot. If they had not neutralized Antropov, then others would have died that night. Now they were just waiting to see who claimed the body. He pushed the autopsy report aside and took a sip of his coffee.

He quickly looked through the return of the search warrant that had been executed at Antropov's residence in Euclid, by the Sheriff's Department and the Secret Service. Vasily Antropov had lived modestly in a three-bedroom home in a working-class neighborhood. The only son of the late Nikolay Antropov, he had been employed as a manager in his father's Lake Erie Container warehouse. When his father had passed away after a lengthy illness, Vasily was left with mounting bills, and an inability to grow the business. So, he took the easy way out and sold to a holding company named Platt Company, Limited.

Platt Company sent in a team of auditors to determine what the warehouse was realistically worth, and what its potential was as an investment. At the end of the week, they decided that while the real estate and building might have some value, the business was basically stagnant, and was seeing intense competition from larger organizations that could move more freight quicker, much less expensively. They offered Vasily an agreement and a check, and he took it. One of the provisions of the agreement was that he would serve as a property manager and maintain the property until such time as Platt found a new use for it.

Stan looked through the report. The Antropov residence was paid for, as were the property taxes for the year. The yard was mowed, the trash was picked up and his neighbors considered him to be an average guy. He and his wife, a transplanted Norwegian named Ingrid, lived within their means. They had no children. She was shocked at the circumstances of his death and seemed to have no idea that her husband could have been involved in anything illegal. However, at the time of the warrant, it was noted that she had bruises on her cheek and eye consistent with domestic abuse. There were also fist-sized holes in the walls in different rooms indicating that one of them had trouble controlling their temper. Also, of interest to the deputies serving the warrant, was her first question. "Will the fact that he was gunned down in the commission of a felony have any effect on his life insurance policy?"

She was assured that the search warrant was customary following unnatural death, and she should not assume anything about her late husband's character that she had not known before. As for the insurance, she would have to contact their broker to determine the exclusions under the policy.

No firearms were found during the search. Neither were any drugs or unexplainable cash. Their detached garage contained the kind of tools that one would expect to see for a warehouse owner or machinist. The couple shared a computer, which was several years old, and Ingrid provided the password for the deputies to take a quick look at the files. There was nothing sinister. Other than a few porn sites, there was nothing in either party's search history to indicate any type of secondary lifestyle.

Investigators were, however, surprised, that when they asked about cell phones, she was able to produce hers and her husband's. They went through the call and text histories and ask her if she could identify who each of the communications had been with. She readily complied and they determined that the data from both phones showed nothing more than social communications between family and friends. She informed them that to the best of her knowledge, neither of them had ever had any other phones. Stan recalled the night in Medina. Agents had seized the cell phone Antropov had carried and tossed it into the shielded container. He took another sip of his coffee and looked for the forensic report of that one.

It was an anonymous burn phone that had been acquired and paid for in cash from a local carry out. The file history indicated that it had only dialed two numbers, albeit several times. One number was to another burn phone in the 440-area code. It was a number that was found in the phone of a homicide victim several nights earlier; a habitual offender of questionable repute whose body had been discovered in the service area of a seedy used car lot on the East side of Cleveland. Rolando Mendocino.

Further research revealed that the other number was to an unregistered phone in Silver Spring, Maryland. It was from a block of numbers that had been acquired by a company called Prostodelat Global. An investigator's note indicated that the name, when literally translated from Russian meant, "Just Do." A check of records in the Washington DC area failed to reveal any references for any company of such a name.

The text, "IT IS DONE. NO PROBLEMS." seemed to coincide with the timing of the death of Mr. Mendocino.

"What have you got?" Franklin Jones stuck his head in the small temporary office space that had been loaned to Marchand.

Stan shrugged. "I haven't gotten that deep into the data yet, but it looks like Antropov might have been involved in the death of Jared Farmington and his partner at the warehouse. So, if we extrapolate a bit, Antropov whacked the guys who stole the safe out of Moreland Hills. Or, whacked the guy who whacked the guy who did it...this Mendocino character. Their deaths are most likely tied to the safe job and bugging at Moreland Hills. At the time of his death, he was carrying a burn phone that only showed contact between him and Mendocino, and him and a number in Maryland. It could be that the Maryland burn phone is where he got his orders. It would be quite nice to see who owns a company called Prostodelat Global. They own the block of numbers for the phones that he called."

"Prostodelat?" Jones repeated, confirming the spelling. "Okay, we'll check on it. What else have you got?"

Marchand clicked on the summary document that accompanied several spreadsheets. Some of the data had been taken from Martin Jeffers' hard drives, and some had been collected via subpoena from several financial institutions. His ex-wife had received a settlement of a paltry seven hundred fifty thousand, obviously unaware of the true depth of Marty's net worth.

"We need to find the identities of ARCHER and SEMPER, but I've got a feeling, looking at this stuff, that ARCHER is being paid through one of these political fronts, and that SEMPER was an inside guy, at one of the aerospace companies."

"Why do you say that?"

"There are transactions that show that much of SEMPER's payments were made in cash. ARCHER's were by electronic funds transfer to several political organizations. Many of them go through something called the Cramlington Youth Foundation. Cramlington is a city in the UK, but one of their board members has something of a familiar name."

"Who's that?" Jones asked.

"Well, not to start casting stones here, but the one that jumps out at me is a guy by the name of William Archer Layden."

Jones looked at him quietly for a moment. "Wait. Archer Layden?"

"Yes."

"The Senator's son? The Presidential candidate?"

"Yeah."

"Are you fucking sure?" Jones frowned.

"'Fraid so." Stan replied as innocently as he could. "And it looks like he's also served on the board of Platt."

"Who's Platt?" Jones walked over and picked up the file laying on top of the desk.

Platt is the holding company that owns the warehouse where Farmer and Consterdine were killed. Platt's worth over two billion, so I think they probably own a bunch of warehouses."

Jones looked up. "The fire?"

Marchand nodded. "Yeah. Young Layden is into all kinds of businesses, most of which have some sort of foreign connection. If I were the suspicious type, I'd think that he'd been trading on his daddy's name, especially while daddy was the head of the Armed Services Committee."

———— ⬤ ————

Karlsson looked around the frugally decorated office in the NASA Glenn Research Center on Brookpark Road, near the Cleveland Hopkins Airport, as Jackie Biehn perused the Military Personnel *201* file on her screen and read just loud enough that he could hear. "William Jefferson Borchardt, born 16 April 1931, in Shiloh Township, Neosho County, Kansas. Completed two years of Army ROTC, switched to Air Force for another two years. He received a BS in Engineering at Kansas State, and was commissioned in the United States Air Force September 1953. Basic flight training at Randolph and then to Nellis Air Force Base for advanced jet training, graduating in 1954."

It had not been that difficult to track down Lieutenant Colonel Borchardt, the last person known to have handled LEM number fourteen. On a hunch, she had checked the internments at Arlington National Cemetery and found her first lead. With the date of birth and death, and a military branch, her OSI access credentials got her the rest on their network.

"His assignments included 31st Tactical Fighter Wing, Homestead, Florida 1963, something called project SARDO in December of that year. Deployed Bien Hoa, Viet Nam in February 1964, and then Foreign

Technology Division, Air Force Systems Command, Wright Patterson in Dayton; project SARDO again. Hmmm...never heard of it."

"What can you find out?" Karlsson asked.

"Let's see." She exited one file and tried to locate the project name. "Nothing here."

"Nothing?"

She shook her head. "Nope. Whatever it was, there's no reference to it now. Could have been some Black Ops thing. They did a lot of that stuff there." She exited out of the site. "If it is, I'm sure I'll hear about it from the front office soon enough. They track all attempts to get into classified projects."

"SARDO?" Karlsson sat back in his chair. "What was going on in December of sixty-three?"

She smirked. "For the record, I wasn't born yet. The only thing that jumps out about that time period is the Kennedy assassination. JFK was trying to make peace with the Soviets, at least in terms of space exploration, but in November...well, you know."

"Yeah, Dealey Plaza." He ran his hand through his short salt and pepper hair. "And for the record, I wasn't all that old, myself. When was he at Wright-Patt?"

"Sixty-six to seventy-one."

"Wait, so when he was packing up the LEM, he was actually assigned to Foreign Technology?"

She looked again at the dates and assignments. "Yeah."

"What did he do after that?"

"Promoted to *bird* colonel and assigned to the Pentagon; seventy-one through September 1975. He was the Air Force Secretary's liaison to the National Military Command Center."

"Back up. You said he was in Viet Nam in February 1964?"

"Right." She confirmed.

"Viet Nam tours were usually twelve-months long. That would have brought him back stateside in February 1965."

"Yeah." She shrugged. "So?"

"So, what did he do for the year that reached from Viet Nam to Wright-Patterson?"

"I don't know. He might have gone back to Homestead, but the file doesn't say." She made another notation on her yellow pad.

"Where did he go in 1975?" Karlsson asked.

"Retired. Looks like his government paychecks were sent to an address in Titusville, Florida until 2008."

Karlsson leaned around to get a better view of the screen. "Deceased; June 18, 2008. Just like it said on his Arlington grave marker."

She thought for a moment. "I'm not normally paranoid, unless the job requires it, but let me look at something else." She exited out of the official Defense Department site and entered another site using a fictitious email account. There were a couple of minutes of silence before she paused and frowned.

"What is it?" Karlsson asked, reading her momentary facial affectation.

She exhaled purposefully. "Elmwood Cemetery, Chanute Kansas."

"Who's in Elmwood Cemetery?"

"William Jefferson Borchardt, born April 16, 1931. Died February 4, 1933."

Karlsson let it sink in as a discomforting chill ran up his spine. "But the Air Force is sure that he attended four years of ROTC, graduated with a degree in Engineering and was commissioned and sent to flight school. Are you sure it's the same guy?"

"Has to be." She scrolled through some other entries. "Unless there were two different William J. Borchardts born the same day in in Neosho, Kansas. I'm betting there weren't two Willie Borchardts born the same day anywhere in the country. Something's wrong."

Karlsson did some mental math. "He graduated from Kansas State in 1953, so we should assume he started in 1949?"

Biehn nodded. "Yeah. His records show four years there."

"They would have fingerprinted him and done a preliminary background when he started ROTC."

"They do now. I'm not sure what type of background checks they did on students in 1949. I'd have to check." She made a notation on the yellow tablet next to the computer monitor.

Karlsson sat down in one of the uncomfortable plastic and metal side chairs. "That was way before Khrushchev and Kennedy could have been hatching a deal to trade astronauts." He tugged on his earlobe in deep thought. "Can you go back into Borchardt's 201 file? Look at his parents' records and see if they have Kansas birth certificates."

"Hmmm...just a minute." Biehn returned to his personal history. "Parents were Rudolph and Magda Bruckmann Borchardt. Let's see what we have on them." She scoured the net for a couple of long minutes. "Here we are. Rudolph and Magda. No birth certificates, but they were naturalized, Ft. Bliss Texas, September 29, 1947."

"Ft. Bliss?" Karlsson asked.

"Oh shit." Biehn was quiet for a moment. "PAPERCLIP."

Karlsson remembered the name from a military history lecture. "Don't tell me; Rudy and Maggie were German rocket scientists?"

"The timing is right. As is the location." She clicked on a link and read from the summary, "At first it was called Operation OVERCAST, July 20, 1945. The Army Counter-Intelligence Corps rounded up German scientists and their families and sent them to a camp in Bavaria. There, they were interviewed and their potential for de-Nazification and later use by the United States, supposedly to shorten the war in Japan, was evaluated."

"In November 1945, Operation OVERCAST was renamed Operation PAPERCLIP by some senior Ordnance Corps officers, who would attach a paperclip to the folders of those rocket experts whom they wished to bring into the program in America. Truman approved the program and expanded it to include more than fifteen hundred scientists and close to four thousand family members. At first, the participants were considered to be in limited military custody, but by 1947, some were quietly being offered a path to citizenship."

Karlsson remembered the ethical dilemma from a high school history class. The US Government, in a sincere effort to shorten the war with Japan, needed German technology. Technology that had been produced by Nazis, with the help of Jewish slave labor.

Many of the most brilliant scientists of the day had some sort of connection to the Nazi party. Thus, it became something of a public relations quandary for the senior military staff to decide who got hanged and who got a new life and a trip to the United States. "So, the Army gave his parents a new identity and moved them to Kansas after the war."

"That's what it looks like to me. Remember, Werner Von Braun was a member of that group, too."

"Von Braun?"

"Yeah." She exited out of the page. "The guy that got us to the moon."

———((●))———

Despite not having left his chair for over an hour, Marchand was exhausted. He needed a break from the spreadsheets he had been studying, and so the text from the number in Virginia could not have come at a better time. "CHECK EMAIL".

He exited his text app and scrolled through his new emails. When he found the one from Grand Emperor Insurance, he knew that Paul was following through on their discussion from the previous day.

"I have on the desk in front of me, an envelope with the number T12542. Please tell me what you can about it."

The discussion with Paul had brought to light that he and Karlsson were basically on the same team, even though they had different roles to play. Marchand was to be the organization's official front, cooperating and in some cases, leading the Secret Service side of the investigation. Karlsson would be assisting the Air Force's OSI investigation until such time as his part broke away from theirs.

The timing of the request was curious, but the tasking didn't necessarily have to have anything to do with their current case. On the contrary, it was unproductive to allow a viewer to know or even suspect anything about a tasking for fear of front-loading and complicating the noise or overlay that could enter his conscious brain while trying to allow genuine sensations and perceptions to push their way out of his sub-conscious. Nevertheless, he was ready for a break.

He closed and locked the office door and turned out the lights. After stepping out of his shoes, he leaned back in his chair and put his feet up on the desk. He inserted the rubber earplugs that he had been carrying around in his pocket since his handgun qualification a few days earlier. He deepened and steadied his breathing and pushed the ambient noises and distractions out of his head and into the small mental dustpan so that they could be locked away until he needed them again. The traffic noise on Rockside Road was now absent, as were the comings and goings of people in the hallway outside. He was safe, warm, and relaxed.

His mind turned to a blank screen, and he thought about the envelope that someone had on their desk in one of Washington DC's many suburbs. Someone wanted to know more about it. The information was available in the universe. He just had to tap into it and allow it to come through to his conscious brain. He reached for a sheet of blank paper and wrote the tasking number and his initials in the upper left-hand corner, before drawing a random, nonsensical ideogram below that.

It came to him quickly. The target was a person. Marchand made notations on the left side of the page as the perceptions emerged. He tapped the ideogram a couple of times to help draw out additional gestalts about the target. It was a male. Older, but good physical shape.

Lean, assertive, committed.

Short hair. Like a crew cut.

Former military. Civilian leadership position now.

A pilot. Long ago. Retired military. Marchand got the image of dress blues with a white cap. Gold braid on the bill. Marines. Major or Lieutenant Colonel?

Considered himself ethical at one time. Now conflicted.

Living a double life. Can't be truthful with family and friends.

Feels like his secret is about to be discovered.

The secret will ruin him.

Almost caught once before; one or two years earlier. Somewhere overseas. Europe. Maybe Italy. Somewhere near the water.

Marchand tried to sketch something, but his page was filling up. He pulled a blank sheet closer and wrote the date and then drew another ideogram beneath it. An image was trying to push through. He traced over the ideogram and tried to listen to his subconscious. He felt a need to push further back in time.

A jolt went through him as he sensed the speed of something moving. Something in a tube. Underground. Incredible speed. His pencil started to sketch; tubes that connected cities. Underground. Secret. Public not aware of them. Like a subway, but not marked. Entry is through regular looking office buildings. Elevators that go deep beneath the ground. Heavily guarded.

Marchand clumsily drew something that looked like a map of the United States and drew lines that connected some cities. Not necessarily cities, but population centers of sorts. People connected by their occupations. Connected by their common interests. "Maybe, military bases?" He wrote, and then notated *analytic overlay* in parenthesis. He drew lines from Los Angeles to Nevada. From west Texas to New Mexico and Utah. Some sort of subway or underground tram; a railway system. Very high speed. Two or three hundred miles per hour. Impossible.

Marchand leaned back and deepened his breathing again. He quieted his mind as much as he could. Where was his target? What was he doing on the underground rail system? It took a while for images to surface. His target steps off the train and must submit to some form of physical examination. People in white. Take his temperature. Take his blood. Swab his mouth for a DNA sample.

Inside a large area...warehouse? Hangar? He boards a bus... something like a bus, with no windows. Brief ride before he gets out in another enclosed space. Another hangar? Downstairs. Underground walkway. White block walls. Long, like a quarter mile. Passes by some intersections leading off in other directions.

Guards...people in uniform, with rifles, walking with him. Climbs two flights of stairs...comes out in another hangar area. Sleek looking aircraft. Incredible, unlike anything he's ever seen. Far more advanced than the F-4's he flew during Viet Nam. Astounding... fleur-de-lis, like the tip of a spear.

Marchand sketched what he saw and tried to bi-locate; to remove himself from his physical body to psychically put himself in the hangar so that he could learn more about this aircraft. He ran his hand along the smooth dark metal. It was ice cold. He tried to experience everything he could about it. Size, performance, capabilities, propulsion. And then he was startled. He was suddenly alerted to another presence. There was another psychic in the room with him. He could not see the form but could feel the presence. He had to leave. Now!

———————— ((O)) ————————

Karlsson's cell phone buzzed, and he risked the ire of local police and the potential for a multi-car accident, so that he could quickly glance at the text.

"They're holding him in an interview room in Independence."

"Are you sure it'll work?" Jackie Biehn asked as they neared the departures lane at Cleveland Hopkins.

He found an empty space and put the car into Park as he looked her in the eyes with a smile. "I'm never sure of anything these days. My thought is that it will. But call me when you get to DC and I'll give you the scoop."

She kissed him hard on the mouth. "How long before I see you again?"

He shrugged. "A couple of weeks, maybe three." He brushed the hair back out of her eyes. "You know, spring in the desert Southwest can be an invigorating experience. Snow in the mountains, hot sun in the low-lying areas below. There's a lot to do out there if you just want to get away for a while."

She inhaled deeply through her nose. "I think I'd like that, Mr. Karlsson." She reached over and hugged his neck once before getting out of the car. He popped the trunk and went around to grab her suitcase.

"See you in a few weeks." He kissed her again, and as she took the handle of her bag, she gave up another one of those smiles. The smiles he thought about all too often. He suddenly missed her, and she wasn't yet out of his sight. But there was work to be done.

He arrived at the Secret Service office about fifteen minutes later and thought about what he was going to say, and how he was going to say it. Sometimes one can bluff their way through such things, but then sometimes one must be ready to lean across the table and punch someone hard enough that they would not think about calling your bluff. This was a federal office, and the subject was a well-educated US Attorney, who was used to getting his own way. The trick would be to get him to believe the decisions he was going to make were his own idea.

Franklin Jones met him at the door to the suite with two file folders and a suspicious grin. "I've been told to give you these and to get all of the agents into a conference room at the other end of the hall for the next half hour. Will that be long enough?"

He opened the folders and quickly glanced at the documents. "Well, I'm no expert, but I think I'll know in ten minutes if this is going to work or not."

Jones nodded and tapped him on the shoulder. "Good hunting! Marchand is in there with him now. I don't think they're discussing sports, but it's pretty innocuous."

Karlsson found the interview room at the end of the hall and knocked lightly.

"Come in." Marchand shouted. He made a note that while the rooms were relatively soundproof, noise still travelled.

He walked into the room and sat down in the chair opposite an visibly exhausted Peter Pasternak. He was wearing an orange jumpsuit and he needed a shower and a shave. It was obvious that prison garb and prison food did not agree with him. His hands were cuffed, and his legs were shackled with a chain that allowed for no more than a foot of movement with each step.

Karlsson stared into his eyes as he seated himself, gently laying the two folders on the table in front of him. "Mr. Bronstein?"

Pasternak looked at him, a bit confused. "No, Pasternak. Who are you and what is it you want from me?"

Karlsson flipped through the first document and then closed it before opening the second.

When Karlsson did not respond immediately, Pasternak repeated his question with as much authority as he could muster, knowing his predicament. "I asked you a question. Who are you?"

Karlsson closed the second folder and laid the two side by side in front of him as he looked at Marchand. "They're all meeting down in the conference room if you'd like to join them."

Marchand nodded silently and looked down towards the floor as he stood. "I'm sorry Mr. Pasternak. This isn't the way we usually do things, but I'm afraid it's out of my hands."

He tapped Karlsson lightly on the shoulder as he left the room and closed the door behind him.

Karlsson rotated the first folder to orient it so that Pasternak could read it. He slowly opened it to the first page, which was a Bureau of Prisons Intake form in Pasternak's real name, highlighting his service to his country and naming all the seedy souls he had prosecuted for the last ten years. It created a mostly realistic reputation, or *rep* that would certainly cause him trouble if it were leaked to the other inmates when he hit general population in a facility of the government's choice. It would be known that he had put people in prison. Also, inside were lists of names of personal friends and family members that could be called in an emergency. The names just as easily represented the witness pool which would be dragged into court to testify during his very public trial for espionage.

Without comment, Karlsson rotated the other folder around and opened it to the first page. Inside were Pasternak's color booking photo and fingerprints, with the name of Saul Bronstein substituted, as well as other fictitious family information. The second folder portrayed him as a former Agency employee, an informer who had traded information about various Islamic groups operating in the United States, leading to the arrests of several influential members in exchange for cash.

When the silence became too much, Pasternak bellowed. "I asked you who you are!"

Karlsson looked deeply into his eyes. He wanted the frightened man to know that he had nothing more to bargain with. He had gotten himself into a position where the normal rules of jurisprudence no longer applied. "My name isn't really important. I've used many, so don't bother yourself trying to assign a name to me. I am simply the man who is going to shred one of these files this afternoon and leave you to walk out with the other."

Pasternak had spent his brief career in courtrooms. Following and bending the normal rules of the criminal and civil legal systems. He would not allow himself to be conned. "I demand to see an attorney."

Karlsson pushed the two folders closer to him so that he could reach his handcuffed hands out to touch them. "And which attorney would you like to call? Who do you hate enough to expose to the abject fear and lethal consequences into which you are about to descend?"

Pasternak looked back and forth at the two files. "I demand to see an attorney."

"Mr. Bronstein, you're a flight risk. No judge will set bail for you. You're inextricably locked into the system. My system."

"My name is Pasternak! Why do you keep calling me Bronstein?"

"When you leave here tonight, you'll be sent to the United States Penitentiary in Allenwood, Pennsylvania for forty-eight hours. From there, Mr. Saul Bronstein will be traded."

"What?"

"You're going to be traded in a prisoner exchange. The Islamic Republic of Iran has offered to trade us a history professor and a journalist in exchange for the man who identified a number of their colleagues to the US Government for an unspecified amount of cash."

"What? That's ridiculous! I'm not Bronstein and I can prove it."

"How? Your fingerprints will be out of the federal system by sundown. Your driver's license has been cancelled and photos removed. Do you want the Iranians knocking on your neighbors' doors to verify some fantasy story you concocted that you're someone else, and not really their snitch? Do you think they'll waste that kind of time? Do you think you'll live that long?"

His hands trembled and his eyes teared. "I need to call..."

"Who? Who do you want to call, Saul?"

"My name is Pasternak."

Karlsson was relentless. "I don't much care about what name you want to use. I only want one name. One name!" Karlsson retrieved Pasternak's burn phone from his pocket and scrolled through the calls made. "This name. Who did you call in the Beltway? Who was on the other end of this phone?"

"Please. You can't do this to me." He put his head in his hands and wept openly. "It's not like you think."

Karlsson erupted from his seat and swatted the man's hands out from under his face so quickly that his nose almost banged the table. He used the palm of his hand to drive Pasternak's head back with such force that it dazed him. "Haven't you figured it out yet? I am not the fucking police! I'm the guy they send in to make sure that shit doesn't go public! I am a soldier, and you're the enemy! Got it?"

"But..." He whimpered. "I know people. People know me."

"I seriously doubt they're the same kind of people I know. You probably know the kind of people that will demand an investigation when you hang yourself in your cell tomorrow night. My people arrange those suicides."

Karlsson had him on the ropes and kept pounding away. "Look into my eyes, Mr. Bronstein. Look past my eyes and into the darkness of my soul. Do you really think that I play by your rules?"

There was stone-cold silence in the room for minutes that seemed like hours.

Somewhere between hysteria and stoic acceptance, Pasternak could hear himself speak. "His name is Golovkin. Feodor Golovkin. He is the Russian Congressional Affairs Assistant Attaché in Washington. In the old days, before today's Russia, he was KGB, in the Foreign Operations Directorate. I went to law school with a nephew of his and we became close. So close that he became known to me as Uncle Ted."

CHAPTER 20

Jenny Lu sat across the enormous mahogany desk from Meyer Savitch, the balding, diminutive lawyer who was handling Marty's estate. She had listened intently as he read the last will and testament of her fiancé and discussed with her the paperwork she would need to execute to have his Moreland Hills house titled over to her. It was now approaching April fifteenth, tax time, but she knew that the residential asset would not become a tax burden until the following year. She wondered where she would be then.

As he read, she could hear his words, but they were not resonating. She was remembering the previous Memorial Day weekend that Marty had taken her to Nantucket, to experience Figawi. The annual twenty-five-mile sailboat race between Hyannis and Nantucket. Since its beginnings in Baxter's Boathouse in 1972, it had grown into an annual event that drew thousands of sailors, and even more non-boating participants, in a three-day party that was unrivaled in New England. The event raised money for a variety of charities and had some extravagant sponsors that contributed to an indescribably fun weekend. It had gotten its name during an earlier excursion, when the destination of the regatta had been obscured in fog. One of the participants had remarked, "Where the fuck are we?" The local pronunciation of the phrase became the eponymous name for the event. *Figawi*.

She still had the blue sweatshirt and the red race hat, courtesy of Mount Gay Rum, that was usually only given to competitors, but now was considered a collector's item, going for as much as five hundred dollars on auction sites. After one of the officials who knew Marty had given them a tour of some of the competitor's sailboats, they had enjoyed cocktails on the fantail of a thirty-eight-foot Hunter sloop, and then walked from tent to tent to experience the kind of salty nightlife only pirates had seen before them. They walked hand in hand up the hill after leaving the party tents and rejoiced that neither one of them had ever had a better time. They stayed in a romantic bed and breakfast inn, not far from the festivities near the water and awoke feeling as though they were truly on vacation. Neither of them had a care in the world. She had forgotten why she was there.

The next day, through more revelry, they had met Bill and Heidi, a fun-loving couple from Hingham, who kept their boat in Scituate, who introduced them to Ed, an earthy, sixty-something ex-NCAA basketball champ and later a special forces operator during Viet Nam, who married the colonel's daughter and despite being worth millions in his current capacity as the president of a commercial insurance brokerage, had opted not to have his over-bite fixed. He was the life of the party that night, raunchily telling people that now that he had finished SCUBA lessons, he was triple certified in diving: "Sky, SCUBA and *muff*".

It was a fantastic weekend, and she felt that it made her complete. She knew she could love this guy. This was why she had fled communist China. This was why she wanted to be here. If only she could make this work. Marty was not the best-looking guy in the world. Lord knew, she could do better. But it all seemed to make sense. It all seemed to work for her, and she knew that this was the life she wanted, even though it meant going back to a house in the suburbs of Cleveland when the party was over.

"Ms. Lu, I'll need you to sign here, and here." Savitch said as he presented the documents across the desk. "This is the deed to the house, and this is the mortgage you agreed to execute last week."

She gave the documents a cursory look and then signed in the spaces indicated. She thought about the ferry ride back to the mainland. They had politely rejected offers from several of the people they had met, to crew their way back on a boat. But it had been explained that sailboats were simply a way to get very, very sick, while slicing your way through the ocean at great expense. The ferry would get them back quicker, and they could sit in the first-class lounge, play liar's poker, and drink their way back to reality.

Zhou had taken it from her. She had told him early on that she would do him this favor in exchange for a new life. There had always been an understanding that once she had made a life for herself, that she would be out. Free and clear. Now though, she could tell that he intended to use her forever. He had gotten where he needed to be through Marty. But now Marty was dead, and Zhou was the reason. In her mind, she knew that Zhou would never give her her freedom. The freedom she had earned. The freedom she desperately wanted.

She tried to get the words out without tearing up. "I would like to offer Kathryn, Marty's wife... uh ex-wife, the opportunity to walk through and take anything in the house that she would like. I know they did that sort of thing during the divorce proceedings, but, if things had not happened like they did, this would have been her house. Can you set that up?"

"You're very gracious. It would be my privilege." Savitch said stoically.

Jenny nodded. She was breaking her problems down into manageable elements. She knew what she had to do.

———————— ((O)) ————————

Matthias Karlsson dialed the number and waited until the voice in the control room told him that he would try to find Paul. He thanked him, knowing that they bloody well knew where Paul was twenty-four hours a day. When he finally answered, Karlsson could sense that his superior was under some level of organizational pressure. Maybe that was typical these days.

"Good morning. I trust you had a chance to read Agent Biehn's report?"

Karlsson thought for a moment before answering. "Yeah. But...I don't know what to make of it. And I'm assuming this is not a secure line?"

"I've told you a dozen times, there is no such thing." Paul chided.

"Fine." Karlsson looked around the parking lot to see if anyone was nearby. "Biehn's research has told us that except for an engineer from Pittsburgh, everyone who handled the missing LEM... number fourteen, is dead. Mostly, from old age. The Chinese took possession of an uncompleted Lunar Module back in 1970, courtesy of William J. Borchardt, lieutenant colonel, United States Air Force. He sent the crates to a San Francisco company called Millennium Equity. But Biehn's research also indicates that the shipment was hijacked by the CIA or the Russians, or whoever was hijacking Chinese shipments at the time, and reverse engineered. She is of the belief that it was most likely the Soviets, because we found that they were already embedded in our own space program throughout the nineteen sixties. It was some kind of brain exchange that Kennedy dreamed up to keep us from shooting each other in space."

Paul did not appear to be the least bit surprised. He had been working on that part of the problem from his own perspective for several months and it had come up several times in conversation. "Go on."

"Millennium Equity went through a number of iterations and incarnations through the years but is now a part of a larger financial investment group that has significant ties to the fundraising efforts of a certain presidential candidate. The son of said candidate now holds board positions with a dozen companies, some of whom are defense contractors. We haven't tied anything concrete to the kid other than the fact that he likes to use daddy's name and influence for his own financial gain. The problem is that there's a lot of smoke, but we haven't found the fire."

Paul seemed deep in thought, and it was a long time before he continued. "Do you remember a congressman named Hale Boggs?"

"Not really, but I've heard the name."

"Boggs was a Congress member from New Orleans. By way of biography, when first elected, he was the youngest person ever to serve in that capacity. He was unseated in 1942 and joined the United States Navy. After the war, he was elected again to Congress in 1947, and on his successful climb up the political ladder to becoming the House Majority Leader, he happened to become the youngest member appointed to the Warren Commission. He was also reported to be a critic of its findings early on."

"He made a run for the Louisiana governor's office in 1951 but lost when his opponent pointed out that he had been a member of the American Student Union, back in the thirties. The ASU was rumored to be a communist front for subversive activities. Nevertheless, he continued getting re-elected to national office, and had a storied career in Congress."

After a brief silence Karlsson spoke. "I'm sorry sir. I'm not getting it."

"I'm just thinking out loud. Boggs disappeared in a plane crash in Alaska in December 1972. I cannot help but remember that a twenty-six-year-old campaign aide who drove him to the airport for what was to be his last campaign trip, eventually became President of the United States. The same aide, who years earlier, at sixteen, had shaken hands with John F. Kennedy."

"Clinton?" Karlsson sensed that Paul was trying to get to a point but was afraid to make it until he had connected more dots. Over the years he had become tolerant of these occasional ruminations simply because Paul was the boss, and the reflections usually got them both closer to the answer, whatever the question might be.

"Yes." Paul replied. "Washington is, and has always been, a unique place. An animal with a life of its own. The key to success and survival, which are tantamount to being the same thing here, is that the participants are judged not by what they bring to the table, but rather, how well they play ball."

"Excuse me?" Karlsson asked, genuinely confused.

"I'm just thinking of another former Naval officer, who was in Congress at the same time as Boggs. From 1965 until 1973, Gerald R. Ford was serving along side Boggs, and had risen to being the House Minority Leader. He also served on the Warren

Commission, investigating the death of President Kennedy. Similar career paths."

"Regardless of his personal beliefs, he officially supported the findings of the Warren Commission. But, in March 1966, his home state of Michigan was awash with reports of Unidentified Flying Objects. The famed J. Allen Hynek, who was the Air Force's expert on the subject, adamantly stated that what the people actually saw in Michigan was nothing more than swamp gas. Ford did not believe that and demanded further investigation into the phenomenon. At the time, he was the highest-ranking politician to call for any type of public inquiry into the topic."

"Ford eventually backed off his challenge and was brought on in 1973, by Richard Nixon, to replace Spiro Agnew. And, of course, later to be his running mate for the next campaign. When Nixon resigned over the Watergate mess, he then became the President of the United States. Nixon had had some of his own UFO experiences but agreed to keep silent about them in public. Ford, sensing a career opportunity, kept mum as well, and once elected to the Oval Office, dropped his UFO pursuits and steadfastly refrained from commenting adversely about the Warren Commission findings. He played ball and survived."

"On the other hand, Boggs perished when his twin engine Cessna crashed in 1972, with a Congressman from Alaska also on board. They were headed from Anchorage to Juneau and the wreckage was never found."

"And your point, sir?"

"You either have to play ball with the people in power, or you suffer the consequences. It doesn't matter which party you are affiliated with, or what your constituents think of you."

Karlsson looked around the parking lot again out of habit. "Situation normal, sir."

Paul went on quietly. "Special Agent Biehn has some additional information relative to her case that wasn't in her report. She has completed her investigation and officially determined that there was no unaccounted-for spacecraft found on the lunar surface. If there had been one, it would have contained the bodies of one Russian and one Chinese astronaut who died in the service of their respective countries, under unknown circumstances, while working hand-in-hand in the peaceful exploration of space. But, since there is no spacecraft, it is no longer of concern. What she saw in the photographs shown to her was nothing more than a digital artifact that occurred during processing. The photographs and the data have been destroyed. So, they say."

Karlsson listened to the information and tried to put everything into perspective. Things were not always as they seemed, but it did not matter to him. He didn't need perspective. Just a time and a place.

Karlsson's silence allowed Paul to finish his thought. "Prometheus, this will be our last contact for the foreseeable future." He paused, the use of Karlsson's code name striking a chord. "The money that Zhou wired you several months back...can you move it to another account?"

Karlsson frowned at the dashboard of the rental car. "Say again?"

"Can you move it?"

"That's technically government money, sir. Where would you have me move it?"

"The money doesn't exist. This operation never existed. For the next few months, you don't exist."

Karlsson had heard a similar script years earlier and felt like he was re-living something of a nightmare. "That bad?"

After a while, Paul responded. "Sometimes the stars and the planets align a certain way and the people who think they have all the facts must make decisions. Weighty decisions. The incumbent is not without sin, if you know what I mean."

"I'm not sure."

"He's not perfect, but he is...uhmm, suitable for office for another four years. He is better for the country than the alternative. If we are to preserve our democracy and try to stabilize our political system, we will have to take an action that history may judge to be inappropriate. Or, illegal."

Karlsson closed his eyes and considered the gravity of what was about to come. "I'm waiting. Sir."

"In forty-eight hours, I will text you a target and a location. Once your assignment is complete, you will return to retired status. Our records will indicate that you never left your ranch in Santa Fe. Your personnel file will be re-assigned to the inactive list."

"I think I'm following you. Will I need support, or is this a solo engagement?"

"You'll have support and logistics. Watch your text."

———⊳«◊»⊲———

Stan Marchand looked at the spreadsheet he had created and checked each line as Deputy Director Vince Catalogna read off the targets for the warrants. It was to be a nationwide sweep, simultaneously executed. This would be huge for the Secret Service. Jerry Lee had successfully played out his role and the agency was prepared to swoop in and bust the lot of them. In six major cities around the country, they were taking down a counterfeiting operation that had perniciously infiltrated commerce in the United States for several years. It would certainly grab national headlines but would have deeper reaching consequences for the upcoming election.

Jenny Lu had been in town the week before and offered the use of Moreland Hills to Stan and Tricia with the explanation that she would feel better if someone were staying there until the operation, now dubbed SWANSONG, was over. She had been in Cleveland for a night to look around and to feel Marty's presence one more time before returning to Chicago and her rigorous campaign schedule. She had done her part and the Service was appreciative.

Jerry Lee had done a superlative job of gathering information about each of Zhou's contacts, while Jenny had deftly arranged to have the unassailable phantom come to the US to meet with an ambitious presidential candidate. Everyone was getting what they wanted. The Secret Service would have Zhou on US soil during the sweep, and would get him, along with his confederates, at the stroke of ten o'clock, or twenty-two-hundred hours Eastern time. The field offices in New York, Miami, Jacksonville, Los Angeles and San Francisco had been notified and were coordinating their raids on warehouses of suspected businesses as well as the residences of the operators listed in the warrants. Huge, indeed. And all without anyone outside of the operation knowing about it. Their investigation had gone deep, and they did not want someone with political influence mucking it up.

From there, the Service's cyber analysts were poised to watch communications traffic between thirty other suspected players. Some were wealthy businesspersons and others had political connections of one kind or another. The following morning, there would be shock, chaos, and a gnashing of teeth throughout the country, and especially in Washington. Generic press releases were on stand-by in the Office of Communications and Media Relations, awaiting names and places, and a special hotline had been set up in the Director's office to field the anticipated pleas and threats coming from tycoons and office holders who would demand to know why they were not consulted.

Others affected would be creating the spin. Manipulating the media to get the story to go their way. The Potomac Two-Step would be in full swing. But, at any given time, each political party could only count on half of the media outlets to support their side. Regardless of which networks proposed that this was nothing more than political posturing, other networks would still push the story and air the facts. Minor heads might roll, but in the end, the same elected politicians would keep their jobs. The voters would believe what they wanted to believe, depending on who they thought was going to deliver a government that would suit their personal needs. But the voices of the people who paid most of the taxes would be quashed with superficial name-calling and gaslighting, just like they were when any of them disagreed with the party in control of the media. Contrary to Lincoln's premise, the country was no longer *of the people and by the people*, but rather of who controlled the message.

It was just after three in the afternoon when Marchand decided that he should take a break and head to Moreland Hills to see Tricia and get a nap before returning to the office to monitor the operation. From the conference room he would have direct links to the offices serving the warrants, and to the Headquarters section that would be monitoring electronic traffic. It would probably be three or four in the morning by the time the field offices finished their sweeps and reported in.

Out of habit, he backed his car up the driveway so that he would be able to pull out quickly when he was ready to return to the office. It was a cop thing. Once inside, he found Tricia on the couch watching some smarmy cable movie that focused on the countless aspects of love and promised a happy ending. When she saw him come in, she leapt off the couch and ran to give him a hug.

"Hey sweetie! You're home early!"

"Yeah. I'm fucking drained and I need to rest before heading back in." Marchand replied as his keys bounced across the counter.

"Tonight's the night, huh?"

"Yeah." He whispered in her ear as he drew her close to him. "By tomorrow, this will all just be a dream. Or a nightmare." He forced a smile.

"Do you want me to fix us something for dinner? I stopped at the store and got some pork chops. I didn't know if you would feel like grilling, or if you just wanted to order something. Pizza?"

"Maybe we could grill tomorrow. I think we'll be in the mood to celebrate by then."

"You want to lay down for a while?"

"Definitely. Want to join me?"

She smiled. "I might be able to move some things around on my calendar. Give me a minute to clean up down here and then I'll be up."

Marchand climbed the stairs in a mental fog. He truly enjoyed the job and Tricia's company, but missed his home in Texas. He took in the sights and scents of the Moreland Hills house and wandered briefly from room to room, remembering his first night there. He visualized what his furniture might look like in this place. Then he visualized the cold winters and shook his head. He wandered back into the bedroom and stopped to look in the giant walk-in closet. Marty's suits still hung on the rack, but he remembered the night they had discovered the secret room and the treasure it concealed. He ran his hands over the sleeves of the suits and looked at Marty's gun safe. A lot of good they did for him at the end. He kicked his shoes off and turned back to the large king-sized bed that awaited him.

"How about a massage?" Tricia asked as she entered the room behind him.

Marchand smiled and kissed her on the cheek. "I would welcome it like a kid welcomes Christmas!"

He unbuttoned his shirt and stepped out of his pants before throwing himself face down on the comfortable bed. He could smell the oil that she used to soften her hands, and within moments he was drifting off to sleep as those magical hands vigorously worked the muscles of his neck and shoulders. Paradise.

Hours seemed to pass within seconds and when he awoke with a start, it was nearing seven o'clock. He could hear Tricia downstairs in the kitchen and realized that he needed to get showered and dressed and drag himself back to the office. And so, thirty minutes later he was a new man; physically and emotionally recovered from the stress of the day. He finished dressing and returned to Marty's closet to retrieve his shoes. Carefully, acknowledging his age, he bent to pick them up.

And then he stopped.

The gun case. Something was missing. When he looked at it earlier, something troubled him, but he was so mentally exhausted, the thought did not bubble to the surface of his consciousness. He tried the door but found it to be locked. Inside, there were the two shotguns and the three bolt-action rifles. The AR-15 carbine was missing. He thought back to the day the Secret Service had carried out the cash and the gold bars. They did not touch the rifle case. He had not really paid any attention to the closet over the past few days because Jenny Lu had moved some of her things in, and he and Tricia had been living out of their suitcases in the bedroom down the hall. Jenny Lu?

He briskly took the stairs down as Tricia was starting up. "Am I going the wrong way?" She asked.

"Huh uh." He replied, barely noticing her. He sprinted into the kitchen and opened the cupboard where the wine glasses were kept. Quickly, he moved them out of the way and used his fingers to feel for it. It wasn't there.

"What are you looking for?" Tricia asked, hands on her hips. "If you're headed back to the office, you probably shouldn't have wine right now."

"It's not here."

"What's not here?"

"The key."

"What key?"

"There was a key up here the last time I checked. It looked like it went to the lock on the secret room where we found Marty's stash. It's not here."

"But you said the secret room was empty. Why would anyone want back in there?"

"There could have been some compartment we missed or another concealed space somewhere else in the house that we never found. The AR is gone too."

"The what?"

"Marty had an AR-15 carbine with a tactical stock and red-dot optic on it. It was here before, and now it's gone."

"Maybe Jenny took it?"

"That's what I'm thinking. But why? AR's are illegal in Chicago, and she's going to be moving in here in a couple weeks anyway. Why would she..." Whether it was a psychic connection or his training and experience through years of threat assessment sounding an alarm, he froze. Jenny was in Chicago. Zhou was in Chicago.

Zhou had flown in the week before to spend some time in his new home on Lake Michigan in Pleasant Prairie Wisconsin. It was a modest four-thousand square-foot place with four bedrooms and three bathrooms, elegantly designed and equipped so that he could feel like the businessman that he portrayed himself to be. The property had a private stretch of beach in the back yard, and a wooded lot to assure his privacy. It was located a half mile north of the Prairie Harbor Yacht Club, a private, gated facility where Jerry had reserved a slip for him.

Zhou was scheduled to attend a ten-thousand-dollar-a-plate fundraiser for Layden's campaign at the Park Hyatt on Michigan Avenue this evening, with a private meet-and-greet to follow the dinner. The Chicago Field Office had agents watching Zhou's home and a team of agents in Washington were also able to monitor the cameras and microphones that they had secreted in the residence before Zhou ever took possession. Of course, the Secret Service also had several teams of agents at the hotel and banquet venue in preparation for the campaign event. Zhou was covered.

They had meticulously worked through the details in a way that would not make Zhou suspicious. Since he was not a threat to the Protectee, he could be allowed to proceed through the metal detectors and have dinner prior to the nationally coordinated bust, which would take place at nine o'clock Central Standard Time. The invitation-only dinner meant that Zhou would be by himself and seated where they wanted him. In fact, the attractive young couple seated across from him were, in fact, Secret Service agents masquerading as a local businesswoman and her husband.

This was the kind of public event he needed to help maintain his air of legitimacy. He would not want to miss this opportunity. The private meeting for the high rollers was scheduled for nine thirty local time, which left agents plenty of time to apprehend Zhou and escort him out of the area before he got close to the candidate.

Marchand waited until he got into his car before calling Jenny Lu. It rang straight through to her voicemail. Either she was on her phone or it was turned off. He knew he could not call Jerry Lee because he was entrenched his Liu Wei character for one last sting and would not have his official cell phone with him. He drove for a couple of miles and entered the freeway ramp before calling Paul.

"How is the operation progressing?" Was the brief greeting after the second ring.

Marchand signaled, glanced over his shoulder, and then merged into one of the southbound lanes of I-271. "We're set in all of the venues. It is scheduled to go down at ten o'clock eastern tonight, in a few hours. Jerry will call me when the San Francisco warrants are served."

"I see. And Mr. Zhou?"

"That's why I'm calling. We might have a slight glitch with Zhou. We know he is scheduled to attend the fundraiser tonight and agents are waiting for him. The problem is that he left his house several hours ago and surveillance lost him on the ninety-four tollway somewhere around the Lincolnshire-Bannockburn area."

"Lost him?" Paul asked calmly.

"Since they had his house wired and pretty much knew where he was going, they only had one car behind him, and wanted to stay back far enough that he didn't get spooked. When they closed the gap in traffic, they realized he must have gotten off the tollway at some point when he was temporarily out of view."

"What time is he scheduled to be at the Hyatt?"

"The invitations specify arrival at least an hour before the event, so it should have been around six local time. The team at the Hyatt say that he hasn't picket up his credential yet. But neither have several of the other attendees. Some people don't want to sit through the cocktail hour. They just go for the dinner and photo opportunity."

"I see. Well, thank you for the update."

"There's more. We're missing a rifle at the Moreland Hills residence. An AR-15 carbine. It was there last month, but this afternoon I noticed it was missing. The only person we know to have been in there is Jenny Lu."

Paul thought for a moment. "The young lady is in Chicago tonight?"

"Yes. She's helping coordinate the fundraiser for Layden's campaign."

"She's at the Hyatt?"

"Yes. She checked in two hours ago." Marchand replied as he moved around a slower vehicle and accelerated.

"Hold on for a minute." Paul said mechanically as he muted his line. The phone was quiet for a couple of minutes and Marchand's mind drifted between a range of scenarios that could be about to unfold. None of them good.

When he came back, he was somewhat solemn. "Ignore the Jenny – Zhou problem for now. I have someone looking into it." Paul paused for a second. "Check in with me in four hours."

⸺⸺◈⸺⸺

Zhou checked his gold Rolex President and made his way from the hotel lobby through the hall to the Marriott Theater. Founded in 1975 and attached to the Lincolnshire Resort Hotel, it boasted a track record of a hundred eighty productions for almost eleven million people since opening. It was considered a prime venue for launching Broadway shows in a regional market and featured a variety of local and international talent. It was still sparkling after a 2017 flood of the Des Plaines River forced an evacuation, one guest reportedly refusing to leave until she had finished her dessert. At the time, the property was in the middle of a twenty-five-million-dollar renovation anyway and was able to close for a week without significant losses.

Zhou stepped lightly across the brilliant carpet, colorfully comprised of reds, oranges and yellows with musical staffs, notes, bars and sunbursts to create an aura of dynamic energy, while carefully disguising any stains left by food or drink. He proceeded towards the exit and tugged his collar up around his neck. It was still cool in Chicago, and Jenny Lu had suggested wearing an overcoat to the event. Her message said she would pick him up by the Theater entrance on the south side of the resort at 6:15. But he went five minutes early so that he could enjoy a cigarette. US hotels no longer permitted smoking inside their facilities; a practice Zhou considered a barbaric attack on human rights.

He stepped to the end of the portico and while reaching into his pocket for his cigarettes, appreciated the lights from the marquis above him that were illuminating the parking lot with stimulating color. He flipped open the cap on the genuine gold-plated Dunhill lighter and exhaled a plume of smoke against the northwesterly wind that was blowing in. The show at the theater did not start until seven thirty, so the parking lot was still relatively empty. A couple of vans had pulled up to drop off materials or goods needed for the performance, and there were a few vehicles parked further out in the lot that presumably belonged to employees or vendors. People with carts and dollies worked feverishly to get set up for the evening's performance.

One hundred seventy-one feet away, Jenny Lu sat in the dark, on the floor of the Ford Transit Connect cargo van that she had rented the day before from one of the agencies near O'Hare. She had driven through the theater's lot earlier in the week, searching for a specific parking space that would allow her to pull head-in, angled slightly to the left, enabling a clear shot from the side door while it was partially ajar. She had measured the distance in the daylight using the range-finding app on her iPhone and calculated that with the weapon sighted in at one hundred yards, the bullet might strike a half an inch high on the target.

The parking space was at the northwest end of the row, under a tree, with the parking lot lights behind her. This cast the right side of the van in silhouette, making it difficult for anyone standing obliquely near the entrance to make out any detail. Marty had taught her well, gleaning what he could from civilian instructors through the years and occasionally infusing tactical tips he had seen in movies. Techniques which were, of course, usually unsafe, or incorrect. Hollywood was not interested in safety or reality. They wanted action.

As she sat in silence, she reminisced about their visits to the range and the professionalism Marty employed when teaching her about the characteristics of the rifle. He was an engineer, and it showed. Because of the significant difference between the bore line and the optic's sight line, the AR-15 was a weapon that required the user to factor in bullet rise and drop at certain distances. Especially distances less than the one hundred yards at which range it had been sighted in for. She remembered his hand on hers, as he patiently showed her how to shoulder the weapon and carefully press the trigger while keeping the sights aligned on the target.

She checked the suppressor once more. Because it had been acquired illegally, Marty had chosen to store it in a different hideaway. The one that had not been discovered by the Secret Service's search of their home. And because it had been illegally obtained, he had not wanted anyone to discover it, or the other prize stored there. His parents had taught him never to put all his eggs in one basket, so he had created another covert storage space under the floor of the attic, over the garage. Whether he had anticipated a search at some point, or was just paranoid, it had paid off. The Secret Service had not found it. And luckily, as the chain of events played out, Jenny had not known about it. It was not until the reading of the will that she learned that there was another private stash over the garage, and where she could find the key. Otherwise, had she known of this other compartment, she never would have been able to pass the polygraph that the Secret Service had administered prior to her being brought on to the case.

Things just fell into place. She had been considering her options since Marty's death, but the discovery of the suppressor and another half million dollars in US currency helped her make up her mind. In her manner of thinking, Marty was providing the tools and the funding to avenge his death.

She quietly unlocked the right-side cargo door and stepped into the back. She had rehearsed it mentally a dozen times; she would slip into the back and wait for Zhou to present himself under the lights. By firing from the back of the van, the brass would eject inside and bounce around for later retrieval. The silencer would muffle the shots, even though the sonic crack would be heard in the air because she was not using subsonic ammunition. Nevertheless, witnesses would not be able to tell from which direction the shots had originated.

She did her best to quiet her nerves, rocking forward onto her knees every few minutes to see if her target had arrived at the pick-up point under the marquis yet. After a few tense moments, from her nest in the rear of the van, she could see over the passenger seat, Zhou lighting his cigarette. His eyes scanned the parking lot as the winds gusted from the northwest. She quietly opened the side door and allowed it to slide backwards as she took her kneeling position on the towel she had brought. She steadied her breathing.

She remembered what Marty had taught her. *Put the reticle on the chest because the head moves around too much.* Zhou's ciga-rette lighter had given her an excellent mark to aim for and she me-thodically placed the red dot just below his hands as she pressed the trigger gently. She could feel the slack end and the trigger's break point begin. One more ounce of pressure and the rifle fired. She quickly brought the sight back down to follow up, but could see Zhou on the ground, the Dunhill a few inches from his hand. It was too easy, and she had to be sure. She fought her impulses to flee, and carefully lined up a second shot, aiming at the top of his head which, the way he had fallen, was presented to her almost face-down on the pavement. The rifle fired again, and she mechanically drew the side door of the van shut.

She fought the urge to wretch and tried not to think about what she had done as she made a calm exit out of parking lot, crossed North Milwaukee Avenue, and turned left into Walker Brothers Original Pancake House. Having closed at 2:30 that afternoon, the parking lot was empty, and she was able to take a couple of deep breaths before disassembling the gun and stashing it in her lug-gage. She quickly collected the two shell casings and then ripped the home-made temporary Ohio license plate out of the back win-dow before using her battery-operated screwdriver to replace the local license plates that belonged on the van.

The idea to use a temporary Ohio plate came after her last visit to Moreland Hills, when she noticed how easy it was to re-create one with a variety of computer software. She had simply photographed one in a parking lot at a grocery store, and then estimated the correct dimensions and typestyle to fabricate a copy on her printer. In most states, when someone bought a new vehicle, or transferred the title of a used one, the dealer gave the new owner a temp-tag that could be secured somewhere inside the car or even on the bracket. Most people just taped them to the back window. In many states, the motor vehicle bureau did not keep temp-tag license information in their files, so when witnesses provided police with the number, it oft times proved less than valuable.

She looked at the checklist she had created on her iPhone to ensure that she had not forgotten anything. The brass was collected, the plates were changed, and it was time to return the vehicle. Satisfied, she deleted the checklist, left the parking lot, and headed north on North Milwaukee, east on Half Day Road and then back south on the Tollway to the airport to pick up her car. Twenty minutes later, she threw the luggage in the trunk of her own car and returned to the Hyatt.

She looked at her watch. It had been one hour and fifty-two minutes since she had left the gala, feigning illness. She parked her car in a garage six blocks away and walked the remaining distance to the delivery entrance at the Park Hyatt, through which she had a Secret Service event credential to pass.

She went through the checkpoint with ease as the female agent waved the electronic wand around her body. The agent checked her credential and then confirmed the name against the list they had of authorized attendees. "Oh. You were here once, and then you left?"

"Yeah." Jenny shrugged. "Aunt Flo." She winked at the agent who understood the complications of one's monthly cycle.

The agent smiled back. "Thank you. Have a nice event."

When she was again in the cleared area around the Green Room, her associate Caroline McKamish saw her pallor. "You look like shit. Are you sure you're okay?"

She nodded with a forced smile. "Yeah, better now."

"Come with me. We have to do something with your hair!"

The woman grabbed her arm and dragged her down the hall towards the lady's restroom. "Didn't you have a foreign associate who wanted to meet the Senator tonight?"

She nodded, somewhat embarrassed. "I did, but he said he had a schedule conflict. Is there a chance we can set something up for another time?"

"If there's money involved, I'm sure we can get him on the schedule somewhere. His son is making the rounds as well." She tilted her head.

"His son?" Jenny Lu recalled the party in Shanghai years earlier. "Oh, yes. Archer. I think I've met him. What is he selling these days?"

"Access."

Natalie Richards lightly rinsed the dishes off before stacking them in the dishwasher for a thorough cleanse. Adrian, her twelve-year old, sat at the kitchen island working on his homework. He wanted to impress his mom with his report card because he had a birthday coming up soon and wanted to be sure he was on her good side. His sister, Kristina, was already getting straight A's and since she had already finished her homework, was helping her dad paint in the living room. Because she really was not excited about house painting, and she was the closest to the front door, when the bell rang, she dashed to open it.

Her dad looked up from the corner of the room to hear her say "Just a minute...", before closing the door and running into the kitchen.

"Mom!"

Natalie dried her hands. "Yeah honey. What is it?"

"There are two men in suits here to see you."

"Well then, let's go see what they want." She hung the towel over the stove's handle and went to the door. By the time she got there, her husband, Thomas, had become curious as well and was wiping his hands on an old t-shirt that he had been using to touch up paint drips.

She opened the door and saw, as her daughter had described, two men in fairly expensive suits, holding leather credential cases. The one who had presumably rung the doorbell introduced himself.

"Natalie Richards?"

"Yes. Can I help you?"

"We're Special Agents Frye and Donner, with the Federal Bureau of Investigation." They simultaneously opened their credential cases and held them close enough so that she could read the names and see the photographs clearly. "Do you have a moment to talk... uh, privately?"

Thomas had quietly come up behind her and with his legal senses in full gear, responded to them before she could answer. "What's this about?"

"Are you Mr. Richards? Thomas Richards?" Special Agent Donner asked.

"Yes. What's this about?" He repeated.

"Please excuse our intrusion at this hour, but we wanted to catch you at home so that we could speak privately. We would like to come in, but if you're not comfortable with that, we can speak here."

Natalie pushed the door open all the way so that her and her husband could both stand in the doorway together. "What can we do for you?"

Donner produced a color booking photograph of a slender white male in his forties, thinning brown hair. "Do you know this man?"

Natalie and her husband leaned closer to look at the photo. She shook her head. "No, I'm afraid not. Who is he?"

"His name is Pasternak. Up until recently, he was an Assistant US Attorney up in Cleveland."

She looked again at the picture and then at her husband, shaking her head. "No. Where would I know him from?"

"He says that a couple of months ago, he dropped an electronic device off at your exercise studio, wrapped to look like a child's gift. We'd like to talk to you about what was in the box, and what you did with it."

She could feel a biological electrical current pulse through her body and knew in that instant that her face was flushing and would betray her reaction. She could deny everything and close the door. But that would only delay the inevitable. They would be back. Thomas would want answers as well, and they had never lied to each other. Much. "Excuse me for one second."

She looked at Thomas. "Can you get the kids ready for bed and then join us in the dining room? This might take some time."

Thomas nodded and steered Adrian and Kristina towards the stairs. Natalie stepped out of the way and waved them into her home. "Won't you come in?"

She closed the door behind them and then gestured towards the kitchen. "We can talk in here."

The agents pulled stools out from the island and sat down. Donner had an iPod and Frye opened a zippered folio on the counter between them, as Natalie joined them.

"Would you like to wait for your husband, Ms. Richards?" Frye asked.

"No. That's okay. I think I know why you are here. It's probably about Uncle Ted, isn't it?"

"Yes, Ma'am." Frye replied. "Feodor Golovkin. He's not your biological uncle, is he?"

She shook her head. "No. He was a very close friend of my father's. In the old days. The old country."

"He was KGB?" Donner tapped something into his iPod.

"Yes. As was my father." She admitted.

"When was the last time you saw your father?" Donner asked, still tapping on his iPod screen.

"It has been two years. Naturally, we exchange cards and have Runet now. Russian internet."

"Is your husband aware of your past?" Frye asked suspiciously.

"Of course. Why wouldn't he be?" She leaned forward. "I came here from the former Soviet Union to attend college. It was during that time I fell in love with this country...about the same time I was falling in love with my husband, and decided I wanted to be an American. My allegiance is to the United States."

"You never met Peter Pasternack?"

"No. I told you that. Uncle Ted sent me a text to expect a package from someone, with instructions on where to deliver it. I did not know who would be bringing it, and since it was already wrapped, I had no idea what it contained. When he dropped it off at my studio, I was on a call and by the time I was free, he was gone."

Frye made a note. "And, if we asked someone in your studio to verify that, they would?"

Natalie shrugged as Thomas found an empty stool in the kitchen. "Just a moment." She punched a series of numbers into her phone and waited for a response. "Jenny, it's Natalie. Do me a favor and download our security TV files for..." She looked across at Frye. "What dates would you like?"

Donner briskly flipped through a printed copy of a report and turned it around so that she could read it. "Jenny, just download the entire month of February and put it on a flash drive for Agents Donner and Frye from the FBI. They will stop by in about a half hour to pick it up. No. Everything is fine. Don't worry about it."

Natalie gently laid the phone on the counter. "Is that good enough?"

Donner and Frye glanced at each other before both nodded. Frye continued, "Tell me about Golovkin, your Uncle Ted."

"What is to tell?" She got up and opened the refrigerator door. She pulled out a bottle of water and held it up to the two agents. "Would you like something to drink?"

Both men shook their heads and she returned to the island and sat down. "My father sent me to college in the United States in 1990, with Uncle Ted's help. I felt I owed him, so occasionally we would get together in Washington for dinner just to catch up. Twice, he asked me to bring him something."

"Twice? You acted as an intermediary once before?"

Thomas interrupted. "I would urge you to strike the term *intermediary*. My wife is confirming that on two occasions, upon request, she took a gift to a family friend."

"Duly noted, counselor." Donner nodded. "Ms. Richards, are we correct in assuming that prior to receiving a gift-wrapped box from the man we identified as Peter Pasternack, that you made another delivery to Feodor Golovkin?"

"Yes. A couple weeks earlier, some other guy dropped off a box that Uncle Ted wanted. I did not get his name, but his face should be on the security tapes we're giving you. Late fifties or early sixties, crew cut. Well-dressed."

"Had you ever seen him before?" Frye asked.

"No. Never. He came in, dropped the box off and said that it was a gift for my uncle."

"And what did you do with it?" Frye made some notes.

"I took it home, gift-wrapped it, and tossed it in my luggage. I drove to the Shoreham Hotel in DC, gave it to Uncle Ted over dinner, and came home the next morning."

"Did you look inside before you wrapped it?"

She smiled. "Of course."

"What was in it?" Donner leaned forward.

Natalie shook her head. "I have no idea. Some metal component thing that looked like it might have belonged in a car or an airplane."

"How was it packaged?"

"It was in a white box, about so big, with blue printing. I think it said Echo Aerospace on the outside of the box."

"Didn't you think that Golovkin's request was a bit strange?"

She shrugged. "Maybe. But he was a family friend, and there was nothing in the box that was illegal. I mean, it was not drugs, and it didn't look like any kind of weapon. So, where is the harm?"

Frye looked at her and then Thomas. "Ms. Richards, that was a highly classified piece of US technology that you turned over to a Russian agent."

Thomas started to speak but Natalie gently put her hand on his arm. "Where did it say that on the box?" She asked matter-of-factly.

Donner realized that she wasn't going to allow herself to be bullied and decided to change their approach. "You have done quite well for yourself. You worked hard, built a business, and raised a fine family. Do you feel that you made the right decisions in your life?"

She smiled again. "I think so. I do not know how my life would have been if I had stayed in Russia. I am blessed with the American Dream. I have everything that I ever could have dreamed of."

The agents were both quiet for a moment, and then Frye asked, "If we subpoenaed you, Ms. Richards, would you testify in open court about your participation...check that. Would you testify that on two occasions, you made deliveries to Feodor Golovkin of items that had been delivered to you by unknown individuals?"

She looked at Thomas for a moment, and without a word, he nodded. Her reply was succinct. "Sure. Why not?"

The agents got up and Frye asked, "Can you excuse us for a minute?" They walked into the next room and could be heard whispering.

Thomas leaned close to his wife and lowered his voice. "Do you want me to call someone to officially represent us on this, or are you okay?"

She kissed him on his cheek. "I'm fine. I love you. I love my family. And I love my country. We will get through this."

When the agents returned and took their seats, Donner folded his hands in front of him on the countertop. "Ms. Richards, have you ever heard of someone by the name of Antropov?"

"No." she said truthfully.

"How about Sardius?"

"Sardius?" She shook her head and glanced at Thomas. "No. Never."

"How about someone named Obval?"

"Obval? O-B-V-A-L? No." she looked at Thomas again. "Obval is not a name. It is a Russian word."

Frye looked up. "Meaning what?"

"It means collapse. It could mean a landslide or something like that."

Frye looked at Donner with a shrug. "What the hell. Let's ask her."

Donner looked across the counter at Natalie. "Ms. Richards, we believe that you are a decent human being and a respectable US citizen, who only took certain actions out of a sense of loyalty to her family. Your old family. However, the time has come to, well, choose sides and stand up for your country. We are going to ask a favor of you."

"A favor?" Thomas asked, the concern showing through in his response.

"A simple favor." Donner explained. "We want you to arrange a meeting."

"A meeting?" Natalie asked. "Between whom?"

After a moment of silence, Frye answered her. "Between the man with the crew cut and his Russian connection."

She nodded in quiet acquiescence. "Sure. It is only a day out of my life."

CHAPTER 21

It was five thirty in the morning by the time Stan Marchand switched off his computer and headed for the parking lot. Jerry's team had served the warrants and arrested more than two dozen people, with the media following the case closely as it unfolded through the night.

After shaving and putting on a clean white shirt for the cameras, Deputy Director Catalogna made a public statement for the press and other interested parties, sometime after midnight. "As the result of a two-year investigation, the US Secret Service and the Federal Bureau of Investigation have arrested twenty-nine people in connection with a global criminal operation that attempted to introduce counterfeit goods, including illegally manufactured and distributed computer boards into the US economy, potentially compromising our national security. Also thwarted was an attempt by some members of the Chinese government to interfere with, and alter the outcome of, US elections by supplying motherboards and software to several companies that manufacture and distribute voting equipment to state and federal government clientele. Among those arrested were Simon Parks, Executive Vice President of Pinnacle Voting Systems."

"The suspected mastermind of the operation, a Chinese citizen named Zhou Zemin, was found shot to death in the parking lot of a Lincolnshire resort hotel yesterday afternoon before an arrest warrant could be served. Police and federal agents suspect that he was assassinated by a rival gang as a consequence of ongoing turf battles among competing counterfeiting organizations. Federal agents across the country have a number of other suspects in custody and are conducting interviews to determine the extent of their involvement in the plan to subvert the US election process."

"The US Attorney's Office from the Northern District of Virginia believes that the plan, carried out by individual conspirators, but with perhaps a limited level of knowledge by some elements within the Chinese government, was to substitute various hardware and software components in Pinnacle election machines so that final tallies could be remotely manipulated. The US Attorney further believes that at least one other executive from Pinnacle was involved in this artifice to defraud the American people and to weaken the integrity of our elections. At this time, we are not releasing that individual's name. This investigation continues and another update will be issued tomorrow by five PM Eastern time."

It was almost six when Marchand arrived at the Moreland Hills house to find Tricia asleep on the couch in the family room. He punched in his code to disarm the alarm system, and gently laid his keys and his briefcase on the counter with the intent of not disturbing her. However, when she heard the alarm chirping, her instincts kicked in and she was up.

Her hair was mangled as one would expect after a night tossing and turning on a sofa. "Hi baby." She smiled and moved into his arms for a comfortable embrace. With her head on his chest, she sighed. "Did you get them?"

"We got them." He answered. "Most of them. The Bureau is working some of them right now to see where it all leads. But our part is done. Jerry is writing up the final report from his end and his will be combined with mine and Headquarters'. I feel like I could sleep for a week. How was your evening?"

She looked at him with a mock frown. "Boring, and anti-climactic. My part of this was done months ago, and I feel like I've just been hanging on like some sort of action groupie. I need to get back to work. Somewhere."

"I've been giving that some thought." He said as he lifted the cap of the coffee pot. She had put ground coffee in the basket and filled the reservoir with water. He was exhausted, but the coffee smelled good, and it stimulated him. He punched the button to make a pot. "You know, you have some pretty unique skills, and an active security clearance. Is there any reason you couldn't do what you do in a place like...Texas?"

"I know a golf instructor there." She smiled coyly.

"I haven't been a part of a couple in a long time, but the last few weeks have been really good. I mean, if you'd like to come down for a long visit, I'm sure we could find you gainful employment somewhere."

She looked up into his eyes and smiled. "Special Agent Marchand, are you asking me to move in with you?"

"That's Special Agent, Retired, to you young lady." He kissed her full on the mouth and squeezed her tightly next to his body. "Why don't we have a cup of coffee, and then get cleaned up. If I'm still vertical after that, I'll take you to breakfast."

She nodded and disappeared up the stairs as Marchand looked for some coffee cups. When he heard the shower running, he opened his leather briefcase, found the report he was looking for before dialing Paul.

The phone rang twice. "Congratulations. It appears that the operation went well, and none of our people were injured in the process."

"Yes. I have to say that I was excited with the result. Now we'll have to sit back and see what comes of it all." Marchand replied.

"I am glad that you have tempered your elation with a bit of healthy skepticism." Paul remarked. "With the financial research you supplied we were able to identify SEMPER as Jonathan Julius JJ Carroll, retired Lieutenant Colonel, United States Marine Corps. We'd had our eye on him for a couple of years, and now we think he may have cheated the executioner in Massa, Italy two years ago. After leaving the Marines, he worked briefly for Naval Intelligence and had become involved in exposing some very lethal characters in a group that we did not know much about. They were for all intents, the descendants of the Red Brigades; the grandchildren, if you will, of the group that had snatched Aldo Moro."

"Our unit was assigned to take out their leader, as well as the individual that was supposedly supplying them with funding. However, by pure chance, or because he had prior knowledge of the trap, the unidentified banker did not show for the meeting. The terrorist leader was eliminated, but we were not able to identify the individual with the money. At the time, we certainly could not connect Carroll as being anything other than an intelligence officer working the case. Now we think that Marty's records of cash disbursements have led back to him."

"Carroll, huh? The Banker? Where is he now?"

"He's an executive vice president of Echo Aerospace in Cleveland. He has been hiding under our noses for fifteen years, supplying the Russians with aerospace technology, while also helping them ferret out their Chinese counterparts. He had a vested interest in stopping Zhou's operation. Carroll has been a capable and successful executive at Echo, so it was good for them, but it was also good for Feodor Golovkin. One might say that Carroll's non-official cover with Echo provided immeasurable benefits to all concerned."

"He was with Naval Intelligence all that time?"

"Yes. More or less; on a contract basis. It's not unheard of, you know. You recall the story of Robert Ballard, the explorer who found the Titanic wreckage in 1985?"

"Of course."

"Ballard was a reserve Naval Intelligence officer. The Navy had another assignment for him and told him that as long as he found what they were looking for first, then he could look for the Titanic after that. The Navy hired him to find the wreckage of two nuclear powered attack submarines, the USS *Scorpion* and the USS *Thresher*, which sank in the 1960s. Without that support, he would not have been able to mount the search for Titanic. And, without the cover of being an expedition to find Titanic, the Russians might very well have figured out what they were really doing in the Atlantic."

Paul took a noisy sip of coffee. "We intend to use SEMPER for a while. He will have value to us in his current position, with the right persuasion."

"Complicated." Marchand mused.

"Things are not always what they seem." Paul noted. "Will you be heading back to Texas soon?"

"Probably in a few days. Why?"

"I am eager to get you back on some projects that require your special abilities."

"Sure." Marchand said. He was anxious to get home, but some things were still troubling him about the case. "What about the Zhou piece of this?"

Paul cleared his throat. "Didn't you hear your Director? Zhou was taken out by a rival element last night. That works for us and when I spoke to your Director last night, he determined that it would work for them as well. It will remain an unsolved Chicago gang-crime, of little interest to anyone this time next week."

"So, that's that then?"

"It is."

"The Air Force is satisfied that they found their missing LEM?" Marchand asked.

"There was no missing LEM. All government equipment that was the subject of any official Air Force investigation has been accounted for." Paul said calmly.

"What about Golovkin?"

He answered thoughtfully. "As near as our investigative and intelligence agencies can tell, Golovkin probably funneled more than a hundred fifty million US dollars to various companies and individuals to support a program that was, at least ostensibly, focused on the exploration of space. We have no idea what the source of the funds were but believe that much of it came from otherwise reputable charities that the Russian government set up years ago. We just do not know. Marty was probably scheduled to make a payoff to someone before his untimely demise, but we caught him while he still had the cash at his house. Bad timing for them."

Stan grunted. "What happens to him?"

"Mr. Golovkin will be retiring to his dacha somewhere, enjoying a well-earned retirement, I am certain. His financial network among defense contractors will certainly be restructured. From the legal standpoint, he is untouchable. From a strategic standpoint, he is no longer of interest to us. But, since you ask, we do have a plan designed to cause him some minor embarrassment."

Marchand grinned at the phone. "And ARCHER? Layden's kid?"

"We have a plan for him as well, but it is outside the scope of your role."

Marchand listened to the message and interpreted the context as well as the content. It was sobering. "Okay then. I'll let you know when I am back home."

"Thank you for your service. Stay safe." Paul said in his characteristic monotone and clicked off the line.

By the time Tricia and Stan were ready to leave, they saw the familiar shape of Jenny Lu's Honda rolling up the driveway, so they waited for her to grab some of her things and enter. She was weary from the all-night drive from Chicago and when they all saw each other, she had the apprehensive look of the child who had just been caught with their hand in the cookie jar.

"Can I help you with those?" Marchand asked as he reached to grab one of her suitcases.

"Thanks. There are some more in the car."

"Staying a while?" Tricia asked with a laugh.

"Yes. I turned in my notice after the rally last night. I had already made up my mind that it was time for a change. I need something that doesn't involve politics or politicians."

"Have you talked to Jerry?" Marchand asked with a smile.

She nodded with exuberance. "Yes. Several times. He needs a couple weeks to get his paperwork straight and then he gets to make a whistle-top tour around the country to testify at arraignments. After that he gets his choice of assignments. He's thinking about Cleveland." She paused. She was searching Marchand's face for clues to what he might know. "I heard you got quite a few last night."

Marchand looked away for a moment and then back at her. "Most of them. I think we got all the ones who needed to be gotten."

"So, it's over?"

Marchand suddenly recalled a tasking from months earlier. It was her. The foreign-born beauty who was both sensitive and cunning, who was torn between two masters. She had grown up abused and used her inner strength to get out of it and make a new life for herself. Paul had somehow known that she would go after her abuser. That was why Paul had told him to *ignore the Jenny-Zhou connection.* "It's over." He answered with a warm smile.

"What's next?" She asked innocently.

"Breakfast." Marchand replied. "I'm buying. Care to join us?"

•───))(((•)))((───•

Using the onboard navigation system, it was not difficult to find the place from the water approach, even in the dark. A warmer April than usual, even though Lake Erie had thawed, the wind was still cold. The chop had been down for a couple of days and Karlsson decided that the surface was as smooth as it was going to get. Smooth enough for his purposes, anyway. The lake was by no means crowded. He had only seen two other boats, well off in the distance, peacefully drifting in search of Walleye.

After he had presented his plan to Paul, his organization arranged to have the twenty-six-foot stern drive made available for immediate use, with no questions asked. Even though the boat had a powerful Volvo-Penta V-8 engine that could guarantee a speedy departure upon command, it had not really been picked it for that.

It had an eight-and-a-half-foot beam with one of the largest swim platforms he had seen on a boat that size. With the concrete block anchoring system Karlsson dreamed up the previous week, he figured that he could prone out on the platform just long enough to take the shot. There was a critical trade-off on the technical side. Karlsson had taken some shots out to almost 800 yards, but those had always been on dry land. The problem encountered when shooting from a rocking boat is that one not only had to time the shot consistent with the target's movements, but also had to factor rock and drift.

The anchor system would not remove all the movement but would mitigate it enough that he could still use the four-power scope. No higher though; the bigger the power of the scope, the more important it was to stay still when setting up for the shot. It would not do anyone much good to be sighting through a twenty-power scope in three-foot seas, because they would be damn lucky to even find their quarry in the eyepiece.

But, getting out at this early hour, the lake was almost as smooth as glass. By setting up his nest on the swim platform, he could pretty much stay out of view as he waited. Obviously, a fisherman with a scoped rifle laying across the transom might draw unwanted attention. So, he anchored into the wind, and let the boat swing around until the swim platform was perpendicular to the back of the house, before tossing the concrete blocks over and cinching the lines down on the cleats.

The range finding reticle showed that it was about one hundred thirty-five yards to the back door. With the shoreline as rocky as it was, he calculated that he had gotten about as close as he could. It was a little past six and he could see daylight beginning to break loose in the east. In the distance, he could hear the freeway getting busy with morning rush hour traffic. From his vantage point, of course, he would not be able to see his target arriving on the other side of the house. However, he was able to see the lights reflecting off the trees along the lane, when the first car came in. He guessed that if Frank the house manager, had stayed onsite the previous evening, then one of his targets had arrived. Frank would already be awake, getting the place ready for the arrival of the day's guests: JJ Carroll, and the son of a presidential candidate. However they had managed it, it must have taken one hell of a story to get ARCHER and SEMPER in the same room at the same time. Someone must have called in a favor.

A couple of minutes later, he could see lights coming on downstairs in the big mansion, and eventually could see Frank through the telescopic sight, opening drapes and straightening chairs. About ten minutes after that, he returned to the lower-level conference room with a cart containing the coffee pot and a wicker basket that probably contained snacks or fruit. Behind Frank, now stood another male. Probably six-feet tall, medium build, brown hair and well dressed. Since he had not seen another vehicle drive in, he assumed that Archer Layden must have spent the night at the mansion in one of the lavish guest rooms.

Just a few minutes before seven, Karlsson caught the reflection of headlights on the tree limbs again, but it was nearly daylight, and he was getting cold. Now in his sixties, he no longer had the stamina or patience that he possessed when he was thirty. It was a long five minutes before Carroll appeared in the conference room, talking on his cell phone as he poured a cup of coffee. Karlsson did not know how he did it, but Paul had guaranteed him that he would get them to the conference room at 0700 hours today. And there they were.

From there, it was as automatic as tying one's shoes. No hate. No anger. Just a job to be done. Karlsson pushed the safety forward on the big Weatherby and adjusted his support hand under the base of the stock. He synchronized his breathing with the roll of the boat and moved his finger to the trigger. Remembering that it had been set to just over three pounds, he was careful not to touch it until the roll to port had finished and the return to starboard started moving the scope up the target's body line. He began to take up the slack in the trigger at the point the crosshairs moved over his sternum so that by the time he was on his lower jaw, there was no slack left.

The Weatherby exploded and slammed into his shoulder. By the time he got it back on target, he could see that the 150 grain XBT had done its job. It had punched through the glass in the door, and smashed into the cartilage that up until now, had formed Archer Layden's nose. It had traversed his skull and imbedded somewhere in the wall behind. An autopsy would later show that it had blown through his sinus cavity and found its way into his brainstem, causing an instantaneous death. As they say, he dropped like water.

Methodically and mechanically, Karlsson tossed the empty Vodka bottle he had been given over the side. A gift from the CIA, it contained the last inch of a chewed-up cigar and had Feodor Golovkin's fingerprints and DNA on it. Maybe an ambitious homicide detective would find it. Maybe not. He pulled the lines through the homemade anchors and started the engine. The Volvo-Penta rumbled to life and he puttered quietly west until well out of the area, so as to look like any other fisherman looking for just the right spot early in the season.

Eventually, he made his way a couple of miles out before disassembling the rifle and inserting the parts into the pre-cast concrete forms. The forms had been fashioned to look like rough concrete with the idea that SCUBA divers might intentionally or inadvertently stumble onto a rifle part and think it of sufficient interest to bring it to the surface, and maybe notify those guys with badges who would be in a frenzy. However, most divers who happen upon chunks of rock or concrete, would not give it a second look. Eventually, the forms would settle into the silt and become a permanent part of the bottom-scape.

Karlsson was not in any great hurry. He figured the seventy-gallon tank was more than enough to get him the fifty nautical miles to Sandusky, where someone had arranged to have dock space waiting for him. His math skills were not great, but at 3,500 RPM it only burned about eight gallons per hour, so he could probably make it all the way to Toledo if he had to.

He tried not to dwell on it but remembered the report he had seen. Archer Layden had been selling secrets to the Russians for years. Also, to the Iranians and occasionally to the Chinese. And there was a possibility his dad might become the next President of the United States. Zhou would have liked that. Golovkin too. At least now, if Senator Layden did make it to Pennsylvania Avenue, it would be as the result of an honest election. Zhou's computer equipment had been seized and Pinnacle Voting Systems was under congressional scrutiny, with their executive vice president sitting in a jail cell.

Karlsson shook his head. All this because someone wanted to counterfeit a part that went to an aircraft that didn't exist, that had taken pictures of a disabled LEM that didn't exist. Its occupants no longer officially existed either. Not that they ever had. He quickly looked up over his shoulder into the dawn sky and found it. At least the moon still existed.

A few days later when he had checked in to a very nice hotel in Crystal City, Virginia, he was pleasantly surprised when the clerk handed him a note with his name on it. He opened the envelope on the way up to his room.

"Lounge at 1700??" He recognized the familiar scrawl of a certain AFOSI agent, and it occurred to him that she was a good kid. Kid, hell. She was over forty and old enough to know better than to fraternize with dirty old men like him. He just hoped she didn't have any wacky ideas about changing him or cleaning him up. She didn't.